Praise for

"Tom Wood has don[e] . . . [historica]l accuracy, globe-trotti[ng] . . . keep you guessing t[o] . . . James Bond look like . . .

—Brad Taylor, national bestselling author of
Enemy of Mine

"A hard-hitting and exceedingly smart thriller that races along with intensity and intrigue. Tom Wood grabs the reader from the opening scene and delivers a powerhouse of a novel with equal measures of high-octane action and fascinating details, creating a world for his characters that feels as real as it does dangerous. . . . Fans of Lee Child and Vince Flynn will not want to miss *The Enemy*."

—Mark Greaney, national bestselling author of
The Gray Man

"A truly great read featuring an unforgettable character. . . . Readers will crave to see this one appear on the big screen."
—*Suspense Magazine*

More Praise for the Thrillers
of Tom Wood

"The scenes are vivid and the plot revelations parceled out at expert intervals . . . an impressively intricate thriller . . . exciting."
—*The New Yorker*

continued . . .

Also by Tom Wood

The Killer

The Enemy

Bad Luck in Berlin
(A Penguin Special)

THE
GAME

•••

TOM WOOD

A SIGNET BOOK

SIGNET
Published by the Penguin Group
Penguin Group (USA) LLC, 375 Hudson Street,
New York, New York 10014

USA | Canada | UK | Ireland | Australia | New Zealand | India | South Africa | China
penguin.com
A Penguin Random House Company

Published by Signet, an imprint of New American Library, a division of Penguin
Group (USA) LLC. This is an authorized reprint of an edition published by
Sphere. For information address Sphere, an imprint of Little, Brown Book
Group; 100 Victoria Embankment; London, England EC4Y 0DY.

First Signet Printing, November 2013

ISBN 978-0-451-41754-1

Printed in the United States of America
10 9 8 7 6 5 4 3 2 1

For Emma, my sister

· Chapter 1 ·

Algiers, Algeria

The killer was good. He moved with a fluidity and an economy of motion that made him seem relaxed, almost carefree, yet he was ever aware of his surroundings and always alert. He had a lean, forgettable face that looked a little older than his thirty-five years. He was tall, but of average height for a native of the tallest nation on the planet. A resident of Amsterdam, Felix Kooi worked as a freelance assassin with no allegiances. He sold his services to the highest bidder, whatever the job, in a career that had endured at least ten years. That career was about to come to an end.

Kooi had a room at the El Aurassi Hotel but spent little of his time there, always leaving shortly after dawn and returning only during the evening, never using the same route or the same entrance twice in a row. Each day he ventured around the city like a tourist, always walking, never visiting the same location more than once, but exploring every medieval mosque, museum, and sightseer destination Algiers had to offer. He ate in restaurants and cafés, but only those serving Algerian and North African food. He walked on the seafront but never lazed on the beach.

Today Kooi was in the old town—the casbah—and had spent an hour wandering around the market near the El Jidid Mosque. The market was a huge, sprawling arrangement of tented stalls selling everything from wicker baskets to live chickens. It was centered on an irregular square and seeped along the numerous adjoining alleys and side streets. He seemed to do nothing beyond browsing, enjoying the sights, sounds, and smells of such a vibrant gathering of people and merchandise.

Victor had followed Kooi for three days. In that time he had learned that Kooi was good, but he wasn't exceptional. Because he had made a mistake. A mistake that was going to kill him.

Victor's CIA employer didn't know the reason for Kooi's cover as a tourist in Algiers. Procter didn't know whether the Dutch assassin was preparing for a contract, meeting a broker or client, obtaining supplies, or lying low from one of the many enemies he had no doubt made in a decadelong career as a hired killer. Victor had followed him for three days as much to determine that reason as to devise the best way to kill him, even though he didn't need to know it in order to fulfill the contract. Such knowledge was important because maybe someone was as keen for Kooi to live as Victor's employer was for him to die. Getting caught in the middle of such a tug-of-war was not something Victor was eager to repeat.

Three days shadowing Kooi around the city had been

a necessary aspect of the precautionary measures Victor employed to stay alive in the world's most dangerous profession, but unnecessary because there was no secret to uncover. Kooi wasn't working. He wasn't meeting a contact. He wasn't on the run. He was on vacation. He was acting like a tourist because he was a tourist.

And that was his mistake. He was a tourist. He was in Algiers to relax and have a good time, to explore and see the sights, and too much of his focus was on being a tourist to effectively protect himself from someone like Victor.

A merchant selling carved wooden statuettes caught Kooi's attention and he listened and nodded and pointed and examined the man's wares. He said nothing in return, because he didn't speak French, or else didn't want the trader to know he did. Victor watched from a distance of twenty meters. Kooi was easy enough to see, being at least half a head taller than the locals occupying the space between him and Victor, and Victor's similar height ensured that his line of sight was rarely interrupted unless he chose for it to be.

Kooi was aware and alert, but he was a tourist and his countersurveillance techniques were basic, and basic had never been a problem for Victor. He was more cautious in return, and Kooi hadn't come close to identifying the threat. He had seen Victor, because Kooi was good, and like Kooi's, Victor's height and ethnicity made him stand out in Algiers, but because he was only good and not exceptional, he hadn't marked Victor as anything other than a tourist. Victor knew this because Kooi's behavior hadn't changed, and no one who learned an assassin was following them acted exactly the same as they had prior to the acquisition of that knowledge.

The Dutchman's lack of precautionary measures in his downtime told Victor he hadn't experienced the same kind of professional learning curve that Victor knew he had mastered by virtue of the fact he was still capable of drawing breath. He wasn't envious of Kooi's comparatively charmed existence, because that existence would soon be over.

"Mister," a voice said to Victor in heavily accented English, "you buy a watch."

A young local man stood to Victor's right, showing his lack of teeth with a wide smile. He wore brightly colored linens. His black hair jutted out from the top of his skull in unruly clumps. His sleeves were rolled up to reveal skinny forearms ringed by wristwatches, counterfeit unless the man had several hundred thousand dollars' worth of merchandise weighing him down while not having enough money for a toothbrush.

"No, thank you," Victor said, shaking his head in an exaggerated manner for the kind of emphasis necessary to persuade local traders to try their bartering skills elsewhere.

He didn't seem to notice. "I got for you Tag Hour, Rolax, all the nice ones. Look, look."

"No," Victor said again, his gaze on Kooi, who had a wooden statuette in each hand and seemed to be deciding on which to purchase. He chose one and handed over some cash for the winning selection. The Dutchman was smiling and nodding, pleased with his purchase or amused by the trader's rapid-fire overselling. He slipped the statuette into a thigh pocket of his khaki shorts.

"Look, look," the young watch guy said again, about ten decibels louder. He waved his arms in front of Victor's face.

He gestured with his hands to show he was interested in the watches when his only interest was in stopping the local from attracting attention. Kooi wouldn't hear over the din of the market, but he might notice the young man's waving arms and the shiny watches glinting in the sunlight.

"That one," Victor said, pointing to a Rolex with hands that didn't sweep.

A toothless grin stretched across the seller's face and he unclasped the watch while Victor counted out a fair price for it.

"No, no," the young local said, "not enough. More. More."

Victor obliged him with another note, having followed the bartering convention of underpaying. However much he offered, the local would want more.

He slipped on his knockoff Rolex and left to follow Kooi, who had extended his lead by another five meters in the interval.

"Bye, mister," the young local called behind him. "You have the good day."

Kooi took his time strolling through the market. He took a circuitous route, but only to make the most of the experience rather than for any tactical consideration. He continued to check his flanks on occasion, but Victor walked directly behind his mark. It would take a one-hundred-and-eighty-degree turn for Kooi even to see him—a move that would give Victor plenty of notice not to be there when he did.

Fabric stalls and small stores selling local fashions lined a twisting side street into which Kooi veered. He didn't stop to examine the wares, but he walked slowly, head rotating back and forth in case anything caught his interest. Victor let the distance between them increase, because now that they were out of the main market square, the crowd density had dropped by around thirty percent. Had Kooi been more active in his countersurveillance, or had he simply walked faster, it would have made Victor's task more difficult, but even if he did lose him, he knew where the Dutchman was staying.

Kooi was in Algiers for another week based on his flight and accommodation bookings, so there was no time pressure, but Victor would take the first opportunity that presented itself. Regardless of Kooi's relaxed attitude to his own security, he was a competent professional and therefore a hard target, and there was no guarantee Victor would get more than one chance to see the contract through to completion.

He hadn't identified a weapon, and Kooi's khaki shorts and short-sleeved shirt were not conducive to hiding a firearm, but he could easily have a knife in a pocket or in a belt sheath or on the end of a neck cord. Plus, bare hands could be equally deadly if employed correctly.

There were no requirements to the successful completion of the contract beyond Kooi's death, but Victor preferred not to identify an assassination as one if it could be avoided. He planned to keep it simple—a mugging gone bad. Common enough the world over. He had a folding knife in the pocket of his linen trousers. It was a local weapon, bought from a street vendor not dissimilar to the toothless young watch seller. Not the kind of quality Victor would prefer to work with, but it was well made enough to do the task he'd purchased it for. As long as he could get within arm's length of Kooi, he could cut any one of several arteries that were protected only by the thin skin of the neck, underarm, or inner thigh. A seemingly superficial cut, luckily placed by an aggressive robber, inducing death in minutes before medical help could reach him.

All Victor had to do was get close to Kooi.

The Dutchman continued his exploration of the city, leaving the old town and wandering to the docks, where he gazed out at the Mediterranean and the many boats and yachts on its blue waters. He took a seat outside a restaurant with an ocean view, and used his teeth to pick grilled lamb from skewered brochettes and ate aromatic couscous with his fingers. He was slim and in shape but he had a big appetite.

Victor waited nearby for the hour Kooi spent over his meal and followed as his target headed back into the city. He didn't take the same route back—that would have been too reckless, even for a man as relaxed as Kooi—but he walked in the same direction, taking streets that ran close or parallel to those he had already walked.

Kooi surprised Victor by heading back to the casbah market. That didn't fit with his MO of never visiting the same locale twice. The market crowds enabled Victor to close the distance between them, and he pictured the rest of the route back to Kooi's hotel. There were numerous quiet alleys that would present all the opportunity Victor needed to complete the contract. He could get ahead of

Kooi easily enough, knowing his ultimate destination, and come at him from the front—just another tourist exploring the wonders of Algiers—maybe sharing a nod of recognition as a couple of guys with similar interests, strangers in a strange land, the kind who could end up friends over a few beers. By the time Kooi realized the man heading in his direction was a killer like himself, he would already be bleeding.

A simple enough job. Dangerous given the target, but uncomplicated.

Victor was surprised again when Kooi led him to the same part of the market square they had been in earlier. He wasn't exploring anymore. He had a purpose. The Dutchman removed the wooden statuette from his shorts and set about swapping it for the one he had rejected previously. The merchant was happy to oblige, especially when Kooi gave him some more money.

"Hey, mister," a familiar voice called.

Victor ignored him, but the toothless young man sidestepped into his path, his arms glinting with watches. Kooi headed off.

"You buy another watch, mister? For your wife or lady. She like nice watch too, yes?"

Victor shook his head and moved to step around him, losing a couple of meters on Kooi in the process. The local didn't let him pass.

"I give you good price. Buy the two, get the one cheap. Good deal. Look, look."

"No," Victor said. "No wife. No lady. No watch. Move."

But the young guy, buoyed by his earlier success and

Victor's reappearance, didn't want to understand. He blocked Victor's path, waving and pointing in turn to the women's watches that circled his lower wrists and mispronouncing the brands.

"Please," Victor said, trying to get around the guy before he lost Kooi, but not wanting to hurl the seller away and risk the attention such a commotion would create.

Kooi turned around. He caught something in his peripheral vision, or maybe he decided to examine some novelty after all. He eased himself through the crowd, not looking Victor's way—yet—as he made for a stall.

"Good price," the watch seller said, holding out both arms to block Victor's attempts to get by. "Your lady like you a lot." He smiled. "You know what I say?" He puckered his lips and made kissing noises.

"Okay, okay," Victor said. "I'll take that one."

He reached for his wallet to end the standoff before Kooi noticed, but the Dutchman glanced over when the young trader clapped his hands in celebration at securing a second sale.

Kooi saw Victor.

There was no immediate reaction. He stared for a second, because he realized he had seen Victor before. He stared for another second, because he didn't know where. He stared for a third second, because he was assessing the chances that a lone Caucasian male he had seen before and who had just been directly behind him was simply a tourist too.

And he ran.

· Chapter 2 ·

Victor grabbed the watch seller by both of his scrawny shoulders and threw him out of the way. The young guy was light and Victor was strong, and he crashed to the ground, one arm of watches impacting first, the women's watch he had taken off to give to Victor scattering between sandals and disappearing into the tangle of legs and feet.

Kooi's route was clearer, but he had first to turn back around and lost a little of his lead. He used his height and body mass to shove his way past the smaller Algerians in his path. They shouted abuse and waved their fists. Victor dashed through the gap in the crowd Kooi created, dodging his way around locals as the gap closed up again and shouldering past those he couldn't weave by. He received his own share of jeers.

His target had a fifteen-meter lead, but he was easy enough to keep track of, as he stood several inches taller than those around him. But he was fast and determined and running for his life.

Stalls flashed by in Victor's peripheral vision. A woman screamed up ahead and he ran past where she sat sobbing on the ground, an ornate earthenware jar smashed nearby, the cinnamon it had held coloring the paving stones orange and drifting away in the breeze.

Victor tripped over a foot and stumbled, but thanks to his agility and the mass of bodies in close proximity, he avoided falling.

He glimpsed Kooi veering out of the market square and down a side street shaded from the sun by tall buildings. The back and the right arm of his short-sleeved shirt were orange with smeared cinnamon. Victor entered the side street a few seconds after his target and caught sight of him as he turned a corner up ahead. Beggars sat with their backs against one wall, their legs crossed before them and wooden bowls near their feet, paying no attention to the men who ran by. Victor avoided crashing into a pair of men who entered the alley ahead of him, slipping side-on between them and around the corner Kooi had taken.

The street that Victor found himself on was long and straight and he powered along the center of it after Kooi, who rounded pedestrians and leaped over a bench to avoid a crowd that would have slowed him down. Victor did the same, and someone applauded the show of athletics.

Kooi took another corner and when Victor reached it he saw a short walkway that crossed another. At the intersection he couldn't see Kooi either to the left or right, but he saw to the right a number of locals with expressions of bemusement or curiosity.

Victor headed that way, then turned into an alleyway

where he saw boxes had been knocked over. He exited it and heard a horn blare, dashed across the street, and cut through another alley, moving toward the sound, coming out on a tree-lined boulevard flanked by nineteenth-century French colonial buildings, grand but dilapidated. He caught sight of Kooi as he hurried through a restaurant's entrance.

More horns sounded as Victor cut across the traffic. Insults were cast in his direction. He pushed open the restaurant door and dodged around the tables and waiters before shoving open the only door Kooi could have taken, entering the kitchen and bundling staff out of his way to follow Kooi through a back door.

He emerged onto another winding market alleyway, lined on both sides by ramshackle stalls. Victor headed left, because a stall had been upturned that way and traders were yelling and throwing things. He jumped up and scrambled over the stall, inflicting further damage and shrugging off the angry locals' attempts to grab him.

Kooi's lead was short, but the streets of the old town were a mazelike collection of narrow cobbled walkways that wound and twisted between whitewashed buildings in no discernible pattern. He disappeared around corners and took intersections before Victor could see which way he went. Victor fell farther and farther behind as he struggled to deduce the correct turnings to take, looking all ways to identify Kooi's path or listening to ascertain from which direction the sound of running footsteps originated. Had Kooi known the city, his chances of escape would have been good, but Kooi was a tourist who had spent his days exploring the unfamiliar. He didn't know Algiers. He didn't know where to run. He didn't know where to hide. He was attempting to create enough distance to lose his pursuer. He was trusting to speed and stamina in an attempt to outrun Victor. He didn't yet know such a thing was impossible.

Victor ran into a small arcade, dodging past men and women amused enough by the spectacle to helpfully point out which way to go. The arcade opened out onto the seafront. Kooi was out of sight and the street was wide enough that his flight had not disrupted the foot traffic sufficiently for the wake to mark his route. He could have gone either left or right, but Victor should be able to see him easily enough in the sparse crowd. But he couldn't. Kooi must have backtracked.

Victor turned around and dashed back the way he had come, picturing Kooi running along a parallel route, perhaps even slowing to a walk to attract less attention. He reached an intersection and glanced both ways down the perpendicular thoroughfare. If Kooi had retraced his steps along a parallel route, he would appear after Victor, who had only had to run in a straight line, whereas Kooi had gone in an L shape, having fled a little way first along the seafront.

He appeared, to the left, and Victor was sprinting after him before Kooi realized he had been spotted. The Dutchman ran again, but now had a lead of less than five meters.

After Victor chased him down another alleyway, Kooi ran across a wide French boulevard, in a straight line through the sparse and slow-moving traffic. He slipped off the cinnamon-stained shirt and tossed it aside, because at some point he would want to hide, to blend in, and the shirt would hamper that. He had a white undershirt beneath.

Victor followed, running behind a backfiring car Kooi had run in front of. He headed into an alleyway that was barely shoulder width, scuffing and tearing his own shirt at the shoulders and elbows and scraping the skin beneath. Kooi took a corner eleven feet ahead, using his hands as brakes to pivot him ninety degrees and prevent him from crashing into the wall. Victor did the same, gaining on Kooi because he knew what was coming.

The paved ground sloped upward in a series of long, low steps and then opened out onto a wide residential street where window boxes bloomed with color and bright doors had grilled security windows. Kooi leaped up and vaulted over a wall. Victor did the same seconds later, landing on his feet in a courtyard filled with tall potted plants. Kooi shoved them aside and knocked them over as he ran. Earthenware cracked apart, spilling soil. Victor dodged around the debris, again closing on Kooi, who had to create the path for Victor to follow.

Kooi ran at the wall at the other end of the courtyard and used the ball of his leading foot to catapult him upward, pulling himself up and dropping down to the far side. Victor heard a yell and a crash, and as he landed on the street on the other side of the wall, he saw Kooi scrambling to his feet and a man on the ground, cursing and rubbing his ankle. Victor swerved around him as Kooi jumped onto the hood of a parked taxi, receiving a blare of horn in return from the driver, who got out of his vehicle to yell abuse. Victor had to shove the driver out of the way, and followed Kooi over the hood and up another set of long, low steps.

At the top an elderly woman was exiting the front door of her home. Kooi threw her aside and disappeared into the building. Victor heard his footsteps dashing up the stairwell as he entered the cool interior. Ceiling fans thrummed overhead. He raced after Kooi, not concerned about an ambush because he could hear his target's echoing footsteps ascending above him.

Victor reached the four-story building's top floor, rushed through an open doorway—the only way Kooi could have gone—and into a small apartment where a family sat on the floor, shocked and scared at the intrusion upon their afternoon meal. Glass smashed farther inside and Victor found a balcony door kicked open. Out on the balcony, there was no sign of Kooi. The street was too wide to leap across to the buildings on the other side, and the ground was too far down to drop to, so Victor looked right—seeing nothing—then looked left.

The Dutchman had jumped to the adjacent balcony. Victor did the same, stepping onto the stone railing and covering the distance by the time Kooi had reached the next balcony along. Victor hurried after his target, who had run out of balconies, but who climbed up onto the stone railing and jumped.

He landed on the roof of the neighboring building and rolled to disperse the impact of the two-meter drop. Victor rolled seconds later and Kooi glanced back over his shoulder, face shining with sweat, to make brief eye contact with his relentless, tireless pursuer.

The next flat roof was only a short jump away, but Kooi

stumbled as he landed and slowed his run to keep his balance. An exterior stone staircase descended from the far side of the roof and Kooi hurried down it, Victor now close enough to hear the Dutchman's urgent breaths.

The stairs led down to a small square, at the center of which was an ornate tiled fountain where residents collected drinking water. Kooi grabbed a boy holding a bucket in each hand and heaved him backward into Victor's path. Victor dodged the boy but not the buckets spilling water. He slipped but stayed on his feet, losing a second on Kooi, who vaulted over a small wall and down to a neighboring alleyway.

Victor followed, absorbing the drop with bending knees, and caught a glimpse of Kooi as he rounded a corner ahead. Victor took the same corner moments later and sprinted down the adjoining alley, jumping over baskets knocked over by Kooi, past a small hovel with a red door, out onto a side street. He looked left, saw a long street Kooi hadn't had the time to run the length of, almost no people, no restaurants or businesses, no way to veer off. Victor looked right—a dead end. Kooi could have gone neither way. Victor's memory flashed back. The red door. No splinters of wood near the lock or hinges from a kick, but it was still ajar, having been already open. He spun around and saw—

Kooi, charging from the doorway, the glint of metal from a blade in his hand, meant for Victor's back but now thrusting at his heart.

· Chapter 3 ·

Kooi stopped half a meter from Victor, the tip of the knife centimeters from his rib cage. It was a small weapon, painted black, with a triangular point and a re-curve blade. A fine weapon, better than Victor's own—folded high-carbon steel, wickedly sharp, strong enough to be capable of breaking bone without compromising the blade, but harmless while piercing only air.

He was only a little older than Victor but far more fatigued from the chase. Kooi was about the same height and similarly proportioned, with long limbs, athletic and muscular but compact and lean. Sweat glistened on the Dutchman's face and arms from the heat and the chase, and darkened the front of his undershirt. Kooi stumbled, but didn't move any farther forward. His mouth opened, but he didn't say anything. His eyes stared at Victor, but focused on a point somewhere behind him.

Then he exhaled and wheezed. The black knife fell

from his trembling fingers and clattered on the paving stones near Victor's feet.

The Dutchman blinked, his eyes watery, and placed both hands on Victor's right arm to steady himself while he looked down at his abdomen, to where the knuckles of Victor's right thumb and index finger pressed against Kooi's white undershirt.

The white shirt became red around Victor's hand.

"No," Kooi said, as if defiance could remove the blade from his stomach and repair the hole it would leave behind.

Victor let go of the folding knife's grip. It protruded at a downward angle from just below the base of Kooi's sternum, the short blade buried up behind the breastbone, the tip puncturing the bottom of the Dutchman's heart. He coughed and struggled to breathe as blood drained from the ruptured left ventricle and slowly filled the chest cavity, impeding his lungs' ability to inflate and deflate. Victor eased Kooi to the ground as the stability left his legs.

"No," Kooi said again, but quieter.

He slumped against the alleyway wall, his legs splayed on the paving stones before him, his arms limp at his sides. He didn't try to take the knife from his flesh. He had to know there was no point even if he'd had the strength left to tug it free of the vacuum's pull. Such an action would only quicken his demise. Victor considered what he would do if their places had been reversed—whether it was better to live those extra few seconds in pain and fear or to hurry to the boatman.

Victor patted along Kooi's thighs and around his waist

to make sure there were no hidden weapons that might be employed with the last of Kooi's strength. He knew better than most that when faced with death, people could find a way to stay alive or take their vengeance, because he had done both.

There was a wallet and a room key in one of Kooi's hip pockets and the statuette in the thigh pocket, but nothing else. Victor examined the statuette. It was about six inches in height and lacquered black. Victor didn't understand what it was supposed to be. It looked like a reptilian man, somewhat comical and juvenile. Kooi had strange tastes.

Victor slipped the wallet into one of his own pockets. He didn't need to check the contents because anything inside the wallet was of no interest to him. He would dispose of it later. Taking it was merely to give the police a story. He unclasped Kooi's wristwatch and ripped a pendant from his neck for the same reasons. There was no phone to take, but Victor rarely carried one himself.

Kooi, his face pale while he sat dying, stared at Victor as he was robbed.

"Who sent you?" Kooi asked in a whisper.

Even if paramedics showed up that second, Kooi couldn't be saved, so Victor answered, "CIA."

"Are you . . . ?"

Victor shook his head. "Independent contractor. Like you."

The Dutchman blinked and swallowed while he gathered the energy to speak again. "For the American?"

Victor nodded.

A weak smile. "I knew I should . . . have said no . . .

to that job." He coughed at the effort of saying so many words in succession. He fought to keep his head upright and his eyelids open.

"Greed kills us all eventually," Victor said.

"But me first." Another weak smile. Another cough. Blood glistened on his lips. "What's your name?"

"Ask me again when I join you."

He nodded, accepting the response. "Would you do something . . . for me?" He paused and wheezed. "A favor. It's important . . ." His eyelids fluttered. Blood . . . dripped from his chin. He tried to lift his hand. "Please . . ."

"Maybe," Victor said. "What is it?"

Kooi never answered.

· Chapter 4 ·

Somewhere over the Atlantic, three weeks later

The Learjet cruised at an altitude of thirty-one thousand feet. In the cockpit a pilot and a copilot monitored the instruments and joked between themselves. There was no other crew. On the far side of the cockpit door, a woman and a man sat in the passenger cabin. The woman's name was Janice Muir. The man was Francis Beatty. They sat on opposite tan leather seats, facing each other across a small table. The sky outside the small round window was black.

A tablet computer lay between them. A photograph was displayed on its screen. The photograph was pixelated and slightly blurry, having been shot at distance and then enlarged as far as its resolution could handle. The tablet was rotated to suit Muir's perspective. Beatty used a finger to wipe the screen and bring up other photographs. They showed a man in a suit walking along the street of a European city, then ascending some steps to enter through the black door of a whitewashed town house.

Muir said, "Are we sure he's the target?"

"Possibly," Beatty answered. "Right height. Right build. Right sort of age. The hair is different, though."

"A wig?"

"I'm guessing he's just changed his style."

The woman thumbed the tablet's screen to cycle back and forth through the photographs. "I'd like a little bit more than a guess."

Beatty frowned. "We're working with intel that is out of date. People grow and cut their hair all the time. I don't think it makes a difference."

"We've had two false positives so far. I'd prefer to avoid another."

"Perhaps it will be third time lucky."

This time Muir frowned. "I prefer to deal with facts, not luck."

"Just a turn of phrase."

"Probability?"

He shrugged and rocked his head from side to side. "Hard to say."

"You're being paid to say."

"Then I'd say sixty-five percent, give or take."

"That doesn't fill me with confidence."

"I was trying to be accurate, not reassuring. From what little we can see of his face in these photographs, he seems a good fit. For what it's worth, he matches the description as closely as we could hope for."

"As do a lot of men."

"I said for what it's worth. What do you want to do?"

"We have just one more potential after him, correct?"

Beatty nodded. "But he matches the least criteria.

This guy here"—he tapped the screen—"ticks more boxes."

"But not as many as the two that came before him."

"Maybe that just means he's good at staying hidden. As expected."

She sighed and rubbed her eyes. "Tell me what your gut says."

"That the target has to be one of the four possibles and he wasn't the previous two and he's unlikely to be the fourth. Therefore, on the numbers, this guy has to be the one."

"I'm coming to the same conclusion."

"Shall I deploy a team?"

"Unless you want to take him on with just the two of us."

A smirk. "I don't think that would be a particularly sane move given the target's skill set."

"Scared?" Muir asked.

"I didn't get this old by being brave."

"You're not old, Francis."

"Saying that just means you're getting old too. How do you want to do it?"

"We're running out of time, so I want as many boots on the ground as we can get. But I don't want any dead-weight. They all have to be good. And each and every one needs to know exactly the kind of target they're dealing with."

"Then you need to be prepared to bump up the fee."

She shrugged. "Better than the alternative. I don't want any amateurs with a guy this dangerous. We can expect he's armed. Who knows what he's capable of?"

He matched her shrug. "Put half a dozen guys on him and it doesn't matter what he can do. It doesn't matter if he has a gun. We'll have more. Numbers always win in the end. What about at his hotel? He may have an idea who is staying there, but we can trap him in the building. It's public. We can—"

"*No.*" She shook her head. "Not his hotel. Trust me when I say that would be an extremely bad idea."

"Okay. You know more about him than I do. So where?"

She tapped the screen. "We know where he's going to be so let's wait for him to leave. We'll stay close—but not too close—behind and in front. When the opportunity presents itself—and it will—we move in and surround him. He can't watch every direction at the same time. Speed and surprise before he can process what's happening."

"You make it sound so simple."

"It will be," Muir said confidently. "He won't know what hit him."

· Chapter 5 ·

Vienna, Austria

The patient wore a charcoal suit. It was a smart business garment of obvious quality and cut in a classic style. The jacket was open and a steel-gray tie rested over a white shirt. He was tall and lean but unmistakably strong, and sat with a relaxed yet rigid posture, his hands resting on the arms of the visitor's chair. He looked a little younger than the age listed in his medical records. His dark hair was cut short and neat but was notably free of product or fashionable style. Eyes darker still than his hair betrayed nothing of his personality save for a calm watchfulness and keen intellect. Dr. Margaret Schule, who prided herself on her people-reading skills, found him quite fascinating.

She examined the site of the surgery and asked, "Are you experiencing any pain?"

The patient shook his head.

"What about when I do this?"

The patient shook his head again.

"Okay, that's tremendous. I'm so pleased."

Schule tugged the latex gloves from her hands, bunched them up, and used the toe of a shoe to push down a pedal and open the clinical waste bin. She dropped the gloves inside. The bin was the only object in the room that marked it as the office of a medical professional, and its presence was as unavoidable as its appearance was unpleasant. She kept it in a corner, where it was less likely to draw the eye and disrupt the room's carefully composed ambience.

Her office was on the third floor of a late eighteenth-century Viennese town house that had once belonged to a conductor in the Royal Orchestra in the time of Mozart. Schule loved to tell her patients of this fact. Brightly patterned Turkish rugs covered much of the dark-stained flooring. She refused to have carpets for hygiene reasons. Classically painted landscapes hung from the walls. The furniture was composed almost exclusively of antiques from the baroque period, save for the ergonomic mesh chair where Schule spent a large portion of her time.

"Can I get you a glass of water, perhaps?" she offered her patient.

"No, thank you."

Schule returned to the chair and rested her forearms on her large desk as she examined the man before her. He looked back at her with the same pleasant yet neutral expression he always wore. He made no small talk. He didn't fidget. He wasn't bored. He wasn't nervous. He offered nothing about himself and sat on the other side of the desk as though there was nothing interesting enough to know. Schule wasn't convinced.

The visitor's chair in which he sat was not where it had been positioned when the patient entered her office. She noted the change immediately because she had noted it each and every time the man had visited her and because she lived her life by a rigid desire to see each and every thing in its rightful place. When he left she would reposition the chair so that it sat square to the desk. Then she could look a patient directly in the eye from her own chair, which was also squared to the desk, without having to swivel the seat as she now did and destroy the careful equilibrium of the room. She liked to have her own chair and the visitor's chair aligned with the office door on the far wall. She liked order. She liked straight lines.

The patient's medical records listed him as a resident of Brussels, but those records began only from the day when the patient had first walked into her practice some months before. He had not supplied his medical history prior to that point. She found this somewhat curious, but it was not uncommon. Schule knew herself to be among the uppermost echelon of the planet's cosmetic surgeons. Her clients ranged from Hollywood's brightest and most beautiful to members of several European royal families and the wives of Russia's superrich. Discretion was not only expected by her clients, but demanded. No one at Schule's practice asked any questions that their clients did not want to answer. The man sitting opposite her didn't look like a movie star or a prince, but he had to be as wealthy as one to afford her fees, or else vain enough to justify such extravagance.

As well as offering a complete range of the most common procedures, such as rhinoplasty, face-lifts, and liposuction, Schule was at the forefront of scar reduction. She had studied and taught across the world, and her expertise was always in demand. The majority of her work in this area was in smoothing the results of her less skilled fellow surgeons.

She said, "I think we can say that the procedure has been nothing short of a spectacular success. I'm delighted with the results and I hope you are too. Of course the original surgeon did a perfectly adequate job of putting the ear back together, but alas he didn't do you any favors when it came to minimizing scarring. Fortunately, with the injury being comparatively recent, combined with your relative youth and exceptional level of health and well-being, the techniques I employed could not have worked any better. I'm sure you've seen for yourself in the mirror, but the actual scar tissue, which you know cannot be avoided and will always be present, is limited to a fine line that is only visible at especially close range. Over time its visibility will further be reduced and I would speculate that within a year even you will have a hard time identifying it."

The patient nodded. "Thank you."

Schule wasn't used to such reserved appreciation. She was used to huge smiles and endless streams of tearful expressions of gratitude. She had never known someone so emotionless. When she had first discussed the procedure with him, he had listened intently, made a series of surprisingly astute queries, and showed neither uncertainty nor concern. On the day of the surgery he had been relaxed and without fear. His heart rate had been almost unnervingly low and regular.

He was at least twenty years her junior and it went against her professional ethics, but she found herself wanting to get to know him better. There was something about him she couldn't articulate that went beyond an obvious attraction.

She cleared her throat. "If there is no pain or discomfort, then I don't believe you'll need another checkup, but please do book an appointment if you feel the need to see me at some point in the future."

The patient nodded.

"If I may," Schule began, "I would love to use your case for a paper I'm writing for a surgical journal."

"I'd prefer to be left out of any literature, thank you."

"I can assure you that your anonymity will be protected. Only the injury, procedure, and results will be included."

"The answer is no."

Schule sighed. "Well, that is a shame. But it's your choice. Do let me know if you change your mind."

"I shall."

"Then I think we're all done."

He said, "There is one thing that I wonder if you could help me with."

"Of course."

"I'd like to take any physical records of my procedure with me, and I would appreciate it if any and all electronic records could be deleted too."

Schule smiled, friendly and reassuring. "I can promise you that your privacy is of the utmost importance to us here and no one but my staff and I will ever see those records. I'm sorry if I've made you nervous because of the journal. I respect your wishes not to be included."

He nodded. "I appreciate that, but regardless of your paper, when I leave here I'd prefer that no record of my presence was left behind."

"I'm afraid we must retain your medical records, both for legal considerations and for any future procedures you might have with us. There really is nothing to be concerned about. I've been protecting the privacy of my patients since the very beginnings of this practice."

"Please. I'd like my records." His tone was calm but insistent.

"I'm sorry," Schule said, "but I just can't do that. It comes down to a matter of legality, and I'm not prepared to break the law, even if I was comfortable with what you're asking of me."

"Your name is Margaret Schule," he said. "You are forty-nine years old. You grew up in Gräfelfing, twenty kilometers west of Munich. Your father was a baker by trade. He joined the Nazi party in the summer of 1939. By the time the Second World War ended, he had risen to the rank of lieutenant in the Waffen SS. He changed his name after the war, taking the identity of one of his childhood friends, and took his young wife to Austria. They lived there for over ten years before returning to Germany, where you were born. You studied medicine at the Berlin College of Medicine and spent six years practicing in Germany before working in London and then the United States, where you specialized in cosmetic surgery and taught for a time at several hospitals. You came to Austria fifteen years ago for your father's funeral and eventually established this practice six years later with an investment from your husband, Alfred, whom you first met while you were in London. He owns a fifty-five percent stake in your practice and has absolutely no idea that you've been having an affair with his younger brother for the past eighteen months. You meet every Friday afternoon. He tells his secretary he's playing badminton."

There was no change in the patient's expression. There was no malice. He sat still and relaxed, handsome yet cold, but everything about him demanded obedience.

Schule stared at the patient for a long time before regaining her composure. Her mouth opened to demand answers to questions that she couldn't form the words for. Eventually, she reached across her desk and pushed a button on her intercom, then held the receiver to her ear.

When the line connected, Schule instructed her secretary to do as the patient wished, silencing the secretary's protests with "I don't care. Just make sure they're deleted and hand him all documentation."

The patient stood without taking his gaze from her, repositioned the chair as it had originally been, and left the office without another word.

· Chapter 6 ·

Victor withdrew a pair of sunglasses from his inside jacket pocket and slipped them on. He stood outside the grand town house that housed Schule's practice. The early-afternoon sun was bright and warm. The building was whitewashed, like every building on the wide boulevard. A wrought-iron fence, painted black and topped with brass spikes, flanked a set of marble steps that led down to the pavement. A light wind blew against his face. He descended the steps as he instinctively swept his gaze across his immediate environment.

The building was located on Wiener Street in central Vienna, opposite the Stadtpark. The neighborhood was one of almost identical streets, with identical rows of expensive town houses, all gleaming white with red-tiled roofs and beautifully maintained. Few were residences. Most served as offices for accountants, lawyers, and doctors. The park's maple trees on the far side of the street cast dappled shadows across the pavement and offered shade for parked high-end sedans and hulking luxury SUVs. Victor couldn't see a single piece of litter or trace of gum.

Every thirty meters or so, a bench was positioned on the wide pavement opposite. Men and women in business attire made use of them to eat their lunches and drink coffee, or just to enjoy the sunshine while chatting on their phones.

A bus stop on the far side of the street was the only sign the neighborhood did not exist in a world of pure affluence. Only two buses stopped there because those who lived and worked here shunned public transport, but the stop was useful for visitors to the park. Victor imagined he was one of the few people in the area, if not the entire city, who considered a bus the ideal method of urban transport. His life was one of assumed identities, but if he could avoid it, he preferred not to compromise them with the trail of documentation required to buy or rent a car. Stealing one posed an unnecessary risk, significant enough that it was only to be undertaken when there was no other option. Cars also trapped him, both by confining him physically and by demanding the concentration necessary to drive them. Riding the subway meant he could maintain more vigilance, but at the price of being held captive at least thirty meters underground. A bus, however, was a mode of transport that let him preserve vigilance, yet one by which he could depart frequently and easily without leaving behind a paper trail.

He planned to take a bus out of the neighborhood as the first step of his countersurveillance routine, but not from the stop opposite his destination. A handful of people were waiting—three heavyset men in business suits, an elderly couple holding hands, a young man in a cap, and a woman with two small children—and they stood up from their seats or shuffled forward into a rough line as both buses that stopped there neared, one after the other.

Except for the man in the cap.

Victor slowed his pace and dropped his gaze to the medical notes in his hand while the buses pulled up, the first in front of the stop, the other directly behind the first. A minute later they set off again, the second bus pulling out ahead of the first because they largely shared the same route and most of the waiting people had not wanted to walk the extra distance to the second bus.

The first bus joined the traffic after the second, leaving the bus stop empty.

Except for the man in the cap.

He wore walking boots, jeans, and a sports jacket. Earbuds rested in his ears and the wires extended down and disappeared beneath the jacket. The brim of a cap hid his eyes. There was some logo on the cap Victor didn't recognize. The cap was navy blue and the logo black. The sports jacket was gray. The jeans were faded but dark. The walking boots were brown.

He looked to be in his late twenties, but it was hard to be exact when his face was half-hidden by the navy blue cap. He wasn't tall or short. He wasn't broad or thin. His clothes were ordinary. Most people wouldn't have looked at him twice, if they had noticed him at all. But he'd let both of the only two buses that served the stop leave, and there was a bench less than ten meters away that would have been far more comfortable to sit on than the small plastic stools of the bus stop.

Victor crossed the street to the same side as the man in the cap and headed west. He didn't look back: either the man was still sitting at the bus stop and therefore was of no concern, or he was now walking west as well, in which case Victor had nothing to gain by letting the man know he was onto him.

After one hundred meters the pavement turned ninety degrees to follow the border of the park. Victor waited in the small crowd that had gathered at the street's edge, waiting for the crossing light to change. If the man in the cap was behind him, he would have slowed down or even stopped to maintain a tactical shadowing distance. Again, there was no point looking to confirm whether he was there, and equally no point if he was still sitting at the bus stop.

Victor saw the traffic slowing and crossed a few seconds before the lights changed. The crowd followed. He hurried across—just a man who didn't like to wait. If the man in the cap was alone, he would now be rushing to close the gap, because he wouldn't want to get trapped on the far side of the street when the lights changed back again.

But as Victor reached the other side of the street, he turned left, and in doing so saw the man in the cap on the far side, walking in the opposite direction alongside the park, not rushing because he knew he would draw attention by dashing across the street alone. But in attempting to stay undetected, he had put a busy street between them. If Victor took a turning, then he could easily lose his shadow.

So the man in the cap couldn't be alone. There was a team.

There was no one nearby that registered on Victor's radar, but they wouldn't have known whether he was going to go left or right after leaving Schule's and so couldn't have put watchers ahead of him. So they were mobile. Two cars, because he would easily have noticed one car doing laps in an area of light traffic. Therefore there were at least five in the team, a passenger in each car, as a driver couldn't drive and watch out for Victor and also communicate with the man on foot. But cars couldn't go everywhere, while they couldn't use the same pavement artist for too long and not expect Victor to spot him. So there would be another team member in the back of each car, ready to be dropped off and follow Victor as necessary. That made at least seven, but with two cars there were most likely eight.

A sizable team, and both a serious and telling statement. They knew who he was, or at least they knew of his capabilities, because no one hired eight men or women for a job they felt could be done by fewer.

They were proficient and resourceful, because they must have followed him to the doctor's office and he'd spotted only one so far of at least seven; else they had known of his appointment in advance and had good intel. But no better than proficient, because the man in the cap shouldn't have been waiting at the bus stop and no team put its worst member in such a primary role.

Victor maintained his walking speed. They weren't a surveillance team of some Austrian agency, because if they were, there would be no need to follow him so closely. They could have used a helicopter or the city's CCTV network. This team wanted to keep close to him for a reason, but they weren't going to try anything on a crowded street in the middle of Vienna in broad daylight. If they were unconcerned about witnesses, they could have ambushed him outside the doctor's offices. Instead they were following him, waiting for an opportunity that matched whatever criteria they had to meet.

He didn't know what that consisted of, and there was no way of knowing for sure until it was too late. He'd identified one of the team. He needed to identify the others.

Their reservations about making a move in a crowded locale worked to his advantage. If he stayed where there were people, he would stop them from putting their plan into action. It would force them to improvise. When people improvised, they made mistakes.

He continued walking and calculating, his gaze sweeping across every person to judge and evaluate. He memorized vehicles that passed him. No one stood out. No vehicle passed twice. They were holding back, or the others were a lot better than the guy at the bus stop. Or both.

People walked by. He walked by others. The streets were crowded, but not crowded enough to hide him effectively, and the ever-changing mass of faces made it impossible to keep track of potentials. He could take any number of turnings onto less busy side streets, but maybe that was what they were waiting for so they could move into action. A numerically superior force could not be combated in the open. They had too many advantages.

His best chance was at close range, where he could pick them off. One by one. But Victor didn't want the fallout from another bloodbath in the middle of a capital. Better to avoid a threat than neutralize it.

He needed to get indoors, somewhere they couldn't all follow, yet some could. There were plenty of bars and cafés nearby, which might work, but he needed somewhere that wasn't too busy.

A black and gold sign told him he'd found what he was looking for.

· Chapter 7 ·

Victor wasn't sure what the difference was between a gentleman's club and a strip joint, but the establishment he entered advertised itself as the former. A hulking doorman greeted him when he stepped inside and ushered him to a booth. There he paid a cover charge to an elderly woman, who then instructed him on the rules of etiquette, ending with "Absolutely no touching."

He nodded and descended a few broad steps onto the main club floor. It was light on patrons, being the afternoon. It was light on dancers because of the lack of patrons. The sparse crowd was perfect for Victor's requirements.

To his right, along almost the entire length of the room, stretched a wide bar worked by a lone male bartender who passed the time practicing tricks with a cocktail shaker. To Victor's left were doors leading to restrooms and others marked STAFF ONLY. A U-shaped stage dominated the center of the room, with five gleaming poles spread out along its length at equal intervals. A single dancer performed to generic electronic music. Nine men sitting around the stage, as far from one another as possible, were entranced by her listless routine and either didn't notice or didn't care that her expression was one of vacant boredom. An arched corridor glowing with ultraviolet light led off the back wall to the private performance area.

Aside from those that flanked the stage, there were a dozen round tables, each with four chairs, spread out around the room. Four of the tables were occupied by lone men, again with as much distance between them as could be achieved. Dancers accompanied three of those men.

The music was relatively quiet, because it was easier to convince a man to part with his money when he could actually hear. The chairs had leopard-pattern upholstery, and huge prints of naked women hung from the walls in elaborate gilded frames. The lighting was dim to create a seductive atmosphere and smooth away any imperfections the dancers might have. The aim seemed to be a high-class establishment, but a club wherein men paid to see women take off their clothes could achieve only so much class.

Victor knew he looked out of place. Men who wore suits were at work. The kind of men who frequented a strip club at two o'clock in the afternoon didn't know the difference between single and double breasted. If he had known in advance that he would be operating here, he would have chosen his attire to blend in better. But it didn't matter. He didn't need to convince those already inside the club that he belonged there.

Up close the bartender barely looked old enough to buy alcohol, but he answered Victor's request for an orange juice with a voice like the roar of a grizzly.

From his position at the bar, the club's entrance was out of Victor's line of sight. He didn't want to give anyone who followed any clue to his watchfulness. He didn't need to see someone descend the steps to know whether he had been followed. The room had contained fourteen men when he walked in—nine sitting alongside the stage and four at tables, plus the bartender—and there were no drinks on empty tables belonging to men in the restroom or enjoying a private dance.

He paid for his drink and took it to a table set toward the back wall, from which he could watch the rest of the room. It was basic protocol, and any shadow who followed Victor in would expect him to show that most fundamental level of precaution. Failure to sit with such a view would only make the shadow suspicious. The team didn't consist of seven or eight members if whoever had sent them didn't feel those numbers were needed. They knew who he was. They knew who they were dealing with.

No one new had entered the room by the time Victor took a seat. The chair was sturdy and comfortable. He had an unobstructed view toward the steps. At the top of them, hidden by a wall, were the woman and the doorman in the entrance foyer.

One of the dancers led an unshaven young guy from his seat and across the room into the ultraviolet-lighted corridor. The guy couldn't keep the smile from his face.

Victor was sipping orange juice when a man walked

down the steps from the entrance foyer. He was about forty, casually dressed in jeans and a thigh-length leather jacket. He had long graying hair and a solid build of about two hundred pounds on a six-foot frame. The man reached the bottom of the steps and glanced once around the room. He took a seat beside the U-shaped stage.

Three minutes had passed since Victor entered. It seemed a little soon for a cautious team with two vehicles and plenty of numbers to send in a shadow, but he guessed their caution meant they didn't want to lose a visual on him for any longer. Three minutes was plenty of time to slip out of a back entrance.

Thirty seconds after the man had sat down, another man entered. He was about ten years older than the first, somewhere in his early fifties. He wore branded sportswear—navy jogging bottoms and a brown sweatshirt. He stood a couple of inches shorter than the first guy and looked fit and healthy. His thinning hair was trimmed short, as was his beard. He bought a bottle of beer from the bartender and found a table he liked the look of on the opposite side of the stage to Victor. It was two minutes before the new guy took his first sip.

At which point a third man entered the club. He was about the same age as the first guy, but wore a smart black business suit beneath a tan overcoat. He carried a brown leather attaché case in his left hand. He was average height and a little out of shape. His hair was dark and curly and his cheeks had a red tinge, as though he was hot or out of breath. Like the guy in the sportswear, he headed to the bar and ordered a drink. The young bartender with the bear's voice worked the coffee machine while the businessman waited, looking a little nervous and excited at the same time.

Three men. Three potentials. But which was part of the team?

On first impressions all gave Victor cause for consideration and reason to dismiss. The first guy had the right physicality for a professional. His leather jacket was long enough to easily conceal a weapon—anything from a handgun to a compact submachine gun. But he had entered sooner than Victor would have expected from a member of a team with plenty of numbers.

The second man entered in what Victor judged to be the right time frame and was in shape, but he was a little older than Victor would have expected. The branded sportswear wasn't the best choice of attire for this neighborhood, but the colors were muted and he would have blended into the crowd in less affluent areas of the city. He was taking his time over his beer, either because he was taking his time or because he didn't want the alcohol in his bloodstream.

Judging by appearances, the businessman looked the least likely. His waistline wasn't fitting to the speed and fitness that were a part of the profession's job description, but he was in the most common age bracket and had entered more or less when Victor would have anticipated. The man looked very much like someone on his first anxious venture inside a strip club, but the suit and attaché case suggested he had come straight from his place of work. Yet lunchtime was over. And if he didn't need to get back to the office, coffee was not the best drink to calm his nerves and cool him down.

Victor dismissed the man in the leather jacket, not for the timing of his entry into the club but because he hadn't bought a drink at the bar. A shadow would have felt an overwhelming compulsion to purchase one to establish his bona fides. The man in the leather jacket knew he didn't need to spend his money on alcohol to watch the dancers so long as he spent his money on them. Because he was a regular.

The other two men both had beverages. They had both entered within the right time frame. There was nothing to single out one as more likely than the other. Both could be civilians, and either could be a shadow.

Which, Victor realized, was the point.

Both were part of the crew. Each was a shadow. The team was maintaining its cautious approach. They were concerned about the club and Victor's motives for entering it. They were worried he had made the surveillance and was attempting to draw it out or shake it off. They couldn't avoid sending a man inside, because they couldn't afford to lose visual contact in case he was trying to dump them. But if he was trying to draw out surveillance, he would be expecting a shadow to follow and would almost certainly make whoever followed him in.

But they couldn't know for sure whether he was in fact trying to draw out surveillance or just interested in naked flesh. They had to send one man inside to reestablish a visual on Victor, and if they were overestimating his aggressive countersurveillance tactics, it didn't matter if they sent in another man needlessly. But they had gambled that if the club was a countersurveillance ruse, then he was already onto them, and sacrificing the anonymity of an additional man was no great loss when they had to send one in regardless. But with two entering shortly after a civilian, there was a chance at least one watcher would remain undetected.

Three of the crew identified left either four or five that Victor hadn't seen. They wouldn't all be men, because a competent team wouldn't limit its options needlessly, but a woman couldn't enter a strip club inconspicuously. Discounting the two drivers and the two passengers needed to relay information, there were between three and four pavement artists. The young guy in the cap wouldn't be involved again for a while to avoid the risk of standing out, especially as they feared Victor might have spotted him, so that left two or three. And as the two shadows that had followed him inside were both men, then at least one of the remaining team members would be a woman and that woman would almost certainly be on foot.

Victor left his orange juice on the table and strolled over to the bartender, a casual walk, in no rush. The young guy straightened up as Victor neared and placed his fingertips on the edge of the bar.

"What can I get for you, sir?"

"I've got a delicate problem I'm hoping you could help me with."

"Problem?"

"Yeah," Victor breathed. "I think my wife might have followed me here."

The young guy suppressed a smile and nodded. "I understand, sir."

"You do?"

"Sure. It does happen from time to time. Wives can

get funny about this kind of thing. We can let you out of the back whenever you're ready to go, and she won't be allowed in on her own. Women have to be accompanied by a man. Which is not as uncommon as you think. Couples looking to add some spice often—"

"That's very kind of you," Victor said, "but I'm wondering if you could ask the doorman to check if she's out there."

The bartender hesitated a moment, then nodded. "Yeah, sure. No problem at all."

"Thank you. You're a lifesaver."

The bartender produced a smug look, as though he considered this favor to have equivalence with saving a life. "What does she look like?"

Victor said, "She's a brunette." A blonde or redhead would be too noticeable. "She's tall." A shadow had to be at least of average male height to be effective in crowds. "She'll be on the opposite side of the street if she's there." The best vantage point. "I don't know what she's wearing—sorry." Better than supplying an incorrect guess.

The bartender nodded along as he committed the details to memory. "I'll go ask."

Victor turned and rested his elbows on the bar behind him while he pretended to be captivated by the bored dancer on the stage. He didn't look at either of the two watchers, but he knew they would glance his way or keep him in their peripheral vision.

It took a little less than three minutes for the young bartender to return. He was already nodding before he reached Victor, who would have preferred the absence of such an obvious gesture so as not to draw the curiosity of the watchers, but short of shouting to the bartender to stop, there wasn't anything he could do.

"She's out there, all right," the bartender said, happy to be playing a part in the apparent drama. "On the opposite side of the street, just like you said she would be. Unless there's another brunette hanging out for the sake of it, of course. Not especially tall, though, but I guess it's a matter of opinion. You want me to show you the back way out?"

"Where does it lead to?"

The bartender said, "There's an alley that runs parallel to the street out front. You can take a left or a right and she'll never know you were here."

Victor pretended to think. "I appreciate the offer, but if she is out there, then she knows I'm here. Slipping out the back won't change that. I don't want her taking it out on you guys instead of me. I'll deal with her. Thanks for the assistance."

The bartender nodded and went to serve another customer. With maps available at the touch of a screen, the team would know about the alley and its two exits. If they were concerned enough about losing a visual on Victor to send two watchers inside the club, then they would have both exits of the alleyway under surveillance. Which meant each of the two vehicles would now be parked instead of doing circuits. The man in the cap would be in the backseat of one of the cars, because they couldn't take the risk of putting him on foot again.

Two inside the club. Five sitting in cars. One woman outside. All possible routes watched. No way to go without being watched. No way to escape the surveillance.

But the team had made one crucial mistake. In sending in two watchers they had inadvertently given Victor all of the team's positions.

So there was no longer any need to escape.

· Chapter 8 ·

From the archway glowing with ultraviolet light, the unshaven young guy with the big grin emerged with an even bigger grin. He walked a little awkwardly. The dancer followed a few paces behind him. She used her fingers to comb the knots out of her hair extensions and had a look on her face that said it was just another day at the office. Her eyes met with Victor's as his gaze swept her way, and she smiled, practiced and sultry as though he had brightened her life with his mere presence. He didn't need to gesture for her to head in his direction.

She had a slow, awkward walk because her skintight dress hugged her legs to her knees and let only an inch of air pass between them. She was no older than twenty, with hair so blond it was almost white. Her skin was a deep caramel color. Her smile widened as she drew closer to Victor, recognizing the quality of his garments and speculating on the limit of his credit card. He made sure to smile back and stare lustfully for the benefit of the two watchers. He held open the chair next to him, patting the seat with his palm for the dancer to sit beside him.

"I'm Claudia," she said as she sat, one manicured hand immediately resting on his nearest thigh.

"Alfred Schule," Victor said back.

"Pleasure to meet you, Alfred."

He let her ask him a few pointless questions that were designed to relax him and make him feel as though she was genuinely interested in what he did for a living and where he lived, and not purely concerned with how much money he might spend on her. He played along and soon she was laughing at everything he said.

"I need you to do something for me, Claudia." He took his wallet from his jacket and placed some cash on the table, watching her gaze lock onto it. "I want you to slap me across the cheek."

She smiled despite her confusion. "I'm sorry, what?"

"I want you to slap me as hard as you can. As though I've stepped out of line. Then I want you to grab a friend and tell her to entertain the man in the sportswear near the bar. I'll buy him a dance." He placed some more cash on the table. "And I'd like to pay you to make sure the man with the briefcase sitting in the corner has a similarly good time. I want you and your friend to make them feel extra special. Tell them it's on the house because they're first-timers. And they're both pretty shy, so don't take no for an answer. Okay?"

She looked at him and back to the cash and then nodded. "Sure, whatever you want. It's your money." She scooped it off the table. "But I'd really rather dance for you."

"Another time, perhaps."

She folded the money and slipped it under her dress. She frowned. "Are you sure you want me to slap you?"

"Hard as you can."

"No one's ever asked me to slap them before. On the face, at least." She laughed. "I'm not sure I can do it."

"Don't think about it. Just do it."

"Hard as I can?"

"Yes, please. Slap me. Hard as you can."

"Are you sure?"

He nodded. "Pretend I've insulted you or tried to grab you."

"But you seem like a nice guy."

"Trust me, I'm really not."

She raised her right hand a fraction and her gaze fell to his cheek. She tensed and frowned but didn't slap him.

"I can't do it." She laughed again.

"But if I asked you to strip naked, you could do that, right?"

She didn't answer. Her smile faltered.

He said, "Is taking your clothes off the absolute limit of your skills?"

The bait and tone worked.

It was a good slap.

She caught the side of his face with the entire inside of her hand, her fingertips making contact between his cheekbone and ear, her palm spread across his cheek. She was no stranger to slapping, and knew how to put her weight into it. The result was a significant sting to Victor's face and a notably loud noise. He felt moisture form in the corner of his eye.

She glared at him and stood.

He sat looking sheepish as she sought out a friend. He didn't need to check to know both watchers would have seen the incident. He bought another drink from the bartender and sat back down with it at his table, knowing the watchers would see him do so and expect him to remain in the club for at least as long as it had taken him to drink the first orange juice.

He took a sip and noted Claudia making her way over to the guy in the suit with the briefcase, while another dancer headed toward the one in the sportswear. They were both predictably good at their jobs and, having already been paid for their services, were fast and efficient in their actions. The two watchers didn't try to turn them away. They had to go along with the attention, or else risk identifying themselves as men who weren't interested in strippers and therefore shouldn't be in a strip joint.

Victor waited a minute, until both watchers were sat with their hands on their thighs and their knees apart, while the women danced between their legs and on their laps, their writhing bodies and swaying hair impeding lines of sight.

He stood and headed for the exit, knowing it would take only ten seconds until the watchers noticed he was gone. But that didn't matter. They couldn't hurl the dancers away for the reason they couldn't say no in the first instance, and similarly they couldn't send an update through their throat mikes with a woman on top of them.

He figured he had a thirty-second head start. He only needed twenty.

The doorman saw him approach and opened the door for him.

Victor nodded his thanks and said, "I've got a feeling there are a couple of guys back there who are going to try to slip out without paying."

"Yeah?"

"Just thought I'd give you a heads-up. One's in a suit, the other in sportswear. They came in separately, but I think they're a team of con artists."

"Oh, right. Thanks for the information."

"You're very welcome."

"Have a good day, sir." The doorman looked very pleased the dull afternoon shift was about to liven up.

Victor emerged onto the street outside. The sun stung his eyes a little after twenty minutes inside a dark club. He saw his "wife" straightaway. On the far side of the street, a woman stood in front of an antiques store. Her dark brown hair, chestnut where it reflected the sunshine, was tied up. She wore casual clothes—jeans and a corduroy jacket—and had a large patent leather handbag over her left shoulder. She wasn't tall and that told Victor a significant detail about her. He couldn't see her face, because she had her back to the street as she seemed to browse the furniture and ornaments in the store window—an action that let her watch the strip club's entrance via its reflection in the glass. He saw no other potential watchers nearby. She was alone.

The weak link.

· Chapter 9 ·

Victor knew she'd spotted him leave the strip joint. She couldn't fail to. She stood in a good position, at a good angle. No one could enter or exit the club without her knowledge. He knew she was watching him as he stepped off the curb and onto the street. She didn't move. She couldn't. She stood pretending to browse the goods displayed through the window of the antiques store. She didn't yet know he had slipped his shadows. She had to maintain her cover. If she reacted in any way, she might needlessly identify herself. She was hoping there was something she didn't understand; that walking in her direction was coincidental; that whatever he was doing, wherever he was going, it didn't involve her. She was still hoping when he was three meters away.

He hurried across the street to avoid the steady flow of traffic, the increased speed of his walk expected and entirely innocent. Except it wasn't.

When he hadn't changed direction at two meters, she

must have known he was coming for her. By that point she still had time to react, and began to turn so that her back was not presented to him, but she hesitated because she was distracted by the shadows in the club yelling updates into their throat mikes.

The loud voices in her ear served to distract her for only a second, but by the time she had shaken off her surprise, Victor was less than a meter behind her and it was far too late.

He put his open left hand on the small of her back, stepped around to face her as she swiveled in his direction, and thrust the tips of his locked fingers against her abdomen, an inch below her sternum.

She was underweight, with a wafer-thin layer of body fat on her stomach, which would have made it easier for Victor to find the spot with his fingertips had he not known exactly where to apply pressure. She gasped at the sudden and intense pain and instinctively tensed her stomach against the attack, but it did no good. Victor's fingertips pushed against the linea alba—the narrow strip of connective tissue that ran vertically down the center of the wall of abdominal muscle. Protecting her intestines from the pressure of Victor's attack was just a few millimeters of soft flesh.

He used his left hand to push her face into his shoulder, as though they were embracing, to muffle her cry as he pushed harder, knowing from experience how debilitating the resulting waves of agony and nausea could be. Her hands gripped his arms, but the pain weakened her and she didn't have the strength to push him away or fight. He closed his eyes and smiled for the benefit of anyone who should happen to look their way.

Her legs trembled and Victor felt her begin to fall, so he eased the pressure on her stomach to prevent her collapsing, and held her upright. He led her away, walking fast and pulling her along with him, knowing that the two shadows would be rushing for the club's exit but when they did there would be a huge doorman to get past first.

"No, wait . . ."

Victor led her to the mouth of an alleyway between two storefronts, stabbing his fingertips hard against her stomach when he felt her tense and try to slow. He could hear the muffled sound of commotion emanating through the woman's earpiece. One of the watchers had left his radio on send. Victor couldn't discern the exact nature of the sounds, but it seemed that they were tangling with the doorman.

The alley was wide, and empty of garbage or bins or anything else that would stop a delivery car or van backing into it. When they had gone three meters into it, Victor reached into the woman's patent leather handbag, having felt nothing hard against his torso as he'd held her close and her clothing offering no other room for a hiding place. He felt a document folder against the back of his hand as his fingers closed around the grip of a handgun. He knew it was a Glock 19 before he withdrew it from the bag.

He only had to give her a light shove to create distance, as she was too weak to resist. She was weaker than he thought because she stumbled a few steps, wildly off balance, and couldn't stop herself crashing to the ground.

But she was smart and resourceful and well trained, because she immediately rolled over to face him regardless of any shock or pain of impact, showing her palms as he pointed the muzzle of the Glock at her forehead.

"Wait," she gasped, eyes wide behind black-framed glasses that were skewed from the fall.

Panic warped her features. She looked about thirty. Her face was thin and drawn.

"Wait," she said again. "I'm no threat to you."

"Your entire team is no threat to me. So, now that you're unarmed and prone, what does that make you?"

Her breaths were quick and short. White showed all around her eyes. "Put the gun down, please. You don't need it. Please."

"Anyone who has seen my face up close, heard my voice, and knows enough about me to lead a surveillance op is a problem I can do without," Victor said. "So I would recommend thinking very carefully before you speak again, because the next thing out of your mouth will determine whether I walk from this alleyway or run."

There was no hesitation. She said, "My name is Janice Muir. I'm CIA. Roland Procter sent me."

"Then," Victor said as he heard a horn blare and tires screech on the street behind him, "you had better tell your team to back off, because two of them are about to get killed."

He pointed the Glock at the mouth of the alleyway.

Muir took a split second to process the situation, then thumbed her throat mike and yelled, *"Stand down! Stand down!"*

· Chapter 10 ·

The two watchers from the club—the one in sportswear, the other in a suit—had their guns drawn but lowered as they entered the alleyway. Both had hard stares that told Victor they didn't much appreciate him pointing a firearm in their direction, but they didn't comment on it and he didn't care. They came in slowly and obviously because Muir had told them what to expect, but for the same reason they were deliberate and cautious.

The guy in the sportswear said, "Are you all right, Janice?"

Muir was on one knee and bent over because of the fall and the pain in her stomach. "I'm fine, guys," she assured him, straightening her glasses so they sat properly. "Honestly. We're just talking here."

"Doesn't look like just talking," the man in the suit said, his eyes fixed on Victor.

"We were having a lively discussion," Muir joked with a cough, and said to Victor, "Weren't we?"

He didn't look at her. He didn't answer. He kept her handgun steady and extended at the two watchers. The guy in the suit was younger and probably faster than the older man in the sportswear, but his suit jacket was buttoned up, which would add a fraction of a second to the time it would take him to snap his own Glock up to shoot. Victor had the gun's muzzle pointed at the gap of empty air between their heads. They were equally quick and he couldn't predict who was likely to make a move first if it came to it.

The one in the sportswear said, "He's got your gun."

"He's just borrowing it," Muir replied. "He's going to give it back to me any second now. Aren't you?"

"Any second," Victor echoed.

"So give it back to her," the one in sportswear said.

Muir struggled to her feet. "Come on, Francis. Leave us alone for a minute. I'm giving you an order. Stand down. Please."

The watcher in the sportswear gestured over his shoulder and said, "We'll be right around the corner if you need us." He tapped the man in the suit on the arm.

Who said to Victor, "And we can be back in a flash, pal. Don't you forget that."

"He won't," Muir answered for him.

"In a flash," the man in the suit said again.

Both watchers backed out of the alleyway, but didn't turn around while Victor had the Glock aimed at them.

"You could have made that a lot easier," Muir said, and thumbed her throat mike.

Victor lowered the gun and faced her.

There was lots of communication back and forth between Muir and the remaining members of the team as she updated the others on the change in circumstances and assured them everything was fine.

She was half a foot shorter than him and he took a step backward so he didn't have to look down at her at such an acute angle. She was wiry, but so thin she was almost emaciated. He weighed close to twice what she did. When he had grabbed her upper arm to lead her to the alleyway, the tip of his index finger had almost reached his thumb, but the arm was firm with muscle, used to doing a job. She found time in her schedule to work out even if she didn't make time to eat proper meals. Her gaunt features added a couple of years to her appearance. He could see the vitamin D deficiency from her skin tone and the lack of protein in her hair.

She rubbed her stomach and said, "I need your help."

"Credentials," Victor said.

She handed them over. The ID was genuine but said she worked for the Justice Department. Common practice. Spies didn't carry laminates identifying themselves as spies.

"I need your help," Muir said again.

He handed back her ID. "You said Procter sent you."

She grimaced. "That's correct. He's my boss at the agency."

"If he really sent you, then you should have been told that I'm not of a particularly charitable nature."

"Okay, perhaps I should have phrased myself a little differently. When I say I need your help, what I really mean is I want you to do a job for me. I want to hire you."

Victor released the magazine from the Glock, then pulled back the slide so the round in the chamber ejected. He caught it and handed the gun, the mag, and the bullet to Muir.

"Thank you." Muir took the items and slipped them back inside her bag.

"The answer is no."

"You don't even know what I'm asking you to do yet."

"The specific details of the contract are immaterial. Procter should have explained to you that I don't talk business with clients in person. Even those who don't put a team of watchers on me."

Muir shifted her weight. "Look, I'm sorry about that. I really am. But you have to appreciate the position I was in. I know how things work between you and Procter. I had to meet you in person. I couldn't have just sent you an e-mail and expected you to take me seriously, could I?"

"I don't have to appreciate anything. But what you need to understand is that Procter is my broker. I don't deal with anyone else. Whatever your job is, if you wanted me to even consider agreeing to it, you should have allowed Procter to make contact. He's the one I deal with. No one else. I'm going to leave now. I've given you the courtesy of not killing you or your men because of your relationship with Procter. And that's a courtesy I'll only grant once."

"Procter's in the hospital," Muir said. "He was hit by a DUI. Some wasted guy in a Hummer. Procter's got a shattered hip and a bruised spine, and even if he wasn't high on opiates nine hours out of ten, he's got a broken jaw the size of a balloon. He's not in a position to contact anyone, least of all you. At an absolute minimum he's going to be out of action for the next few weeks and won't be back at the company for at least a couple of months. I can't wait that long."

Victor remained silent for a moment, then said, "Tell me what you know about me."

Muir stopped rubbing her stomach. "I know you're a professional assassin. Formerly freelance. Currently an unofficial asset for the agency. Which I find amusing seeing as the CIA has a crisp termination order with your name on it. Well, code name. You're also wanted by the Russian SVR and FSB, French Secret Service, Israeli Mossad, and half of the police forces in Europe. That's pretty much all I know."

"Then, when you claim to have so little information about me, how can you possibly know I can do what you need me to?"

"Because no one else can." She winced and rubbed her stomach again.

"The pain will come and go for about an hour. After that, you'll be fine. But you might want to skip the sit-ups for a few days."

She sighed. "Thanks for the advice."

"What about the rest of your team?" Victor asked. "What do they know about me?"

"They know even less than I do. The older guy is Francis Beatty. He's been at the agency forever. He's assisting me. The rest are a contract surveillance team purely here to establish if you were who I was looking for. They don't know what I want with you. All they were told is that you were a contact, albeit a highly dangerous one, and that you would spot them if they were anything less than perfect."

"They weren't close to perfect."

"And they'll be reprimanded appropriately, but I didn't have a lot of choice using them. You're not exactly the kind of man that you can walk up to and ask if he's really the assassin you're looking for. But whatever, they're of no danger to you now."

"They were never any danger to me."

"All I'm asking you is for thirty minutes of your time. That's all. Just half an hour. Let me tell you what the job is. You don't like what I have to say, you can walk away and you'll never hear from me again. You've got nothing to lose. I'm just asking you to listen to me here. See what I have to say first before you turn me down. I'll even buy you a coffee. You do drink coffee, don't you? Or tea if you prefer. You English guys like tea, right? Earl Grey or something like that. I don't know. I never drink it."

"Who said I'm an Englishman?"

"No one. I just thought that . . ."

"Okay," Victor said after a moment. "I'll listen to you, but I'll give you ten minutes of my time. Not a second longer."

"Great," Muir said. "Thank you. But let's talk somewhere else."

"There's a nice place round the corner where we can talk."

"Sounds great," Muir said. She touched her stomach. "I could really use a sit-down, you know?"

· Chapter 11 ·

The French bistro was small and cramped, with tightly packed tables beneath a low ceiling. Black-and-white photographs of famous French nationals covered the walls. Framed and signed soccer jerseys had pride of place behind the bar. The lunchtime rush was over and there were plenty of empty tables, but the close proximity of neighboring diners meant there was little chance of privacy, especially with the affable—and slightly drunk—owner making the effort to chat with all of his customers.

Victor selected a table outside on the pavement where there were no other patrons. He chose the table farthest from the entrance and took the chair against the wall, so Muir sat opposite him, her back to the street. Pedestrians passed in sparse enough numbers to ensure that they were not overheard.

Sunglasses shielded Victor's eyes from the glare of a sun unobstructed by clouds. The photosensitive lenses of

Muir's own glasses had darkened automatically to compensate for the brightness.

A waiter was quick to arrive with menus, but Victor motioned for him to keep hold of them.

"Just coffee, please," he said. He looked at Muir. "Espresso?"

"Sure. Whatever."

"Two espressos."

The waiter nodded and smiled.

After he was back inside the bistro, Muir placed her phone on the table between them and slid it over to Victor. He didn't reach for it. He didn't look at it.

"Procter being out of action changes nothing about the way I conduct business. I'm not assessing a target in person and especially not in a public space. Put your phone away. I'm here only to listen to what you have to say. So say it. The ten minutes begin now."

Muir shuffled her chair closer to the table and leaned across. She tapped the phone. "Do me a favor and look at it, okay? It's just a photograph. Just a guy's face. That's all. Just take a look."

"No," Victor said. "If you don't want me to stand up and walk away right now, you do things my way. I'm here to listen. That's all. Ten minutes isn't a long time. I suggest you use it economically."

"You don't have to touch the phone if you don't want to." She manipulated it briefly and the screen lit up in Victor's peripheral vision. "Just look at his face. It'll make all this a lot simpler. And quicker. Please, it's someone you know."

"I'm not sure why I'm failing to make myself understood. I'm not looking at the photograph. I don't care who it is. I'm not killing him."

Muir smiled a little. "You can't kill him. He's already dead."

That got Victor's attention, but Muir waited a minute until a couple of teenaged girls had passed on the pavement. He overheard something about a double date gone spectacularly wrong.

Muir slid her phone back and slipped it away into a pocket. "And the reason why this guy is currently horizontal is that you made it happen."

She sat back in her chair and watched him process the information.

He said, "My previous contract."

She nodded. "Felix Kooi. Dutch national. Citizen of Amsterdam. Professional contract killer. Killed almost a month ago. Stabbed in a back alley in Algiers. A mugging gone wrong, according to the authorities."

"You told me you didn't know the details of the work I've done for Procter."

Muir showed her palms. Her hands were small and glowed white in the sun. "I only know because it's relevant. And it's all I know. I promise."

"I'm not sure how much your word counts for at this particular moment."

"Hey, I don't lie. All right?"

"I imagine that stance poses significant problems for your chosen profession. Deception is inherent to spying, is it not?"

"I'm not sure if we really have spies anymore, at least

in the traditional sense." She glanced around. "I'm an intelligence officer for the CIA. I gather information on the bad guys and sometimes I act on it, or on information supplied to me."

"All without a single untruth."

"Okay," she conceded, exhaling heavily, "sometimes I might take a liberal attitude with the truth. But only for the greater good."

"How commendable of you."

"I'm not sure what you're trying to achieve with this."

"We're having a discussion about how much your word is worth. Or not. I'm sure you can appreciate how that is pertinent to this conversation."

"Listen. I'm playing straight with you. I am. I wouldn't go through all this to try to BS you."

"Very wise."

Muir glanced at her watch. "I'm going to continue, if that's okay with you?" She didn't wait for a response. "You were supplied with a significant amount of intel on Kooi, of course, so I won't waste what little time you've granted me regurgitating what you already know. The salient part of his bio is that he was responsible for the assassination of an American diplomat in Yemen two months ago, which is why Procter sent you to deal with him. He—"

The waiter appeared outside with their coffees. He smiled as he placed them down on the table. The tiny white espresso cups were ringed with lines of red glaze.

"Would it make you more comfortable if I explain how I found you?" Muir asked once the waiter had left them. She tentatively sipped the steaming espresso. "Procter figured you'd want to know."

"I already know."

"How?"

Victor remained silent and drank some coffee. He'd picked up the injury to the top of his left ear in the aftermath of his contract prior to Kooi. Procter, with his considerable power and insight into events and those responsible for the injury, could easily have found out the specifics. He knew enough about Victor to know he wouldn't be satisfied with a noticeable scar. Given the uncommon nature of the injury, it would have been a relatively simple task for supercomputers and analysts to sift through the patient records of cosmetic surgeons for a man fitting his description.

Muir said, "Procter just told me to say 'your ear.' He wouldn't tell me anything else."

Victor nodded.

"You're our third of four ear guys," Muir continued. "Today marks my third straight week of tracking down men with cosmetic ear surgery within the past twelve months."

"Procter's a good boss."

Muir nodded. "Of course. He's the best."

"Even though I imagine he hasn't told you he's doing it, he's looking after you. There's a good reason he's supplied you the absolute minimum of information about me. Do you know why that is?"

She nodded again. "So you wouldn't consider me a liability."

"Most people wouldn't be so careful. They wouldn't even think about that." Victor sipped from his little cup. "You should send him a card if you haven't already."

"I sent flowers."

"The last victim of Felix Kooi," Victor began after a nod. "When you say he was a diplomat in Yemen, what you really mean is he was a CIA nonofficial cover operative, correct?"

She hesitated a moment, then said, "That's classified."

"Of course it is, Miss Muir." Victor swallowed the rest of his espresso and placed his cup back on its little saucer. "And hence I'm afraid to say that you've wasted the past three weeks. Because one thing about me that Procter should have made unequivocally clear is my intolerance for the withholding of relevant information. Perhaps, if you would like to know more about why I am so inflexible on this particular issue, you can ask your boss. He knows." Victor stood. "Thank you for the coffee. It was delicious."

· Chapter 12 ·

Andorra la Vella, Andorra

The man with sandy blond hair watched. He'd been watching all day. He would be watching into the night. He would watch the next day. Maybe even the day after that. Nothing but watching.

Some people didn't like to watch. They got bored with the monotony of it. They grew complacent. They became irritated. They missed details. They didn't do the job they were supposed to. They were lazy.

Not the man with blond hair. He didn't get bored. He wouldn't become irritated. He was never lazy. He maintained focus whatever the hour. However long he'd been watching for. No matter what the circumstances. It was the way it should be, even if it hadn't always been so. As a young man he had lacked patience. He had hungered for excitement. Such was the folly of youth. Now he would appreciate the quieter moments of life. He appreci- them because they were so very rare and therefore precious. Yes, he liked to watch.

It was such a simple thing, to watch, but no small skill was required for that simplicity. Anyone with sight could watch. Yet to watch successfully meant to remain unseen in return. The man with sandy blond hair knew himself to be not unmemorable. He had enough height and breadth to make him stand out. His face had sharp features. His eyes imprinted themselves forever on anyone who looked into their depths. Yet, despite his conspicuous appearance, he shrouded himself in a cloak of the mundane that few could hope to peer behind.

The scenic locale and the sunshine made watching a more outwardly agreeable experience than perhaps it could have been, but a pleasant temperature and environment were quite unimportant to him. It would have made no difference had he been lying on frozen ground with an inch of snow across his entire body. He took his pleasure in the watching, not in the circumstances of the watch.

A riotous mob of pigeons flapped and crowded before his feet, eager enough for the bread he threw to them that they passed underneath his legs and between his feet. Across his lap lay a baguette that had been baked that morning and gave off the most wondrous of homely fragrances.

He was seated on an ornate iron bench set in Parc Central in the heart of the town that served as the capital of Andorra. It was a tiny settlement of less than twenty-five thousand people, and where often he discovered the charm of a town was in direct disproportion to its size, Andorra la Vella broke the rule he had witnessed the world over. He found it a horrid, soulless place, its buildings concrete monstrosities. Even the surrounding mountains failed to make a favorable impression. They were lumps of ugly rock fit only for the most ironic of picturesque postcards. He would not be sad to see his excursion here come to an end.

The man with blond hair carefully pulled chunks from the baguette's soft innards. While he rolled them into little balls between finger and thumb, he tore off pieces of crust and fed them between his lips.

The pigeons waited impatiently for the bread, but he only flicked it among them when he was happy the ball was perfectly spherical. Such attention to detail greatly mattered to him.

When the ball of bread sailed through the air, the resulting melee caused him to suppress a smile. Many times he'd watched the stronger pigeons shunt the smaller birds aside as they chased after the bread, else the fastest or most cunning pigeons would get to the food first and flap away before they were relieved of their prize. The weak and the slow were left hungry. It was life's eternal struggle played out in miniature at his feet. He silently applauded the actors who performed with such passion. So savage and yet so very beautiful. *Bravo*.

A middle-aged woman strolled by, draped in finery, dragging along a dog with bulging eyeballs and so small even the pigeons showed no fear of it.

"You shouldn't feed them," the woman called to him. "They're a nuisance. Pure vermin."

"As are we all, madam," the man with blond hair said back. "But at least the pigeons have no pretense of grandeur."

She frowned and quickened her pace.

"Everyone's a critic," he whispered to his actors.

He flicked another sphere of bread. It landed near the woman's feet, and the pigeons whooshed in her direction. She yelped and fled, jerking the tiny dog with her. It yapped.

This time he didn't suppress his smile.

Parc Central was one of the few green areas inside the town, but the surrounding valley was green under the summer sun. The pretty young mother and her son came here so often because it was so close to the boy's school. The child still enjoyed playing on the swings and roundabout and climbing on the frame. They came most days after school and sometimes on the weekends too. The man with blond hair knew because they never went anywhere without his knowledge—without his presence.

They lived in an apartment nearby. Although only a small dwelling, it was located in one of the town's most exclusive neighborhoods. The mother worked part-time as a sous chef in a fine restaurant and earned each month less than half the sum of the apartment's rent. He had eaten at the restaurant and found the food to be quite excellent, if a little heavy on the saturated fats.

The mother saw him on occasions, of course, as she saw other people on the street or in the park, but she strolled through a simple existence unaware of just how dangerous life could be. She failed to see through the mundane cloak that encased him. She dismissed him as just another man. A local, perhaps. Uninteresting and harmless. She didn't see the monster. But she would when the time was right.

That time was coming.

· Chapter 13 ·

Vienna, Austria

Victor's hotel had a fitness suite located on the ground floor. It was open twenty-four hours a day, which meant Victor could use it in the middle of the night when there were no other guests around. Beneath a high ceiling the room was fitted with rows of exercise bikes, cross trainers, treadmills, step machines, and rowing machines that occupied about three-quarters of the space. The rest was filled with resistance machines. No free weights.

It was quiet. His footsteps echoed. There were speakers positioned throughout the room linked to a music system that could be operated by the guests, if they so chose. Victor left it alone. The only other sound was the thrum of air-conditioning that kept the temperature low.

Including the main entrance, there were four ways in and out. The other three consisted of two short corridors leading to the male and female locker rooms and a door that would open into a room containing maintenance, cleaning, and first aid equipment. He tried his hotel key card on the lock for the other door but was greeted with a red light.

The female locker room was small, with no more than twenty lockers lining two of the four walls. Benches stood before them. A small toilet and a smaller shower room led off from the main area. Victor found no one. All the lockers were unlocked and he checked inside each one to make sure they were empty of anything forgotten by a guest who might come to collect it at this time of night. Nothing.

He exited it, walking fast, shaking his head and looking embarrassed for the benefit of any security guard who happened to be watching the fitness suite via one of the two cameras. The men's locker room had a similar layout and was similarly empty of people and belongings.

The suite's only entrance was set in one corner, and even with mirrors on most of the walls, it was impossible to watch from the majority of the cardiovascular and resistance equipment thanks to several pillars and the machines blocking line of sight. But the door pushed inward. Victor took a two-euro coin—the only money on him—from a pocket of his shorts and balanced it on the top of the inside handle.

He began his workout by doing a circuit of the resistance machines. He kept the breaks between sets short and used light weights and high repetitions to maintain his strength without adding excess bulk to his lean muscle mass. It took him an hour to do the circuit and he paused to refuel on protein and carbohydrates from a supplement shake before beginning the second part of his workout with cardiovascular exercises.

He rowed for thirty minutes, creating intense fatigue in

his upper body already weakened from the circuit training. His workout gear now soaked in sweat, he moved to a cycling machine. He kept his heart rate at ninety percent of maximum for half an hour and moved to the treadmill as the first light of dawn began to brighten the city outside.

The cardio machines all faced windows that ran along one wall beneath rows of TV screens. Normally, Victor would not have remained exposed before an unarmored window for any length of time, but to protect the privacy of the hotel's guests, the fitness suite's windows were one-way. In addition, he used machines adjacent to or behind pillars to provide cover and limit line of sight for any marksman across the street.

Midway through his run on the treadmill, he heard the echoing clink of metal striking a hard surface. The sound was quiet compared to the whine of the treadmill's machinery and the thump of his feet on the belt, but Victor had chosen a machine close to the door to make sure he heard it.

He glanced over his shoulder to see a woman enter. She was in her mid-twenties, dressed in workout gear, with blond hair pulled back into a tight ponytail. She was slim and toned and he didn't have to look at her longer than half a second to know for certain there could be no hidden weapon on her person. Victor dismissed her as a threat and continued his run.

Her fragrance would have informed him of her approach even if the mirrors had not let him keep track of her movements. He was on the end of the row of treadmills. There were another five to his right. She chose the one next to him.

He glanced again in case he had missed something the first time, but there wasn't room to hide a pencil in her clothes, let alone a gun. She was looking his way and saw his eyes flick in her direction.

"Hey," she said.

He nodded to acknowledge the greeting, but didn't say anything in return.

In his peripheral vision he saw the young woman tap the screen of her machine to set up her workout and began at a quick walk. She looked across at his readout.

"Wow," she said, "that's an impressive time."

He nodded again, and smiled briefly—polite but distracted. "Thanks."

"Where are you from?"

"Sorry," he said, speaking between inhales. "I'm in training for a race. I need to concentrate."

"Sure, no problem," she said. "Oh, by the way, did you drop this coin?"

• • •

Victor found Muir waiting outside his room. She didn't see him straightaway, because she was looking left in the direction of the elevators as Victor rounded the corner from the stairwell. She didn't hear him approach because his footsteps were quiet even without athletic shoes and carpet to further muffle the sound, only facing him as he entered her peripheral vision. Her shoulder blades came away from the wall next to his door, her legs straightened, and she arched her back. She'd been waiting there a long time. She had a key card between her fingers.

"I took a wild guess that you wouldn't like it if you

found me inside your hotel room," she said, waving the card for emphasis.

"Not as much as you wouldn't."

She wore gray trousers and a blue blouse underneath a smart leather jacket that was tapered at the waist and flared out around her hips. It made her look less thin than she had the day before but could do nothing for the sunken cheekbones. Her boots had a two-inch heel. Her dark hair was loose and wavy. Behind her glasses her eyes looked tired, but she had applied extra makeup to try to hide the dark circles and bags.

"My body clock is still all over the place," she explained, "and I figured you would be an early riser."

He ignored her and moved to insert his own key card in the slot.

Muir took a rapid step back. "Why don't I wait for you downstairs while you take a shower?" She wrinkled her nose. "You really hum."

He looked at her.

She said, "Shall we say I'll see you in the lobby in about twenty minutes?"

"We have nothing further to discuss. If you had managed to get clearance to answer my question, you would have said so by now."

"You're right. I don't have clearance. I spent half the night trying to get it."

Victor pushed open his door. "Have a good flight back to Washington, Miss Muir. I trust you understand it's in your best interest to forget you ever met me."

"Wait," she said, and went to grab his arm.

Her fingers didn't find their target. Instead they were

twisted back on themselves, and her wrist joint hyperextended. She gasped and sank downward as he applied pressure. He released her before any serious damage was caused, but only just.

"Go back to Washington, Miss Muir."

"Wait," she said again, grimacing as she rubbed her wrist. "I haven't got clearance, but I'm going to answer your question anyway. I'm going to break the rules because I need your help and I don't have time to waste waiting for a guy in an office to grant clearance on facts you've already worked out for yourself."

"That's a sensible attitude to take."

"I thought you'd agree. I'll tell you everything you want to know downstairs, okay?" She sucked in air between her teeth and tried to rub the pain from her wrist.

"Not in the lobby," Victor said. "But I'm going to get some dinner when I've cleaned up. You can join me if you wish."

She glanced at her watch. "Don't you mean breakfast?"

"I'm unlikely to get the two confused."

"Sure, okay. Let's go get some dinner. At six a.m."

· Chapter 14 ·

Dinner consisted of two hot dogs loaded with onions and ketchup bought from a street vendor. Muir settled for a cream donut, along with a black coffee into which she added three sachets of sugar. Two brown. One white. The sun shone through wispy clouds and they walked along the river, where it was quiet. It was windy and Muir wore a band to keep her hair back. Joggers passed them by on occasion.

Victor saw nothing of Muir's team. There were still three he hadn't identified and he knew they wouldn't be far; nor would the young guy who had been waiting at the bus stop, the sportswear-clad fifty-year-old called Beatty, and the one disguised as a businessman. They would be tracking Muir easily enough with GPS via her cell phone. Beatty would have argued they needed to maintain visual contact, but she would have insisted otherwise. She knew as Victor had spotted them the first time that he would do so again, and she didn't want to antagonize him. He appreciated that uncommon courtesy.

"The diplomat who was killed in Yemen was CIA," Muir said, looking away. "Nonofficial cover operative. A NOC. Stanley Charters. Guy was a real hero."

"What was he doing in Yemen?"

"He was running agents linked to the black market plutonium trade. Which I'm sure you can appreciate is a very rare and complex operation. Anything radioactive automatically becomes the hardest illicit commodity to identify and track. And not just because the traders go to such great lengths to hide it."

"Because more often than not it's mostly smoke and mirrors."

Muir nodded. "There's a million bad guys out there who want to get their hands on it, so there are countless opportunists claiming to have access to hidden Soviet stockpiles and suitcase nukes. It's ridiculous. Have these people never heard of a half-life? Even the few genuine traders out there are mostly trying to sell junk that stopped being detonable over a decade ago, else it was never weapons grade in the first place. As long as the Geiger counter crackles, most buyers don't know any better. But ninety percent of sellers don't even have access to waste product. They're just charlatans looking to rip off rich jihadists eager to turn up in the middle of nowhere with briefcases full of cash money."

"But your NOC was onto traders who had the real thing?"

"Charters had a solid-gold link to a chain that supposedly ran all the way to the enrichment plants in Pakistan."

"Hence why he met with a premature demise."

Muir nodded again. "We don't know how he got

found out, but the body was discovered in his apartment with a straight razor buried in his throat. Yemeni authorities were happy to put it down as a suicide."

"How did you identify Kooi as the assassin?"

"One of the agents Charters was running was terrified he'd be the next victim. He turned up at the U.S. consulate for protection. He was just one of the network's smugglers, not that he ever came near anything radioactive, but he'd overheard his boss boast that they had a Dutchman on the books who was cleaning up problems for them. Then it was pure grunt work; a process of elimination. Only so many Europeans entering and exiting Yemen in the right time period. Only so many men. Then of those only one traveling from Amsterdam who also happened to have flown into Pakistan the same week as an asset for the Pakistani Secret Service, who was supplying them intel about plutonium smuggling, committed suicide by slitting his wrists. You'll never guess what he cut them with."

"Sloppy," Victor said.

"Don't approve of the MO?"

"A suicide takes some skill to pull off convincingly, especially with someone more prone to violent death than a regular civilian. But to use the same method for two separate targets for the same client is leaving an unnecessary trail. Perhaps the razor is symbolic to these guys. Whoever is in charge is sending a message to everyone in the network: *Wherever you are, I can get to you.*"

"Makes sense. Kooi likely thought there was enough difference between slit wrists and a razor in the neck that a connection wouldn't be made, but he could still satisfy the client's wishes."

"His intent would have been to slit your NOC's wrists as he'd done with the Pakistani asset to create a convincing suicide. A razor in the neck is not. He would have been waiting in the apartment for when he came back. Either he made a mistake or the NOC knew he was there, because they fought. Kooi had no choice but to stab him in the neck. But that wasn't his plan."

"The Yemeni police report mentioned nothing about signs of struggle in Charters's apartment."

"Then they're lying."

"Or Kooi covered his tracks."

"Possible, but unlikely. Unless the NOC lived in a soundproof apartment, neighbors would have heard the commotion. Kooi wouldn't have had time to clean up and set the scene. Easier to bribe or threaten the investigator."

Muir frowned and withdrew her phone. "I've got to pass this on. Give me a minute, please?"

Victor nodded and stepped away to give Muir a little privacy while she made a call and explained to whoever was on the other end of the line what had just been discussed. She hung up.

"Thank you for accommodating me."

"No problem."

They walked on for a minute in silence. Then Victor said, "Why was I sent to kill Kooi? Why not pick him up and find out who hired him to assassinate your man?"

"If only it were that simple. Kooi was a citizen of the Netherlands with no criminal record. He ran a small charity that required him to travel all over the world as an alibi. There was no evidence against him that would stand up in court or would convince the Dutch authorities to extradite him. And we couldn't just lift him from the middle of Amsterdam and smuggle him out of the country without risking stirring up a hornet's nest. More important, however, we didn't need to sweat him for intel. The Pakistani asset who turned up crying at the embassy gave us everything we needed to track the client down. He's now rotting in a prison that doesn't exist, wishing he was dead, and spilling his guts of everything he knows in the hopes he'll be let out one day. He won't, of course. We think we've identified about sixty percent of the plutonium smuggling network so far. It's only a matter of time until we get the rest. We didn't need Kooi and we like old-school justice at the agency when it comes to our own. We had the opportunity to deal out a little karma that wouldn't lead back to us, so we took it."

"In other words, you had me."

"Yes," Muir admitted. "And I'd like to thank you for that. Charters was a good guy. We worked together some time ago."

"You didn't just work, though, did you?"

"What do you mean by that?"

"I mean you've lost fifteen pounds. Recently, because your clothes don't fit and you haven't had the time to go shopping for ones that do, except for that leather jacket."

"Stan and I had a thing while on an op together a couple of years ago. It hurt when he died. It still hurts. So what? I'm still objective here."

"I didn't say you weren't. But you said you'd be honest with me."

"It was personal information. It's got nothing to do with this conversation."

Victor finished off the last hot dog and used a napkin to clean his fingers. Muir said, "For a guy who works out so much, I'm surprised you're not more careful about what you put inside you."

"I'm not without my vices." He dropped the napkin and the greaseproof paper from the hot dogs into a bin. "Perhaps it's about time you told me what I have to do with this sequence of events, aside from Kooi's death."

Muir watched him, then took a breath and said, "A few weeks ago the client informed us that he hadn't hired Kooi directly. He'd used a broker. After Kooi was dead we had some of our people go searching for proof through his personal laptop and phone, but they were clean. We hadn't expected to find anything, but it doesn't hurt to be thorough, right?"

"Absolutely."

"But they didn't find a link to any broker to support the client's claims, and we dismissed it as hot air to try to shift some of the blame."

"Until you checked out Kooi's charity."

"Correct. It was more than just a front so he could jet all over the place without drawing suspicion. It was how he handled his business too."

"Let me guess: Kooi had erased anything that might link to a previous job. But since his death, the broker, not knowing Kooi's dead, has made contact."

She nodded. "Just once."

"A new contract?"

"It's instructions for a meeting: a date and a time and a location. I think it must be a follow-up, part of an ongoing dialogue. There's nothing about a job. Nothing about a target. The title of the e-mail is 'First Date.'"

"How romantic."

"I think the title is significant. I think it's their first face-to-face."

"I made the same association."

"The client who hired Kooi said he never met the broker. Never saw him. Never spoke to him. We know absolutely nothing about him except for the fact that Kooi is supposed to meet him."

"And you would like me to go instead."

She nodded and said, "Yes," even though he hadn't been asking a question. "This isn't a contract. You just have to go to the meeting in Kooi's place. You don't have to kill anyone."

"Then have a team stake out the location and see who turns up thinking they're going to meet Kooi. I'd recommend using different people than the ones you put on me yesterday."

"That isn't going to work. I don't believe the broker will be at the location to meet up with Kooi personally. At least, not initially."

"What is the location listed in the e-mail?"

"Budapest International Airport."

"Ah," Victor said.

"Exactly. The airport isn't random, is it? There's going to be someone waiting in arrivals with a card to collect Kooi. That person isn't going to be the broker. I pick him up and when he doesn't turn up where he's supposed to when he's supposed to or make the scheduled call or e-mail or whatever, the broker is going to vanish. And the guy I pick up? Maybe he's only there to ferry Kooi and he knows nothing about the broker. What if he's just a taxi driver? It's just not going to work. I need someone to go in Kooi's place. I can't just send one of my guys because I don't know what has or hasn't been discussed between Kooi and the broker. I can't brief the person I send in. He'll have to improvise."

"Which is why you need someone who knows the industry well enough to bluff their way through the encounter."

"I'm authorized to pay you your agreed fee," Muir said. "Whether the meeting lasts all day or three minutes, whatever the outcome, you'll get the money."

"What are you hoping to achieve?"

"It's about taking down a bad guy and preventing an assassination. Plain and simple. I don't want the broker hiring some other killer when no one turns up to meet him. These people aren't exactly knocking off bad guys."

"That's not all you want."

"Kooi may have killed Charters, and the guy rotting in a black-site jail wanted him dead, but this broker made it possible. He shouldn't be the only one who gets away with it. We look after our own at the agency, and we make sure they get justice."

"You need an answer now, don't you?"

"I do."

"Desperation is stamped all over your face. So this meeting is going down soon. Don't tell me—tomorrow?"

She shook her head. "Tonight."

· Chapter 15 ·

The waters of the Danube were gray and choppy. Ferries and pleasure cruisers passed in both directions. A seagull floated on the waves. Muir leaned against the low stone wall and watched it. The breeze pulled loose strands of hair from her hair band. Victor saw a kid waving at them from one of the passing boats and returned the gesture.

"How old are you?" he asked.

Muir didn't hesitate because she found the question embarrassing, but she also didn't answer automatically. She watched the gull take off from the water and flap away. She looked over her shoulder at him, answering his question with one of her own: "How is my age relevant to what we're discussing?"

"Any question I ask is relevant."

She considered for a moment. "Okay, if you believe it's important to know my age, I turned thirty last week."

"Happy birthday for last week."

"Thank you," Muir said after another pause, this time to decide on his sincerity. She turned around to face him properly and leaned against the stone fence.

"Law or history at college?"

"I majored in law."

"Never wanted to be a lawyer?"

"Sure I did."

"So why aren't you one?"

"I don't have the right qualifications on my résumé: I have a conscience."

"CIA straight out of college?"

"Yes."

"No gap year? No seeing the world?"

She shook her head. "On whose dime? I worked three jobs to help pay my tuition."

"So you've been at the agency for about eight years."

"That's right," she said, hesitantly.

"You're a little inexperienced to be running this kind of show."

"I'm good at my job."

"I don't doubt you are, but that's not the only reason you're speaking to me now, is it? And if you're as good at your job as you say you are, then you've already worked out that reason for yourself."

She didn't want to say it. For a moment it looked as though she would change the subject, but she said, "You're saying Procter chose me to deal with you because he believes you'll find it harder to say no to a woman."

"I'm not the only one who thinks that, am I?"

Muir's eyes narrowed a fraction. Behind her glasses, he almost didn't see it. She adjusted them. They didn't need adjusting. "The thought has crossed my mind. It's the twenty-first century, but that doesn't mean some guys aren't still cavemen at heart. Procter thought you're less likely to say no to a woman. He also thinks you'd be less likely to kill one if you reacted badly to being contacted like this."

"Why would a man be more deserving of death than a woman in a given scenario?"

"Chivalry. I don't know. It's how we're wired as a society. Women receive lighter sentences for the same crimes as men. I'm not saying it's right; it's just how it is. If it's not true in this case, then why would Procter think it?"

"Because a good man—or woman—hopes to see the same good in others."

Muir stared at him, attempting to identify any subtext, but found none.

"Do you believe I'm more likely to accept this job because you're a woman?" Victor asked.

She shrugged. "It doesn't matter what I think."

"It matters to me."

Frustration was obvious in her expression. "Yes, okay? I believe it does. I think it has to make a difference; otherwise Procter wouldn't have sent me. He hasn't got a concussion, and like you said yourself, he's good. He's smart. He considers everything. If it didn't matter he wouldn't have sent me. There are guys who would have been more suitable."

"'More suitable'?"

"Better," Muir said. "Men who have twice my experience."

"Most people don't care how or why they get a break. They just want one."

"I didn't enter the intelligence business so I could be a pair of legs."

"You want an op assigned to you based exclusively on your proficiency, not your gender?"

"Of course. It's an insult that my gender is even considered relevant, let alone if it actually is relevant. It makes me angry—so what? It pisses me off. Wouldn't it you in my place?"

"I don't get angry," Victor said. "And please correct me if I'm wrong, but an essential contributing factor to my suitability for this job of yours is the fact that I, like Kooi, am male."

She stared at him, trying not to show her annoyance. But she couldn't stop the capillaries widening beneath the skin of her cheeks any more than she could stop her pupils dilating.

"If you're trying to jerk my chain, then let's not waste any more of each other's time, okay?"

"I'm simply trying to understand you."

Muir examined his face, trying to determine what he was thinking. She hadn't yet worked out the futility of such an attempt, but the annoyance became confusion that became hope. "Does that mean that you'll do it?"

After a moment, he said, "Yes."

"Because I'm a woman?"

"Do I seem like a knight in shining armor to you?"

"Then I can only assume you trust me."

"I trust that you understand the consequences of showing yourself to be untrustworthy."

She nodded. "I'm here to play fair with you. I don't know how to do anything else."

"Good," Victor said, "because if I'm played in any way, the one thing I won't do is play fair in return. Procter can tell you about that too."

"Understood. You don't need to be concerned about being compromised. You'll deal with me and me alone. We're going to be a two-person show. Procter said that's the only way you would do it."

"He was right. I take it you have all the information on you that I will need."

She reached into a pocket. "Everything I have is right here." She withdrew a tiny flash drive. "Don't lose it."

Muir passed it to him and he pocketed it, thinking briefly about what had happened the last time he'd had a memory stick on his person that contained valuable information. He turned his mind away from the past because he would only survive the future by concentrating on the present.

"There's not as much intel as I would like," Muir began, "but that's why I need you to fill in the blanks. Once you make contact we have absolutely no idea what's going to happen next. But I think we can assume that after you've been picked up at the airport you'll be taken—"

"If you've supplied me with all the facts you have, there is nothing you can speculate on that I won't consider myself."

A pause, then, "Okay."

"If I'm blunt it is because we're operating on a limited time frame, and, unless you've been withholding a significant amount of your personal history, I know more about this business than you do."

She nodded. "Yes, of course. I understand. No offense taken."

"Good, then you also need to understand that once I accept a job I'm in charge. I'm not an employee. You supply me with all the intelligence you have and I'll make the decisions on how to proceed with it. Agreed?"

"Sounds perfectly fair. What I'm asking you to do is meet the broker and learn as much about him as you can. If that means accepting a job, great. I want to know about that too. I want this broker and the client too. So agree to anything he wants as long as it keeps him talking and gets you hired. Be his perfect assassin. You'll need to wear a wire so we can record what he has to say, and I'll have some of my guys follow you from the airport."

"No."

"Excuse me?"

"No wires. No guys. Whoever this broker is he isn't stupid. He's used Kooi before but he's never met him in person. But he plans to now, because whatever this job is it's big enough to require a face-to-face. He's having someone else pick him up at an airport for a reason. He knows Kooi wouldn't risk trying to carry a gun on a flight, and collecting him straight from the airport means he wouldn't be able to get one on the ground. This broker is cautious. He's careful. There's a very good chance I'll be searched or he'll have electronic countermeasures. So no recording device of any kind. And your guys just aren't good enough. I'm not having my life balancing on their skills at remaining unseen."

Muir sighed and looked away. "Then it's a no-go. I can't send you in without backup, and if we don't get anything useable on the broker, then there's no point going through with it."

"If I get hired the broker is going to tell me the target and the job specifications. With that you can work back to the client."

"Maybe."

"Yes, maybe. But that's the risk you're going to have to take."

She stared back out at the river. "I don't exactly have a lot of choice, do I?"

Victor remained silent.

"Okay," she said eventually, "we'll do it your way if that's what it's going to take." She turned back around. "You're supposed to meet the contact tonight at twenty fifteen, in Budapest. Which means you need to be on the seventeen twenty-two flight from Vienna International. We've already got you a ticket. We weren't being presumptuous, just so you know. We didn't want to risk the flight selling out. It's business class, by the way, courtesy of the U.S. government."

"Scrap it. I require an economy seat."

"There's no need. We've already got the ticket. The price isn't coming off your fee. Consider it a bonus, but it's practical too. You'll be more alert on arrival."

"Kooi used a charity as a cover for his contracts. A business-class ticket costs several times that of an economy. No small charity is going to blow its budget sending employees business class. So neither would Kooi. If you don't believe me, check his flight history."

Muir sucked in air through her teeth and grimaced. "You're right. Damn. I should have considered that."

"Yes, you should. Because maybe this unidentified broker knows as much about Kooi as you do and has the resources to check on these things."

"I know; I'm sorry. I don't know what else to say."

"Nothing more needs to be said on the matter. Everyone makes mistakes."

"Do you?"

"You'll get your answer if I return," Victor said. "And if I don't."

· Chapter 16 ·

Andorra la Vella, Andorra

Peter Defraine loved school. He absolutely loved it. He had cried on his very first day because it was the first time he had ever been parted from his mother for any length of time. But that was ages ago and he hadn't cried since. He was a big kid now. A very brave boy, as his mother often told him. He wasn't quite sure why he was brave. It wasn't as though school was scary. It was fun. Lots of fun at break times when he played games with the other children, but also fun in the classroom, and not just when he got to draw pictures. Drawing pictures was the best.

Every day he enjoyed learning new words and how to spell them and how to write them down. Every afternoon he told his mother about the new words he knew and she was always so impressed by how clever he was. He was clever. He knew more words than anyone in his class and he knew the most multiplication tables. Some of his classmates pulled faces when he thrust his hand into the air to answer questions. He didn't get why they did that.

It was almost home time and Peter sat on his chair with his bag packed in front of him and resting on the desk, as did all the other children, while they waited for the clock to tick round to three o'clock. Then they would be dismissed and everyone would rush out of the classroom and down the corridor and out the big doors.

When the teacher told them to go and the other children leaped to their feet, Peter slowed himself down because his table was near the exit and Eloise sat on the far side. They'd held hands once one lunchtime—but didn't talk—and Peter had eventually got bored and gone to play football. Eloise's friends had then told him she didn't want to go out with him anymore. He didn't know they had been going out. He didn't know what that meant. All he knew was that Eloise wouldn't even look at him anymore and left her place in the queue for the cafeteria and went to the back when he'd tried to play with her hair.

The other children rushed out. Peter slowly put his coat on and slowly looped the strap of his backpack over one shoulder and slowly put his chair on top of the table—why did they all have to do that?—and slowly headed for the door.

Eloise and her friends rushed past him and he was left alone with the teacher.

He felt Mrs. Fuentes pat him on the shoulder, and she said, "Better luck next time."

He didn't understand.

• • •

Outside, the sun was shining and Lucille Defraine waited for her son, hoping he would be wearing his coat as she'd asked him to. He argued he didn't need one because some of his friends didn't and he was just getting to that age when fitting in was starting to matter more than staying warm. She waited on the pavement outside with the other parents, in the same spot she always waited. She smiled when she saw Peter and he smiled back. He skipped over to her and she pulled him into a tight hug.

"*Ow,*" he said. "You're squashing me."

She kissed him on the top of his head. "Don't be silly."

"You're silly, not me."

"Any particular reason why you're not wearing your coat?"

He looked away as if by not meeting her gaze she would forget all about it. He said, "I learned lots of new words today."

"That's great, honey," his mother said, smiling to herself at her son's attempt at cunning. "Why don't you tell me all about them on the way to the park? But put your coat on first."

• • •

Peter left his coat and tie and his bag with his mother and sprinted to the climbing frame. It was big and painted in bright colors. Peter loved to climb to the top. Some of the other kids his age didn't climb all the way. They got scared. He didn't understand what there was to be afraid of. He'd fallen off the climbing frame twice, once grazing both knees and both elbows and once hurting his ankle. He'd cried both times and again when his mother used stinging liquid to clean the grazes. That didn't stop him going back on it. He didn't remember what the pain felt like. He'd never fallen from the top before, but he was a whole year older now and it didn't seem that far down anymore. Sometimes he felt like jumping from the top just to see if he could, but his mother always knew when he was thinking about it and would shake her head and give him *that* look, and he knew he would be in big trouble if he did.

She watched him from one of the benches while she smoked a cigarette and drank coffee. Both smelled horrible. He didn't know why she liked them. He knew from school that smoking was very bad and he told his mother as often as he could. She always agreed with him, but she still did it. It made her clothes stink. She never smoked inside their home, though. She stood on the balcony with the door closed. How good could it be if she had to go outside in the cold to do it?

When he'd finished on the climbing frame, he played with some of the other children on the swings, taking turns between pushing and swinging, and then on the roundabout, sometimes heaving and pushing to make it go faster and faster so the girls screamed and he fell away because he couldn't run as fast as it could spin around, other times hanging on while others spun it, but he never screamed. It never went fast enough to make him scream.

Just like always, it was time to go too soon. Peter pretended not to hear his mother's calls and instead chased one of the girls up the path and through a crowd of pigeons that all took flight in one big flapping mass.

"Peter," his mother called again.

The girl ran off to her own mother and Peter turned to trudge back down the path.

"You'd better hurry," a man said.

He was big and had short blond hair. He was old like Peter's mother but not really old like Mrs. Fuentes and sat on a bench with a half-eaten baguette of bread across his legs. Peter had seen him before, but he didn't know where or when. He was smiling and looked a bit like a friendly giant from one of the storybooks they read in class.

"You don't want to make your mother late for work at the restaurant, do you, Peter?"

Peter didn't know how the man knew his name. He didn't ask because the man was a stranger.

"You take care of yourself," the man said. "You're a very special little boy. I look forward to seeing you again soon."

Peter pretended not to hear and sprinted toward where his mother waited.

· Chapter 17 ·

Budapest, Hungary

The plane touched down a minute behind schedule at Budapest Liszt Ferenc International Airport. Victor remained in his economy-class seat while the cabin emptied around him. The harried business travelers were first to get up from their seats to try to beat the rush to the exit, followed by the tourists and finally the old or infirm and families with young children. There were a few solitary passengers who, like Victor, were in no rush, and he briefly wondered what had brought them to the city and why time didn't hold the same power over them as it did so many others.

He made his way off the plane, pausing in the aisle to let a woman use a walking stick at her own pace. A slow walk through the jet bridge tunnel brought him to the arrivals hall, where a stewardess smiled and nodded at him as he passed. He smiled in return and gazed around while he walked, as though he were visiting for the first time and every mundane feature of the airport fascinated him and required him to stop and examine it.

The passport and visa check was conducted with swift efficiency by a round woman in her fifties, but was significantly delayed when Victor had trouble locating his passport. He checked the pockets of his trousers and those of his jacket. He searched through his bag twice. He laughed along with the woman when the passport was eventually found to have been in his inside jacket pocket all along.

He waited near the baggage carousels until only a scattering of people remained, all anxiously waiting for their suitcases to magically appear through the black rubber curtain, but slowly accepting the fact that their trip had been ruined before it had even begun. His overnight bag did three laps until he exhaled, shook his head, and lifted it away. It contained a change of clothes and some toiletries, but he wasn't expecting to use any of the bag's contents. Whatever guise the meeting with the unidentified broker took, it wouldn't last all night, but Victor had the bag for another reason.

He strolled through customs, head angled down, trying not to make eye contact, shoulders bunched defensively, and was waved over by an official who looked as bored with life in general as he was with his job. The official checked Victor's bag and sniffed the contents of the numerous unnecessary miniature bottles of shampoo and shaving balm. The lack of anything even remotely interesting had a palpable effect on the official, who waved Victor away with a heavy sigh, his face a picture of disappointment and hopelessness.

By the time Victor descended the escalator to the ticket hall, there were only nine passengers from his flight who hadn't gone before him. The rest had dispersed throughout the terminal and were now drinking coffee, queuing for taxis, or on their way to parked cars, or else were boarding buses and trains. What would have been a dense crowd of people waiting to meet the arrivals had thinned to just four. Two of those four were holding signs with names, where before there might have been dozens. Both of the signs were held no higher than chest height, their holders having endured gravity's unyielding effect for some time.

Victor ignored the two without signs. If Muir's intel was correct, Kooi had never met the broker or anyone affiliated with him. There could be no visual recognition to identify Kooi to his contact, or vice versa.

Of the two signs, one was held by a man, the other by a woman. The man was about forty and wore a suit and an overcoat and a neck brace, and didn't look at Victor once. Acute disappointment that had once been expectant excitement was etched into the man's face. Victor had seen no single woman waiting in baggage collection, so the man in the neck brace wasn't going to break into a huge grin anytime soon.

When the waiting woman saw Victor, she grew a little taller as her back straightened and she raised the sign above shoulder level. It was a taxi company whiteboard with a name Victor didn't recognize written on it by hand in thick black uppercase letters. The name had no doubt been agreed by Kooi and the broker in one of the deleted e-mails Muir's team hadn't been able to recover, or else had some significance to Kooi that would have enabled him to identify who was picking him up. Already the gaps in the information were showing. Victor knew there would be others. Now there was no fallout. Later might be different.

There was relief in the woman's expression, but no recognition. There was no first name on the whiteboard, but either she had been given one and therefore knew she was collecting a man, or she had been told she was. She wore faded blue jeans, flat shoes, and a baggy checked shirt that hung down to her hips. A trucker's cap covered her long dark hair, which was unwashed and tied back into a loose ponytail. She was pale skinned, five feet seven inches tall, and he estimated about one hundred and thirty pounds. She looked somewhere in her late thirties, a little tired and overworked, but attractive despite the lack of grooming and the clothes that went a long way to hide her figure.

The woman pointed at the name on the sign, then at Victor as he approached and then back to the sign. Victor nodded.

She reached for his bag, but Victor moved it outside her reach and shook his head. She shrugged and led him through the airport, walking fast in an attempt to make up some of the time she had lost because of his deliberate tardiness.

Her taxi was parked outside in the allotted area. It was a dented Saab that was painted white but looked gray with pollution under the unforgiving exterior lights. Decals for the Budapest taxi company ran along the bodywork and rear windshield.

She shivered in the chill evening air and rubbed her hands together as she hurried to open the trunk. This time Victor let her take his bag and watched as she dropped it inside. The woman hurried again to open the rear passenger-side door. He nodded his thanks and climbed in. She slammed the door shut and he shuffled across the backseat until he was on the far side of the car.

He watched as she moved around the hood and climbed into the driver's seat in front of him. There was a rattle from the beaded seat cover. She started the engine, cranked up the heat, and held her manicured fingers against the air inlet.

Victor had no information as to where in Budapest he was supposed to meet the broker, so if the woman asked him where he wanted to go, Muir's deception would fail at this early stage. But she didn't ask.

She wriggled against the beaded seat cover to get comfortable while she waited for the heat to warm her hands, then released the handbrake, put the Saab in gear, and pulled away from the curb. She glanced at him in the rearview mirror.

The taxi driver's license that hung from the dashboard stated that her name was Varina Theodorakis. It was a Greek name. The photograph looked exactly like the woman driving.

They followed the airport road around the short-stay parking lot and joined the main highway to the city. Liszt Ferenc was about sixteen kilometers from the city center.

"Where are we going?" Victor asked in German.

She glanced at him again in the rearview mirror and shrugged and shook her head, not understanding him.

"Where are we going?" Victor asked in Hungarian.

She didn't look at him. "Speak English?"

He nodded. "Where are we going?"

"Don't you know where?"

"Why would I ask if I already knew?"

She tapped the screen of a cell phone sitting in a holder on the dash. "The address is in the sat nav. I don't know the area."

"Who supplied you with that address?"

She glanced at him in the rearview again and said, "The company."

Victor nodded back, as if her answer explained everything he wanted to know.

The woman kept the Saab at a conservative speed. She passed some cars. Others passed her. She turned on the radio and cycled through several stations until she stopped at one playing seventies dance music. She increased the volume.

It was louder than Victor would have preferred and he did his best not to listen to any music composed after the end of the nineteenth century, but he didn't comment. He ran through the little intel Muir had on Kooi and the even less intel she knew about the broker. One wrong assumption or one piece of missing information about either could give him away.

After fifteen minutes the driver indicated and slowed to take an exit. She fidgeted in her seat, briefly stretching her back and shifting position. The satellite navigation system on the phone supplied her with directions, but the voice instructions had been disabled. Victor could see the phone over the woman's shoulder but didn't have a clear enough view to see the directions. She occasionally glanced at him in the rearview, but he pretended not to notice.

They drove along quiet urban streets that passed through run-down neighborhoods. The sky above Budapest was cloudless, but light pollution hid the stars, if not the half-moon. The mix of commercial and residential buildings slowly faded into industrial complexes. Alongside the street were factories and warehouses.

Victor said, "Pull over here, please."

"What?" The driver decreased the radio's volume.

"Pull over here," Victor said again.

"We're almost there."

"I'm going to throw up. Stop the car."

She glanced at him in the mirror, then pulled over and stopped alongside the curb.

As soon as the handbrake had been applied, Victor reached forward with his left hand and thumbed the release of the driver's seat belt. It was a standard three-point Y-shaped belt, and with no tension on the spring-loaded retractor, the strap whipped across her torso. Victor caught the clasp in the same hand when it was near her sternum, pulled it up while his right hand extended slack from the belt feeder, wrapped the diagonal strap around the woman's throat, hooked the clasp around the horizontal strap to lock the noose in place, and let go with both hands.

The mechanism reeled in the unfastened belt, and the remaining slack was gone in a split second. The looped straps immediately tightened around the woman's throat, and her scream became a gasp as her airways constricted under the considerable pressure.

She panicked. It was almost impossible not to when being strangled. She thrashed and bucked in her seat, clawing and pulling at the belt around her neck, but the centrifugal clutch inside the reel did exactly what it was designed to do and locked the belt against the rapid and jerky movements. She was too terrified to act calmly, but managed to jam some fingers of her right hand between the belt and her neck while her left hand went for the gun at her waist in a pancake holster that had been hidden by her baggy shirt.

But the gun wasn't there.

Victor examined it while the driver wheezed and choked. It was a small Cold War–era Soviet pistol. A Makarov. Outdated, inaccurate, but still deadly in the right hands. The gun bore none of the marks or scratches of a long life of use. He released the magazine and checked the load. It was filled with eight 9x18 mm copper-cased rounds. The chamber was empty and the safety was on. It was a backup weapon—for protection, not aggressive use.

The woman made a continuous coughing, spluttering noise as she struggled and suffocated. The fingers of her right hand were still wedged between the strap and her throat in an effort to relieve the constriction, but any benefit would be minimal. It might keep her alive an extra twenty seconds, but it was only delaying the inevitable and extending the pain. Her left hand was reaching up and behind her head in an attempt to unhook the clasp, but it was an impossible feat with one hand. She could have freed herself in seconds by employing both sets of fingers, but she was terrified and panicking and full of adrenaline and in agony.

She had no longer than a minute before she passed out. She would be dead soon after that.

Victor shuffled across on the backseat so he could lean sideways between the front seats to reach for the woman's taxi license. She batted him with her left hand, but the blows weren't hard enough for him to counter. She had no leverage and was weak from oxygen deprivation.

The license was in a plastic sleeve fixed to the dash with a clip. He ripped the sleeve away from the clip, used a knuckle to silence the radio, and sat back in his seat to examine the license.

The driver's movements were growing increasingly sluggish and her wheezing was quieter.

He pulled the license from the plastic sleeve. It was the size of a credit card and he dug a nail under a corner of the photograph of the woman driver that had been glued to its surface. He then peeled it away to reveal the real Varina Theodorakis's face. She had a big smile that showed almost every tooth in her mouth. She was about the same age as the woman in the Saab's driver's seat, but she had olive skin and curly black hair cut short, and from the plumpness of her cheeks and double chin weighed fifty pounds more.

In the rearview mirror the driver's face was turning from red to purple.

Victor pocketed the license and the photograph. He gripped the seat belt near the reel and pulled it slowly outward to slacken the tension on her windpipe.

She gasped and sucked in air before coughing violently. He kept his grip on the belt for the minute it took before her coughs subsided and the sound of her breathing approached normal.

Victor met her reflected eyes with his own. "You have exactly ten seconds to convince me not to let go of this strap."

"Please . . ." she gasped. "I'm only here . . . to . . . drive."

Victor held up the Makarov. "Yet you were armed with this."

She swallowed and rubbed her throat. "I only had it . . . to defend myself." She grimaced and swallowed again.

"How's that working out for you?"

"I'm just a driver. I—"

A fit of coughs cut off her words.

"Who am I going to meet?" Victor asked.

"I can't tell you that."

Victor released his grip on the seat belt. Immediately the inertia reel sucked the slack from the strap and it tightened around her neck. This time she didn't try to ease the pressure with her fingers or unhook the clasp. She went straight for the strap protruding from the reel housing, to mimic Victor and create slack. He didn't let her. He grabbed her wrist and pulled her hand away.

"Nod when you're ready to tell me everything you know. It's worth remembering that I can wait longer than you can."

She didn't hesitate and nodded as much as the belt around her neck would let her.

Victor released her wrist and she tugged on the strap, too hard, and it didn't reel out. She panicked and pulled and jerked on it, panicking more and more when the strap didn't slacken.

He prized her hand away and did it himself. "Slowly, remember."

"Robert Leeson," she spluttered out between heavy breaths. "My boss is Robert Leeson . . . That's all I know about him. Please . . ."

"And what's your name?"

"Francesca Leone."

"Well, Francesca Leone, stay still for a moment."

Victor unwrapped the belt strap from around her neck and she collapsed forward, coughing and wheezing, traumatized and out of breath, but alive.

"There won't be any lasting damage," Victor said. "But it wouldn't hurt to get a doctor to check you out."

"You're a bastard," she hissed as she sat back. "You didn't need to do that."

"You didn't need to pretend to be a taxi driver."

She glared at him.

In return, Victor showed no expression.

"How did you know?" she asked as she rubbed her throat.

Victor saw no immediate harm in answering, but he wasn't used to explaining his methods. "You'll work it out eventually. It wasn't hard."

She stared at him, unsure whether he was being truthful or if he knew something he wasn't revealing. He had revealed as much as he was going to.

He said, "Take another minute to recover and then let's get going. I don't want to keep our mutual friend waiting any longer."

· Chapter 18 ·

This time the woman calling herself Francesca drove without her seat belt fastened. It was generally the preferred approach of professionals for reasons including, but not exclusive to, those Victor had just demonstrated. Though last summer being forced to wear one had helped save his life. He swallowed an unpleasant taste from his mouth.

Francesca glanced at him every few seconds, expectantly fearful of what he might do, but it was useless. Even if she was somehow able to identify the moment before he elected to act, she was driving the car and could hardly throw herself out of the line of fire should he decide to squeeze the Makarov's trigger. Victor kept both hands in his lap to defeat her attempts at using mirrors to see which hand held the gun and where it was pointed. It was tucked in his waistband. He didn't need it.

She said, "We're almost there now."

"How long?"

"Five minutes maybe."

Victor nodded and said nothing more.

After four minutes she indicated and slowed, before turning onto a narrow access road flanked on both sides by a tall chain-link fence topped with razor wire. The road surface was cracked and potholed. It ended after thirty meters where a metal gate divided the road from the compound beyond, but the gate was already open.

The Saab rolled through the opening and onto an open area of asphalt that suggested a nearby factory or plant, but the wash of the headlights disappeared into darkness. Victor pictured a vast area of wasteland where a huge industrial complex had been demolished.

The ground changed from unmaintained asphalt to earth that was uneven and rutted. It hadn't been completely cleared from the demolition, and the tires threw up fragments of rubble that clattered against the wheel arches and pinged off the Saab's underside. With two-wheel drive the car struggled on the terrain and its soft suspension caused it to rock and sway.

Francesca turned the steering wheel to the left and the headlights swept over a barren expanse of wasteland that seemed endless and empty until the lights bounced off the polished bodywork of another car.

A black Rolls-Royce Phantom was parked on a large flat area that comprised industrial-sized concrete slabs. Grass grew along the gaps between slabs. The concrete was cracked and split where plant life had forced its way through. The Rolls-Royce was a limousine, beautiful and monstrous at the same time.

Francesca stopped the Saab when it was parallel to the

limousine, leaving about six meters of open space between the two vehicles. She applied the hand brake and
killed the engine and sat motionless with her palms on
her thighs, her reflected gaze locked on Victor.

"This is it. We're here."

"What happens now?"

"He's waiting for you in the back of the Rolls."

"Apart from the limousine's driver, is he alone?"

She nodded.

"Is the driver armed?"

"I wouldn't know."

"If you were armed, is there any reason the driver
would not be?"

She shook her head.

"I take it you're supposed to call when I get out of the
taxi, yes? To give the all-clear."

She nodded. "But it's not all clear, is it? I'll have to say
about the pistol."

Victor nodded back. "I imagine you will."

"He won't be happy about it," she said. "I'm just
warning you."

"I expect he won't. Do whatever you must."

Her eyes widened. "Really?"

"A couple of points for consideration, though. If this
is a setup, then you should know that it's not going to
work, and if you mention the gun I'll have to kill you
with it after I've killed whoever is in the other car. The
Rolls can carry six people including the driver, so even if
it's at full capacity, which of course it isn't, that still leaves
one bullet in the Makarov for you and one spare in case I
decide to make you suffer first."

Her eyes widened farther.

"However," Victor continued, "if this isn't a setup, then you can have the gun back after I'm done speaking with your boss, so if you tell him about it on the phone the only thing you'll achieve is to inform him that you can't be trusted to do your job properly. If your boss is the kind of man who will have no problem with that, then by all means let him know I disarmed you. But it's up to you."

Victor placed his hand on the door handle.

She frowned and said, "I can really have it back after you've finished?"

"Sure you can," Victor answered. "Now give me your car keys."

• • •

A cold wind blew across the wasteland and rippled Victor's jacket when he stepped outside the Saab. The cold air found its way under his shirt and he saw his breath cloud in the night air. He left his jacket unbuttoned and looked around. The half-moon was the only source of light, but Victor's eyes had adjusted to the night while he'd sat in the back of the taxi.

The Rolls-Royce limousine was painted black and polished to a gleaming shine, with blacked side windows. Whoever was in the car would be able to see him, even if the darkness would disguise his features. If Kooi's broker knew what he looked like, then he would know Victor wasn't him before he got much closer.

He looked to his right, back toward the gate and the razor-wire-topped fence. He couldn't see them, but they were there, approximately two hundred meters away. A short distance, but a long way to sprint in the dark if pursued by cars and armed men.

Running wasn't an option. Nor was fighting—the limousine's ground clearance was about an inch less than it should have been because it was carrying six hundred extra kilos of reinforced steel and polycarbonate. The Makarov tucked in Victor's waistband wouldn't make a dent. He would sooner face a tank, because at least a tank's crew had limited visibility and the Rolls-Royce, even one carrying extra weight, had twice the top speed of the fastest main battle tanks in the world.

Which meant the Saab behind Victor was the only option if things went wrong. Ejecting Francesca from the driver's seat, whether she was alive or dead when he did so, would take time. Inserting the key into the ignition, starting the engine, releasing the hand brake, circling toward the exit, would all take time. And he wouldn't have that time.

Because he looked to his left, to the empty blackness that extended seemingly into infinity, and pictured someone lying out there, about a hundred meters away, peering at him down the scope of a rifle.

This Robert Leeson had sent an armed subordinate disguised as an unthreatening female taxi driver to pick him up directly from an airport to ensure that he had no weapons. He was a cautious man. His precautions in Budapest wouldn't end with an eight-shot Makarov. He sat in the back of an armored limousine. He hadn't ordered Francesca to leave so much space between the two cars for some arbitrary purpose, and if she had received no order she would have parked closer. Leeson wanted the space for a specific reason. The same reason that meant they were meeting on empty wasteland for more than just privacy.

The marksman had to be to Victor's left, because the entrance was to his right and the Saab's headlights might have given him away as Francesca drove through the gates and across the site. Victor looked away so as not to let the marksman know of his deduction.

The only remaining question was whether the marksman was out there as a precaution, or whether he was there because Leeson wanted to erase the link between himself and the NOC's death. He might have learned about the client's disappearance and arrived at the correct conclusions.

That question would be answered when Victor was equidistant between the two vehicles, in the killing zone, with no cover and nowhere to run. Even if this wasn't a setup, it was conceivable that Francesca would reveal that Victor had taken her gun and Leeson, ever cautious, would give the order to shoot rather than risk a face-to-face with an armed killer.

He waited next to the Saab. He was protected while he stayed there because the marksman had no need to take a shot that might miss and hit the car or Francesca, or else spray Victor's brain matter over the Saab's bodywork. Simpler to wait until Victor was in the open. Fewer risks and less cleanup.

He looked expectantly at the limousine, as though he had misinterpreted how the meeting was to be conducted and was waiting for Leeson to step outside too. Whether

Leeson complied would tell Victor a lot about the situation and the man, but he didn't believe Leeson would give up the protection of the armored car. If anyone got out, it would be the driver.

He did. The wind disguised the sound of the limousine door opening on the far side of the vehicle, but Victor heard the scrape of the driver's shoe on the concrete. The driver climbed out with no discernible effect on the Rolls-Royce's suspension, because even before the extra weight from the armored bodywork and glass, it weighed more than three thousand kilograms straight from the factory. Ninety kilos didn't make a difference.

The driver wore dark clothing and momentarily faded into the gloom as he rounded the limousine's long hood. He approached Victor, who walked toward the driver, meeting him in the center of the killing zone, but veering to the right a little to put the driver between himself and the marksman.

The skin of the driver's face was tanned and weather-beaten. His head was shaved, but he wouldn't have had much hair had he let it grow. A broad chest and broad shoulders advertised a build packed with muscle. He was a couple of inches shorter than Victor and moved as though all that muscle were weightless. He wore black boots and trousers and a navy Windbreaker. Black leather gloves covered his hands. He was somewhere around thirty-five, and looked as though he had reached that age purely through brute strength and an enjoyment in using it.

He spent a moment examining Victor and then stared into Victor's eyes, unimpressed with what he saw.

"In the back," the driver said, his voice a raspy growl.

Victor said nothing in response and they headed toward the limousine. Victor stopped a few feet away.

This confused the driver, who stopped himself and gestured to where the two cabin doors led into the limousine's rear compartment. Victor nodded and waited. The driver gestured again, stabbing his finger in the direction of the doors. Victor waited.

The driver's face warped and contorted in frustration and bewilderment. He went to gesture yet again, but then understood. He scowled at Victor, his jaw muscles bunching into hard balls beneath his skin, and opened the rear of the two coach doors.

"There you go," he snarled between clenched teeth, "Your Majesty."

There was no attempt to frisk Victor, because he had been picked up straight from the airport. He now knew Francesca had kept the fact that he had her gun to herself, trusting Victor's word that she could have it back more than she trusted her boss's capacity for forgiveness.

He ducked down and climbed into the back to meet Kooi's broker.

· Chapter 19 ·

There were four individual seats in the rear compartment of the limousine, each covered in cream-colored leather; two where the backseats would be in a conventional car, and two facing them with their backs to the divisional wall that separated the compartment from the driver's cab. On the far side of the vehicle, on the seat positioned directly behind the driver, sat a man.

He had one leg crossed over the other and sat with both hands resting casually in his lap. He wore a three-piece suit, silvery gray, with the jacket open to reveal the waistcoat and a striped red-and-white dress shirt underneath. His tie was ruby red and affixed to the shirt by a gold tie bar shaped like a pirate's cutlass. His shoes were brown tasseled loafers with the toes polished to a mirror sheen. Light brown hair was swept back from a face that was far more youthful than Victor had expected. He looked no older than twenty-eight or -nine.

Victor slid onto the nearest seat so that he sat diagonally opposite the man. Blue eyes free of fatigue or emotion locked with his own.

The driver, still scowling, pushed the door shut and it made a solid clunk.

"Please accept my most sincere thanks for meeting with me, Mr. Kooi," the man said, with the accent of someone who divided his time equally between the two sides of the Atlantic.

"My pleasure," Victor said back.

Muir didn't know the name of Kooi's broker, nor if Kooi had known it, and Victor wasn't about to trust that Francesca had told the truth, but the man dispelled any doubt when he said, "My name is Robert Leeson."

Victor showed no reaction. Leeson watched him with an intense, searching gaze, but his expression revealed nothing of what he might be looking for, or have found.

"I trust that you had a pleasant flight."

"It was uneventful."

Victor heard the driver's door open and then the creak of leather as he slid onto his seat, but there was almost no reaction from suspension that balanced so much weight. The sliding window between the back and the driver's cab was closed.

Leeson saw him look. "For privacy," he explained. "It's completely soundproof."

Victor imagined the sound of three and a half grains of gunpowder exploding and the sonic crack of a bullet breaking the sound barrier within a confined space, and nodded.

"I expect you must grow weary of all the air travel necessitated by your line of work," Leeson said.

"It affords me time to think."

"Then it is good that you can derive some benefit from it. To me it's a simply odious way to travel. I don't know how you do it. When you can breathe in marvelous sea air as pure and unsullied as a newborn, I cannot abide the thought of sharing that recycled garbage with all and sundry on an airplane."

"Beats walking," Victor said.

A corner of Leeson's mouth turned upward in what Victor took to be as much of a smile as the younger man was willing to placate him with.

"I hope the taxi ride from the airport proved agreeable."

"Fine," Victor said.

Leeson nodded, satisfied with the response. He hadn't moved since Victor had entered the vehicle. He seemed relaxed and in no rush and showed not even the smallest evidence of trepidation in the company of a hired killer.

"I have to say," Leeson began, "that you don't look quite as I expected."

"Then I'm glad."

Leeson acknowledged the remark with a little nod. "Your accent is curious. Which part of the Netherlands are you from?"

"All of it."

"I sense that you aren't keen on revealing personal details about yourself."

"Are you surprised by this?"

"Not at all. Perhaps you would like a beverage?"

He motioned, but did not look, at a crystal decanter of amber liquid that sat with fat tumblers on a silver tray.

The tray rested on the console next to Victor, set between his seat and the one next to it. An identical console was positioned opposite, between the backward-facing seats. They had various buttons and dials for climate and sound control. There were compartments for a fridge and drinks cabinet and all sorts of other necessities the wealthy required when traveling.

"Thank you for the offer, but no."

Leeson's face showed a trace of surprise. "You're not a drinker?"

"On occasion."

"It's twenty-four-year-old Scotch," Leeson explained. "Perfect for any occasion."

The decanter was full. Seven hundred milliliters of whiskey. An entire bottle. The tumblers were clean. There was no smell in the air. Perhaps Leeson had not touched it because it had been purchased especially for Kooi's tastes and Leeson was demonstrating etiquette by not having drunk any before now. Or there could be any number of reasons why Leeson hadn't touched it himself.

"I'm fine without," Victor said.

Leeson interlaced his fingers. "And I thought you were a sailor."

Victor tried to read the younger man's expression, but there was nothing there except the same searching gaze.

"Not while discussing business," Victor said.

"Though we are yet to discuss any."

"Then what are we doing?"

"Getting to know each other a little better."

"With all due respect, I'm not interested in getting to know you."

Leeson said nothing. There was something new in his eyes.

"My time is precious, Mr. Leeson. So if there is no business for us to discuss, then I'm afraid I shall need to depart."

Victor reached for the door release and Leeson held up a hand.

"Please, Mr. Kooi. Stay. Please."

Victor let his hand fall away.

"Mr. Kooi," Leeson began. "I know you are a busy man. I know you are a man whose services are in much demand. I'm not trying to waste your time. I invited you here because I wish to discuss a contract with you, a contract that has specifics I feel require more than just inflectionless words bounced by satellite across the world."

"I'm listening."

Victor used an index finger and thumb to pick up a paper napkin from the tray next to him, unfolding it and using it to cover his fingertips as he removed the decanter's stopper and poured himself a measure of whiskey. Leeson watched him the whole time, expressionless.

Victor poured a second glass and offered it to the younger man, who made no move to take it.

"I don't drink alone," Victor said.

Leeson reached out a hand, but didn't lean forward, and Victor had to stretch farther to bridge the gap. A power game. He sat back down and rested the tumbler on his thigh, the paper napkin still between his fingertips and the glass.

"You're a cautious man," Leeson said, and took a sip from his glass.

"Is that a problem for you?"

"Not at all, Mr. Kooi. I believe in reliability and trust. And I trust that a cautious man is a reliable man."

Victor sipped too. "I've had no complaints thus far."

"I can imagine," Leeson said with a nod. "My last client was most pleased with the way you dealt with those problems in Yemen and Pakistan."

"My pleasure."

"But not his," Leeson said, watching how Victor reacted. "He has disappeared into the ether." He made a rippling motion with his fingers. "Rumor has it that he has been captured or killed by friends of your previous target."

"I don't see the significance," Victor said, because he did see it.

"This is a great shame for two reasons. Firstly, I expected a number of similar contracts to pass my way from him, and therefore to you. That business has now vanished along with the client."

Leeson paused, and Victor knew he was expected to ask, "What's the second reason?"

"Ah, the second reason. If the first reason was a great shame, then this second is highly troubling, because if the client were apprehended, then it raises doubt as to the quality of your work."

Victor didn't respond. He looked at Leeson while thinking he could put a bullet through his skull and be out of the Rolls-Royce before the driver could respond. But that would put him in the kill zone between the two cars. The Makarov was a poor copy of a much better, but still outdated, pistol. It had limited effectiveness against anything beyond point-blank range. Victor couldn't hope to face the marksman and live, even exploiting the limousine's armor plating as cover. He would have to go out of the left side to put the limousine between himself and the guy behind the rifle, but that meant scrambling over the seat and past Leeson's corpse. That delay could mean the driver would be ready for him. He might have a better weapon, perhaps body armor underneath his jacket, and would have an easy shot as Victor leaped out of the door. If the limousine's armor extended to the partition between the rear compartment and the driver's cab, then a 9 mm round from the Makarov had no chance of penetrating it. There was more chance a ricochet would kill Victor if he attempted to kill the driver by shooting from where he sat. If the partition was unarmored, Leeson's corpse would still be in the way and shooting at a trajectory that would avoid the body meant a significant chance the luxury seats and partition wall, thickened by the angle, would deflect the round or slow it enough to render it ineffective. If he attempted to open the partition window, it would give the driver enough time to be out of his seat before Victor could shoot through the window.

"Well?" Leeson asked. "Do you have anything to say for yourself?"

"Yemeni authorities ruled that my last victim committed suicide, as per the stipulations of the contract. Same as the Pakistani informant."

"I've read the Yemeni report," Leeson said. "The target died from a stab wound to the neck. Hardly a common way to end one's life."

"He was a hard target. A CIA operative. He was

smart. He took precautions. When you passed me the contract you should have known it would be a difficult ask. And, lest we forget, it was still ruled a suicide."

"So why has the client disappeared?"

"I don't know enough about the client to offer a considered opinion and I'm not the kind of man who likes to guess. That said, if I had given the target's associates enough reason to convince them he was murdered, and I say convince because they would automatically suspect given his occupation, then how would they have learned of the client? Certainly not through any mistake I made, because I don't know enough about the client to leave clues leading to his doorstep. Any mistake I made, and I made none, would have led back to me and me alone. I'm still here, even if he's not. Hence, the client's disappearance is nothing to do with my last job."

Leeson didn't respond.

Victor said, "You must have come to the same conclusion yourself. At least, I sincerely hope you did if we're to continue this business relationship."

"Of course."

"So why even bring it up?"

"Because I wanted to hear what you had to say about it."

"To what end?"

Leeson produced a little smile. "Call it peace of mind."

"Then I hope I've provided you with some."

The younger man nodded. "Please know that I have been satisfied with your work, which is no small thing. Your good work reflects favorably on my reputation, and a reputation is perhaps the most valuable trait for men like you and me."

"I don't take a job if I don't believe I can fulfill my part."

Leeson nodded again. "Though, lest we forget, a reputation is nothing but hearsay."

"I don't remember suggesting otherwise. But I didn't stab the CIA operative in the neck with my reputation."

"True," Leeson said, smiling again. "And there is no hearsay in a man's eyes. There is only truth."

"What truth do you see in mine?"

He didn't answer for a moment. He just looked at Victor, then said, "I see a man of experience. I see a man without conscience. I see a man who sold his soul before he knew he possessed anything of value."

"Shall I tell you what I see in yours?"

Leeson shook his head. "Not necessary."

Victor sipped some Scotch.

"The work I'm offering is dangerous," Leeson began, "but I expect it to be no more dangerous than other contracts you will have successfully completed. But I don't just need a man who can pull a trigger. I need a man who can be relied upon. I need a man who can be available where and when I require him to be. I need a man who will follow orders but a man who can improvise. Can you be that man for me, Mr. Kooi?"

Be his perfect assassin.

"For the right price, absolutely."

"I'm delighted you said that." Leeson rested his whiskey on the console and extended his left arm in front of him. He used his right hand to pull back his shirt cuff to reveal a gold watch. He unclasped it and tossed it at Victor, who caught it while sipping Scotch. "That's a diamond-encrusted Rolex Super President. Solid twenty-four-karat gold for the most part. Weighs a ton. I think it's hideous, but I wear it because the circles I mix in require such classless and revolting displays of wealth. Amusing, of course, because the members of such circles do so like to believe they are of a higher class."

Victor turned the watch over in his hand. It was heavy and extravagant and as obviously genuine as the Algerian trader's stock had been counterfeit. He didn't know the price tag, but the watch was worth tens of thousands of dollars.

"It's yours," Leeson said.

Victor looked back up. "In return for what?"

"A mere ten seconds of your time."

Victor remained silent.

"I know you said your time was valuable, Mr. Kooi, but a diamond-and-gold Rolex for one-sixth of a minute must be a good deal, even for you."

"That depends on how those ten seconds are spent."

"I want you to do what you do best."

"I'm listening."

"I want you to climb out of this limousine and walk over to the taxi and then I want you to kill the driver."

"Why?"

"Because she's not a taxi driver. She works for me, and she has failed me far too many times. Kill her any way you like and don't worry about the mess. We'll take care of the cleanup and we'll even drive you back to the airport. I would have paid you in cash, but large amounts of money can be so bothersome to pass through an airport with."

"What's her name?"

"If it's important for you to know, her name is Francesca Leone. I'd like you to kill her for me. Right now, if you please."

Victor paused for a moment, then said, "No."

"Perhaps we don't understand each other," Leeson said. "You're a hired killer and I'm hiring you to kill. There is nothing to say no to. Ms. Leone has outlived her usefulness. Ten seconds' work for a Rolex. Child's play."

Victor placed the watch on the silver tray next to the decanter. "The answer hasn't changed."

"She's pretty, isn't she? Is that why you're refusing to kill her? Did she give you an erection while she drove you here?"

"Just in case you didn't hear me before, the answer is no."

"I'll double your fee. You can take the Rolex now and I'll make a sizable donation to the bank account of your choice."

Victor's lips stayed closed. He didn't blink.

There was no surprise in Leeson's expression, but there was some kind of calculation running behind his eyes. He sat still and considered Victor in silence.

"You invited me here for a reason," Victor said. "You know who I am. My reputation speaks for itself and I won't change how I conduct myself for anyone, for any price. No amount of money will send me into a situation that I have not fully evaluated beforehand. But as long as I am able to prepare for a job properly and unrushed, there is nothing I won't do for you. I won't kill the woman because I am here to discuss taking a job. I'm not here to do a job. When you require my services you present the work to me in a manner of my choosing and I, not you, will determine the appropriate fee after I have that information. That fee will not be up for negotiation."

"You make a lot of demands for a man being interviewed."

"I'm not the only one being interviewed."

Leeson nodded, neither displeased nor pleased. He said, "Then I think this conversation has come to its natural conclusion."

· Chapter 20 ·

Victor climbed out of the limousine. The air was cold. The wind rippled his jacket. He heard a jet pass overhead. As he shut the door behind him, he thought about the marksman lying on the hard ground approximately one hundred meters to his left. He would no doubt be using a thermal imaging scope on which Victor would appear as a stark white shape against a black background. Victor preferred heat as black against a white background, but he knew he was in the minority. It would take a little more than three-hundredths of a second for a high-velocity rifle round to cover the distance between where the marksman lay and where Victor stood. The sound wave produced by the gunshot would take more than twice that time to cover the distance. Victor wouldn't hear it. He would already be dead when the sound reached his ears. He would never know a shot had been fired. He would just die. One second alive; before the next second was out, dead.

Not a bad way to go, considering. He knew that better than most.

But the bald-headed driver didn't exit the car, so Victor knew he wasn't going to die just yet. If Leeson had given the marksman the order to fire, the driver would know about it, and he wouldn't have stayed in his seat. He wouldn't have been able to see from there. He would have climbed out. He would have wanted to watch.

As Victor crossed the killing zone, he saw Francesca looking his way. If she knew of any prearranged course of action, she wouldn't want to see it go down, whatever he had done to her. She didn't have the driver's fondness for violence or Victor's detachment from it.

He climbed into the back of the Saab taxi and shuffled on the backseat so he sat behind her. She was rubbing her throat. It would be sore for several days. She stared at him via the rearview.

"How did it go?" she asked, not because she was interested but because he made her nervous and conversation always induced less fear than silence.

"Hand me your phone."

She hesitated, confused and scared. "Why?"

"Because I have a gun and you don't."

Francesca continued to stare for a moment, then twisted and tugged on the phone until she had freed it from the holder on the dash. She looked at it and hesitated, and Victor could read her thoughts clearly enough. He didn't say anything because he didn't need to.

Eventually, she swiveled in her seat so she could look at Victor as she held it out for him to take. She gripped one corner between her thumb and index finger and pointed the opposite corner his way to create the maximum distance between her hand and his when he took it from her. She didn't want his fingers to touch hers.

"Thank you," Victor said.

"You're welcome."

It was a reflexive response, politeness infused into her from an early age. Even now, with someone who had nearly killed her, she couldn't escape the conditioning.

The phone was clean and unmarked. A thin rectangle of protective transparent plastic covered the screen. When the screen came out of hibernation, the service provider's default background lit up. There was no pass lock and he checked the call log. Just one number. Four entries. The most recent call lasted nine seconds and was made eight minutes ago, moments after he had stepped out of the taxi. The others were spaced out over the evening. The earliest was three hours ago. He loaded the location app.

Francesca was watching him through the rearview mirror while she gently massaged her throat.

Victor turned off the app, put the screen back into hibernation, and held out the phone and the car keys in one palm.

She looked at him, suspicious of a trap. She was right to be cautious of him now that she had an idea of what he was capable of, but at this particular moment there was nothing to fear.

He said, "Take them."

Francesca twisted in her seat again and picked the keys out of his open hand, careful not to make contact with his skin. She snapped her hand away, then paused when he made no movement to grab at her, before taking back the phone. She looked at it suspiciously.

"There's nothing to be concerned about," he said. "I haven't tampered with it."

She didn't believe him, but also didn't know what he could have done to the phone in such a short time. She stared at his reflection as she slipped it into a pocket.

"You shouldn't be working for Leeson," Victor said.

"Really? And why exactly shouldn't I?"

"You haven't got what it takes for this kind of life."

Her eyes narrowed. "What makes you say that?"

"Because I know a little something about it."

She spoke through tight lips. "What do you care?"

"Who says I care?"

"I can look after myself, all right?"

"Like you did on the way here?"

"Well, I'll be ready next time, won't I? Now I know there are assholes like you in the world."

"But that's the problem," Victor said. "There are people even worse than me out there."

She huffed. "I find that hard to believe."

"And that's what will get you killed."

She didn't respond. She just stared at him.

He sat back and looked out of the side window. He wondered if the marksman was still in the same position or whether he had moved to another. Had their roles been reversed, Victor would have moved so that on its way to the exit the car would pass horizontally through his field of view, so if necessary he could shoot someone in the backseat with minimal risk to the driver.

"There's a flight leaving soon," he said. "I'd like to be on it."

Francesca turned the ignition key and shuffled on the beaded seat cover to get comfortable. "Can I have the pistol back as well?"

"That's up to you. Either you can have it back when we get to the airport or you can have one of the bullets now."

She frowned and released the hand brake.

· Chapter 21 ·

Vienna, Austria

The flight arrived after midnight. On board were no more than half the passengers carried by the inward flight. Victor was one of the first off the plane. He walked briskly through baggage reclaim and found Janice Muir waiting for him at the bottom of the escalators, as Francesca had been in Budapest. She looked tired.

"Well?" she said as he approached her.

"Come with me." Victor didn't stop. "I'm hungry."

He ordered a sandwich at one of the many restaurants in the airport that were still open. There were only two other tables for the waitress to serve, and she was delighted to have Victor's business. He asked for a coffee for Muir. She didn't ask for one, but she looked as though she could use it. She looked as though she could use it as an IV drip.

As soon as the waitress had left them, Muir said, "What happened?"

"I was picked up at the airport by one of the broker's

people. A woman, disguised as a taxi driver. She drove me where the broker was waiting. It was an interview, as expected. We only spoke for a few minutes, but he spent every one assessing me. We didn't discuss a contract, however."

"Did you get a name?"

"He introduced himself as Robert Leeson. The bogus taxi driver also supplied me with that name."

"Genuine?"

"Absolutely not."

"How can you be so sure?"

"He had a subordinate pick me up from the airport to make sure I didn't have a weapon. We met on an empty area of wasteland. He had an ex-military meathead driving him around in a Rolls-Royce Phantom fitted out with top-of-the-range armored paneling and windows. A guy with a rifle covered me while I crossed between the taxi and the limousine. Someone that cautious does not give out his real name to a man like Kooi."

Muir's eyes widened. "Just who is this guy?"

"A man of considerable means. I'm sure you can imagine an armored Rolls-Royce limousine is beyond the buying power of any but the considerably wealthy. His watch was worth more than the Saab taxi that took me to meet him. His suit was from Savile Row in London and cost twice what you take home in a month."

Muir pursed her lips, a little insulted, but didn't act on it. She said, "Describe him, other than his wealth."

"Average height and build. Late twenties. Brown hair. Blue eyes. His accent drifted between British and American, so he was born in one but spends most of his time in the other. His taste in clothes and cars might suggest he's from the U.K. originally, but there's no reason why he couldn't have been born in the States but adopted the style of the British upper classes."

"Subthirty doesn't seem old enough to be doing what he's doing."

"My eyesight is reliable," Victor said.

"That's not what I meant. I mean he's younger than you or I, but he's got himself in a position where he's brokering contract killing. That's some feat. I want to know how he managed it."

"The answer could be as simple as he's good at what he does."

Muir nodded. "Maybe it's a family business."

"Then it's one he's been involved in for a while. Kooi isn't the first killer he's dealt with like that."

"How do you know that?"

"Because he wasn't afraid of me in the least."

"But you said he had an ex-military bodyguard and a sniper as backup. They're two good reasons not to be scared of you."

"I was in the back of the limousine with him for several minutes. The marksman couldn't have seen me, let alone intervened, while I was sitting within a couple of feet of his boss and behind the best armored glass money can buy. There was a partition between the rear compartment and the driver. I could have snapped Leeson's neck before the driver even knew Leeson was in trouble."

"Well, when you put it like that . . ."

The waitress appeared with Muir's coffee and a glass of iced water for Victor.

"Thank you," he said.

She smiled and left.

Muir slurped her coffee, then said, "Tell me about the fake taxi driver."

"She said her name was Francesca Leone. I have reason to believe that name is more likely to be genuine than Leeson's."

Muir gave him a look. *"Reason to believe?"*

"I can be very conducive to honesty."

Muir raised her eyebrows briefly. She drank some more coffee. "Thanks. I needed this. What was the bodyguard like?"

"Six feet tall. Two hundred pounds. Mid-thirties. I didn't get a name and I'm not sure of his accent."

"The guy with the rifle?"

"I didn't see him."

"Then how do you know he was there?"

"Experience. The marksman presented a neat and easy way of bringing things to a close if Leeson hadn't liked what he saw."

"So he must like you; otherwise we wouldn't be talking here now. But I thought you said you didn't speak about a contract?"

"That's correct."

"But he did like what he saw, yes?"

"I believe so."

Muir put down her coffee cup. "So what happened?"

"He gave me a test."

"I take it you don't mean a written multiple choice."

"He asked me to kill the driver, Francesca."

Muir sat back and stared at him, her eyes wide behind her glasses. "And did you?"

"No."

"Why didn't you?"

Victor said, "That's not how I operate."

"You're not supposed to operate like you. You're supposed to be Kooi."

"Would you have preferred it if I had killed her?"

She hesitated, then ignored the question. "How did he react when you refused to comply?"

"He attempted to persuade me to accept his offer. When I wouldn't, he drew the meeting to a close."

"Shit."

Victor sipped some water.

"Sorry," Muir said. "Procter told me to watch my language around you."

"It's okay."

"You said you didn't discuss the contract. But maybe Francesca was the job."

"No, it was a test. Leeson didn't need to have me fly in to do it. The marksman or the limousine driver could have killed her. He could have shot her himself. She wasn't a hard target."

"Okay, but job or not, you didn't kill her. So you failed the test. It doesn't matter if he liked you before that point. If you aren't going to follow his orders and kill when he asks, why would he hire you for anything else?"

"I didn't fail," Victor said.

Muir frowned. "Come on, I'm not judging you here. I didn't expect you'd have to kill someone to get hired. That wasn't part of the plan. Thank you for trying."

"I didn't fail," he said again.

Muir stared at him.

"Killing Francesca was the test," Victor explained. "But I never said if I had killed her I would have passed that test."

"I don't understand. I must have missed something because you've lost me."

"Francesca was dressed in casual, shapeless clothes because she is an attractive woman. Beautiful, in fact. Leeson had her play down her appearance because someone who looks like that doesn't spend her nights driving a cab. And that someone also isn't an errand boy for a guy like Leeson who he's going to kill for some unspecified spurious reasons."

"Why not? He could have used one of the other two guys as the taxi driver instead of her."

Victor shook his head. "No, because he knew there was no way the meathead could pull off pretending to be a taxi driver. He couldn't even hide being a psychopath for the eight seconds of contact I had with him. Either the marksman couldn't either, or he's by far the better shot and Leeson wanted him and only him behind the rifle. Francesca, though not the best choice to try to make a taxi driver because of her looks, was the only option."

"So you're saying this Francesca is just *so* damn pretty that it's impossible Leeson could actually want her dead?"

"In short, yes. We've already established that Leeson is notably wealthy. He has the money and the contacts to have who he wants at his side. Francesca is at his side for a reason, and that reason is not her aptitude for fieldwork."

"Okay, fine," Muir said, conceding. "So why ask you to kill her if he wanted you to say no?"

"Because Leeson wanted to see if Kooi was the kind of killer who would execute someone without the proper planning and prep work. That kind of man is reckless and unpredictable. He told me how much he valued reliability. He wants someone careful. He doesn't want someone who is going to be impulsive and take undue risks; he doesn't want someone who is going to rush in and make a mistake. There's an old SAS saying, the seven p's: Proper prior planning prevents piss-poor performance."

"I thought you didn't swear."

"I was quoting."

"I agree it sounds plausible. But you can't know for certain Leeson wanted you to decline."

"Of course," Victor agreed, "but I can make a logical deduction based on what I know. And while we've been talking I've been thinking back to the meeting because something has bothered me about Leeson's security. I told you I thought there was a marksman covering me as a security precaution or in case Leeson didn't like what he saw."

"That's right."

"But there was only about twenty feet of ground between the two cars. That's a very narrow killing zone if I was a danger, and Leeson's Rolls was armored. I could have used it as a tank, had it come to it. It would have made much more sense to have another man up close, sitting in the back with Leeson. So the marksman wasn't there if I was trouble, because Leeson never expected me to be."

"So the guy with the rifle was there if Leeson didn't like you."

"Exactly. He was there in case I agreed to Leeson's offer. Had I said yes to killing Francesca, the marksman would have dropped me as I made my way to do it. He was there purely to protect Francesca. Leeson wasn't taking any chances with her safety."

"So she's his woman, surely?"

"Seems likely."

"But if you're wrong about any of this, then Leeson is going to vanish into the wind and hire some other killer to do his bidding. And all we've got is nothing but some descriptions and some names that are most likely bogus."

"We have a little more than that. Do you have a pen and paper?"

"Sure."

Muir fished a slim notebook and ballpoint from her inside jacket pocket and placed them on the table between them. The waitress reappeared with Victor's sandwich.

Muir said, "Can I get another coffee?"

Victor took a bite from his sandwich and slid over to her the passport-sized photograph of Francesca he had peeled from the Budapest taxi driver's license belonging to Varina Theodorakis.

"This is the woman who called herself Francesca Leone. The photograph looks exactly like her, so it was taken very recently." He continued to eat with one hand while he wrote a series of numbers on a page of Muir's notebook with the other. "This is the cell phone number of the woman in the photograph. The phone was brand-new, probably bought within the last twenty-four hours.

She hadn't bothered to take the screen's protective film off. It'll be a prepaid handset and SIM, as will be the phone that this number belongs to."

He wrote another number beneath the first. "That's the only number Francesca called. It'll belong to either Leeson or his driver. Like Francesca's, it's no doubt a prepaid bought just for this meeting. But maybe they haven't ditched them yet and if you're quick you might be able to use GPS to track their locations. It's a long shot, but worth the effort." He wrote down a series of numbers and letters and then another. "This first one is the license plate number of the taxi that picked me up from the airport. It's a genuine cab, so that will be a genuine plate. The second number is the Budapest city taxi license of Varina Theodorakis, a Greek woman who the license belonged to before Francesca Leone got hold of it. Either Theodorakis is a clueless victim of theft or she's compliant and has information."

He wrote down a sixth number. "That's the serial number of the Makarov pistol Francesca was armed with. It's at least thirty years old and it'll be part of a batch commissioned before the collapse of the Soviet Union. Chances are you won't be able to trace ownership, but you might get lucky because there wasn't a single scratch in the paint and I could still smell packing grease, so it hasn't been long out of the crate." He wrote down another long series of numbers and characters. "The site where I met Leeson was a demolished industrial complex approximately thirty minutes' drive north from the airport. There's likely no connection to the site and Leeson, but it was gated so either they broke in or they had keys. I don't know the area, but that's the latitude and longitude of the location."

Muir slid the notebook back to her side of the table, looked at it, then sat back, the whites of her eyes obvious behind her glasses. "Procter told me you were good."

· Chapter 22 ·

Budapest, Hungary

The man who some people knew as Robert Leeson relaxed in the back of the Rolls-Royce Phantom. He had removed his handcrafted brown loafers and rested his feet on the chair opposite. The seating position that resulted was exceptionally comfortable. The window curtains were drawn and the partition between the compartment and the driver's cab was closed to provide Leeson with the privacy he both required and relished. He lounged in darkness, cocooned and protected from the savagery of the world outside. The compartment was so well insulated that Leeson was barely aware of the fact that he was inside a moving motor vehicle. The ride was wonderfully smooth. No jolts from the suspension. No vibration.

No exterior sounds were audible to dilute the glorious music that emanated from the Rolls-Royce's top-of-the-range sound system. The London Philharmonic Orchestra Choir was performing a stirring rendition of Thomas

Tallis's *Gaude gloriosa Dei Mater*. Leeson sipped twenty-four-year-old single malt and sang along in Latin.

As the anthem finished he dabbed his watery eyes with an Egyptian cotton handkerchief and thumbed a button on the console to mute the speakers before he was enraptured by more beauteous sound. Tallis made Mozart and Beethoven seem like amateurs.

From one of the console's compartments he took out a satellite phone and powered it on. He entered a phone number known only to himself and to the person who answered when the line connected. The satellite phone sent out a signal scrambled by a custom encryption algorithm created by a code-writing genius currently rotting in a Siberian prison because he refused to use his skills for the Russian intelligence services. He would change his mind eventually, Leeson knew, when youth faded into maturity and blind idealism became secondary to the pursuit of life's little luxuries. Leeson knew this because he had once been an idealist. But he had grown up, albeit younger than most did.

"How did it go?"

The voice that sounded through the phone's speaker was clear but did not belong to the person on the other end of the line. It had been manipulated by a scrambler that altered the tone, tune, volume, and pitch of the speaker's voice. The result was a perfect disguise only identifiable by the slight electronic quality that occasionally affected words in a way similar to that of the tuneless studio-enhanced singing star. Leeson's own voice was similarly scrambled.

"Kooi was a most interesting individual," Leeson answered.

"Tell me about him."

"He wasn't quite what I was expecting from the information I had."

"In what sense?"

Leeson considered for a moment, before answering, "He was well mannered and patient and clearly of more experience than I had believed. He had no complaints about how we met. He seemed in complete control at all times, yet had to understand he was at my mercy."

"A front?"

"I can tell the difference," Leeson said.

"Calm?"

"Supremely."

"He seems very promising thus far. But, of course, everything hinges on how he reacted to the proposal."

Leeson topped up his Scotch from the crystal decanter. "He said no."

"Was there hesitation?"

"Not a second's deliberation. He didn't hesitate. He didn't think about it. He looked at my watch as if it was a piece of junk."

"Did you increase the offer?"

"Of course. I offered to double the money. It didn't even tempt him."

"Fascinating," the voice said.

"He was a fascinating individual."

"Do you think he'll be suitable?"

"That would first depend on how the insurance policy is coming together."

"Perfectly," the voice said.

"Excellent to know."

The voice said, "So is he suitable for the position?"

Leeson considered again. "Yes and no."

"Yes and no?" the voice echoed.

"Yes for the reasons already discussed. He can do what we need him to."

"But?"

"But there is something about him that is dangerous."

"As he is a professional killer, I would have been most surprised had he exuded no danger."

"That's not what I mean," Leeson said. "There was something in his manner I have not encountered before. Something I cannot articulate."

"It's not like you to be lost for words."

He swallowed some Scotch. "I am equally aware of the anomaly."

The voice said, "I'm not sure how much consideration we can give to a feeling that you can't even describe."

"I'm not saying we should. But it is necessary to be frank and honest in my assessment. We need to hire the right man for a very specific kind of job. Neither of us can afford to make a hasty decision."

"And it would be, had your discussion with Mr. Kooi not been the last step of a journey begun long ago, and your assessment of him need only include your conclusion of his suitability. So my advice would be to discount any inexpressible feelings you might have about the man, and tell me whether we can proceed with him. Yes or no?"

Leeson drained his glass and delivered his answer.

· Chapter 23 ·

Iceland

The pickup was a rugged Toyota Land Cruiser modified to cope with the unpredictable and sometimes extreme weather and diverse geophysical conditions of Iceland. The tires were extra large and could handle snow, rock, and sand and provided the height necessary to cross the many glacial waterways. The fuel tank had one hundred and fifty percent of the standard capacity, to cover the long distances it would need to travel. The vehicle was also equipped with GPS and VHF radios, additional lights, a high-powered winch, and an air compressor.

Wipers swung back and forth to fight the relentless sleet from sticking to the windshield glass. Fog lights bounced off the waterfall of partially frozen raindrops, and the world beyond was an impenetrable mass of gray. The cab's temperature was pleasant thanks to the Land Cruiser's heating. The FM radio managed to pick up a single station that ran a talk show Victor didn't understand more than a few words of.

He gathered that the host was discussing global finance with a banking expert, but between the weak signal and Victor's limited understanding of Icelandic, they could have been discussing pretty much anything. Still, it was something to pass the time.

It had been two days since he'd left Muir and he was about fifteen kilometers south of the small town of Húsavík, heading south along the main road that looped around the coast, linking Húsavík with Akureyri. Each town had fewer than five thousand inhabitants, and they were as remote as human civilization was ever likely to, or would want to, get.

Another kilometer and Victor slowed. Visibility was poor through the sleet and in the featureless terrain, the turning would be easy to miss. Satellite navigation would have informed him when he was approaching it, but it would also inform anyone else with the resources to hijack a GPS signal. Victor had plenty of enemies capable of doing just that. He kept it disabled.

He didn't see the turning until he'd reached it, whereupon he headed off the highway onto a track, heading east, slowing down further because the track was unsurfaced and uneven. He flicked off the wipers now that he wasn't driving into the sleet and he could see the landscape extending away into the distance. The terrain was flat with no elevation or depression for at least ten kilometers in every direction.

Victor liked what he saw.

• • •

He applied the hand brake and turned off the engine some thirty kilometers from the coastal road that linked the two towns. He pulled up the hood of his coat, opened the driver's door, and stepped outside. The sleet had eased but had been replaced by raindrops that didn't fall down but were pushed horizontally by the wind and peppered his face. The ambient temperature was somewhere around minus two, but the wind chill pushed it down much further.

A building lay approximately three hundred meters to the north. It was a two-story cabin with a triangular red-tiled roof that extended down almost to the ground. Little but Icelandic moss grew on the tundra that extended to the horizon to its south, east, and west. To the north were mountains, but no area of high ground within anything close to a rifle's effective range.

Victor drew an FN Five-seveN handgun from a pocket of his coat and racked the slide to put a high-velocity 5.7 mm round in the chamber. He approached the cabin, seeing no signs of recent vehicles or people, but the sodden ground made any such signs difficult to spot.

When he was two hundred meters away, he circled the cabin, keeping low and moving quickly because there was no cover, only the downpour to help make a shot from the cabin more difficult. Seeing no evidence of visitors, but aware the snow made his tracking attempts unreliable, he sprinted toward the building, moving in a line that offered the best protection from gunmen at the windows.

Victor reached it with no shots fired and proceeded to examine the exterior. The two doors were locked and the windows closed. He checked along the door and window frames and examined the ground before them. Nothing out of the ordinary. He double-checked everything.

He returned to the Toyota, and by the time he'd driven it three hundred meters and parked it close to the cabin, the rain had stopped completely. Victor saw the sun shining and areas of pale blue sky appeared through openings in the clouds. He used his set of keys and unlocked the cabin's front door.

• • •

He checked every room of the cabin, first the lounge, kitchen, and bathroom on the ground floor and then the two bedrooms on the second floor. Each room was compact and had a minimum of furnishings. A diesel generator in a small shed outside the kitchen supplied electricity to the building and Victor spent an hour cleaning it and performing some basic maintenance before he could get it working. The kitchen contained a boiler supplied by water heated deep below the surface, and Victor started it up now that the electricity was running.

He pulled back the weatherproof sheeting from the Land Cruiser's trailer and heaved off a sack of smokeless coal, carrying it over his shoulder to the kitchen. He fed the stove with fuel and poured the rest into a coal cupboard. He made himself a cup of black tea and ferried in supplies from the pickup until half of the lounge was full of boxes and bags and he was sweating beneath his coat.

The windows were the first areas that required modification. He would have liked to replace them with armored glass, but it had proved impractical to have such specialist materials shipped to Iceland without attracting attention. Instead he drilled holes in the brickwork on the inside of the windows and screwed in metal frames, across which he stretched high-tensile steel mesh. The mesh wouldn't stop a rifle bullet, but he had learned his lesson the hard way never to dawdle in front of a window, no matter how well protected he believed himself to be. He bolted steel sheeting to the insides of the shutters. He calculated that when the shutters were closed, the sheeting and mesh would stop all but the highest-velocity rifle rounds.

It took him two days to finish the windows and another day to replace the doorframes and doors with ramproof steel. He fixed the original wood over the steel to disguise the reinforcements from outside.

The next morning he drove to Húsavík to buy supplies and materials with which to continue his planned renovation of the cabin into a safe house fit for purpose. It would take some weeks until it was finished, but with each day's work it took on additional layers of protection. As soon as the modifications were complete, he would leave it, returning only when he needed to lie low. He'd learned the hard way never to stay in one place too long.

Each morning he examined the doors and windows for tampering, and powered on a rugged custom-made laptop computer based on the model used by military personnel in combat situations. He attached the computer to a satellite phone and unfurled the minidish. The encrypted signal was bounced via satellite to wireless receivers in Europe.

This time he hijacked the Wi-Fi transmission of a café in Bonn, Germany, and used it to access the e-mail account he'd given to Muir so she could reach him.

On the morning of his sixth day in Iceland, he found a single e-mail in his in-box: *We need to meet.*

· Chapter 24 ·

London, United Kingdom

Some actors Victor didn't recognize were promoting the premiere of a film he hadn't heard of. From the huge posters, it didn't look as if he would enjoy it. The hordes of people crowding behind the barriers in Leicester Square to get a glimpse of their idols told him he was in the minority when it came to modern cinema. Or cinema in general. He used to enjoy watching Harold Lloyd, but far preferred books to films. The special effects were more realistic.

It was Friday evening, nineteen forty-five hours, and the sky was just beginning to darken. He'd flown in that morning, from Reykjavik to Helsinki, then to Amsterdam, and finally to London. He had no concern that Muir would try to track him, for whatever motive, but he knew stringent adherence to protocol had saved his life several times. He couldn't quantify how many times such precautions had saved his life without his knowledge. The longer he stayed alive, the more enemies he created. The more enemies out there, the greater importance protocol took on, and the more disastrous the consequences of breaking it.

A chorus of claps and cheers sounded from the crowd as the film's star climbed from a limousine. Victor clapped too. He didn't know the man's name.

"I think he's a bit wooden, personally," a woman's voice said from Victor's flank.

He turned to see Muir and acted as though he hadn't tracked every inch of her circuitous route through the crowd toward him.

"But," she added, "when he's that handsome, who cares?"

"It would appear no one does."

"Are you a movie fan?"

"Absolutely," Victor said. "Who isn't?"

She looked at him for a moment, debating whether to take him seriously or not. Instead she asked, "Shall we take a walk?"

"Your team having trouble keeping eyes on me in the crowd?"

"I didn't bring one."

"Sure you didn't."

He knew she'd come alone. But he didn't want her to know that, for the same reasons he didn't want her to know he'd seen her approach. Regardless of how this job turned out, there was no guarantee he wouldn't find himself on a different side from Muir at some point down the line. The less she knew about how he worked and what he was capable of, the better his odds in that hypothetical future. Not against Muir specifically—she wasn't on his level—but against the organization she worked for and those of its employees who were.

"I didn't bring a team," Muir said. "Honestly."

"Okay, I believe you," Victor said, sounding as if he didn't. "Let's take a walk."

He wasn't sure when the decision had been made to use *1984* as a blueprint, but London was one of the most Orwellian cities on the planet. Closed-circuit cameras were everywhere and the number of routes through the city Victor preferred to take got smaller with each visit as new cameras appeared. But even with the risk posed by the cameras, the huge city offered a great deal of anonymity.

He led Muir down a series of cobbled side streets and alleys until they had left the West End and the crowds of partiers and tourists and miserable Londoners who hated anyone capable of producing a genuine smile.

He said, "I take it Leeson sent another message to Kooi's e-mail account."

Muir nodded. She walked next to him, alongside the curb because that was the only room he'd left her. He wasn't expecting an attack from a car or across the street, but some habits came too naturally to ever change.

"The e-mail is from the same address as the previous one," Muir explained. "This one's subject is Second Date. You must have made quite the impression."

"When?"

"The message said at your earliest convenience."

"Where?"

Muir shook her head. "No location this time around. But there's a phone number to call."

Victor nodded. "Makes sense. He's met me once.

There's no need to go through another face-to-face, especially as the first was set up purely to test Kooi's reliability. I take it you've checked out the number." He gestured. "This way."

He turned onto another side street lined with independent coffee shops, record stores, and fashion boutiques. He smelled marijuana on the breeze.

"The number you're supposed to call is a cell phone. It matches that of a prepaid handset and SIM card bought together last week in Romania."

"Before or after I met with Leeson?"

"Before."

Victor nodded again. "The meeting wasn't simply a formality, if that's what you're deducing from that."

"I get that it's just Leeson being cautious and prepared. If you didn't pass the test, he could just ditch the cell. A few bucks down the drain isn't likely to make him lose any sleep. Purchasing the phone in the same city where you met is just a smokescreen. He doesn't know how much you can know or find out. But you know he was in Budapest. If he bought the phone in some other city, he's just giving away needless information about his movements. Give me some credit, please."

"I didn't doubt you for a second. What about the industrial site?"

"Owned by a Swiss real estate developing corporation. They're going to build condos on it. The textile plant they demolished belonged to some industrialist whose business took a nosedive when the banks did the same. They're clean. Rich people clean, if you know what I'm getting at."

They were quiet for a minute while they walked past a crowd drinking on the pavement outside a pub. Pint and wineglasses rested on the pub's broad windowsills.

The next street was quiet and Muir continued. "As predicted, we couldn't trace the Makarov to Leeson. Like you said, it was Cold War era and commissioned by the KGB a few years before the collapse. It sat with about a thousand others in crates in a warehouse outside Minsk for a couple of decades, gathering dust until they vanished."

"Quite a magic trick for a thousand pistols."

"You got that right. Especially when the crates of AKs and RPGs they were stored with disappeared too. Coincidentally not long after, a Russian multinational bought shares in the company that manages the warehouse and several others like it, which in turn is owned by a very unpleasant Minsk Mafia crew. ATF is all over it because one of those rifles turned up in downtown L.A., but they're being stonewalled by Moscow because that Russian multinational just happens to have a guy called Vladimir Kasakov on their board of directors. You heard of him?"

Victor shook his head.

"Heavyweight arms dealing scumbag. Literally heavyweight. Word on the street was that his business was in turmoil or he'd retired, but whatever. People always want guns. That's never going to change, I suppose. So, how your driver got hold of the Makarov is anyone's guess. I've passed the serial number to a friend inside ATF and they'll add it to their file, and in return if anything comes up, I'll be first to hear about it. I know a little more about the driver."

"Hold that thought."

A pair of police officers appeared ahead, rounding the corner at the end of the block about twenty meters away. They were both male, both in their thirties, both of useful dimensions. They wore standard-issue stab-resistant vests, but as they weren't armed response officers, the only weapons they carried were truncheons and Mace.

One spoke into a shoulder-mounted radio, and all Victor read on the man's lips was some code he didn't understand.

Victor glanced around. Alleys led off both sides of the street. Foot traffic was light. No cars passed. No other police presence.

Muir registered his reaction, and whispered, "Are they here for you?"

"No," he replied. "They're alone. Just on patrol."

"Evenin', ma'am," one officer said to Muir as they passed each other.

When they had reached the end of the block, Muir glanced back over her shoulder to check that the two officers were out of earshot, then turned to Victor and said, "That was tense."

"Was it?"

"What would you have done if they were there for you?"

"You don't want to know."

She gave him a look.

"The driver," Victor prompted.

"Her name really is Francesca Leone. She was born in Italy but she's what you would call a citizen of the world. I'd struggle to name all the countries she's lived in. She's thirty-seven years old, from a wealthy family, and a graduate of the University of Florence. Art history, if you're interested. But what she's been doing for the last fifteen years, aside from globetrotting, is a little sketchy. She's been a painter and sculptor; she was a curator in a gallery in NYC; she's modeled, been married a couple of times. She never stays in one thing in one place for very long, and there are large swaths of seeming inactivity in her résumé. If I had to label her, I'd call her a nomad."

"Criminal record?"

"She was arrested for possession of cannabis resin in Munich twelve years ago, but no charges were pressed. Daddy's lawyers took care of that one. He's dead now and she inherited a tidy sum to help her through the grieving process."

Victor thought for a moment. "How is Varina Theodorakis involved?"

"She's not. She reported her taxi missing before you'd even landed. The plates had been changed. She doesn't know anything."

"And Leeson himself?"

She shook her head. "Nada. There are quite a few Robert Leesons hailing from the U.S. and the U.K., but none of them were in Budapest at that time or own a Rolls-Royce Phantom. Do you know how much one of those costs?"

"A lot."

Muir's cheeks puffed as she blew out a breath. "And the rest. There aren't that many of them out there, thankfully, and I'm in the process of compiling a list of the owners, but the kind of people with the money to buy one also like their privacy. You haven't asked me how Procter's doing yet."

"Why would I?"

Muir raised her eyebrows and didn't say anything for a moment. "Whoever the target is, he must be a major one for Leeson to go through all this to find the right man for the job."

"Quite."

"But what I don't understand is why a man as careful to cover his tracks as Leeson would risk a face-to-face with an assassin he's never met. It doesn't fit with his MO."

"It fits exactly with the kind of man he is. It was the only way to truly know if Kooi could be trusted to do the job he needs doing. Leeson knew enough about him from the contracts in Yemen and Pakistan to confirm his operational skills, but he needed a measure of Kooi's personality. He wanted to see exactly how he reacted when asked to kill Francesca there and then, and sitting opposite Kooi was the only guaranteed way to see if he passed the test. It wasn't just about yes or no, but how Kooi responded. From Leeson's perspective it's preferable to hire someone who knows his face but won't get caught than someone he's never met who gets picked up by the authorities two minutes after the target is dead. Or two minutes before. He couldn't have got the same level of insight any other way. If Kooi had agreed to kill Francesca, Leeson would have known he couldn't be relied on, and would have had his marksman execute him. Nice and clean, no comeback, and he looks for someone else. But I passed the test and Leeson's still clean because he knows I'm trustworthy."

"Except you're not."

Victor nodded. "Except I'm not."

"Trust aside, I'm not sure I'm convinced with the reasoning. It still seems too much of a risk, but I can't justify it any other way, so I guess I have to agree."

"There is another reason."

She read his look and stiffened slightly. "Stan?"

"Kooi didn't fulfill the contract in Yemen exactly how he was meant to," Victor explained. "It was meant to be a suicide just like the one in Pakistan—slit wrists—but Stanley Charters was too good and Kooi didn't pull it off as planned. That made Leeson doubt Kooi's suitability. He wanted an explanation. He needed to hear it from Kooi's mouth. He needed to see his face while he explained."

"Then I don't know how you sold yourself with that mark against Kooi."

"Neither do I. And it presents us with a significant problem."

"Why?"

"Because it shows that Leeson didn't want to hire just any suitable killer. He wanted to hire Kooi. Specifically him, so he was willing to overlook the Charters snafu."

"So what did Kooi have about him that made Leeson so keen to use him instead of someone else even though he made a mistake?"

"I don't know," Victor admitted, "but we need to work it out before Leeson brings it up. Otherwise, this is all over."

· Chapter 25 ·

There had been a time when the humble public telephone was never more than a street or two away in any Western city. Though those days were long gone, they hadn't yet disappeared entirely. The next morning Victor found a pay phone near Charing Cross Station and inserted a handful of coins into the slot, punching in the number with the knuckle of his right index finger.

Muir had requested to be present for the call. She'd wanted it played through a speakerphone, and recorded and traced. Victor had politely declined.

Electronic blips and clicks sounded through the receiver before the dial tone began. It rang for five seconds before the line connected.

A male voice he didn't recognize asked, "How old was the Scotch?"

"Twenty-four years."

"Which seat did you sit in?"

"Right side rear."

Silence. It lasted eighteen seconds.

Then Leeson's voice said, "How nice to speak to you again, Mr. Kooi."

"Pleasure is all mine."

"Thank you so much for calling."

"No problem," Victor said. "But I didn't think I would be hearing from you again after how we parted company."

"Ah, yes. Please accept my apologies for the abrupt nature of that conversation's ending."

"No problem," Victor said again. "I don't imagine you are used to people saying no to you."

"Very true, Mr. Kooi. Though there are salient facts you are not privy to at this moment that affected my response. I shall explain all in good time. But before we reach that point, I do hope there are no hard feelings between us."

"I'm a hard man to offend. And besides, I make sure my professional life has no bearing on my emotional state. And vice versa."

"Is that right?" Leeson asked, and Victor detected there was more to the question than just the obvious.

"No hard feelings," Victor assured Leeson as he watched the world outside the phone booth. Not for curiosity's sake, but because a phone booth presented the kind of confinement and risk Victor preferred to avoid.

"Tremendous," Leeson said. "I'm so pleased to hear you say that, Mr. Kooi, because I would like to offer you employment."

"I'm listening."

"You don't seem particularly surprised to learn I want to hire your services."

"Like you," Victor replied, "I'm good at hiding what I'm really thinking."

Leeson chuckled. "Touché."

A series of horns sounded in the street. A black cab had performed an illegal U-turn, blocking traffic going in the opposite direction in order to pick up a fare.

"What's the job?" Victor asked.

"I prefer not to discuss such delicate matters on the telephone, as I'm sure you can appreciate."

"Yet we're speaking on one now."

"I thought it both necessary and polite to communicate with you directly, so I might assure you of my intentions. I doubt you would have agreed to another faraway meeting after how the first ended. And e-mails can be so very impersonal when one doesn't want to leave a detailed record of intent."

Victor inserted some more coins. The call charges for a foreign mobile number were rapidly draining his credit. "Where would you like to meet this time?"

"I thought perhaps you might like to suggest somewhere."

"So I can be assured of your intentions?"

Another chuckle. "Something of that nature, yes. How would you feel about somewhere hot?"

"The ambient temperature is perhaps the least important factor to me."

"Then why don't we get some sun while we talk? I could use a little color."

"Sure." He paused as if he needed to think. "How about Gibraltar?"

"An especially fine choice."

"Glad you approve. How about next Tuesday?"

"As you decided upon the location, I would prefer to elect a date and time." He paused briefly. "If that is agreeable, of course."

"I have no objection. But I'll need twenty-four hours' notice."

"Noted," Leeson said. "I look forward to doing business together, Mr. Kooi. Good-bye."

The line disconnected.

• • •

Muir waited in the dinosaur hall at the Natural History Museum in central London. For a while Victor watched her and those who came and went through the exhibits, paying particular attention to unaccompanied men and women who were neither young nor old. There were a lot of tourists and families, but no one whom he made as surveillance. He hadn't expected Muir to bring anyone, but he would never stop checking.

She took her time, reading every card, examining each exhibit because he'd told her where to wait but hadn't specified an exact time. She was early. He had been earlier.

A case of fossilized eggs had captured Muir's genuine interest, and his reflection in the display's glass protector informed her of his approach. She acted as though she hadn't seen him and he approved of the attempt at deception. He did nothing to let her know she'd seen him only because he'd allowed her to, because he wanted her to continue building an inaccurate opinion of him.

"Hello," he said.

She turned, and acted as though a little surprised. "Hey."

"Are you enjoying the exhibits?"

"Are you kidding me?" She put her elbows on her stomach and pulled in her forearms to her chest, clawing her hands in an impression of a *Tyrannosaurus rex*. "I love all that roar-roar stuff."

She surprised him. "What are your thoughts on the hypothesis that the T. rex was a scavenger, not a predator?"

"I was kidding."

"Oh."

"Don't tell me you're a dinosaur nerd?"

"I have an interest in natural history."

She smiled and gave him a doubting look. "Keep telling yourself that. I bet you had the dino lunch box and everything."

He ignored her and glanced at a procession of schoolchildren filing into the hall.

"Let's move on."

• • •

Victor took her into a wildlife photography exhibition for which there was a charge for entry and hence fewer people. The lighting was dim so that the illuminated photographs could be better appreciated. They were almost uniformly spectacular, if the winning shot was uninspiring—a political, instead of an aesthetic, choice. He took her to a position from which he could watch the entrance to see who followed. He recounted the phone call with Leeson.

"He's still being cautious," Muir said when he'd finished.

"He may want to hire me, but he doesn't trust me."

"Is there going to be another test?"

He shook his head. "No. He may not trust me as an individual, but he trusts I can do whatever it is he needs doing."

"Any idea yet who the target might be?"

"No."

"I don't like the idea of you meeting him again without knowing what you're walking into."

"Why not?"

"Because we've pushed our luck once already."

"I don't subscribe to the concept."

"Of luck? Then call it whatever you want. I'm talking about factors outside our control here. I assume you subscribe to those?"

He nodded and said, "Leeson had the opportunity to kill me in Budapest when I stepped out of his limousine. He didn't take it, and that was the best chance he's ever going to get."

"If you're sure you want to go through with this."

"I'm sure."

"Okay, good. Because I'm not going to make you do anything you don't want to."

"You couldn't make me."

"That's not what I meant. I'm not going to ask you to do anything you don't want to do. Better? Are you always this pedantic or am I a special case?"

"I always prefer to be exact when my life is on the line."

"Okay, I can appreciate that," she said, nodding. "I'm just a little tense, you know."

Victor nodded as if he knew. "I'll arrive in Gibraltar tomorrow."

"You could end up waiting there a long time. Leeson didn't indicate when he'd meet you, right?"

"He didn't, but it will be soon."

"Why do you say that? He doesn't seem to be in any kind of hurry."

"He's not improvising here. He's working to a specific timeline. He's gone to a lot of trouble to make sure Kooi is the right man for the job. If he waits too long his perfect assassin might get caught, or killed, or take some other job. Besides, if time wasn't a factor he would have sent Kooi on another contract first after he failed to make Charters's death look like a suicide. Leeson isn't the kind of man to accept less than perfect if he can help it."

"Plausible. But he gave you the choice of where to meet. You could have picked anywhere in the world. Anywhere can take a long time to get to and back from."

"He didn't give me a free choice. He was trying to use suggestion to influence me. He asked me to pick somewhere, but suggested somewhere hot. Where's guaranteed to be hot at this time of year in Europe?"

"You didn't have to select Europe. You could have gone to a hundred different places."

"I could have, yes. But before he asked me where I wanted to meet, he justified the phone call by saying he wouldn't have expected me to agree to another faraway meeting. Like I said, suggestion. Besides, going halfway across the world isn't something Kooi or anyone else would choose to do without a good reason. It would make no sense to choose somewhere like Peru just for the sake of it. If I had, Leeson would have politely suggested somewhere closer to home. He wanted me to think I had a choice. As he said, to assure me of his intentions, but in reality he was trying to manipulate me into going somewhere that suited him. I played along, but I knew what he was doing."

"Even so, you could have chosen Greece, Italy, Morocco . . . There are plenty of hot places that aren't a world away."

"And what do all those countries have in common?"

It took her three seconds to work it out. He would have preferred her to do so in two or less. "The Mediterranean."

Victor nodded. "Leeson suggested somewhere hot because he wanted me to pick a country that bordered the Med."

"But why?"

"Because when I meet him, we're going on a little trip."

"To where?"

"I don't know, but somewhere that can be reached by boat. Could be France, Italy, Egypt, Cyprus. Maybe even up to the Black Sea."

Muir nodded too. "Easier to slip into a country unnoticed that way."

"Which is why you're having such a hard time tracking Leeson. He doesn't use planes. He either takes a boat or uses that huge car of his. He can get from one end of Europe to the other and never have to show his passport or have his name in a computer."

"Just what the hell is this guy up to?"

"That's what you want me to find out."

"I know this is probably a redundant question, but how do you know he'll set the meeting soon?"

"I offered him a date next week, but he said he'd let me know when. The implication was that it was too soon for him, so he'll think I'll expect it to be later than the date I suggested. Therefore he'll choose earlier, to catch me off guard. The less warning I have, the safer he'll feel. Kooi's account will get another e-mail, either tomorrow or the next day, and I want to be in the city well before he wants me there."

"He really doesn't trust you, does he?"

"He's right not to. But this is just how he operates. This isn't purely because of me. He doesn't trust anyone."

"I don't know why anybody would choose to live like that. Surely there are easier ways to make a little money."

"Not everyone has a choice."

Her eyebrows appeared above the rim of her glasses. "Don't give me that BS. Everyone has a choice. Everyone has free will."

"It's comforting to believe that, isn't it?"

"Very." She smiled a little. "You're going to need to wear a tracker. If he's going to take you from Gibraltar to who knows where, then we have to keep you in our sights."

"Not an option. I'll be searched."

"Trust me, we can hide it. You wouldn't believe how small these things are these days. They won't find it."

"I said it's not an option."

"Then you can't go through with it. He could take you anywhere. We still don't know that this isn't some kind of elaborate trap. Maybe Kooi killed Leeson's wife. Maybe this is revenge."

"I told you, he could have killed me in Budapest. He didn't. He needs me. The only danger is that he finds out I'm not Kooi."

Muir took a breath. She considered. "Okay, we'll do it your way, as agreed. But you'll have to find a way of getting hold of me as soon as you know what the job is, or where you're going. Soon as you can. Don't wait for us to meet in person. Call, text, e-mail, whatever. Okay?"

Victor shook his head. "That might not be as simple as you think. He's not coming to Gibraltar to discuss the job with me. There won't be any more tests. There won't be any more discussion. Phase one is over. We're moving into phase two. Planning."

· Chapter 26 ·

Gibraltar

Victor had arrived the day after leaving Muir in London. He had flown in from Berlin, having departed London for Zurich and taken the train north across the border. He had a room in a small guesthouse on the outskirts of the town, which he had booked for four nights but where he didn't expect to stay even three. He'd paid in advance so he could leave at any time without creating a problem.

For two days he explored the town, playing the role of a tourist, acting not dissimilarly to Kooi a month before. Victor paid more attention to countersurveillance than the Dutchman had, however, but witnessed nothing to make him consider he was the object of anyone's attention.

On the morning of his third day in Gibraltar, Muir contacted him to say that Kooi had received an e-mail from Leeson, requesting a meeting the following day. The timetable was longer than Victor had expected, and though he was not unduly concerned by being proved wrong in this instance, it was the kind of gap in his understanding that could prove fatal at a later date.

The weather was hot and dry. The streets were busy with tourists and locals. Victor wore loose trousers and a long-sleeved shirt, sleeves rolled up to midforearm. Doing so would have been impossible the previous year when the twin scars on his outer and inner left forearm had yet to blend in with the surrounding skin. They were needle thin, thanks to a cosmetic surgeon in Quebec who had been far more accommodating in handing over Victor's medical records than Schule had in Vienna.

He had arranged to meet Leeson on the seafront, near a harbor full of yachts and pleasure boats, all gleaming white on the azure water. Wind from the sea pushed back Victor's hair and flattened his shirt against his torso. Sunglasses kept him from squinting and let his eyes scan the area without the risk of his watchfulness being noted.

There was a low but wide wall separating the promenade from the harbor. Victor had told Leeson to meet him nearby at noon. It was a little beforehand. Normally, Victor would have preferred to arrive at least an hour before to scout out the area, but if Leeson wasn't alone and had people around, Victor didn't want to take the risk that he would be noticed, for the same reason he gave Muir a false impression of his behavior and skills. He didn't want Leeson to understand how he worked. He didn't want Leeson to know how careful he was. He didn't want Leeson to understand how little Victor trusted him. He wanted Leeson to underestimate him.

He walked with a large tour group led by a couple of

loud local guides who wore louder shirts and delivered their facts and anecdotes with practiced enthusiasm. The tour group was from a Mediterranean cruise ship and happily returned Victor's small talk.

"My wife couldn't make it to shore," he explained to a personable couple from Scotland.

"The prawns?" the husband suggested.

"Too much sangria," Victor said with a raised eyebrow.

Not conducting a proper recon of the locale increased the risks, but it was a poor spot for an ambush, which was why Victor had selected it. The promenade was full of slow-moving pedestrians, few wearing enough clothing to conceal weapons. The street itself was narrow, with tall buildings on one side and the sea on the other. Numerous cramped alleyways and side streets led off into the town. Vendors offered their wares to the continuous flowing mass of tourists. If Leeson had backup it would be a significant challenge for them to spot Victor walking alone. As part of a tour group, it would be almost impossible.

Victor said his good-byes to the Scottish couple, claiming he wanted to pick up a present for his wife and promising to join them for a drink that night in one of the cruise ship's many bars.

"We can't wait to meet her," the Scottish woman said in a thick Aberdeen accent. "She sounds like a lovely wee girl."

• • •

When the tour group had wandered away and the Scottish were out of sight, Victor veered over to the agreed meeting point, where a woman sat on the low wall, one long smooth leg crossed over the other. She wore a figure-hugging white dress that stopped midthigh. The skin of her bare legs and arms was pale and showed no signs of tanning. She wore a hat with a huge brim that shadowed her face and almost her entire body. The wind tossed her wavy black hair back and forth across her face.

"Where's Leeson?" Victor asked when he was within speaking distance.

The woman turned to look his way and tipped her head back so the brim of her hat didn't block her view. She stood when she had identified him. The dress showed as much flesh as it covered and accentuated her figure.

"Surprised to see me, Felix?" she asked, a smile playing beneath the shadow of her hat. Her eyes were invisible behind black sunglasses. Mauve lips glistened in the sun.

"I'm surprised the marks on your neck have faded so soon."

The hat hid her frown, but Victor knew it was there. "Yes, well," she began, "it's amazing what a bit of time and a little makeup can do for a girl."

"I'm glad to see there's no lasting damage."

"Is that your way of apologizing? Because I didn't hear a sorry."

"I gave you the Makarov back, didn't I?"

"I wasn't planning on using it. I know you know that."

"Nevertheless, carrying a gun isn't the best way to make friends."

She laughed briefly. "Says the man who strangled me.

Fortunately for you I try not to judge men on first impressions. I'll put it down to nerves."

"So what do I call you?"

"Francesca, of course. That is my genuine name. I'm not exactly one for hiding who I really am."

Victor raised an eyebrow. "Your dress makes that very clear."

She grinned.

"Where's Leeson?"

She pretended to take offense. "Don't tell me you'd have preferred he had met you instead."

"I'd have preferred to never see you again, Francesca. I had hoped you'd have taken my advice and reconsidered your chosen career path."

"Still playing that record, are you?" A smile failed to hide her irritation.

He ignored it. "This is not the kind of life you want for yourself."

"And who made you the expert on what kind of life I want?"

"No one would want this if they had a choice."

"Who says I have a choice?"

"You're responding with questions because you're defensive. You're defensive because you've chosen this life for yourself and I'm challenging you about that choice."

She exhaled and briefly looked away. "You're really quite arrogant, aren't you?"

"Am I wrong?"

"Am I?"

"A woman of your age has had a life before this one—"

Francesca shook her head as she interrupted. "Arrogant and so full of compliments . . ."

"A woman of your age has had a life before this one," Victor repeated. "And a woman of your attractiveness doesn't need it. You're—"

"Don't think you can reverse my opinion of you so quickly. I'm not that easy to manipulate, Felix."

"You're cultured and intelligent—"

"Hmm, better. More, please."

"You have other options available to you," Victor said. "It's not too late to walk away."

"You see, I knew there was a sliver of a gentleman behind that icy front of yours."

"You're playing the most dangerous game there is, Francesca. It's not too late to walk away, but at some point it will be."

She laughed. "You're really quite sweet, aren't you?"

"Where's Leeson?" he asked again.

Francesca smiled once more and remained silent, enjoying her power. "Let's grab a drink, shall we? I'll pay, and you can pay me back with some more compliments."

"I'm not in the mood."

"Don't be a spoilsport. I fancy a cocktail: something tall and opaque."

"Where?"

She made an exaggerated sigh and pointed without looking in the direction of the harbor.

"He's on a boat?" Victor asked.

"No, silly boy." She turned and pointed, this time past the harbor, out to sea, out across the Mediterranean. "He's that way."

· Chapter 27 ·

Andorra la Vella, Andorra

The restaurant was a chaotic place to work, but Lucille Defraine enjoyed that chaos. She had been a sous chef there for three years; no longer terrified of the giant Turkish chef who ran the kitchen, she now found his explosive outbursts bordering on the hilarious. All the junior kitchen and waiting staff cowered before him and Lucille remembered what it had been like to be afraid of coming to work. It was a stressful environment where the chef demanded perfection and the staff either learned to cope with the verbal assaults or quit. When they did, the chef put another red X on his scoreboard.

"You'll be on there one day," he'd promised her during her first week.

She went about her job with a quiet efficiency that kept her off his radar for the most part, but if she let the risotto stick or a length of asparagus bend in the middle he would unload abuse on her that was a mix of French and Turkish. She had spoken French and German fluently since her childhood, and now could claim to be trilingual—but her Turkish was limited to expletives and insults, though she did know dozens of them.

One of the juniors dropped a pan and boiling water flooded across the floor. Green parcels of ravioli slid along on the flow.

The Turkish chef launched a tirade of insults at the junior, who scalded his fingers picking up the ravioli. Lucille tried not to smile, but failed.

This did not escape the attention of the chef, who turned his abuse her way.

Lucille laughed. She couldn't help herself. The chef's face went so red she thought he was going to burst.

She pointed at the scoreboard and said, "You'll have to do better than that."

• • •

Her shift ended at midnight and she walked home stifling yawns and looking forward to kissing Peter's forehead as he slept soundly in his bed. The night was cool and the stars above bright and beautiful. She lit a cigarette and tried not to hear Peter's voice in her head, regurgitating what he'd learned at school about the dangers of smoking. She promised herself she would quit before he was old enough to be influenced by her behavior, as she had been by her parents who smoked strong French cigarettes every day from breakfast until bed. Neither had made it past sixty-five.

The babysitter was prostrate on the couch, eyes shut, mouth open, a light snoring rumbling in the air, but she snapped upright when Lucille flicked on the light. "I wasn't asleep," she was quick to say.

"Don't worry about it."

The sitter smiled and yawned. "He's been a good boy. We watched a show about Romans. Did you know that they—"

"That's great. What time are you getting picked up?"

The sitter shrugged. "I'm not. Marcel's car won't start, so I've got to take the bus. I hate the bus."

Lucille frowned as she handed the sitter her fee and said, "It's far too late for you to be standing alone outside. I'll just go and check on him and then I'll walk you to the bus stop, okay?"

• • •

The stop was at the end of the street. A one-minute walk there. A one-minute walk back. Hopefully no more than three minutes to wait. Peter would be alone for five minutes. Lucille didn't like it, but she didn't have the heart to let a seventeen-year-old girl go by herself. The town was very safe, but most crime was opportunism. She would never forgive herself if something happened.

There was a group of three young men at the stop. They had the buzz cuts of soldiers and the builds to match. It was not uncommon to see soldiers here. There was a French military base to the north, and its young male residents would often come south to blow off steam in Andorra. They looked harmless enough beyond being drunk, but Lucille was glad the babysitter wasn't alone. She felt the three soldiers watching her and the sitter, but men were never subtle, especially young men, and least of all young men who had been drinking.

The bus arrived and Lucille waved the sitter good-bye as it left.

The young men were still at the stop. They had spread out. They must be waiting for the next one. She didn't look at them as she turned to head home to Peter.

"Hey," one called.

She didn't respond. She went to walk around another one, but he held out his arms and stepped into her path.

"Excuse me, please," she said, her heart racing.

"Hey," the one behind her called again.

"I want to go home."

"I just want to talk to you."

She turned around. "My little boy is waiting for me."

"You left him alone?"

The speaker was the eldest of the three men, but no older than twenty-five himself. He had a smooth face and acne at his temples.

"I need to go," Lucille said. "Please."

He approached her and she backed away until she bumped into the one behind her.

"Why don't you come with us?" the young man with the acne said. "We can have some fun."

"I'll scream."

There was malevolence in his young eyes. "Do you think that will do any good?"

She slapped him.

She didn't think about it. She just did it.

Shocked, he glared at her for a moment. His cheek was red.

His return slap knocked her to the pavement. She didn't feel the pain of the slap because she hit her head on the pavement and darkness encroached at the edge of her vision. Images became blurry and sounds somehow distant, but she detected footsteps nearing.

She lay on her back and found standing impossible, so she rolled her head to the side to see a man crossing the street.

"There was no need for that." His voice was a low growl.

He was tall and broad and blond. He seemed vaguely familiar, but she couldn't make his face come into focus.

"She slapped me," the soldier with acne answered, "so I slapped her back. An eye for an eye."

"Yet the result was not the same," the blond man replied.

The young soldier opened his mouth to retort, but the tall man slapped him. The sound was thunderous. He seemed to fly backward into the bus stop, then collapsed into a heap.

The blond man said, "Now there is parity."

Lucille, still dazed, watched as the young man sprang to his feet, the blade of a knife protruding from his clenched fist. He lunged at the blond man, who moved to the side as he grabbed the thrusting hand and drove the knife up to the hilt in the young man's chest while his own hand still gripped it.

He shrieked and fell to his knees.

The blond man looked to the other two soldiers, who stood dumbfounded. "You should have already started running by now."

He moved, fast and without hesitation, wrapping an arm around the neck of one of the soldiers. He placed his free palm on the young man's forehead and did something Lucille didn't see, but she heard a sickly *crack* and the soldier fell straight down as if his limbs had turned to liquid.

The third soldier—the one Lucille had bumped into—ran. She didn't see him, but she heard his heavy footsteps. She watched with wide eyes as the man with blond hair calmly tugged the knife from the chest of the kneeling man, adjusted his grip, turned, and threw it.

She heard it whistle over her; then an instant later the sound of running footsteps ceased, replaced by a thump and a clattering.

The young man with acne on his temples was crying, his hands pressed over the hole in his chest, still on his knees, but swaying back and forth. Blood bubbled out from between his fingers.

The blond man walked over to Lucille and pulled from his hands bloody latex gloves she hadn't noticed he'd been wearing. He stuffed them into a pocket and helped her to her feet. She could stand, but only just. He kept hold of her to make sure she stayed upright.

"My son . . ." she managed to say.

"I know," the blond man replied. "I'll take you to him."

The soldier with acne fell forward and lay with his face in the gutter. His skin was white and his eyes didn't blink.

"We need to hurry," the blond man said.

Lucille hung on to him because her legs had no strength and the world swayed back and forth before her.

The street came in and out of focus. Her head began to hurt. She realized her head was wet where she'd hit it on the pavement.

"You're okay," the blond man said as she reached to touch her head, "but you have a concussion."

"Those men . . ." she said. "You killed them."

He didn't respond. He led her into her building and sat her down at the foot of the stairs. He took her keys from a pocket of her coat.

"I'll be back in a minute," he said. "Wait there."

"Peter . . ."

"I'll bring him to you."

She heard him walk up the stairs behind her and tried to stand, but she couldn't get her knees to straighten and slumped back down. Not long after, she heard him descend behind her and then watched him pass her. He carried Peter in his arms. Peter was fast asleep.

The blond man exited the building.

Lucille panicked. She forced herself to stand. She used a hand to brace herself against the wall and followed. The blond man walked with Peter along the pavement to where a white panel van sat against the curb. She went after him, stumbling and swaying, grabbing hold of a lamppost to stop herself from falling. Terror drowned out any pain in her head.

The man put Peter over one shoulder so he could open the doors at the back of the van, and then climbed inside, carrying her son.

"Peter . . ."

She pushed herself from the railings to give her the momentum to cross the pavement. She grabbed hold of the van to stop herself tumbling into the street. The blond man reappeared and dropped down.

"Let me help you," he said.

He took hold of her waist and easily hoisted her up so she sat on the cargo deck. Grabbing her calves, he swung her legs up so they were on the cargo deck too.

"I'm sorry he hit you. I assure you I did not instruct him to do so."

"What?"

"I was merely supposed to scare them off. So you would trust me."

"What?"

"It was never my intention to kill them. But at least now you know I'm not the kind of man you want to anger." He examined her head and then her face. "You won't need stitches, fortunately. The concussion will be gone soon. You'll have a little redness on your face for a few days, but don't worry; no one will see it."

"Why are you—?"

"Go to Peter."

She peered into the darkness of the compartment, seeing Peter lying down on a mattress at the other end. She shuffled closer to him and looked back at the man.

Lucille gasped and he swung the van's rear doors shut, one at a time. She heard a bolt slide into place.

She crawled to where Peter lay, now in complete darkness, and pulled him into a hug. He didn't stir, his breathing still deep and regular. She held him tightly until she felt the van rock as the blond man climbed into the cab. She realized the floor was soft and spongy. She checked the walls. They were spongy too. She climbed to her feet and banged a fist on one of the rear doors but made no noise. It was the same as the floor and walls. She pushed her fingers against it. They sank into a thick layer of foam rubber.

The engine started and the van pulled away.

Lucille lay down next to Peter and began to cry.

· Chapter 28 ·

Lazio, Italy

The last time Victor had been in Italy, he had been lying low while he recuperated from a bullet that had torn a groove across his right triceps. That injury had not been severe and had healed well, but it had added another scar to the many hidden beneath his clothes that no surgeon in the world could fully remove. The oldest scars were souvenirs of mistakes not to be made again or considerations never to be forgotten. The newer scars were permanent reminders that no matter the considerations he took, he could not control every facet of every situation, but that he still had to try.

A chartered yacht had ferried Francesca and Victor across the Mediterranean through the night, and by dawn Francesca was driving a dusty Fiat up the coastal roads from Terracina, seemingly heading to Rome, but veering east into countryside when they passed Latina.

She spoke as she drove, talking about her experiences, her travels, and especially her husbands, and asking no questions in return. Victor was happy to let her talk—it wasn't the nervous chatter of someone afraid of silence like the last time they had been in a car together.

"The only thing I've learned for certain over two marriages is that all men are pigs."

"All men?"

"*All* men." She gave him a look for emphasis, then a different kind of look. "Though I'm always on the hunt for the exception to the rule."

They drove along winding roads through a rural landscape dotted with medieval villages. Woods of chestnut, hazelnut, and oak broke up the vast swaths of vineyards and groves of olive trees. The countryside glowed green under the morning sun.

"Beautiful scenery," Francesca said, glancing across to him.

He nodded. "Stunning."

"We're nearly there, by the way."

She turned off the narrow lane and onto an unlaid track that meandered between groves of olive trees. She drove fast despite the frequent blind corners created by the hedgerows that lined the track. The track's surface was uneven and rutted. Dust billowed from the vehicle's tires.

"Hope I'm not driving too fast for you?" she asked, hoping she was.

He raised an eyebrow at her. "This is fast?"

She grinned and applied more pressure to the accelerator. She buzzed her window down all the way and rested an elbow on the sill. The draft threw her black hair around and it whipped across her face, but she seemed to like it.

Her carefree attitude to speed told him that the track led only to a place from which no other vehicles would be coming. Their destination. Given the acres of olives trees, it would be an old farmhouse, built on a hill at a time when higher ground was the first and best line of defense.

After another kilometer a small hill in the distance began flashing into view between gaps in the hedgerow and olive trees. Buildings stood on the summit.

Victor pretended not to have seen until it became obvious. The hill was about thirty meters high and the farmhouse had a sloped roof composed of ochre tiles and walls the color of sand where the bricks weren't covered in climbing ivy. He guessed sixteenth century. The barn that stood perpendicular to it was maybe a hundred years old.

"This is it?" Victor asked.

Francesca smiled in response.

"Leeson's?"

She didn't answer.

She slowed as the gradient increased. Victor expected to see some kind of gate blocking the road and a wall surrounding the property, but there was none. Francesca drove onto the dusty patch of ground that served as a courtyard and driveway to the farmhouse beyond and stopped the car sharply, causing Victor to jerk forward in his seat and then back again. She laughed. He smiled, because she expected him to and because people who smiled were more trustworthy than people who didn't.

The Fiat rocked back and forth on its suspension, and a cloud of dust drifted around them, obscuring the view through the windshield. Victor heard footsteps crunching on grit and sharp stones. When the dust cloud dissipated he saw Leeson standing on the driveway. There was a dark blue Toyota minivan parked outside. The paintwork shone and reflected the sunlight in glowing white pools.

Francesca looked at Victor and he looked at her.

"Always best not to keep him waiting," she said.

The Fiat's door creaked as Victor swung it open. He climbed out and let it fall shut behind him. The weather was hot and dry. Thin clouds drifted from west to east in the sky above. The bright sun from behind the farmhouse made him squint. Leeson stood in the building's shadow.

He wore a suit, this time a two-piece, made from linen. His sunglasses were black as ink. He looked at Victor without expression and made no movement until Victor had crossed the distance. Leeson held out his hand.

Victor shook it.

"Mr. Kooi," Leeson said after they'd released hands. "Welcome to our humble abode."

Victor glanced around. "Thank you for inviting me here."

"That thanks should be shared out between us, for I'm positive we shall both benefit tremendously from our association."

"I'm sure I'll get a great tan at the very least."

Leeson smiled a little. "I hope Francesca kept you from becoming bored on the long journey."

"Her company was gratefully received."

Leeson rotated his head slightly to watch Francesca's approach. "Oh yes, Mr. Kooi, she can be most grateful."

He watched her as she passed them and entered the farmhouse through a wooden door that Victor expected to lead into the kitchen.

"Let me apologize that I couldn't meet you in person in Gibraltar," Leeson said.

"I would have been happy to come straight to Italy."

The younger man nodded. "I'm sure you would have, but I have my little tics that must be satisfied, as I'm sure you understand. Men in our business must never grow complacent, after all. And you will be paid for each and every hour of travel."

"Thank you."

"Don't mention it. I appreciate that you have been inconvenienced by all these escapades and this is not how you conduct your other affairs. I assure you it will prove worth your while."

"I have no doubt it will. What's the job?"

"All in good time."

"I'd like to know now."

"Of course you would."

Leeson said nothing more. Francesca reappeared from the farmhouse, the door hinges creaking to announce her. She held her elbows by her ribs and her forearms perpendicular to her torso, parallel to each other, palms turned upward. A neat pile of folded clothes sat on them. On top of the pile was a pair of hiking boots and a canvas bag.

"I'm sure you're tired from the traveling, but before we go inside and I show you to your room, I wonder if you might accommodate me."

Leeson gestured to Francesca, who stopped nearby.

"Another tic?" Victor asked.

"If you wouldn't mind."

"Not at all," Victor said back.

He emptied his pockets of his money, wallet, passport, and gum and placed each item inside the canvas bag. He handed it to Leeson, who held it open with both hands.

Victor unbuttoned his shirt and took it off. He stuffed it into the bag. He unlaced his shoes and they too went into the bag. As did his socks. Francesca's sunglasses were not as dark as Leeson's, and Victor saw her eyes moving as he undressed. Leeson watched Francesca watching him.

Victor unbuckled his belt and removed his trousers. He pushed them down into the bag to make room. His underwear followed.

He redressed in the clothes Francesca held.

She said, "I hope they fit okay."

"They'll do." He looked at Leeson. "I hope these aren't the only garments I'll be provided with."

"There are more inside." He pulled the string to close the bag and handed it to Francesca. "If it becomes necessary, she will shop for you. Any questions before we continue?"

"Just one: Are the other members of my team already here?"

· Chapter 29 ·

Leeson didn't react but Francesca did. Her eyebrows rose a little above her sunglasses, and a sliver of a gap appeared between her lips. Then she glanced at Leeson, but he didn't return the look. He was focused on Victor. The breeze pulled loose a few strands of hair from the grip of whatever product had held them in place and they danced lazily in the breeze above Leeson's head. He didn't show it, but he was as surprised by Victor's question as Francesca. Though, unlike Francesca, he ran through the connotations and came to the conclusion Victor had expected.

The younger man smiled a little. "How long have you known about the team?"

"Not long."

"Does that mean before or after you arrived in Italy?"

"I suspected beforehand."

Leeson nodded. "And Francesca said or did something to confirm that suspicion?"

She stiffened, ever so slightly, but Victor saw it. Leeson didn't.

"Not at all," Victor said.

He saw that Leeson wanted to press him further, but not wanting to appear as if he cared how Victor had come to his conclusion, he took a slightly oblique approach: "How many do you think are in your team?"

"Do I get a prize if I'm right?"

Leeson smirked.

Victor paused for a moment, as if he had to think. "That people carrier will fit six in the back, plus a driver and passenger. Eight maximum, then. You, Francesca, and I make three, so there can't be more than five more." He glanced at the farmhouse. "Four bedrooms. One for you. One for Francesca. Two left. Two beds in each. One for me. Three left."

He ignored the Fiat's presence and its capacity to carry another four.

"Is three your conclusion?" Leeson asked.

"It's a deduction. Am I right?"

Leeson smiled again. "Shall we go inside?"

Victor nodded in response. Leeson and Francesca walked ahead, Leeson putting a hand on her lower back and drawing her closer to him to whisper in her ear. When he pulled away again she glanced over her shoulder.

Victor winked at her.

• • •

The doorway was low and narrow, the farmhouse having been built centuries beforehand when people were slimmer because food was scarce and shorter because nutrition was poor. Victor dipped his head forward and felt his hair brush the frame. He stepped into a kitchen that looked as though it had remained unaltered in the hundreds of years since it was built. There was a big table in the center, thick and dense, bearing the scuffs and marks of endless use, the polish worn down to almost nothing. At each of the long sides were similarly old and worn benches. Copper pans hung from hooks, as did strings of onions and garlic. The cupboards were made of the same wood as the table, but the polish had endured a little better. The brass knobs were scratched and dull. It was old but tidy and clean. There wasn't a single cobweb among the heavy beams that crossed the low ceiling. The air smelled of herbs and coffee.

"Quaint, isn't it?" Leeson asked.

Victor nodded. "Beautifully rustic."

Francesca huffed. "It's a hole. Practically medieval."

"It *is* medieval, my dear," Leeson said. "But please ignore her, Mr. Kooi. She's a pure urbanite. Not like you and me."

Victor acknowledged the remark with a little smile. He wondered if Leeson's reference was merely to the fact that both he and Victor had expressed their liking for the farmhouse, unlike Francesca, or if he knew more about Kooi's background than Muir believed. If the latter was true, then he had also revealed a little about his own.

"I notice the absence of a refrigerator," Victor said.

Leeson waved a hand in the direction of one of two doors leading farther into the farmhouse. "Yes, no refrigerator. But that's a pantry on the left, which also leads down to the basement. It's much cooler down there, so that's where the perishables are kept."

"No freezer either," Francesca added. "No anything. Like I said, medieval."

"They had neither half a millennium ago," Leeson sighed.

"And this is the twenty-first century."

Victor asked, "No electricity at all?"

"There is a diesel generator outside," Leeson explained. "Purely for lighting at night. There's no phone line and no Internet connection. There's barely any mobile phone reception; enough to take incoming calls on occasion, but you'll struggle to make an outgoing one."

Victor nodded. "I'm impressed."

Leeson smiled. "See, Francesca? Mr. Kooi appreciates the benefits of the simple life."

"Then, like you, he is a barbarian."

"Civilization weakens a man, my dear. And you do so like them strong, don't you?"

Francesca didn't answer.

This seemed to please Leeson, who smiled briefly and opened the second of the inner doors. "Let's continue the tour, shall we?"

• • •

The rest of the ground floor was of a similar age to the kitchen. It was divided into five rooms, only three of which showed any signs of habitation: a lounge and dining area, a bedroom, and a bathroom.

"It's the only room in the building that has anything approaching modern facilities," Leeson explained.

"Approaching," Francesca echoed.

A narrow, winding staircase led to the first floor. Each step creaked and bowed under Victor's weight.

"It's perfectly safe," Leeson assured him.

There were four bedrooms but no upstairs bathroom. Three of the bedrooms were fitted out each with a single bed, bedside table, dresser, and wardrobe. Threadbare rugs partially covered the floorboards. The first two rooms showed signs of occupation—in one the bed was unmade and there were clothes on the floor; in the other a scent of deodorant or aftershave lingered in the air.

"This will be your room," Leeson announced after opening the door to the third bedroom. "Neither Francesca nor I stay here, so I'm afraid you were incorrect in your deduction."

Victor stepped in and turned on the spot, quickly examining each feature and fixture as his gaze passed over them.

Leeson said, "You'll find it basic yet functional."

Victor nodded. "What about the fourth bedroom?"

"Storage."

"Welcome to the Dark Ages," Francesca added as their eyes met.

Leeson sighed. "The medieval period, or Middle Ages, when this farmhouse was built, and the Dark Ages are not the same thing."

"I do so love these history lessons, Robert. Dark Ages, Middle Ages, who cares? This place is a hole."

"My dear, you're not exactly helping to sell the venue to our new friend here."

"It sells itself," Victor said.

A voice drifted up from the stairwell: "That's a good answer."

The stairs creaked as they had done when Victor had ascended. Leeson and Francesca turned to face the open bedroom doorway, ready for the speaker's arrival. Victor did so too, but he knew who was going to appear because he recognized the voice. It was deep and coarse, every word laced with a subtext of anger and resentment and barely contained psychosis.

"You've already met each other," Leeson said as a man stepped into view. "Mr. Dietrich, this is Mr. Kooi. He'll be working with us from this point forward."

The tan that covered Dietrich's face and bald head was deeper than when Victor had last seen him in Budapest. He stepped into the doorway of Victor's room and leaned a muscular shoulder against the frame. He wore khaki cargo trousers and an olive green T-shirt. Sweat darkened a small area over his sternum. The grip of a small combat knife protruded from a sheath fixed to the right of his belt buckle. He stared at Victor. Victor held his gaze.

Neither spoke.

"Mr. Dietrich resides in the room opposite," Leeson said, breaking the silence.

"So you'd better not snore," Dietrich said, then with a smirk added, "Your Majesty."

"Play nice, Mr. Dietrich."

· Chapter 30 ·

Leeson led Victor outside. Dietrich and Francesca didn't follow. The sun was bright and hot. There was an annex separate from the main farmhouse as well as the newer barn.

"The generator is in the annex," Leeson explained. "Wait here for a moment, will you?"

"Sure."

The younger man approached the barn and Victor stood in the sun, pivoting on the spot to look out at the surrounding land. Wherever he looked, groves of olive trees stretched into the distance. Green mountains rose in the east. Farmhouses littered the landscape, but the closest village was about five kilometers to the south.

Leeson opened a door and disappeared momentarily into the barn. He closed the door behind him. When he reappeared he walked back toward Victor, followed a few seconds later by a huge figure.

The man filled the doorframe. Victor had had to duck his head to avoid colliding with the farmhouse's low doorframes, but this man had to bend his knees and angle his shoulders to walk out of the barn, and he ducked his head to one side so his ear almost touched one shoulder.

His head and hands were in proportion to the rest of his body, so Victor knew his physique had not been built with weights but was ingrained in his DNA.

Leeson said, "This is Mr. Jaeger."

Jaeger's shadow fell over Victor and he extended his right hand. It was massive, fingers twice as thick as Victor's own. The wrist was wide and dense. Knotty muscle bulged from the forearm.

"You must be the new guy," Jaeger said.

The accent was German. He was about forty years old. He wore jeans stained with oil and a white undershirt dark with sweat. Hair covered his arms, shoulders, and exposed areas of chest and back.

"I'm Kooi," Victor said.

He shook the hand, maintaining an even expression despite the enormous force he felt in Jaeger's grip. He had no doubt that if he so chose, Jaeger could break his hand without even applying his full strength.

"From Holland, right?" Jaeger asked.

Victor nodded.

"I like your cheese."

"I don't make it."

Jaeger grinned and released Victor's hand. It was red.

They stared at each other for a moment. Jaeger was evaluating Victor, and either he couldn't hide that fact or he didn't feel the need to. Victor returned the favor.

Jaeger said to Leeson, "I'd better get back to it," and then to Victor, "See you around, Kooi from Holland."

"What's in the barn?" Victor asked when Jaeger had angled himself back through the door.

"My Phantom," Leeson said. "But the barn is off-limits to everyone but myself and Mr. Jaeger. Please respect that."

"Of course."

They stood in silence for a moment. Leeson gestured to the red-tiled rooftops and church spire of the village to the south.

"It's a nice place," he said. "Lots of chubby little Italians going about their business as if the world had stopped turning the same time as the first motor car appeared."

"Nothing wrong with leading a quiet life."

"True enough, I suppose. But for men like you and me, quiet is just not enough, is it? Otherwise we wouldn't be standing here now."

"One day it might be."

"When you're old and gray and growing fat from the spoils of a less quiet life?"

"That's the plan."

"If you live that long, you mean?"

Victor nodded.

Leeson patted him on the arm, then looked away, turning and tilting his head back so the sun shone on his face. Victor turned on the spot, memorizing features of the farmhouse, the surrounding countryside, angles and distances and lines of sight. The village was about five kilometers away, downhill, but cross-country because he wouldn't be able to take a road and risk being spotted. A twenty-minute slow jog because he couldn't afford to arrive at the village out of breath and sweating, and because he would have to run back uphill for thirty minutes. If the village was as rustic as Leeson described, there would likely be a pay phone. He needed to make contact with Muir as soon as possible. The farmhouse was old. There were no mod cons. No security measures. He could slip away tonight, update Muir, and be back within an hour.

Footsteps crunched on the gravel driveway. Too light for Dietrich or Jaeger. Too heavy for Francesca. Another member of the team.

"Mr. Coughlin," Leeson said as he turned around. "How good of you to join us."

The man was slight of build, mid-twenties, dressed in khaki trousers and a white undershirt. His arms were thin and tanned brown up to a line where the sleeves of a T-shirt would reach, and pale beyond. His shoulders had reddened in the sun.

"Is this Kooi?"

He was British, from the north of the country.

"Mr. Kooi," Leeson said, "meet Mr. Coughlin."

He was about five eight, about one hundred and fifty pounds. He wore a backward-facing baseball cap and mirrored sunglasses. Three days' worth of stubble covered his cheeks and neck and surrounded his mouth.

"You any good?" Coughlin asked.

"You had better believe it."

Coughlin nodded, but the stubble, sunglasses, and hat made his face unreadable.

Leeson said, a little apologetically, "Mr. Coughlin is something of an expert marksman."

"Royal Marine sniper." Coughlin pointed with his

chin to a tattoo on his left shoulder. "Thirty-two con-firmed between Afghan and Iraq."

Victor said, "Only thirty-two?"

Coughlin's back straightened. "A lot more uncon-firmed. Obviously."

"The marines must have been sorry when you left."

Coughlin said nothing but his smile disappeared. "So, what action have you seen in the world-famous Dutch military? I'm all ears here."

"Who said I'm ex-military?"

Coughlin sneered. "A civilian? Shit. You must be the designated driver, then."

"Mr. Kooi has proved himself very capable," Leeson interjected.

"That right?"

Victor nodded.

Coughlin said, "Then I can't wait to see you in ac-tion."

• • •

When they were back in the farmhouse's kitchen, Leeson said, "Do you know why I hired you?"

"I don't even know what you hired me for, so I wouldn't even guess why you hired me."

"I hired you because you are careful. I hired you be-cause you didn't accept my offer to kill Francesca. You don't act rashly. You do what is sensible."

"I don't understand."

"I think you do, at least partly. For the job I need do-ing I need different people with different skill sets as well as different mind-sets. For example, Mr. Dietrich would brave a storm of bullets in order to earn his paycheck. The man has no fear and no compunction, both of which are traits that are valuable to me. But I only require one Mr. Dietrich. Now do you understand?"

"I imagine one Dietrich is more than enough."

Leeson smiled briefly. "I'm taking a risk telling you this, because perhaps you will react poorly to it, but had you agreed to kill Francesca for me I would have had Mr. Coughlin shoot you with a high-powered rifle."

Victor nodded. "Then I'm glad I declined."

"As I said, I needed a man who was careful and composed, a man who wouldn't do something rash without weighing up the consequences. Alas, there are precious few ways to test such a thing. I hope you can appreciate that."

"I do. And what might have happened had I accepted your offer is irrelevant to me because I did not accept. Had I accepted I would now be dead and my understanding of what caused my demise would not be necessary."

"I'm glad you can see it like that."

"When do I get my things back?"

Leeson nodded, having expected the question would come; no doubt he had answered it already with Jaeger, Dietrich, and Coughlin. "When the job is complete all your belongings will be promptly returned to you."

"How long will it be until then?"

"Are you in a hurry to be somewhere?"

Victor shrugged. "Do I need to be in a hurry to wonder how long I'll be here?"

"You'll remain here for more than a day but less than a year. That is all I will say on the matter for now. During that time you will be my guest and everything you might need shall be provided for you."

"Everything?"

"You have a hand, don't you? You are not permitted to leave the farmhouse grounds unless that is a requirement of your work. In such an instance you will be accompanied by another member of the team at all times."

"Sounds as if I'm more of a prisoner than a guest."

"You may elect to use whichever word you think is most suitable to the situation, but those are the terms of your employment and they will be obeyed without argument."

"Then I want more money."

"Of course, Mr. Kooi. I would not have expected otherwise. Shall we say a twenty-five percent increase in your fee?"

"Thirty percent."

"Agreed. I am now your boss and you are my employee. This is your place of work and you will follow my orders and respect my decisions, and in return I will make you a very wealthy gentleman."

"You still haven't told me what the job is yet."

"For now, Mr. Kooi, the job is to wait. But tonight it will begin with a little excursion."

· Chapter 31 ·

Location unknown

Darkness: all around her, impenetrable black that made her think her eyes were still closed when she knew they were open.

Movement: a swaying and rocking underlined by endless vibration that made her entire body tremble.

Sound: incessant rumbling that filled her ears.

Pain: a throbbing ache that originated in the back of her skull and seeped throughout her head.

None of it made sense. Why had her alarm not gone off to wake her up before Peter surfaced, always hungry for breakfast, decreasingly hungry for morning cuddles? Was it the middle of night? Why was the bed shaking? Where was her duvet? What was going on in the street outside that caused the noise and vibration? Why did her head hurt so much?

Lucille Defraine thought about the bottle of Prosecco in the fridge, not remembering but imagining she had drunk it before bed and now was paying the price of a killer hangover. But that didn't make sense of all that she was experiencing. That didn't explain the lack of light or a scent in the air that she realized was exhaust fumes.

She sat upright, squinting because the movement sent a wave of pain from the back of her head and straight down her body. She touched the source of the pain and found hair matted with crusted blood and a scabbed wound. The sensation made her feel nauseated. An image flashed through her mind.

She put fingertips to her cheek, picturing a slap. A man had slapped her. Who? When? Then she had slapped him; she remembered that clearly. A tall blond man. No, that wasn't right. She'd slapped a young man. A soldier with acne. But she had slapped him first, not the other way around. But why? Then she'd fallen. She must have hit her head on the pavement. That was why the back of her head hurt. That was why she couldn't remember getting into bed. Why was it so dark? Why could she smell exhaust fumes?

The memory strengthened—the Turkish chef trying and failing to rile her; walking the sitter to the bus stop; the three soldiers waiting there; waving the sitter goodbye; the young men harassing her.

The blond man, tall and strong.

He had helped her. He had slapped the man who'd slapped her.

"Now there is parity," he'd said.

Lucille gasped, an avalanche of memories assailing her. He'd killed them. The blond man killed all three of the soldiers. She pictured a white face lying in the gutter, eyes open and staring after her as the blond man carried her away to . . .

Peter.

She cried out and stood, struggling to stay balanced against the swaying and the vibrations. She searched in the darkness, remembering the blond man taking her son and putting him in the back of a white panel van. Then she'd been put inside too. She realized she'd been lying on a mattress in the back of that van. The vibration and fumes were because the van was moving. The blond man had taken them.

Lucille blindly felt along every square inch. She ran her palms over the foam rubber that covered the walls and floor.

No Peter.

She screamed. She banged her fists on the sides and floor and roof, screaming for her son.

The blond man had taken him. The blond man had him.

She screamed and screamed.

Then the van stopped and she was thrown forward. She bounced off the spongy wall and fell onto the floor. She lay on her stomach, crying and screaming.

A noise. Metal. A bolt sliding. Light, as a door opened at the rear of the van. It blinded her. She couldn't see. A shape emerged through her tears. The blond man. Another shape in his arms.

"Peter . . ."

Her son was smiling. "I've been up in the cab like a big boy."

She sobbed, relief and fear overwhelming her equally. She pulled herself to her knees.

"I didn't want him to get bored," the blond man said. "And you needed to rest. He's been having a good time, haven't you, Peter?"

He ruffled her son's hair, and he grinned. "The best time. We've been playing red car."

"And you're winning, aren't you?" the blond man said.

"I've got nine," Peter said, proudly. "He's only got five."

"Your son is very observant. You should be proud of him."

"Give him back to me. *Now*."

The smile fell from Peter's face at her tone.

The blond man said, "There's no need to be like that, Lucille. You don't want to upset your son, do you?"

Lucille tried to control her emotions for Peter's sake. He didn't understand what was happening. She didn't want to scare him, but she couldn't stop the tears spilling down her cheeks. "Come with me, Peter." She held out her hands.

"Why don't we ask Peter what he would like to do?" the blond man said, then to Peter, "Would you prefer to sit with your mother in the dark or ride in the cab like a big boy?"

Peter thrust his hand in the air as if he was answering a question at school. "In the cab, please. *Please*."

Lucille wiped her eyes with the back of a wrist and tried to smile. "Come to your mother, Peter. She misses you."

Peter didn't seem to notice. "Can we play red car again?"

The blond man nodded. "Of course. Go and get back up front." He put Peter down. "But I'm going to win this time."

"No, you won't. No, you won't."

Peter ran out of Lucille's sight, and more tears wet her cheeks. The blond man smiled at her, but his eyes were dead.

"Who are you?" she gasped.

"I am the devil who wears men's skin."

The door swung shut and darkness enveloped Lucille once more.

· Chapter 32 ·

Lazio, Italy

Victor had never driven a Rolls-Royce before. He'd never driven a limousine either. People talked about life being about new experiences, but for Victor new experiences were almost exclusively bad. He didn't know how this one would turn out. He clunked the door shut and adjusted the seat back a notch—the previous driver, Dietrich, was a couple of inches shorter. The driver's seat wasn't as large or as luxurious as those in the back of the vehicle, but it was still exceptionally comfortable as far as car seats went. Still, considering the price tag of the Phantom, Victor would have expected nothing less.

The door windows and rear window were tinted with a dark stain, but the front windshield was left clear. The glass was almost an inch thick with alternating layers of toughened safety glass and impact-resistant polycarbonate. The result was a shield that would stop most bullets. No good against a high-velocity rifle round, but only snipers of exceptional skill in a perfect position could hope to score a hit on the occupant of an enclosed moving vehicle. A monitor on the dashboard received a signal from a camera mounted on the back, acting as a rearview mirror when the privacy screen was closed. Surrounding the monitor, numerous buttons, dials, and readouts occupied the dashboard. A clock displayed the time in both analog and digital formats: eight p.m. A disk-shaped pine air freshener was fixed behind the steering column, but Victor's nose still registered Dietrich's stale body odor.

Victor opened the glove box and searched it, running his hand over every inch to make sure he didn't miss anything. Not even documents or the owner's manual. He checked the compartments in both the driver's and passenger's doors. All empty. He angled down the sun visors. Nothing. He reached under the seats, fingertips touching only carpet and the seat's metal fixtures. No weapons, and no objects that could be used for the purpose. The air freshener could be used as a projectile if it came to it—but only assuming he discovered someone had a lethal allergy to artificial pine scent. He left it alone.

He turned his attention to the set of keys dangling from the steering column. Besides the ignition key, four others hung from the same ring. A small shiny one was for a padlock, presumably the barn. Two older skeleton keys matched the locks he'd seen on the front and back doors of the farmhouse. Lastly, there was what looked like a spare ignition key. It wasn't a spare, however. A spare key kept on the same ring as its counterpart wasn't much use. It was a valet key that would start the Phantom's engine and open the driver's door, but wouldn't enable access to the glove box or trunk. Some valet keys also restricted the performance of the vehicle's engine, ensuring that it could be driven only at minimal speeds. A useful feature when trusting a luxury car to a stranger.

The valet key glimmered in the dim light. No scratches. No scuffs. It had never been used because there was never any need. Leeson always had someone drive for him. He didn't need to trust his limousine and its contents to a valet he hadn't met before.

There was a soft rustle of static and the intercom light glowed green before Leeson's voice sounded from the cab's speakers. "Let's have the partition window open, shall we, Mr. Kooi? I don't think there is any pressing need to be overly formal here."

Victor reached over one shoulder and slid across the opaque window separating the driver's cab from the rear compartment. The window could be opened from either, but there was a catch on the other side so those traveling in the back of the limousine would not be interrupted at the wrong moment.

A slight tilt of the rearview mirror brought Leeson into view. He sat on a rear seat, one leg crossed over the other. He was immaculately dressed in a black three-piece suit, white dress shirt, and navy tie. Calm and relaxed. Victor wore a blue cotton shirt and dark jeans he'd found in his room.

His gaze met Victor's. "Somewhat more civilized, I'm sure you agree."

Victor watched Leeson's mouth move, but the sound that reached Victor's ears came from the speakers, resulting in a disembodied effect.

"Where are we going?" Victor asked.

"Are you hungry?"

"Not particularly."

"Well," Leeson said, looking at his gold watch, "if you're not hungry now, then you will be by the time we get to our destination. And if not, you will be when you smell the food. That I can promise you."

"We're going to dinner?"

"Does that surprise you?"

"A little."

Victor's answer seemed to amuse Leeson. He said, "Take me north, Mr. Kooi."

"To Rome?"

"Yes, to Rome. I can guide us if you're unsure of the route, but kindly ignore the sat nav." He glanced at his watch again. "I have a nine p.m. reservation and the drive is about an hour, so do please take a liberal attitude with the speed limit."

Victor set the vehicle to cruise control and unhooked the valet key from the key ring. It had never been used.

It wouldn't be missed.

• • •

Victor didn't know the exact route from the farmhouse, but he knew where the city was in relation to it and he could read the road signs. He didn't want Leeson to know that, however, and made sure to ask for directions when Leeson failed to supply them.

The limousine had a big engine that as standard put out about four hundred and fifty horsepower to drag its three thousand kilos along to a top speed of more than one hundred and forty miles per hour. Victor had expected the extra twenty percent weight from the armored plating and glass to be offset with extra power beneath the hood to the tune of at least another fifty horses, but he found this wasn't the case. There was no extra power. As a result the Rolls-Royce was painfully slow to accelerate. The brakes were standard too, and the vehicle was equally slow to decelerate.

The twisting country lanes that led from the farmhouse were difficult to negotiate efficiently. Stopping for intersections and then pulling away into traffic was even worse. Victor had no concern about accidents, however. It would take an eighteen-wheeler to put a dent in the limousine. If there was a collision, the small European cars that appeared on the roads would practically bounce off.

"Not the kindest of motor cars to drive," Leeson commented, as the dusk became twilight.

"Something of an understatement."

"You'll get used to it, eventually. If Mr. Dietrich can master it, I have no doubts you can."

The Rolls-Royce was easier to drive once they'd joined the motorway leading to Rome. The sun had set in the west and Victor paid attention to the headlights that glowed in the rearview mirror and the dash-mounted monitor. He paid attention because he always did. He paid particular attention because he noticed a pair of headlights in his mirrors that had been there since he'd left the country lanes. They stayed two cars behind. An innocent position, as there had to be one vehicle occupying that spot, or a tried-and-tested tactical placement.

In the darkness the vehicle they belonged to was too far away for Victor to discern any details, but the headlights were notably higher from the ground and farther apart than those belonging to the two cars that followed directly behind the limousine. The arrangement of the lights didn't match those on the people carrier that had been parked outside the farmhouse on the day of Victor's arrival, but they belonged to a big SUV of some kind.

"Somewhat smoother when you can keep your foot down, yes?" Leeson asked.

"Much," Victor answered, gaze flicking between the road ahead and the rearview monitor.

Behind him, Leeson bent out of sight briefly and Victor heard the clink of glass. When Leeson sat back he held up the crystal decanter for Victor to see.

"Can I interest you in a little something to smooth the edges of your stony demeanor, Mr. Kooi?"

Victor shook his head. "Not the most sensible of ideas when driving."

"I'm sure a man such as yourself can handle his liquor. One tipple of Scotland's finest is hardly going to send us crashing into the embankment, now, is it?"

"Nevertheless, I prefer not to."

Leeson poured himself a Scotch and set the decanter back down. "Your choice, of course. You are the driver."

"Is that why you hired me?"

"To be my driver? Hardly." Leeson laughed briefly. "But I'm paying you for your time and your services, Mr. Kooi. At the current moment I require you to drive."

"I haven't been paid yet."

"All in good time."

"When do I start doing the work you actually hired me for?"

"All in good time," Leeson said again.

"I'm beginning to grow tired of this game."

Leeson smiled. "Then you shall be refreshed soon enough."

Victor glanced at the SUV's headlights. They still shone from two cars behind. "Why isn't Dietrich driving for you, or Coughlin or Jaeger?"

"Mr. Coughlin is currently busy performing his duties. Jaeger consumes even more than you would believe and more noisily than you could comprehend. And can you dare imagine what dining with Mr. Dietrich would be like?" Leeson shuddered. "Horrific beyond words, I'm certain. Besides, I expect he eats leather and drinks motor oil."

"Francesca, then?"

Leeson raised his tumbler in a mock toast. "Far more pleasing to have on the opposite side of the dinner table than yourself, as I'm sure you won't mind me saying."

Victor nodded. "Then why me?"

Leeson pulled back his shirt cuff to check his gold Rolex Super President. The diamonds surrounding the face sparkled. He said, "Because I still don't know you, Mr. Kooi. And I'd really like to. I—"

Leeson's phone rang. Without another word, he leaned forward and slid the partition window shut. No sound came through the speakers. Victor glanced at the intercom's light. Off.

He gaze alternated between the road ahead and the SUV two cars behind.

· Chapter 33 ·

Rome

Forty-eight minutes after Victor had climbed into the limousine, Leeson directed him via the intercom to turn off the motorway. The signing for Rome was obvious, even for someone who couldn't read Italian, but Leeson offered the instruction before Victor had to decide how far to push his supposed ignorance. The SUV turned off too. So did both cars that followed between the limousine and the SUV. But at a traffic island they took different exits. Only the SUV remained.

It was closer now and in the glow of streetlights Victor saw it was a big Jeep Commander driven by a man with a passenger at his side. He couldn't make out many details, but the driver was taller and broader than the passenger, although not hugely so. As Dietrich was to Coughlin. Maybe Jaeger was in the back. The Commander had plenty of room to accommodate him comfortably. The whole team together.

Except Victor.

"Second right," Leeson said, the intercom light disappearing as soon as the words had been spoken.

A minute later: "You just missed the turning, Mr. Kooi."

"My apologies," Victor replied. "I'll take the next one."

He did. The Jeep did too.

"How's your hunger level now?" Leeson said.

"Building."

"Take a left at the end of the block," Leeson said. "And please try not to miss it."

Victor drove down narrow streets alive with light and color. Glowing signs advertised bars and restaurants. The pavements were packed with tourists and natives alike, all out to make the most of life. There were couples and groups of friends of all ages and races. They joked and laughed as they walked by open-fronted establishments bustling with people. No outside table was unoccupied. Victor drove slowly, not because of traffic or pedestrians crossing back and forth, but because the Jeep was no longer following. He hadn't tried to lose it. He had simply taken a turning and it hadn't.

Maybe Leeson had told them to back off to avoid being spotted. Maybe.

The partition window slid open and Victor saw Leeson's face in the mirror.

"Second right and we're there," Leeson said, and checked his watch yet again.

They weren't running late. There was still ten minutes left to meet the reservation at the restaurant, which would be close by. Leeson wouldn't have the limousine parked a significant distance from his destination. There was no point in paying for armor plating only to walk unprotected for half a mile to reach it. They were close to the restaurant and not pushed for time. If Leeson was obsessed with punctuality, Victor would have seen it before now. Perhaps there was another deadline to meet that Victor didn't know about.

He saw their destination as soon as he had taken the turning. Fifty meters ahead a giant sign advertised a multistory parking garage.

"I wouldn't park here," Victor said as they approached the entrance.

"Why ever not?"

"These places are full of blind spots."

"Mr. Kooi, you're sitting behind the best bulletproof armor money can buy. I can assure you there is nothing to be scared of."

"There's no such thing as bulletproof."

"Regardless, there is no reason to be concerned."

"I take it you plan on leaving the vehicle?"

"Of course," Leeson replied. "And that's why I have you."

"I'm unarmed."

"Then you can point out who I need to shoot at." When Victor didn't smile, Leeson said, "I don't think we need to be overly cautious. Rome is a reassuringly safe city. Besides, we can't leave the Rolls on the street, even if we could find a parking space big enough. I don't want some delinquent keying it. The have-nots always despise the haves for working harder than they do."

"I strongly suggest you reconsider."

"Your advice has been noted, Mr. Kooi, and I'm ignoring it. Now find somewhere to park."

Victor buzzed down the driver's window to take a ticket. The barrier opened and he drove through.

• • •

At six meters in length the Phantom required two parking spaces back to back, which proved impossible to find on the first four levels. Victor drove slower than he needed, gaze continuously sweeping the area, half expecting to see the Jeep parked in some corner where it would be missed by a casual glance. It wasn't there. But it wouldn't be far. It hadn't followed them closely all the way to Rome to leave them alone now they'd arrived.

The only level with room to park the limousine was the roof. It was less than a third full, with cars scattered across its space, but concentrated at a slightly higher density near the entrance and exit ramps. Victor selected a spot away from both, but where he could see the entrance ramp and the door to the stairwell when he parked. A corridor of empty parking spaces lay directly between Victor and the exit ramp, some twenty meters away. He applied the hand brake and turned off the engine.

He sat for a moment in the seat, watching the entry ramp, waiting for the Jeep to appear. The roof would be a good place for an ambush. There were no pillars for an assailant to hide behind and fewer cars to provide concealment, but once they were out of the car, there was no protection for its passengers and nowhere to go. But while they were in the limousine, any attack would be doomed to failure. Those carrying out the assault would need a large-caliber machine gun or RPG to get through the armor plating, and Leeson was inside as a human shield. But once Victor stepped outside the vehicle, everything would change. He didn't park close to the ramps because he wanted to see them coming before it was too late.

"Keys," Leeson said.

Victor slid the key out of the ignition and held the ring through the partition window for Leeson to take. Leeson reached out his hand and Victor watched the younger man's gaze drop to the keys.

"Let me get out of the car first," Victor said.

Leeson's eyes angled upward to meet Victor's in the mirror and he swept the keys out of Victor's hand without looking at them. "Of course you get out of the car first," Leeson said with a hint of incredulousness in his voice. "How do you open my door otherwise?"

When the keys were in Leeson's pocket, Victor opened the driver's door and stepped out. The night air was warm. He heard traffic and faint music. He kept his gaze on the entry ramp as he held open the rearmost cabin door.

"Tell me," Leeson said as he glanced at the entrance to the stairwell, "what is the point in arriving in luxury if one has then to walk farther than necessary?"

"Having legs is a luxury."

Leeson nodded as though he was genuinely considering the point, then asked, "Hungry yet?"

"I can eat," Victor said.

"Fabulous. Do you like Japanese food?"

"Who doesn't?"

Leeson gestured toward the exit. "Then you'll love where we're going. I think it's the only one in the city. Italian cuisine is indeed divine, but Italians would do well to diversify their tastes a little. I recommend the katsu curry if your palate can handle a bit of fire."

Victor walked a little way ahead, as Leeson expected, and kept the door in his line of sight as he glanced at the overlooking buildings, picturing Coughlin at a window or on a roof, peering down the scope of his rifle as he had watched Victor on the wasteland in Budapest.

He motioned for Leeson to stop about three meters from the door. Victor opened it, peered inside to check there were no surprises, then ushered Leeson through.

"Elevator or stairs?" Leeson asked.

"Always stairs."

"Making use of the luxury of having legs, I take it?"

"You need to be alive to make use of them."

Leeson looked at him with a little smile as he processed the point. "I have to say, Mr. Kooi, I'm impressed with your level of caution. Neither Mr. Dietrich nor Mr. Coughlin has expressed anything close to the same level of awareness to security."

"And Jaeger?"

Leeson looked at him. "I would imagine that it is the world that needs to be cautious of him. Not the other way around."

"No talking as we descend," Victor said, then added when Leeson raised his eyebrows in confusion, "Our voices will echo in the stairwell and carry farther. Any threat will be able to pinpoint our location with a higher degree of accuracy than with footsteps alone. Plus, if we're speaking it will be harder to hear any threats in return."

He wasn't expecting threats. He wanted to listen out for the rumble of a big SUV's exhaust on one of the levels they passed.

"It's comforting to know you are at my side, Mr. Kooi," Leeson said, and checked his watch.

In return, Victor would take comfort in knowing where Dietrich, Jaeger, and Coughlin were, and more important, what they were doing there.

"Worried we'll be late?"

The younger man looked up and met his gaze. He shook his head as if the fear of tardiness was the very last thing that would ever occupy his thoughts.

They descended the stairs with Victor leading. Leeson followed half a flight behind. Their shoes clattered on the concrete steps and echoed in the stairwell. The exit opened out onto the ground floor of the parking garage, next to the automated ticket machine. The level was bright with fluorescent lights, reducing the shadows to blurred outlines around cars and pillars.

"How far is the restaurant?" Victor asked as his gaze roamed their surroundings.

"Not far," Leeson answered. "A couple of minutes maximum."

Outside they turned left. Victor walked alongside Leeson as would a well-trained bodyguard. If he walked ahead he could better handle threats from the front, but would be useless at any originating from behind Leeson. The reverse was true if he walked behind. Next to Leeson provided the best compromise. He could also shove him to the ground or behind cover if necessary. Victor wasn't a bodyguard, he wasn't guarding Leeson against potential threats, but he wanted him to think he was.

The street was relatively quiet, with intermittent passing cars and a steady but light flow of pedestrians. Opposite the parking garage was a line of stores, all closed for the night so those on foot had no reason to use the street as anything other than a thoroughfare. Except a man standing on the corner up ahead. He stood on the opposite side of the street, outside the glow of a streetlamp that silhouetted him and hid his features. His height and build were a match for Dietrich.

Victor glanced over his shoulder, searching for sign of Coughlin or Jaeger, but saw no one. Leeson did not react, but Victor wouldn't have expected him to. The silhouetted man was about thirty meters away. As they neared he turned around and stepped through the light, and Victor saw a knitted hat covering the back of the man's head, a black leather jacket, stonewashed jeans, and thick-soled boots, but no recognizable features. By the time Victor was twenty meters away, the man had rounded the corner.

Leeson glanced Victor's way. "I'm looking forward to this."

"And me," Victor said.

· Chapter 34 ·

Leeson was right about the proximity of the Japanese restaurant. It took one hundred and eighteen seconds to reach its front door from the point Victor had asked how far it was. They crossed the intersection on the opposite side of the street from where the man in the leather jacket had waited and walked twenty meters farther along the street. Victor held the door open and Leeson passed him with an expected lack of thanks.

Inside, Victor's nostrils were assailed by the smell of the open kitchen at the room's far end. The room was dimly lit and the tables were set with plenty of space between them. It was more than half-full, mostly with couples, except for a table of businessmen in suits celebrating the closing of a big deal. It had the unmistakable air of somewhere that served excellent food at massively inflated prices—somewhere Victor would not have chosen to eat, if only because the portion sizes would be such that he would leave hungry, or else be forced to eat half the menu.

An immaculately dressed maître d' glided between the tables and greeted them with impeccable manners. She wore a black trouser suit and lots of makeup.

Leeson gave his name. "I have a nine p.m. reservation for my very good friend and me."

The woman took menus from a stand and led them to their table. It was in the center of the room.

"Not here," Victor said. He'd already selected the most suitable of the available tables. He pointed. "That one, please."

The woman nodded and changed direction, seating them at a table that lay along a wall, halfway between the door and the stone counter that divided the restaurant from the open kitchen. It was far from a perfect spot, but it would do. Victor drew back a chair for Leeson, who sat down facing the open kitchen, the restaurant entrance behind him. Leeson checked his watch as he shuffled the chair forward a little.

"On time?" Victor asked.

"Precisely," Leeson said with a smile.

Victor glanced around the restaurant. There were no teenagers or children. The youngest person was at least twenty-five. Every diner was well dressed except himself, Victor noticed.

"Don't worry about it," Leeson said. "So you are a little underattired. Everyone will assume you're so rich you've long since ceased to care about your appearance."

"Reassuring," Victor replied.

As they perused the menus, a waiter came by to take their order for drinks.

"Two large Glenmorangies," Leeson said. "No ice."

"One," Victor corrected. "And a San Pellegrino for me."

"Ah yes," Leeson said once the waiter had gone. "You're driving."

Victor nodded.

Leeson ordered shark fin soup and katsu curry. Victor asked for a green salad and stir-fried teriyaki vegetables with rice noodles.

"Can you ask the chef to make the sauce extra sweet?" he said to the waiter.

Leeson huffed. "A man can't be sustained on such a meager meal. At least have some chicken or fish with your stir-fry."

"My stomach is a little raw today. I don't want to upset it."

"Extra-sweet teriyaki sauce?"

"I want the sugar."

The younger man laughed. "You never cease to surprise me, Mr. Kooi. You might be the only gentleman I've ever met who can lay claim to such a thing."

"There is a first time for everything."

They made small talk over their starters. Leeson revealed nothing about himself while asking nothing probing of Victor in return. The primary topic of conversation was the Rolls-Royce. Victor was happy to discuss it while he maintained a vigilant watch of the pedestrians and vehicles that passed by the restaurant's plate-glass front.

The waiter cleared their tableware and they assured him of the starters' quality. Victor asked for a replacement for his empty bottle of mineral water.

Leeson toyed with the Scotch in his glass. "Thirsty?"

"It's important to stay hydrated."

A smirk. "And how did I know you were going to say that?"

"Then my run of surprising you was short-lived."

Leeson said something in return, but Victor wasn't listening. A car drove past on the street outside, and its headlights momentarily illuminated the mouth of an alleyway on the opposite side of the street and the two men standing there. One taller than the other, and broader. One in a knitted hat, black leather jacket, blue jeans, and boots. The second wearing the same outfit, except his leather jacket reached his knees. They were too far away and the illumination too brief to see their faces.

Dietrich and Coughlin.

Their surveillance had been obvious from the beginning when Victor had spotted the SUV tailing him on the motorway, and then on the street corner. He could put the first two incidents down to underestimating him, or maybe even overeagerness, but standing across the street with only the most basic attempt at concealment was too sloppy for men of any skill if they wanted to remain unseen. Which made Victor doubt there was an ambush waiting to be initiated. More likely they wanted him to see them. Leeson wanted him to know they were never far away. He trusted Kooi enough to go to dinner with him, but not enough to be unprotected. If Leeson was testing his trustworthiness, they would have kept themselves hidden.

Something didn't sit right with the assessment, however. He knew there were facts he wasn't privy to, and so any conclusion he reached was unreliable. He survived primarily by constantly assessing the odds, by predicting threats before they appeared and acting instead of reacting.

Another car passed and again Victor glimpsed the two men.

Far too sloppy.

Something was wrong.

"You told me the cell reception at the farmhouse is unreliable," Victor said.

"That's right."

"Yet I saw both Coughlin and Dietrich have phones."

"Indeed."

"Then call them."

"Excuse me?"

"I'll explain later and I'll apologize if I'm wrong. But for now do exactly as I tell you: Call Dietrich."

"I think you're forgetting your place, Mr. Kooi. You should remember that—"

"Call Dietrich. Now."

Leeson scowled, but recognized that arguing further with Victor was not in his best interests. He placed his tumbler on the table and fished a phone from the inside pocket of his jacket. He thumbed a code to unlock it and made the call.

"It's ringing," Leeson said. "What do you want me to say?"

"Hand me the phone when he answers."

"You need to explain yourself immediately or there will be—"

Victor leaned across the table and tore the phone from Leeson's grasp and held it to his ear. Leeson's eyes narrowed and his face reddened, equally furious and humiliated.

The dialing tone cut off and Dietrich said, "How's your dinner?"

Victor didn't reply. He waited. A car drove past on the street outside the restaurant.

He hung up and looked at the call log. There were no names, only numbers. "Which one is Coughlin's?"

Leeson said nothing. He glared at Victor.

Victor stared at Leeson, eyes unblinking, every iota of his lethality succinctly expressed in the gaze. "His number?"

"It ends with oh nine," Leeson whispered between clenched teeth. "It'll be the last but one."

The phone was already dialing before Leeson had finished speaking.

"Sir?" Coughlin answered.

Victor remained silent.

"Sir," Coughlin said again, "is everything all right?"

Victor remained silent.

"Are you there, Mr. Leeson?"

A bus passed on the street outside. The glow from its big headlights washed over the two men in the alleyway. One had his hands in his pockets. The other's hung loose at his sides.

It had been the same when Dietrich had answered.

Victor disconnected the call and tossed the phone to Leeson, who just managed to catch it.

"Just what the hell is going on, Mr. Kooi?" he snarled.

"Do you have any enemies?"

Leeson didn't seem to hear. "I've had as much as I can take of your insolence, Mr. Kooi."

"Listen to me carefully. A Jeep Commander followed

us to Rome. There's two guys now standing across the street. I thought they were Dietrich and Coughlin. They're not."

Leeson's brow furrowed. "Of course they're not. They're both busy on my orders."

"So I say again: Do you have any enemies?"

Leeson sat back, anger starting to fade, but he wasn't grasping what Victor already understood. "Do you think a man in my line of work does not generate enemies?"

"Who could have known about the farmhouse?"

"No one. It's an impossibility."

"The Rolls, then. Who knows about the limousine?"

"I, uh . . . I'm not sure."

"Tell me who might know."

Fear crept into Leeson's expression. "Georgians."

"Mob?"

Leeson nodded. "An organization in Odessa. Half of them are former KGB and SVR. God, I—"

"I don't care what you did to them. If you want to survive this, you're going to need to do exactly what I say. No questions. No hesitation. I say; you do. Understand?"

Leeson nodded frantically. "You've got to protect me, Mr. Kooi. These people are animals. They're absolute animals."

The waiter arrived and placed Leeson's curry and Victor's stir-fry on the table. He bowed briefly and left.

Victor grabbed his fork and began eating.

Surprised, Leeson stared at him for a moment. "What . . . what the hell are you doing? We need to go. Right now."

Victor spoke between chews. "I haven't eaten in a long time. I need to fuel up."

Leeson's eyes widened in disbelief. "We need to get out of here. I'm ordering you to." He pushed his chair back.

"Go and die on your own if you wish." Victor waved a hand toward the door. "Or you can stay with me and live."

Victor ignored Leeson while he shoveled into his mouth the crispy vegetables that wouldn't bloat his stomach or weigh him down, along with the sauce packed with simple carbohydrates that would load energy into his blood. He'd ordered it in preparation for facing Dietrich and Coughlin, not Georgian criminals, but the benefits were the same.

"Drink some water," he said to Leeson.

Leeson reached for his Scotch.

"No, drink water."

The younger man did, downing half the glass in one go. His face was pale.

"Don't worry," Victor said. "They're not going to make the attempt while you're in here unless we give them reason to. So get ahold of yourself."

Leeson wiped his mouth with the back of his shirtsleeve, took a breath, and nodded. "What do we do?"

"Go to the men's room. Put your gun in the bin. Then come back here and wait while I go and get it."

"Okay."

"Don't forget the spare mags."

"I don't have any."

"Then just leave the gun."

Leeson nodded again and stood. He looked unsteady.

"Keep calm," Victor said. "Don't let them know we know."

Leeson sucked in a large breath, relaxed his face as best he could, and headed for the toilets.

Across the street, the two Georgians waited.

· Chapter 35 ·

Victor retrieved Leeson's gun from the bottom of the bin that stood next to the paper-towel dispenser in the restaurant's men's room. He had wanted to find an FN Five-seveN that fired supersonic bullets capable of penetrating most conventional body armor and held twenty in its magazine. He would have been pleased with a reliable Glock or a Beretta with plenty of bullets to shoot, whether 9 mm or .40 or .45 caliber. He would have been content with a compact pistol that held fewer rounds but still had enough stopping power for a one-shot drop. He had to settle for a SIG Sauer that fired .22-caliber bullets.

A .22 had enough power to kill—Victor had done so using one several times—but he had also seen a .22 bullet ricochet off a man's skull. The SIG's barrel had less than four inches in length through which to spin the subsonic round and create accuracy. Its magazine held just ten rounds.

It would have to do.

He tucked the gun into his waistband and headed back to the table where Leeson waited. He hadn't touched his food, but he seemed as if he'd shaken off a little of the panic.

"If you live through this," Victor said, as he sat down opposite, "get yourself a better sidearm."

"I called Dietrich," Leeson said. "He's on the way with Coughlin."

"They won't get here in time."

"They're not at the farmhouse. They're in Rome. They can be here in less than twenty minutes. We just have to stay in here. We just have to wait."

Victor shook his head. "No, we have to get to the car."

Leeson shook his head too. "We wait. I'm ordering you to wait."

Victor stood. "Waiting won't do any good. They know."

"What? How do they know? How do you know they know?"

"Because they're not across the street." He looked around the room. "Did you make the reservation yourself?"

"Yes. This morning."

"You've eaten here before?"

"Yes. Why?"

"With a member of the Georgian cartel?"

Leeson's face dropped. "But it was years ago. Before our relationship ended. I don't understand . . ."

"The time is irrelevant. You should have known better

than to come to the same place twice, especially when the people you betrayed are former Russian intelligence. Someone overheard your calls to Dietrich and Coughlin."

Turning on his chair to face the open kitchen, Victor saw the waiter staring straight at him, backing out of a door on the far side. He looked terrified. He knew what was about to happen.

Victor was already reaching for the SIG as the man in the knee-length leather jacket burst through the same door. He had a pump-action Mossberg shotgun clutched in both hands, the galvanized steel finish glinting under the bright halogen lights of the kitchen. His face was rigid with controlled aggression. His head immediately swiveled to his left, to where he knew his target sat, the muzzle of the Mossberg trailing a fraction of a second behind. Trained, but out of practice.

His right eye exploded in a haze of blood and gelatinous fluid.

There was no exit wound because the low-powered .22 bounced off the inside of the skull and deflected back on itself, tumbling end over end through the Georgian's brain.

The man's turn continued after death, momentum pirouetting the corpse as it collapsed forward into a kitchen worker, who screamed and fell beneath it.

Victor shot again, twice, because he knew the second Georgian from the alley would be following behind, and as the dead man collapsed, the next appeared, moving into the line of fire, the second of the bullets catching him in the left shoulder before he was even through the door. The shock and pain halted his charge and he tried to aim with his own shotgun, but another .22 hit him in the throat.

A spray of blood arced through the air.

He fired—whether deliberately or from the reaction of his nervous system jerking his finger on the trigger—and the plate-glass window at the front of the restaurant exploded.

Glass rained to the floor.

Diners were screaming and ducking or throwing themselves off chairs. Panicked kitchen staff dropped to the floor or scrambled into cover.

Victor squeezed the trigger again and the bullet zipped past the Georgian's head. Blood continued arcing from his neck in staccato spurts as he racked the Mossberg. The expended shell was ejected from the chamber and spun through the air trailing a gray wisp of gunpowder smoke.

Terrified diners and staff moved into Victor's line of fire. He tried to sidestep to get an angle, but people were dashing to the door and blocked his way.

The shotgun roared and the maître d's face contorted in front of Victor. She dropped at his feet, opening up a corridor of air between the SIG and the guy with the shotgun.

Victor put a double tap through his heart.

Among the tinnitus ring in his ears and the screams of terrified civilians, Victor heard Leeson's panicked inhalation and the screech of hot rubber sliding on asphalt.

Twisting, Victor saw the big Jeep Commander skidding to a stop on the street in front of the restaurant. The passenger was already looking their way, the barrel of an AK-74SU protruding through the open window.

"Down!" Victor yelled.

Leeson was slow to react, but Victor leaped forward to send them both crashing together to the floor as the submachine gun opened fire.

The AK-74SU was a shortened version of the AK-47, designed to be used at close quarters. The Jeep's passenger aimed low to follow his target, but the SU's recoil lifted the muzzle as it spat out a cyclic rate of more than five hundred rounds per minute in a wild uncontrolled spray because the shooter wasn't braced in a proper firing position.

Bullet holes appeared in brickwork, tables, diners, kitchen cabinets, and even the ceiling.

The roar of the gunshots drowned out the screaming.

Victor rolled onto his back as Leeson lay facedown with hands over his head as if those hands could stop bullets. Victor squinted to protect his eyes from the fragments of masonry and brick dust that peppered the air and the blood that misted above him. He counted off the seconds—*one*—because he knew on continuous fire—*two*—the SU would unload its thirty rounds in—

Three.

He jumped to his feet and drew a bead on the Jeep's passenger as he released the spent magazine and fumbled for a new one, but he didn't shoot straightaway. The man was twelve meters away, blurred by gun smoke and shadow, presenting a narrow side-on profile, fifty percent of his body concealed by an SUV's door that might as well have been armor plating to a low-powered .22-caliber round.

Victor waited until the SIG's tiny iron sights were perfectly aligned and squeezed the trigger three times.

The man jerked and slumped in his seat. Blood splashed across the driver's face.

The Jeep's tires squealed and smoked as it sped away.

"Move," Victor said to Leeson.

· Chapter 36 ·

When he didn't move, Victor grabbed him by the collar and wrenched him to his feet. He shoved the empty SIG into his hands. "Put this away and follow me."

Victor pushed and shoved his way through the crowd of cowering and wailing diners. He vaulted over the stone counter and into the kitchen. The tiles were slick with a lake of blood from the guy shot in the neck. At about six feet tall and two hundred pounds, he should have had nine liters of blood in his body. About half of that was spread across the floor. As Leeson followed, awkwardly climbing over the counter and dropping down the other side, he slipped in the blood and fell onto his back.

There wasn't time to search the corpses, but Victor patted underneath the armpits and around the waist of the first dead Georgian, finding nothing. He did the same with the second and found a pistol tucked into the back of his jeans. It was a Daewoo DP-51.

"Get up," Victor said to Leeson.

He thrashed and fumbled on the blood-slick tiles, horror etched into his young face, his tailored wool suit soaking up blood.

Someone in the kitchen screamed at Victor in Japanese. He ignored him, released the Daewoo's magazine to check the load, shoved it back into the grip, pulled the slide, and, gun leading, hurried to the open back door through which the two Georgians had appeared. It didn't lead directly outside. A corridor lay on the other side. It was narrow and bright. Closed doors lay to his left. They would lead to walk-in cold cupboards, storage, maybe a small office or toilet. Another door at the end of the corridor hung open. Victor saw an alleyway on the far side.

Leeson scrambled to his feet and scooped up the first Georgian's shotgun.

"Take the other one," Victor said.

"This has more shells, surely."

"But we know for certain the other one works."

Leeson swapped weapons and edged up behind Victor, who had the Daewoo trained on the open doorway at the end of the corridor.

"More?" Leeson asked.

"Only one way to find out."

Victor walked quickly along the corridor, gun out before him. Leeson followed, cradling the Mossberg with whitened knuckles.

"Keep your finger outside the guard," Victor said, glancing over his shoulder.

"But—"

"If you squeeze the trigger while you're behind me,

you'll shoot me in the back. Then who will get you out of this?"

Leeson nodded. "How are we going to get back to the car?"

Victor ignored him. He kicked open the first door to his left. There was a small toilet on the other side. He kicked open the next door. It was a pantry, full of boxes and shelves of nonperishable food and kitchen supplies. He glanced around, gaze fixing on cans of chopped tomatoes. He grabbed one and tore off the label to reveal the bare metal beneath. Leeson watched but said nothing.

Back in the corridor, Victor made his way to the doorway leading to the alley beyond. He listened. Nothing from the left. A dead end. Muted sounds of traffic and fleeing diners coming from the right. He tossed the can through the doorway so it sailed diagonally to the right. It was dark in the alleyway, but the reflective metal sheen of the can caught what little light there was.

Muzzle flashes illuminated the alleyway in strobes of orange and yellow.

Bullets chipped brickwork and tore through the open door.

Leeson stumbled backward away from the door, his soaked suit leaving a bloody smear on the wall as he leaned against it, his legs weak with fear. Victor pushed past him and dashed back into the kitchen.

Overturned tables and chairs lay strewn throughout the restaurant. The body of the maître d' lay facedown near where Victor and Leeson had sat, the back of her clothes a mess of blood and torn fabric. The room was empty except for the corpses. Diners and staff alike streamed out of the restaurant exit or climbed through the destroyed window. There was no sign of the Jeep or the Georgian mobsters. But they were out there, waiting for the crowd to disperse and ready to open up with automatic fire if Leeson or Victor was among them.

"Go back into the corridor," Victor said. "Lie down facing the exit. Aim the shotgun halfway up, at the center. You'll see a shadow on the alley wall an instant before anyone enters. They'll be hurrying, so squeeze the trigger as soon as you see the shadow. Do you understand?"

Leeson nodded. He spoke in disconnected bursts. "Lie in the corridor. Aim at the door. Shoot the guy who comes through the doorway."

"No. Shoot the shadow. Don't wait for the guy to appear. You'll be slower to react than you think because you're scared—he'll be faster because he isn't. If you wait, he'll kill you."

Leeson nodded again. "Shoot the shadow. Don't wait. What are you going to do?"

Victor didn't answer. He grabbed the first Georgian's shotgun. Broken glass and crockery crunched beneath Victor's shoes as he stepped across the destroyed room. The last of the fleeing crowd—the kitchen staff who had been farthest away—scrambled faster when they saw him coming behind them.

"Get across the street," Victor called after them. *"Don't go to the left."*

Those fleeing were already going straight ahead or to the right because guys with automatic weapons were to the left, but Victor didn't want anyone to go the wrong way in the elevated panic caused by his proximity. They were even more afraid of him than they were of the Georgians.

He looked over a shoulder to check that Leeson had moved as instructed, saw him lying on the other side of the open kitchen door, turned left side on to the restaurant's exit, stepped out, and immediately squeezed the Mossberg's trigger.

It roared and a huge blast of white-hot gases exploded from the muzzle. The recoil kicked in his hands, jerking the unsupported barrel upward.

He missed because he hadn't aimed. His eyes took in a snapshot of the scene before him—the rear of the big Jeep stationary in the center of the street eleven meters away; a guy with an AK-74SU covering the alleyway; another, kneeling in the gutter, aiming a submachine gun Victor's way—and he retreated into the restaurant before the crew could respond.

The kneeling Georgian fired, reacting a fraction of a second too slowly—though fast enough had Victor taken the time to aim. But he wasted only a few rounds as he controlled the burst. A calmer operator than the guy in the Jeep's passenger seat, and therefore a more dangerous one.

Victor racked the Mossberg and fired it again single-handed, extending only the gun and his arm through the door. He didn't expect to hit either of the men, and he couldn't see if he had, but the minuscule pause before the return burst from an SU told him he hadn't.

"What's happening?" Leeson yelled over the din of automatic gunfire.

"Stay where you are," Victor called back as he racked the shotgun. "Remember what I told you."

He fired blind again. Another smoking shell landed among the debris on the restaurant floor. After the roar of shot dissipated, he heard a clattering—windshield glass pebbles raining on the street.

He glanced at Leeson. "Be ready."

The Rome police would have been called by now. Average response time for reports of gunshots was sub three minutes across the developed world. Less than two minutes left. The Georgians might not know the statistics, but they knew they didn't have much time left if they wanted to complete their job and stay free long enough to celebrate a share of the purse gone up three hundred percent.

"Be ready," Victor said again. "Shoot the shadow."

Three shots fired. Three remaining in the feeder.

Then two.

"Shoot the shadow," Leeson repeated.

Victor squeezed the Mossberg's trigger a fifth time. Before he'd finished racking another shell into the chamber, he heard the roar of Leeson's weapon and dashed back across the restaurant, vaulted over the counter, and pulled Leeson to his feet and into the kitchen. He didn't need to look down the corridor.

"I got him," the younger man whispered. His eyes were wide. Unsteady legs because there was more adrenaline in his bloodstream than there had ever been before in his life.

"I know," Victor said. "You couldn't miss."

"I shot the shadow. Like you said."

"You did good." Victor used one hand to drag Leeson around the stone counter and onto the restaurant floor.

Leeson's voice was still little more than a whisper. His face was pale. "What now?"

"We wait," Victor said. "There's two left. One with an AK. The other behind the wheel of the Jeep. Neither will try coming in here. They've lost two-thirds of their team trying that. No one's that brave. If they've got any sense, they'll get out of here before the cops show."

"What if they don't have any sense?"

"They'll try to wait us out."

"Will it work?"

"Yes. We have to be gone before the police arrive and arrest us. But it's suicide for them to wait until then. They'll be caught too."

"These people *are* crazy," Leeson said.

But they weren't stupid. Tires squealed for traction and a big V-8 engine sounded. Victor ditched the shotgun and readied the Daewoo.

Leeson was still in shock. "I killed a man."

"Join the club," Victor said, and tapped Leeson on an arm with the back of a hand. "Let's go. It's not over yet."

· Chapter 37 ·

Victor peered out of the restaurant to confirm that both remaining Georgians had gone in the Jeep and one wasn't waiting behind to catch them as they came out—as he would have done. The street was empty. He saw the Jeep rounding a corner at the end of the block.

"Drop the shotgun," Victor said.

Leeson did.

"Take off your jacket."

Leeson did, but his movements were slow and awkward. Victor helped pull it off him and threw it to the floor. Blood stained one sleeve and almost the entire back.

Victor turned him around on the spot to check that the blood hadn't soaked through to the white shirt. It hadn't. Stains darkened the backs of his trouser legs, but would draw less attention than a man in his underpants.

"Are those sirens?" Leeson asked.

"Yes. Time to move."

Leeson swallowed. "You saved my life, Mr. Kooi."

"Not yet."

"But they've gone. You said—"

"And they know where we're going."

Leeson reached for the shotgun.

"Leave it," Victor said.

"If they're waiting I'll need it."

"If you take that shotgun out onto the streets, you're asking for the police to spot us. I take it you don't want to be arrested?"

"I don't want to be killed either. I need a gun."

"Then you should have selected your sidearm with a little less thought to its appearance and a little more consideration to its usefulness."

"But—"

"Do you want to continue this discussion at the farmhouse or in jail?"

Leeson didn't answer, but he nodded.

"It's a two-minute walk to the right to get to the parking garage, but we can't go direct. So we go left, and we walk quickly but we don't run. Soon as we get to an intersection, we take it and circle the block, walking like a couple of regular guys. No looking over your shoulder. No watching the street for the Jeep. We just walk."

"But the Georgians went left."

"And by now they'll have already circled the same block and will be waiting for us in the parking garage. Until we get there our priority is not getting picked up by the police. No more questions. I've got you this far. Do as I say when I say it and I'll get you the rest of the way. If you don't like my methods you can try making your own way back."

"No, no. I'll do what you say. I will. Sorry. Let's go. Don't leave me. Please."

They went, turning left, hurrying along the pavement as the sound of sirens grew louder behind them.

"Don't look back," Victor said.

Leeson nodded.

They walked past the scatter of glass pebbles on the street surface where Victor had shot out the Jeep's rear window. Expended brass shell cases from the AK-74SU glinted. The wail of sirens intensified and Victor was aware of Leeson tensing next to him, but after Victor's brief he managed to resist the compulsion to look back. Then tires screeched and the sirens grew no louder.

Victor took the first turning that presented itself—a side street that cut through the block. Closed boutiques lined both sides of the twisting throughway. A young couple were making out in an alcove, oblivious of the shoot-out that had occurred less than one hundred meters away, or unconcerned by it. Maybe it helped the mood.

Walking quickly by with Leeson had no effect on the lustful moans and gasps. They reached the end of the cobbled street and turned left.

"Act normally," Victor said as he slowed the pace.

They reached the intersection and waited for a moment to cross the flow of traffic. A police cruiser sped toward them. Leeson tensed.

"Relax," Victor assured him. "It's not slowing."

The cop car shot past and Leeson exhaled.

"Containing the scene is the first priority. The emergency call won't have provided enough intel to act upon. They don't know who they're looking for yet."

Leeson gulped and nodded.

"Unless we do something to draw their attention," Victor added.

"Okay," Leeson said. "Okay. I understand."

"Understanding and doing are two separate concepts."

Anger was in Leeson's gaze. "I'm not in the business of fucking up, Mr. Kooi."

"That's the spirit."

A gap in the traffic appeared and they hurried across. The signage for the multistory parking garage glowed up ahead.

"Do you have a plan?" Leeson asked as they neared.

"I always have a plan."

"We're going to the limousine?"

"Yes."

"Won't they be waiting for us there?"

Victor nodded. "Of course."

"Then all they have to do is wait on the top level until we're out in the open and then we're dead."

"Is that what you expect?"

"Of course."

"Is that what you would do?"

"Yes."

"Then why would they do it?"

"Because it will work."

"There's two ways onto the roof—the ramp and the door to the elevator and stairwell."

"There's two of them. One can cover each."

"What happens if one of us appears at the door?"

"The one covering it will shoot."

"What about the other one: Will he join the gunfight or stay covering the ramp in case we've split up?"

"That depends on if we split up."

"But they don't know what we'll do. If one is engaged in a gunfight and the other can't assist, then it's riskier for them than it is for us, because maybe we're both shooting back. Then it's two-on-one in our favor. If the other does assist and we have split up, then their flank is exposed and they get shot in the back."

"My weapon is empty."

"They don't know that."

"I don't know how to do this kind of thing. I'm not trained in combat. I don't know how to—"

"They don't know that either."

"What does it matter? It doesn't change the fact that they have more guns than us because you made me leave the shotgun."

"They don't know that," Victor said again, "so they'll act as if we're both armed. They won't be on the roof, for the reasons I just explained."

"Then where will they be?"

"On a level below with the Jeep abondoned elsewhere so we don't see it. They'll ambush us as we make our way up, knowing we'll expect them to be on the roof."

"Unless they can think like you can."

"In which case why are four of them already dead, yet we're still alive?"

Leeson didn't answer.

· Chapter 38 ·

They waited. All they had to do was wait. It was simply a matter of time. And patience. The target—the man named Leeson—would return to his car. He would never leave it behind. Of this they had been assured by those who had sent them to kill him.

They were enforcers in an expansive organization who had been paid up front with a sports bag crammed with bundles of euros and dollars. That money was to be split between six, based on seniority and experience. Now there were only two of them to divide it. There was no consideration of taking the money and running. The brotherhood would find them, wherever they went, and all the money in the world was not enough to buy the protection they would need to live long enough to enjoy it. They knew trying to finish the job that so far had killed four of their six was dangerous, but if they did not see it through they would need to return the money and beg for forgiveness from an organization that knew no mercy. So they waited.

The Rolls-Royce limousine was parked on the roof floor of the multistory parking garage. Only two ways led to the roof: the stairwell and the ramp. Only two ways Leeson and his bodyguard could come. Only two ways the Georgians needed to cover. And there were two of them.

They were up against two, but it was only the bodyguard who concerned them. They had not been told about him when the job had been explained. They had been told Leeson wouldn't be alone, but they had not been told the man with him would be death himself. They took some comfort in the fact that their leader, who had failed to supply them with the appropriate information, now lay slumped in the passenger seat of the Jeep Commander, two bullet holes vivid against the white skin of his forehead.

The bodyguard was the threat. Neither man relished the idea of facing him again. They had seen and heard the fates of those who already had. He was a killer of men who was not easily ambushed. He would expect another attack. He would expect his enemies to lie in wait near the limousine. He would be ready for that ambush. He knew they would cover the stairwell and the ramp.

But they were cunning men.

They would cover the stairwell and the ramp, but not from the roof. They would strike on the level below, when Leeson and his bodyguard were making their way to the roof, when they were vulnerable, when they weren't expecting it.

One was armed with a pistol, the second with a submachine gun. The former had driven the Jeep and now had the dried blood of the leader smeared across his face. He'd wiped off the chunks of brain and fragments of skull. The latter had exchanged fire with the bodyguard. He was a former soldier. He knew more about battle than the driver, whom he had ordered to cover the ramp. He didn't believe the bodyguard would come that way, but it couldn't be left unguarded. The man with the submachine gun believed the bodyguard would come up the stairwell. Leeson would follow him because he wouldn't want to be parted from his only protection.

The gunman crouched in the stairwell on the floor below the roof. He kept the AK-74SU aimed down the stairs. He didn't move. The only sound he made was that of his quiet, regular breaths. His right index finger maintained gentle pressure on the trigger. All it would take was a single squeeze and the bodyguard—who would be leading—would be blasted by a burst of 5.45 mm rounds before he knew he'd been outthought. Another five bursts would follow before his corpse rolled down the stairs. The gunman knew himself to be an excellent marksman. At this range, with an automatic weapon, there was no way he could miss.

He could then reload and kill Leeson at his leisure. Maybe even with the knife he had with him. He had never killed a man with a knife before. He wondered what it would be like. He imagined it would be fun to watch the life fade from a man's eyes. Killing from a distance was so impersonal.

Police would be swarming the restaurant by now. They would find the abandoned Jeep soon enough. But none of the Georgians had carried ID or personal effects.

They had no criminal records in Italy. It would take a long time to identify them and trace their movements, leaving more than enough time to complete the job. It had gone bad, but the gunman had come too far to let a little setback like the deaths of four of his fellow brotherhood members stop him from seeing it through and enjoying the money. And it was a lot of money. It had been a lot of money split six ways. It was a huge amount split two ways. A thought occurred to him.

It would be a monumental amount if it was not split at all.

It wouldn't be long. Leeson and his bodyguard couldn't wait as long as the Georgians could. Witnesses had seen them up close. Maybe their names were in the restaurant's reservations list. They had to escape. They had to come this way. The ramp was too risky. There were too many blind spots and choke points and too much cover to worry about. The bodyguard wouldn't risk that. They had to come this way. They had to come soon.

The gunman realized that there was another, better benefit to completing the job than just the monetary reward. When he returned to the brotherhood with Leeson's head in a cool box and the brutal story about how four—five—of his teammates had been killed by the bodyguard that he had managed to kill single-handed, he would be hailed as a hero. His value to the brotherhood would be elevated to an unprecedented level. He would be respected and feared and every boss would want to use him. He had succeeded where five had failed. What better evidence of his skills could there be?

A sound.

Muted by distance and the attempt at muffling, but the sound of the stairwell door opening several floors below. The bodyguard.

A civilian or the target would have made more noise. The gunman tensed slightly, then relaxed and concentrated on listening. He expected to hear the quiet footsteps of a cautious man when he was two floors below. Such a man, moving at a careful pace, would take about a minute to climb the four flights of stairs in between.

It took thirty seconds.

The gunman considered. There was only one set of footsteps. Leeson had to be waiting at the bottom for the bodyguard to get the car and drive it down. The bodyguard was moving faster than the gunman had expected, so he was arrogant. He had underestimated his opposition. Not unsurprising as four of them were already dead, but not the man waiting on the stairs. He was alive. He was smart.

He listened to the footsteps. Two floors below. Then one.

This was it, he told himself. In moments the bodyguard would appear. A moment after that, he would be dead.

The gunman stayed focused. He'd seen combat in Chechnya. He knew the danger of distraction. A blink at the wrong moment could spell disaster. Any second now.

He heard the stairwell door open behind him.

He glanced back to shoo his partner away so he didn't ruin the ambush, but the man who came through the door wasn't dressed in their uniform boots, blue jeans, and leather jacket. The man wore no shoes or socks. His shirt was dirty and scuffed. His sleeves were rolled up.

The bodyguard.

Disbelief, shock, and questions assailing the gunman's mind slowed his reaction.

He twisted, turning his body and swinging his arms, and the submachine gun, but the bodyguard was already too close.

The barrel of the AK-74SU was pushed aside. The edge of a hand struck the gunman in the throat. He gasped and choked, but his experience and training kicked in and he released the gun and grabbed his knife. But the bodyguard had a hand in his hair and a palm under his chin and he was wrenching the gunman's head backward and—

Crack.

The second and third vertebrae of the Georgian's neck broke, rupturing the spinal cord. He slackened and collapsed and rolled down the stairs in a tumble of uncontrolled limbs.

• • •

The Georgian didn't die instantly because Victor had to rush the maneuver and the broken vertebrae failed to fully transect the spinal cord. But he would be dead soon. No messages from the brain could reach the body. The diaphragm couldn't expand or contract. No air could be sucked into, or expelled from, the lungs.

Leeson rounded the motionless, dying man and moved cautiously up to Victor, his face pale and sweaty.

He pointed back down the stairs to where the Georgian lay.

"He blinked. I don't think he's dead."

"He's dead," Victor replied. "His brain just doesn't know it yet."

Leeson looked Victor up and down, noting the scuffed and torn clothes, scratched bare feet, hands, and arms.

"I can't believe you actually did it," Leeson whispered. "You climbed the building."

"Just the one level," Victor corrected. He used a thumbnail to scrape some grit from his palm and said, "Never attack from the front when you can do so from behind."

"What now?"

"The last one is still out there. He's covering the ramp and is dug in well between a pair of Mercs."

"How do we deal with him?"

"Easily," Victor said.

• • •

The last Georgian breathed in short, panicky bursts. He was the youngest and most inexperienced of the team. His job was to drive. That was it. He was armed with a handgun, but he wasn't supposed to need to use it. He'd never even fired a gun before. He knew how to, and he knew how to kill—he'd beaten a liquor store owner to death as his initiation into the brotherhood—but he didn't know how to do *this*.

The other guy had told him what to do. He'd told him where to wait. He'd told him where to aim. He'd told him their target and said the bodyguard wouldn't come up this way. He had to watch the ramp anyway—just in case.

The other guy was going to handle it. He knew how to fight. He'd been a soldier. He was one of the proper killers who had murdered and tortured for the brotherhood numerous times before. Such men terrified the younger Georgian, but he aspired to be one, one day. He wanted to have such a reputation for skill and brutality. He wanted other men to be intimidated by him, not the other way around.

It wouldn't take long, the soldier had told him. He would trap them in the stairwell and then they would split the bag of money. The soldier had not explained how they would split it, but the younger man would be happy with his promised cut and his life. He didn't want to end up a rich corpse like the four dead men.

An engine roared into life behind him.

He turned and headlights momentarily blinded him. He heard tires squealing for traction on the ramp above, the noise echoing around the level.

The target's limousine.

It took the young Georgian a few seconds to react. He watched it accelerate down the ramp, toward him and then past him.

He squeezed his weapon's trigger.

The gun barked and twitched in his hand and a mark appeared on the rear window of the limousine. He shot again, and again, and then ran from cover—not thinking, just acting—and chased the Rolls-Royce, shooting wildly as he ran, missing more than he was hitting.

He chased the car to the level below and his gun clicked empty as the limousine disappeared out of sight.

The young Georgian stopped running and became aware of his heart hammering inside his chest and sweat dripping from his nose. He used a palm to swipe it from his face, realizing that the older soldier must have failed in the stairwell and was likely dead and that the target had escaped.

He'd failed and would have to accept whatever punishment the brotherhood deemed appropriate. There was no other option. He hoped they would show leniency as he was just supposed to be the driver. If five experienced killers couldn't get the job done, how was he supposed to? He needed to get out of the city. Now.

He didn't care about the money anymore. He was just grateful to be alive.

He turned to head for the stairwell and stopped dead as he found himself staring into the black eyes of the bodyguard standing directly before him.

· Chapter 39 ·

Location unknown

Lucille was waiting near the van's doors when they opened. She had been on her feet as soon as she had felt the vehicle coming to a stop. She'd been sat on the mattress positioned across the width of the back compartment and next to the front wall. The mattress was queen-sized and newly purchased. There was no protector or linens and no pillow, but with her back against the padded wall, it was comfortable enough that she had no aches or pain from the long hours of traveling. She didn't sleep, though. She couldn't.

He had her son.

In time she had become used to the darkness and the constant rocking and swaying and noise and the heat of an insulated room with no ventilation. The pain in Lucille's head had eased throughout the day, but she felt sick with fear and weak from the hours of crying and screaming. She hadn't drunk anything since leaving the restaurant, however long ago that was now. Her throat was dry and her lips were cracked and sore.

She didn't know where she was. She could have been taken south to Spain or north into France, but she didn't know how long she had been unconscious. They could have reached almost anywhere by now.

This time when the door opened, light didn't flood inside and sting her eyes, though she had been braced for it. Outside it was dark. Nighttime. The blond man stood alone against a backdrop of starry sky and flat countryside. He held a backpack in one hand. For the first time Lucille saw him with her vision unimpaired. He was tall and powerful, dressed in loose jeans and a loose workman's shirt with the sleeves rolled up to reveal thick forearms covered in fair hair. He looked to be somewhere in his forties, his skin weathered and tanned. His lips were thin and surrounded by a short beard that reached high on his cheeks. The blond hair was clipped short and even across his head, receding at the temples and flecked with gray. Blue eyes that caught the starlight and reflected it like those of a wolf stared at her and she forced herself not to cower.

"Where's my son?"

"How's your head?"

"I want to see him."

"I would have been aghast had you not. He's sleeping in the cab."

"What do you want with us?"

He didn't answer. "Your eyes are focusing better, aren't they? I imagine the headache has dulled over time too. That's good. Could you turn around so I can see the wound?"

"Let us go. Please. I'll do"—she paused and breathed to stay composed—"anything you want."

He stared at her. His wolf's eyes didn't blink.

Her heart hammered. She braced herself, disgusted and terrified, but thought about Peter and how she would willingly endure anything to save him.

The blond man stepped forward. He held up his hand. Lucille looked at it. It was large and callused. A monster's hand. She swallowed and reached for it.

Laughter.

A loud, coarse sound that permeated every inch of her being and made her wince and shudder.

"You need to fear me, Lucille," the blond man said once he'd finished laughing. "But not in that way."

An image flashed through her mind: a bench, pigeons, a man feeding them.

"I know you," she said. "From the park."

"Excellent," the blond man replied. "You're over the worst of the concussion if you remember me."

"How long were you watching us for?"

"Does it matter?" he asked. "With that knowledge could you bend space and time and travel back to warn yourself of my presence? And if you were able, would such a warning do any good? Could you stop me? Could anyone?"

"God will punish you for what you are doing."

"When he has already done so by granting me life, how can any further punishment be worse?"

Lucille couldn't stop the tears. She wanted to be strong. She didn't want him to know how terrified she was. But she couldn't help it.

"Give me back my son," she wept.

"When he wakes he can rejoin you."

"He needs me."

"He likes it up front. It's fun. I let him win almost every game we play. Not all, of course; otherwise he'll suspect. He's a smart little child. You should be proud of him."

"What do you want with us? Why are you doing this? Don't hurt him. Please, don't hurt my son."

The blond man said, "You should know, Lucille, that there is no safer place for Peter in all this world than at my side. You should also know that whether it stays that way is up to you."

She sobbed.

"Take your time," he said.

It took a little while until she was able to hold back the tears. She wiped her eyes with the back of her wrist.

He hoisted up the backpack and placed it inside the rear compartment of the van. "In there you will find some water, food, and basic medical supplies. There are also some clothes and other items." He gestured to the countryside behind him. "I'm sorry I didn't let you out earlier and I may not be able to do so again for some time, so go and relieve yourself now while we have the opportunity."

Lucille peered at the countryside. Low verges lined the road. Beyond were fields that stretched to the horizon. There were no lights, no sign of human habitation.

"Where are we?" she asked.

"That does not matter."

"Where are you taking us?"

"Find yourself a quiet spot. Climb over a verge into one of the fields."

She looked at him.

"I'm not going to come with you," he said. "Can't leave a young child on his own even for a few minutes, now, can we?"

The words stung her deeply. More tears wet her cheeks.

"I'll stay here with Peter," the blond man said. "Take all the time you need."

She glanced at the road, then looked away in case he'd seen. He had.

"I won't try anything," she said.

"You're an intelligent woman. You know this isn't some deserted track, so there's a reasonable chance a car might pass. You know you could flag one down to help. But you also know the occupants will fare no better than those soldiers." He shrugged. "Or maybe you'll get lucky and a convoy of armed police will happen by. But could they stop me before I ripped your boy's head from his neck? It's an interesting question. How does one weigh the odds of that which is beyond common comprehension?"

The blond man held up his hand again and she took it. He helped her down from the van and onto the road. Standing next to him, without the artificial perspective gained from the height of the van's cargo deck, she realized just how weak and insignificant she was in comparison. If he didn't want her body she had no weapon to use against him. She was powerless.

"I won't try anything," Lucille said again.

His wolf's eyes shone in the starlight. "I know you won't."

· Chapter 40 ·

Lazio, Italy

Victor found the Rolls-Royce waiting for him a couple of kilometers south of the parking garage. It had been too much of a risk to have such a recognizable vehicle in close proximity to two crime scenes and a heavy police presence, so Victor had told Leeson to drive it away while he took care of the last Georgian. The limousine sat along the curb of a quiet street, out of the direct glare of any streetlights, as Victor had instructed. As he neared, Leeson climbed out of the driver's seat and greeted Victor with a smile and a handshake.

"Thank you, Mr. Kooi. Thank you so very much."

"All part of the service."

Leeson gripped his hand tightly with both of his own. "You saved my life. I don't know how the hell you pulled it off, but you did. Six of them against the two of us, but here we are, alive and breathing and nothing but some sweat and a few scratches to show we've ever been in battle. I really think that—"

Victor opened the rearmost cabin door and gestured. "Why don't you tell me what you think on the way back?"

Leeson smiled, in a different way. "Yes, of course, Mr. Kooi. Anything you want. Any problems with the last one?"

Victor shook his head.

The younger man climbed into the back and Victor shut the door before getting into the driver's seat. Leeson pulled open the partition window and then slouched back in his seat.

"Did you call Dietrich and Coughlin?" Victor asked.

"Yes. As you said, I told them to stand down and head back to the farmhouse."

Victor pulled away from the curb and set about taking a circuitous route out of Rome. He saw Leeson was smiling and drumming his fingers on the console next to him.

"Happy to be alive?"

Leeson nodded. "I've never experienced anything quite like this."

"Post-battle elation," Victor explained.

"It's exhilarating."

"Don't be alarmed if you find yourself experiencing strong sexual desire."

"Wouldn't that make me a psychopath?"

"That's not exactly how one is defined, but regardless, it's nothing to be concerned about. The violence doesn't cause it. You came close to death. Your subconscious wants you to reproduce while you still can."

Leeson laughed. "I'll remember you said that if I find myself with an inexplicable erection." He fixed himself a drink. "Now I understand why men like yourself can do what you do. For the first time in my life I'm actually happy—no, ecstatic—just to be alive. It's more satisfying than anything I've ever experienced. I would happily do it all again just to recapture this sensation."

"It diminishes each time."

"Do you still feel it?"

Victor shook his head again. "I don't even remember what it really feels like."

"Then what do you feel after something like this? What do you feel right now?"

"Nothing."

"No joy?"

"No joy."

"Then I feel sorry for you, Mr. Kooi. I really do. Aren't you glad to be alive?"

"Of course," Victor said. "Life is always preferable to the alternative."

"Ah, so you are a man who believes there is nothing waiting for us beyond the grave."

"No," Victor said. "That's the problem."

"Then why do what you do?"

"It pays well."

Leeson laughed.

• • •

He barely stopped smiling for the entire journey back to the farmhouse. He also barely stopped talking. He wanted to relive the experience. They talked through what had happened, their individual roles and how they worked as a team. Leeson described every detail of when he had shot the Georgian attempting to flank them. The panic he had shown in the restaurant was long gone and didn't seem likely to return in the dead of night, tearing him from sleep and drenching his body in sweat. It wouldn't be long before he believed he had been fearless.

Victor stopped the Rolls-Royce on the driveway in front of the farmhouse, but kept the engine running.

"You need to open the barn," he said.

"The barn is off-limits—"

"It doesn't bother me who does it," Victor interrupted. "But you need to hide this vehicle. It'll have been picked up on CCTV and witnesses don't forget seeing a Rolls-Royce limousine. It's a bull's-eye to any aerial surveillance. And you don't want another visit from your Georgian friends, do you?"

"Why not?" Leeson asked with raised eyebrows. "We dealt with the last lot easy enough."

We. Easy.

"And what about the authorities? Are we going to easily deal with a police helicopter spotting the Phantom and a tactical team knocking down the farmhouse door?"

Leeson nodded. "Okay, you win. Sensible as always. I'll have Mr. Dietrich do it."

Victor nodded too, wondering why Dietrich was allowed to take the limousine into the barn and he wasn't.

. . .

Inside the farmhouse kitchen Francesca, Dietrich, Jaeger, and Coughlin were waiting. Jaeger sat eating a sandwich; the rest stood around the table—Francesca closest to the door, the other two men at the far side, leaning against the countertop next to the sink. Dietrich's arms were folded in front of his chest, defensive. Coughlin looked bored.

Francesca smiled. "The warriors return. All hail."

She spoke while looking at Leeson, whose back instantly straightened in a rush of pride and arrogance. Francesca knew exactly how to play him.

"My dear," he said, and embraced her.

Victor made sure not to make eye contact as she glanced his way.

"Well?" Dietrich spat.

Leeson released Francesca. "Do you want to tell the story, Mr. Kooi, or shall I?"

"Be my guest."

"Though first, Mr. Dietrich, would you be so kind as to house the car in the barn?" Dietrich nodded and Leeson handed him the keys as he passed. "And I think before I begin, a glass of vino is appropriate." Leeson motioned to Francesca. "Pop down to the cellar and fetch a bottle, there's a good girl."

Francesca nodded and smiled and left the kitchen. Victor got himself a glass of water. She returned after a minute and poured everyone a drink. Victor shook his head when she came to him.

Leeson waited until Dietrich had also returned before he recounted the events of the last few hours. He was a good natural orator, who did an excellent job of underplaying his own role just enough to encourage clarifications and inquiries for more details. Details he was only too happy to embellish under the veneer of false modesty.

Francesca gasped and exhaled at every chance and

when Leeson had finished, said, "I didn't know you had it in you, Robert," with wide-eyed rapture and a little excited clap of her hands. Leeson was a good orator, but Francesca was his perfect audience.

Jaeger nodded with raised eyebrows, reserved but impressed.

Dietrich and Coughlin were not.

"So, His Majesty here pinged five of this crew, right?" Dietrich asked, doubt creasing his forehead.

Leeson nodded. "That's correct. Mr. Kooi was truly formidable."

"He kills a bunch of amateurs and I'm supposed to be awed? Don't think so."

"Your evaluation of the quality of the opposition is immaterial here. Had Mr. Kooi not been present, I would now be a corpse and you, Mr. Dietrich, would be without an employer."

Dietrich scowled. "There's nothing this guy could have done that I couldn't have myself. And easier. I wouldn't have needed a civilian to help me get the job done over a bunch of amateurs."

Victor tried—badly—to hide a laugh.

"Got something to say, Your Majesty?"

Victor remained silent. But he smiled at Dietrich. Just a little smirk, but enough to further antagonize the man. There was nothing Victor could do to make Dietrich reverse his opinion of him, and there was a good chance they would eventually find themselves as enemies. Victor was happy to let Dietrich go into that potential future encounter with the disadvantage of genuine dislike and hatred.

Dietrich stared. "Too afraid to talk, are you?"

"I'm afraid if I do I might use words you don't understand."

Dietrich took a step forward. "You won't be talking so tough when I gut you and leave you in the basement for the rats to gnaw on."

"Good luck with that."

Francesca laughed. "Such pathetic displays of testosterone-fueled arrogance. Who are you both trying to impress besides each other? Because it's not working."

"Don't flatter yourself," Dietrich said.

She laughed again. "Do you think anyone cares who could have killed more or done so easier? Is that the only way you can measure yourself against him?"

"Why don't you shut the fuck up?"

Her eyes widened.

"Don't talk to her like that," Victor said.

"I'll talk to her however I wish."

"Try again."

Dietrich stared at him. "Mind your own business or maybe I'll start minding yours."

Victor stared back. "You say that like it actually means something."

"Better for you if you don't find out what that something means."

"I can't wait to find out."

Dietrich smiled at that and inched away from the countertop. There were two meters between them. His back straightened and his fingers curled toward his palms. He was strong. He was dangerous. But he couldn't hide what he was about to do if his life depended on it.

Which it did.

But Leeson saw what was coming and held out a hand. "Let's leave this posturing right there, shall we? You are both valuable men to me in different areas. Whoever harms the other will lose that value. Do I make myself clear?"

Dietrich's eyes were locked with Victor's. Neither answered.

"Well?" Leeson asked. "Do I need to start looking for replacement personnel who will actually do as I ask?"

"No," Victor said, because he knew Dietrich would rather fight to the death right there than answer first.

Dietrich smirked at him—satisfied at this perceived victory—and shook his head at Leeson.

"Very good," Leeson said. "When you two are no longer in my employment, you can settle your differences in whatever manner you see fit. For all I care you can beat each other until what remains is not enough to fill a bucket. But for now, you behave yourselves. If you cannot be respectful, be silent. And, Mr. Dietrich . . ."

"Yeah?"

"I don't ever want to hear you speak to Francesca like that again. Apologize, immediately. And need I remind you of the potential consequences of such discourtesy?"

Dietrich stared for a moment until he did understand, then nodded. He looked at Francesca and said, "Sorry."

"Accepted."

Coughlin, who had been silent since their return, asked, "How exposed are we?"

"Minimally," Victor answered when Leeson didn't right away. "The crew were competent enough not to have any ID on them or other identifiable evidence, so they are unlikely to have left an obvious trail elsewhere. The restaurant has Leeson's name." He looked at Leeson. "But I assume that's not a problem. The parking garage had CCTV, obviously, and the recordings will match witness descriptions from the restaurant, but there won't be recordings of our faces."

"And how can you be so sure of that?"

"Because I'm good at what I do."

"Then let's hope you're right, because you've left a trail of destruction through a city all of thirty miles from this position."

"Way to go, putting us all at risk," Dietrich added.

"It's not a problem," Victor said.

"That remains to be seen," Coughlin said.

"It's not a problem," Leeson repeated after a moment's thought. "We're still good here," he said after another pause, and Victor wondered what conclusions he'd come to and why the involvement of the two of them in a firefight in the middle of Rome didn't compromise whatever it was they were here for.

· Chapter 41 ·

Later, Victor found Leeson outside the farmhouse, sipping wine while he looked at the night sky. There were no clouds, and bright stars littered the blackness of the eternity above. Victor looked too. Stars and constellations had fascinated him as a young boy. He looked at them on clear nights with a telescope he'd built out of materials raided from junkyards and landfills, making up his own names for them because he didn't know the correct ones. He wondered briefly what had become of the telescope.

"My savior," Leeson said as he turned to face Victor. The younger man was a little drunk, but only a little. "I'm sure you don't mind that I put a slight spin on the facts earlier. Thank you for not challenging those—how shall we put it?—inaccuracies."

"Thank me by telling me what we're doing here. Specifically, what I'm doing here. I've waited long enough."

"You have my gratitude for saving my life. But that changes nothing regarding the nature of our relationship. I am your employer, and you are my employee. What happened earlier tonight affects neither. You will be told your role and what is expected of you when it is necessary, and only then."

"What you and I consider necessary are likely two very different things."

"I'm fully aware of that, but I have every faith in your suitability. I would not have hired you otherwise. And you have nothing to fear regarding the time frame. There will be more than enough time to prepare."

"Again, our definitions of what constitutes enough won't necessarily sync. I told you in Budapest that I won't go into a situation without the full facts and the proper time to plan and prepare. That I'm your prisoner here changes none of that."

"Then when the time comes, if you are not happy with the facts or the time frame or any other consideration, you may step back and depart. No hard feelings."

"Just like that?"

"Just like that," Leeson echoed.

"You don't trust me, do you? Even after I saved your life."

"Answer me this, Mr. Kooi: If our positions were reversed, would you?"

He didn't wait for an answer but headed back inside.

• • •

Victor stayed outside to think. The night air was warm on his face. Moonlight reflected on the padlock securing the barn. The limousine was on the other side of the doors along with whatever Jaeger was working on. In less than a minute Victor could be past the padlock, but he had no source of light with which to explore the interior of the barn, save for using one of the candles he had found in a kitchen drawer. With Coughlin, Jaeger, and Dietrich all residing within ten meters of the barn, it would be far too risky to break in. Even if he didn't wake them up, there was no way of knowing whether all three really were sleeping and not waiting for him to betray himself.

The barn could wait for tonight, but he needed to update Muir. Which presented its own problems.

Francesca stepped outside. He let her think he didn't notice her until she came closer to where he stood.

"Beautiful night," she said, looking up.

Victor nodded.

"Robert was right when he said I was a pure city girl, but the one thing you don't get in the city that you do in the country is the stars. Sometimes it's easy to forget just how breathtaking the night sky can be when you can actually see it. I wish I knew the names of the constellations. I know Orion's Belt, but that's the limit of my astronomical expertise. I can't actually find it, though. Can you see it anywhere?"

"At this time of year Orion is in the sky during daylight, so you can't see it, I'm afraid. The belt isn't a constellation in itself. It's an asterism of three stars within Orion: Alnitak, Alnilam, and Mintaka."

Francesca laughed.

He faced her. "You need to get out of here."

She was still smiling. She gestured to where the Toyota minivan was parked. "That's exactly what I am doing, silly boy."

"That's not what I meant."

Her eyebrows arched. "I'm very well aware of of what you meant and I'm choosing to ignore it."

"I don't know what you're getting out of this. It isn't enough. Trust me on that."

"You're really quite taken with me, aren't you? I'm flattered, but I don't believe you've thought this through. I'm sure even you appreciate that strangling a girl is not the best way to begin a relationship. How would we tell our friends the story of how we met? 'Oh no, you tell it, darling. The way you do the choking sounds kills me.' Which of course you nearly did."

She was laughing but he ignored her.

"Leeson may come across as a gentleman, but he's utterly ruthless. I've known men like him before. Whatever hold you think you have on him, it will only protect you for so long."

"Stick to shooting guns. This kind of thing is beyond your simple male brain."

"I tried to tell you in Budapest that you were out of your depth. I hope you realize it for yourself before it's too late."

"I'm not as stupid as you think I am."

"Oh no, I know you're anything but stupid. But intelligence isn't enough in a situation like this."

"I do have another weapon in my armory." She gave him a mischievous look. "I'm sure you've noticed."

"If you think beauty is enough, then let me take back my previous statement."

She laughed. "What happened to you to make you so serious all the time?"

"Listen to me, Francesca, you need to understand how dangerous this situation is. You need—"

She rested a palm on his chest to stop him. "If intelligence and beauty aren't enough to protect me, I know you will, won't you?"

Before he could respond she kissed him on the cheek and walked toward the minivan. He watched her, wanting her to turn around. She didn't. She knew how to play him as well as she did Leeson, who joined her at the vehicle a minute later.

"Get a good night's sleep, Mr. Kooi," he called to Victor. "Tomorrow is a big day."

· Chapter 42 ·

He didn't sleep. He sat on the end of the bed designated to him the previous morning. The mattress was soft and lumpy. The springs had taken a beating over the years. They squeaked and rattled in the center of the mattress. They were quiet at the end Victor sat on, where they had only had to support the feet of its former owners.

Victor's watch had been dropped inside the canvas bag along with his other possessions, and the room contained no clock, but the minutes ticked inside Victor's head. Leeson and Francesca had left four and a half hours ago. Dietrich and Coughlin had retired to their rooms shortly afterward and Jaeger a little after that. Victor had lain on the floor, in the center of his room, in order to peer through the gap beneath the door at the strip of light under Dietrich's door opposite. He'd remained on the floor until that light had gone out. Then he listened for the creaks and groans of centuries-old floorboards to stop, and waited until his internal clock reached four a.m.

He sat facing the bedroom door, at an angle where he saw the room's small window in his peripheral vision. Those were the only ways in and out. Both door and window were closed. The door had a lock, but Victor had no key. Not that the lock would hold up to a solid kick from Coughlin, a half-decent one from Dietrich, or a gentle shove from Jaeger. The door had been made and installed with a mind to privacy, not security. The window was a little better. It had a latch—which would stop none of the farmhouse's occupants—but its height from the ground offered significant protection, further enhanced by the rendered exterior walls scalable by only the most dexterous of climbers.

If an assailant came through either the door or the window, it would be because Leeson had discovered Victor was not Kooi. Then it would be three against one, or four if Leeson was present for the assault. Victor had seen no guns apart from Leeson's SIG, but he knew there would be others, kept wherever Leeson and Francesca were staying, because he didn't trust his hired killers to have sidearms that could be turned on one another or himself. But those sidearms would be distributed if he knew he had an imposter in his team.

But that wasn't going to happen. At least not yet. Because Victor was awake in a quiet farmhouse and Leeson couldn't arrive with guns for the others without Victor's knowledge. If Leeson merely contacted Jaeger, Coughlin, and Dietrich with the order to go after Victor, the three would do so without firearms. Three against one: they might not see that as a problem, especially with Jaeger's size and Dietrich's cocktail of arrogance, psychosis, and aversion. Leeson's tale of what happened to the Georgians would give a man as considered as Coughlin pause for thought, but Victor had used a gun then. They might not see him as a threat without one because they had no idea what he was actually capable of.

They would simply open the door and attack, but they couldn't do so without forewarning Victor. The farmhouse was too old and creaky to allow for the level of stealth necessary to take a man like him by surprise. And if he felt they would attack, he would pull the bed in front of the door to slow them down and go out the window. Hearing breaking glass, Dietrich, hotheaded and eager for blood, would rush downstairs in pursuit, followed by one of the others—he wasn't sure whether that would be Jaeger or Coughlin—leaving the last man to check the room, maybe even try to spot Victor fleeing by looking out the window. Which would result in a ten-foot drop because Victor would not be on the ground and running, but on the roof above. And if the last man didn't orchestrate his own death or incapacitation by his proximity to the window, Victor would swoop back into the room. Coughlin wouldn't be a problem to deal with, but if that last man was Jaeger, the broken shards of glass from the window would come in useful.

Leaving two against one on Victor's terms. A formality.

But wishful thinking if they did see him as any kind of threat. Then they wouldn't attack him in his room when he could hear them coming. They would wait until morning, pretending nothing had changed. There was already enough tension in the air that Victor might fail to decipher that another layer had been added to it. Then they could corner him in the kitchen or a corridor where there was nowhere to run or pick his battlefield.

He would fight, because while he drew breath he still had a chance. But Dietrich would have a knife and he wouldn't easily be disarmed of it, which would give Jaeger more than enough time to grab Victor from behind. Then it was over.

He knew he could have smuggled up a cup of olive oil from the kitchen to grease the old hinges of his bedroom door, but the muted squeal they made was the only true defense the door offered. Dietrich and Coughlin hadn't made a noise for four hours. Jaeger's snores were loud and regular.

Victor opened the door. He did so quickly, so the squeal was louder than it might have been had he done so slowly, but it was over within a second instead of lasting several. Jaeger's snores didn't change. Maybe Dietrich or Coughlin might have stirred at the sudden sound, might even have awoken, but with silence restored when their eyelids opened and no further sound following, they would fall asleep once more and not even remember the incident come morning. The door stood open for five minutes before Victor stepped through it.

He had the limousine's valet key in his pocket. He wasn't planning on using it—yet—but he wanted to keep it on his person at all times. He walked with his boots hanging from a fist by their laces, keeping as close to the short corridor's wall as possible, so the most worn floorboards in the center did not suffer his weight. He did the same on the stairs. They creaked and groaned with every step. He waited at the bottom for another five minutes to see if the noise drew a response from any of the three killers upstairs. It didn't.

The kitchen's stone flooring was cool through Victor's socks. He left via the kitchen door and circled around the building so he was beneath his window with groves of olive trees before him. He laced up his boots and made his way slowly down the steep slope and into the field. He ran.

The village wasn't far and the stars were bright enough that the journey was easy to navigate. He exited the field and found a gap in the hedge at the far end. He crossed the narrow road into another field, running alongside its boundary hedge to avoid leaving his footprints because the earth felt softer underneath his boots. He jumped a stream and slowed to a stop at the edge of a copse. A two-lane road lay before him. On the other side stood the first building of the village.

It was a tiny habitation of maybe two dozen buildings as old as or older than the farmhouse. Victor made his way to the center of the village, following the road that snaked between the buildings. He speculated that in a village this far from modernization, there would be a public telephone, probably near the center; if not, he would break into a nonresidential building to use their phone. But he found a phone box outside what appeared to be the only commercial establishment in the village: a post office.

He dialed the operator and requested a reverse-charge call to the number Muir had given him. Since it was an overseas call, the operator was hesitant, but did as he asked.

After a moment, he heard Muir's voice say, "Janice Muir speaking."

The operator asked her if she would accept the call. Muir didn't understand Italian.

"It's me," Victor interrupted. "Tell the operator *si, accetto*."

Muir did so and the operator left them to the call. She said, "Don't go anywhere. I'll buzz you back. I'm driving."

Victor set the receiver down on the hanger and snapped it back up midway through the first ring eighty-two seconds later.

She said, "Where the hell have you been?"

"I'm currently in a phone booth in a village about fifty kilometers southeast of Rome."

"What the hell is going on?"

"Stop saying hell and I'll tell you."

"Sorry."

He summarized meeting Francesca in Gibraltar, traveling by boat to Italy, meeting Dietrich, Jaeger, and Coughlin, and the shoot-out with the Georgians. Muir listened without responding until Victor had finished. "This is more dangerous than I anticipated. Far more. I promise you I did not expect any of this. The plan was for you to get hired, not to be a prisoner in a farmhouse in the middle of nowhere, part of a team of mercenaries waiting around for a job to begin at what could be any time, with any target. There are so many unknown variables here that we can't even begin to get a handle on them."

"Every time I accept a contract, I also accept that it could very well be my last, but so far this is no more or less dangerous than I expected. Even the simplest job in theory can end up being a fight for survival in practice, and the most complex and difficult assignment is sometimes the safest."

"We don't even know what the job actually is yet. If you want out, I understand. In fact, it's better for you to walk away now while you still can, before this gets any more dangerous. You didn't sign up for this level of risk, and I wouldn't have exposed you to it had I known about it in advance."

"I know a little more about the risks than you do. At least this time the weather is warm and the scenery is nice to look at."

"I'd feel a lot better if you could take this more seriously."

There was a short pause before he asked, "Do you think I'd still be alive if there was any aspect of my chosen profession that I did not take seriously?"

Muir was quiet for a moment.

"Why did you let Leeson know you knew there was a team?"

"Because I wanted to see how close Leeson and Francesca are. The moment I asked about the team, she looked at Leeson. Not in fear. She wasn't scared that she had said anything to tip me off. But she was surprised I knew. A typical reaction would have been to stare at me. Searching for answers. An explanation. She didn't do that. She didn't care how I knew there was a team. She cared what Leeson thought about it. Because I wasn't supposed to know. Because she knows why there is a team. Because she knew even before there was a team."

"That's a lot to guess from a single look."

"It's not a guess. It's fact. She told me, just without speaking. People say more without words than with."

Muir exhaled.

"Exactly," Victor said.

"What are they like, Coughlin, Dietrich, and Jaeger?"

"Operationally, I don't know yet. But I can't see Leeson hiring them unless they were good. Dietrich is wound up pretty tight and doesn't like me."

"With your charming personality?"

He didn't comment. "Coughlin is more relaxed, but he doesn't trust I can do whatever I'm here for."

"What about Jaeger?"

"I haven't formed an opinion yet because I've had less contact with him. When I do I'll know more about why the other two don't trust me. Or at least Kooi."

"That's expected, though, isn't it? You're the new guy, fresh off the bus. Stands to reason they would take a while to trust you. Especially when they've both known each other for a little longer. You're the outsider. The new kid at school."

"It's more than just being the newest member."

"Bottom of the pack, then."

"Again no. There's a hierarchy, of course. Leeson is at the top, naturally. Francesca is next one down, but also a separate entity. She doesn't give orders, but she is closer to Leeson than the others."

"That close?"

"I don't know," Victor said. "Sometimes it seems that way, then not at others. I'm at the bottom of the pile, but the rest of the team are on the same level.

They don't seem to know any more about the job than I do."

"Could be they're just keeping what they know to themselves."

"They are. They haven't got tans just sitting around waiting for me to join them. Jaeger's in the barn, and while I was with Leeson in Rome, Dietrich and Coughlin were in the city too. I don't know why, but it was something to do with the job."

"See if you can get one of them to open up, but don't push it more than you have to," Muir said, then paused a moment. "I've got an idea. Taking Jaeger out of the equation for a second, we know the rest of your team aren't accepting you as an equal. Even though you've proved yourself by saving Leeson's butt. You okay with the word *butt*?" He didn't answer. "Maybe it's as simple as male pride, testosterone, any of that nonsense. They don't like you because you intimidate them; because they're threatened by you. But I know you'll have gone out of your way to be the opposite. And, as you've just explained, none of you know what you're doing there. You all share that lack of knowledge. Despite all that they don't trust you."

"That's what I said."

"I think you're wrong. I don't think it's a matter of trust; otherwise you would have felt that from Jaeger, regardless of how much contact you'd had with him."

"Then what is it?"

"They don't accept you yet. Because they're reserving judgment."

He was quiet for a moment while he considered that.

"If they're reserving judgment, then what are they waiting for?"

"Won't be until you've proved yourself, because you did that a few hours ago in Rome. Can't be until you've successfully completed some aspect of the job, because they don't know anything about it. So it must be until you've been approved."

"I think you might be right, but I already have Leeson's approval, twice: first by putting me into the team and then by having me save his life."

"And Francesca doesn't give out orders. So it's got to be someone else, surely."

"There's another person involved in this I haven't met yet, but everyone else has."

"Then they must value this other man or woman's opinion over Leeson's."

"Yes."

"Then it has to be Leeson's client," Muir said, excitement making her speak fast. "Has to be. I never thought he'd show his face, so this is too good to be true. If they've all met him, you will too. When we have him in the same place as Leeson and the others, we can take them all down in one go. We won't need any physical evidence. They'll be falling over each other to cut a deal against the rest because they'll be terrified someone else will first. I've seen it happen a thousand times."

"It's not the client," Victor said. "It makes zero sense for a client to have a broker like Leeson running the show if he's going to be personally involved. The broker is the first and most important layer of protection the client has. He wouldn't scrap that. Besides, these guys wouldn't care about the opinion of the man who signs their checks. This other person is another member of the team."

"Who do they respect more than Leeson?"

"Soldiers respect the men who fight alongside them more than they do the ones who send them into battle. That's a given. But this is more basic than a matter of respect. It's more primal."

"Then what is it? Why do they care what this other guy thinks?"

"Because they're afraid of him."

Chapter 43

They went through what they knew, searching for anything they might have missed. Around Victor, the village was dark and quiet. Aside from Muir's voice and his own, he heard only the wind.

Muir said, "I'll have the farmhouse checked out, see if it's been passed to any notable hands in the last few years. But I think we're going to find it's been leased for the occasion, probably paid in untraceable cash by an intermediary to a guy whose only crime will be not declaring that income."

"While you're at it, check for couples matching Leeson and Francesca with hotels, guesthouses, et cetera. The village doesn't have any as far as I can tell, but there must be others nearby. Of course, there's no reason why they couldn't be staying in Rome or somewhere even farther away."

"Leeson would want to stay close to his team, though, surely."

"Yes," Victor agreed. "But there's also no reason why he needs to. Unless he wanted to keep an eye on us at all times. Which he doesn't; otherwise he would be sleeping there too. It's a hideout for the team, nothing more."

"What about the barn? There must be a reason why you're not allowed inside it, unlike the rest of them."

"Jaeger was in the barn when I arrived and Leeson had Dietrich put the limousine inside it last night, but I think that's the only time Dietrich goes inside. Coughlin hasn't been inside to my knowledge."

"So what is Jaeger doing in there?"

"I could take a guess, but that's not how I like to do things. When I know more, I'll pass it on."

"Can you get in there?"

"Not easily. But if the opportunity is there, I'm taking it."

"Leave it for now. Maybe when you've been there longer, Leeson will trust you enough to let you inside too. Better that than breaking in and leaving evidence behind. You'll be top of the list of suspects by default."

"I'm not in the habit of leaving evidence behind."

"Even so, I'm asking you not to."

"Noted."

"But you're going to do it anyway, aren't you?"

"Yes. You want to know what Leeson is planning, and now that I'm here, I need to know. Because he wants Kooi for a specific reason, for a specific skill Kooi has or a specific role he can fulfill. I need to know what that is before Leeson gives me my orders. Finding out what's in the barn might help me get the answer we're both after."

"It might also get you killed."

"So might crossing the road."

"Just promise me you'll be careful, okay?"

Victor didn't.

Muir said, "How are we doing for time?"

"I can give you another few minutes. Then I'll have to get back to the farmhouse. If someone knows I'm gone, I can justify my absence as a middle-of-the-night run because I couldn't sleep, but the longer I'm out, the harder a sell that will be."

"Okay. Let's go back to what happened in Rome. So, we don't know what he's done, but Leeson has angered a Georgian mob enough for them to send a six-man crew over to Italy to kill him. This mob is based in Odessa and some of its members are former Russian intelligence. And you killed the whole hit team?"

"Leeson got one."

"No possible way one of the corpses could be alive in a hospital bed?"

"I didn't shoot to wound."

"I'll liaise with the Italians and get hold of the crime scene intel. With a bit of luck Leeson's prints will be recoverable from his tumbler or knife and fork."

"There's a shotgun he used. A good set of prints should be recoverable."

"Great."

"You understand I couldn't leave his gun behind?"

"Hey, I know. That would have been perfect, but we know that one reason Kooi was hired is that he—you—is calm and careful. Leaving his sidearm behind is something only an absolute amateur would have done. Even if Leeson himself didn't consider it, one of your teammates could have done. Your cover is precarious enough as it is without doing anything to make it more so."

He was glad she could see the same angles he could, and what she didn't understand about the business she learned fast. He wouldn't have taken the job had he not felt she could.

She said, "But even if we can get a set of Leeson's prints, it only helps us if he's on someone's files. Which seems unlikely considering how careful he is the rest of the time."

"Perhaps he's so careful because he's on someone's file."

"We've got a good relationship with Italian intelligence. Once the lab geeks have finished with the crime scene, I'm sure I'll get the results quickly. But it's going to take them a while to sift through all the evidence with a crime this spectacular."

"Spectacular?"

"Complex, then."

"How soon can you get here?" Victor asked.

"This time tomorrow."

"Then you need to call your Rome station and get someone to the parking garage."

"Why? The Italians aren't going to let us near it just yet."

"Then he's going to have to be creative because he needs to go to the third floor. There's a beige Alfa Romeo in the northeast corner." He gave Muir the license number. "He needs to jimmy the door and hot-wire it, so he has to be good at field craft. Then he needs to drive it away and take it somewhere quiet. Are you making a note of this?"

"Yes, yes. What is going on here? What's special about this car?"

"There's one of the six Georgians in the trunk."

"Excuse me?"

"He's young and only the team's driver, but he's been traveling and lodging with the others, so I figured he might know something about Leeson, or he'll be able to point to someone who does. But I didn't have time to interrogate him myself, so I did the next best thing."

"What? Wait. You told me all six were dead."

"No, I didn't. You asked if I was responsible for all the deaths and I said Leeson killed one of the Georgians."

"Oh man, so you're telling me you knocked out one of these mobsters and hid him in the trunk of a car smack bang in the middle of a major crime scene?"

"I didn't knock him out. I tied him up and gagged him. I told him I'd let him out again in twelve hours."

"He won't still be there," Muir said, the volume of her voice a good six decibels louder than it had been previously. "One of the cops at the scene will have heard him by now."

"You don't know how well I secured him," Victor said back. "He couldn't have made much of a noise and I muffled his ears so he wouldn't know what was happening around him. Besides, I told him if I heard him so much as clear his throat I'd kill him like I did his five friends, only I would take my time. He believed me."

"I'm sure he did. What about the garage's CCTV?"

"The system was basic. Cameras covered the ramps and ticket machines, but there were a number of blind spots."

"And what if the car's owner has driven it away?"

"The Alfa Romeo is part of a crime scene, as you said. Rome PD will maintain the integrity of the scene for at least twelve hours before letting cars leave. That gives you six hours to make sure your guy is first on scene when they do. And I'm sure the owner of the vehicle could be persuaded to let you borrow it for an hour if an incentive is offered. But it's up to you how you sort it out."

"Why didn't you tell me this earlier?"

"Because I'm telling you now," Victor said. "Time's up. I need to get back."

· Chapter 44 ·

Victor woke at six a.m. An hour's sleep was not enough to recharge him after the escapades of the previous day, but he wanted to be up before his three teammates. Specifically, he didn't want to be asleep while they were awake. He remained in his room until he heard Dietrich's door open opposite, and then the heavy footfalls of Jaeger a while later. Victor waited another ten minutes and then headed downstairs.

It was cool in the kitchen. Light streamed in through the window above the sink. He filled a cast-iron kettle with water and placed it on the stove. In a cupboard, he found a cafetière and a hand grinder and downstairs in the single-room cellar he located a one-kilogram sack of roasted coffee beans, of which he took a handful. They smelled fantastic.

The cellar was at least ten degrees lower in temperature than the kitchen and made a reasonably cool room. He dropped the beans into a pocket of his trousers, slipped a packet of butter into the other, tucked a loaf of bread under his left arm, and in his left hand picked up a tray of large brown hen's eggs.

Coughlin was sitting at the table when Victor reentered the kitchen. He had left the cellar door open, but still hadn't heard the Brit. Coughlin was not as physically dangerous as Dietrich or Jaeger, and though young he was measured and reputedly good with a rifle and quiet. Victor made a mental note to kill him at close range, when the time came.

"Making coffee?"

Victor nodded. "How do you take it?"

"As nature intended. Looks like you're going to make breakfast too."

There was a hint of hopefulness in his voice. Victor nodded again.

"Scrambled egg on toast, then, mate," Coughlin said, then added, "Cheers."

Victor ground the coffee beans. He stood to the left of the sink so he could see Coughlin's reflection in the window while he had his back to him. Coughlin picked at his nails and tossed the fragments to the floor. He didn't look up at Victor once.

While he waited for the kettle to boil, he cracked eggs into a glass bowl and whisked them with butter and a little water because there had been no milk in the basement, before adding black pepper and salt. He cooked the mixture in a copper skillet while he sliced bread and toasted it.

The kettle took a long time to boil because Victor had filled it with twice as much water as he needed. It started hissing as he placed the scrambled eggs on toast on the table before Coughlin, who wasted no time hacking off a chunk.

"It's good," he said, chewing.

Victor prepared the coffee and left it to brew for five minutes while he made some breakfast for himself. He poured them both a cup and sat down perpendicular to Coughlin, at one end of the table, his back to the stove and facing the door that led outside.

"Ah, that's the shit," Coughlin said after his first slurp. "Much better than that horrible sludge Dietrich makes."

"Where is he?" Victor asked.

"Probably running."

"Jaeger?"

Coughlin shrugged and shook his head. "He's always in the barn."

"What's he doing in there?"

"How would I know?" He gulped down some more coffee. "You should ask Dietrich to make you a cup just so you can see how bad it is." He smirked. "Idiot could get a glass of water wrong."

Victor turned up the corners of his mouth in response. "I take it he's better at his job than he is in the kitchen."

"You can say that again."

"Top-up?" Victor said, gesturing to the cafetière.

Coughlin shoveled the last of the breakfast into his mouth and nodded. "Thanks."

"You've been here for a while, right?"

Coughlin nodded. "Yeah."

"What have you been doing?"

He looked at Victor. "We're not supposed to discuss the job."

"We're just talking here. I don't know anything about what we're doing here."

"Neither do I."

"So what harm is there in telling me how you've been spending your time?"

Coughlin shrugged. He slurped some coffee. "Me and Dietrich stole an ambulance."

"What for?"

Coughlin shrugged again. "Your guess is as good as mine."

"Where is it now?"

Before he could answer, Jaeger entered and washed his hands at the sink, working up a lather with a block of carbolic soap and rubbing his palms together for several seconds. He washed each of his fingers in turn, then the back of his hand, and then did it all over again. Coughlin paid the long and careful routine no attention because he had seen Jaeger often enough for it to be a normal part of the day. After drying his hands on a towel, Jaeger said, "Who cooked breakfast?"

Coughlin pointed. "Kooi did."

"Was it good?"

Coughlin nodded. "Best I've had here."

"Coffee?"

"Kooi too."

"Would you like some?" Victor asked.

"I don't drink it. But you can cook me some food if you want to."

"Not particularly."

"That's pretty selfish."

"It's pretty lazy not to make your own. Takes all of five minutes."

"I don't want any. I've already eaten. I just wanted to see if you would make me some."

"Why?"

Jaeger shrugged his big shoulders. "Just because."

He left the kitchen. Stairs groaned a moment later.

"Dangerous combination," Coughlin said.

"What is?"

"Being that big and that strange. Can't be a good mix. Like cooking with napalm."

Victor nodded. "Was he here before you?"

"Yeah, but I've traded more words with you than I have with him. Did you see the way he washes his hands?"

Victor nodded again.

"And?" Coughlin asked, pointedly.

"Maybe he's got an obsessive-compulsive tic."

"Or?" Coughlin asked, even more pointedly.

"Or he really wanted to be sure there were no traces left behind of whatever it was that had got on his hands."

"Exactly."

They held eye contact for a moment, but Coughlin didn't say anything further and Victor didn't either because Dietrich pushed open the exterior door. He wore khaki shorts and an undershirt dark from sweat. His face and shaven head glistened and his mouth was open. As before, he had his combat knife sheathed on his belt.

He turned on the cold tap and leaned over the sink to drink straight from the flow for almost a minute. Then he wiped his mouth with the back of a hand and said, "What are you ladies talking about?"

Victor said nothing, but Coughlin elected to answer: "Your lack of culinary expertise compared with Kooi here."

Coughlin picked some crumbs up from his plate and ate them for emphasis.

Dietrich looked at Victor. "I leave a woman's work to a woman."

He didn't respond. He heard the rumble of an approaching engine and then the crunch of gravel beneath tires. Both other men looked toward the kitchen window and to the driveway outside. It wasn't just expectation, but trepidation too. Not because they were expecting Leeson or Francesca and the arrival of the two made them nervous. They looked through the window because they thought someone else might appear.

The other guy.

The team member Victor hadn't met yet. The one they already knew. The one they respected. The one they were afraid of.

But Victor knew it wasn't going to be the new guy even before the Toyota minivan came into view, because he knew the tone of that vehicle's engine. So either the other guy drove a comparable vehicle or Dietrich and Coughlin didn't pay the same level of attention Victor did. But few people he encountered did, else he would have died long before now, and his chances of surviving the impersonation of Kooi would be negligible.

Francesca walked through the doorway. She wore a flowing white halter-neck dress, patterned with undulating chrysanthemums, that stopped well above the knee. Dietrich and Coughlin didn't attempt to hide their stares. She smiled briefly at Victor.

Leeson followed after a moment. He wore a different linen suit. Something was different about him too. He still displayed the veneer of confidence that had cracked apart last night in Rome, but his eyes were different. Victor wasn't sure why: whether the weight of killing a man pressed down on his soul—which Victor doubted—or whether Leeson knew something today he hadn't known yesterday.

Victor stood, because he had a dangerous killer to each of his flanks and a wall behind him, while a table blocked his route out of the building. He watched Leeson, ready for the first word or change in expression that would indicate his cover was blown.

· Chapter 45 ·

He would prefer to deal with Dietrich first—the biggest threat—but he was out of immediate attacking range, so Coughlin would get the knife resting next to Victor's plate. It was a blunt, unserrated butter knife, no good at cutting, but driven down with strength and skill would impale the hand Coughlin had helpfully left resting on the kitchen table. That one-second attack would take Coughlin out of the fight just long enough for Victor to deal with the others.

The problem then was that Victor would have used up his closest and most effective improvised weapon to immobilize Coughlin. A fork in the back of the hand wouldn't penetrate to anywhere near the same degree, but he wanted the knife in his hand when he went for Dietrich.

If Victor went for Dietrich first, he would lose precious time covering the distance and present his back to Coughlin while he dealt with Dietrich. Even though Victor didn't consider Coughlin a threat in a one-on-one confrontation, he didn't like the idea of losing sight of him during the attack. He had to immobilize Coughlin fast and first with the knife, which meant he needed another weapon for Dietrich.

The kettle. It was still on the stove. He'd filled it with more water than he'd needed for the cafetière so he would have a short-range missile within reach should he need one. He couldn't miss with a quick throw, and Victor only needed to slow Dietrich down enough to stop him from drawing the knife from his belt sheath before Victor got to it first and used it to expose Dietrich's intestinal tract to the elements.

Which left Francesca and Leeson.

She wasn't an enemy or a threat, but if she got in his way she would slow him down a second or two. And if Leeson knew Victor wasn't Kooi, he would be alert and ready. In the one second it would take to deal with Coughlin, added to the two seconds for Dietrich, combined with the second or two to get past Francesca, Leeson would have gained four to five seconds in total to react to the attack, draw his gun, release the safety, aim, and—

Victor would take a .22-caliber bullet in his center mass.

At this range Leeson wouldn't miss. And even if he didn't score a one-shot drop, Victor wouldn't then be able to reach him in time to stop him firing a second, a third, and a fourth.

He knew his only hope was that Leeson would panic and react too slowly in his shock and surprise. But Leeson wasn't the same man he had been twenty-four hours ago. By having him guard the corridor and kill the Georgian who had tried to flank them, Victor had given Leeson his first experience of facing violent death and triumphing. Leeson would be less terrified in a similar situation now that he knew he could survive one, and less fear meant less shock and less shock meant a faster reaction.

He had given Leeson exactly what he needed in order to kill him now.

Victor watched the younger man. He watched because he was waiting for that first sign. He watched because he would still attack even though it was futile, because while fighting there was always a chance and because even if that chance never materialized, Victor would die fighting as he'd always known he would.

He watched Leeson. Waiting for the first word. The first expression.

"Good to see you boys are getting along," Leeson said.

"We're best buds," Coughlin said.

He slid his hand from the table, robbing Victor of his opening attack, but shifted in his seat to face Leeson. Victor pictured grabbing the fork first, not the knife, and stabbing it into the side of Coughlin's now-exposed neck, puncturing the carotid, leaving the knife free to drive into Dietrich's left eye, saving a second. He would then get to Leeson a second quicker, before he could get his little SIG aimed, enabling Victor to rip it from his hand and use it on Dietrich and then Coughlin if the initial attacks had not been fatal.

Victor watched Leeson. Because now he had an achievable plan.

"Put your tongue back in your mouth," Francesca said to Dietrich, who hadn't yet pulled his gaze from her.

He rested his elbows on the edge of the countertop and said, "Dress like that and men are going to look. Don't want to be looked at, then don't dress like that. It's pretty simple."

"There's a difference between looking and being a pig."

Dietrich smirked and snorted.

"How did you find your room last night, Mr. Kooi?" Leeson asked. "I appreciate it's not exactly five stars here, but I do hope you slept okay on the bed."

"The room and the bed did their job."

"Excellent. Might I have a word in private, Mr. Coughlin?" Leeson asked.

"Sure."

Coughlin pushed back his chair and stood. Any chance of Victor killing him quickly vanished, but Leeson hadn't yet shown any reason to make Victor think his ruse had been discovered. Unless Leeson was going to tell Coughlin when they were out of earshot. The two men stepped from the kitchen and into the lounge. Victor heard the wooden staircase creak as they ascended.

Francesca poured herself a coffee, sipped it, and raised her eyebrows in disapproval. She said to Dietrich, "Something else you're not good at, I see."

"Nice try, sweetheart, but His Majesty over there made it."

She wrinkled her nose at Victor. "I'd have expected much better from a man of taste like you."

She smiled, a thought amusing her, and a mischievous edge changed that smile. Victor knew things were about to get more complicated. She turned the smile toward Dietrich as she stalked over to Victor.

Her hand found his shoulder. "That said," she said to Dietrich as her slim fingers slid down to Victor's chest, then his stomach, "he can get away with it when he has so much more to offer."

Victor couldn't see her face because his gaze was locked on Dietrich, but he knew she winked because Dietrich's perpetual scowling expression deepened.

"Word of advice," Dietrich said. "You're too old to still be playing the whore."

Victor straightened.

"What?" Dietrich spat and edged away from the countertop. "Did I offend your delicate sensibilities?"

Francesca said, "Not as much as you offend your reflection every time you look in the mirror," and laughed.

"You're too old to still be such a whore," Dietrich said again, stepping forward, "but I'll still slap you like one if you're not careful."

Victor stepped forward too.

Dietrich eyeballed him. "You really think you could stop me?"

"Not think," Victor said back.

"I'm not sure why you have such an attitude, but I'm getting a little tired of it."

"I'm surprised it's taken this long."

"You know what, Your Majesty, I'm thinking this bravado is nothing more than a smokescreen." He was close enough for Victor to smell the body odor. Not quite attacking range, but close to it. "All this tough-guy talk is just that: talk. It's all bullshit. Nothing but a bluff, and I'm calling you on it. You're trying to hide it, but inside you're terrified."

Victor slowly raised and held out his left arm, palm facing up. "Would you like to check my pulse?"

Dietrich glanced at the wrist, then back up, and stared into Victor's eyes.

"Da dum," Victor said, low and slow, then paused for a couple of seconds. *"Da dum."*

Dietrich smiled, as if he was about to laugh, as though it was all a joke.

But Victor said to Francesca, "Leave the room," because Dietrich's right hand moved toward his waist.

She was out of Victor's line of sight because she was behind him, but he knew she didn't move because there were no footsteps and he could still hear her breathing.

"Let her stay and watch the performance," Dietrich said as his fingers touched the grip of the knife sheathed to his belt. "I'll show her what a real man can do."

He withdrew his knife from its sheath.

"Okay," Francesca said from behind Victor. "This has gone too far. You're both real men. Each as much as the other. Put the knife away. Remember what Robert said."

Dietrich shrugged. "I think I'm about to take some time off, so at this moment he isn't my boss."

"Leave the room," Victor said again to Francesca, risking a glance over his shoulder for emphasis. "Now."

He didn't have to take his gaze off Dietrich to slide

the butter knife from the table where he knew it sat. He held it so the blade protruded from the bottom of his fist. Fewer options for attack that way, only downward stabs— but the knife was too blunt to be otherwise employed effectively.

Dietrich looked at it without fear and sneered.

"Robert," Francesca called. *"Get in here. Get in here fast."*

"Won't do no good. I'm on a personal day, remember?" Dietrich raised his weapon to sternum level, blade close to his torso, his free left hand out. He smiled at Victor and said in a quiet voice, "Are you ready?"

Victor nodded.

Dietrich attacked.

· Chapter 46 ·

He was fast. But Victor had expected him to be. Dietrich sprang forward into range to slice at Victor's face, his left hand out to control distance and ward off counterattacks. Victor blocked, striking Dietrich's right forearm at ninety degrees with his left, forcing the blade away and stepping forward to stab with his own, aiming for Dietrich's neck but settling for tearing his T-shirt when Dietrich whipped back out of range, bouncing on the balls of his feet, not committing to the attack, testing Victor's speed.

Dietrich shuffled forward, shooting out his arm for a quick backhand slash at Victor's throat, but it was too fast and Victor knew it was a feint to bring up his guard. He was ready when Dietrich followed up with a stab under his left elbow, aiming for his stomach, blocking it by slamming that elbow down onto Dietrich's fist and sidestepping so the blade missed and Dietrich was off balance when Victor countered with a half slash, half stab that caught him on the shoulder and drew blood.

It wasn't deep and didn't slow Dietrich's assault.

"*Robert,*" Francesca yelled.

Although a large space, the kitchen offered little room to maneuver because of the table, but there was enough to move in and out of range while they fought in the same back-and-forth rhythm. If Dietrich fully committed to the attacks and pressed forward, accepting any superficial wounds he sustained in the process, he could easily force Victor back far enough that he would run out of room. Then, without the ability to dodge and create space between them, Victor wouldn't be able to parry Dietrich's fast attacks for long before the blade started finding its mark. But Dietrich was fighting like the experienced knife fighter he was—in and out—relying on his reflexes and speed and skill. He had a total disregard of strategy and tactics because he hated Victor, as Victor had wanted him to.

Coughlin arrived first. "What the hell is going on here?"

Victor didn't answer because it was obvious. Dietrich didn't answer because he was too busy attacking and he couldn't talk and fight at the same time. Victor parried a thrust, blade to blade. Dietrich ducked and dodged back, away from Victor's counter, slashing at Victor's leg as he did so. Victor felt the burn of a hit above his left kneecap. He glanced down. A small cut to his trousers and a small amount of blood.

"Stop this," Leeson said as he followed Coughlin, but he stopped in the doorway, not daring to get any closer. He didn't shout, but he spoke loudly and with authority. "Stop this immediately. That's an order."

Victor hesitated to see what Dietrich would do now that his boss had told him to halt. But his opponent attacked again anyway, trying to capitalize on Victor's passivity—a high slash followed by a low one, aiming for Victor's face and then the inside of his thigh. Victor darted out of range.

Leeson didn't repeat himself because he had to know neither man was going to obey mere words.

"Mr. Coughlin, would you please—"

Coughlin cut him off. "I'm not getting between those two."

"For God's sake, Robert, do something," Francesca barked. "You have a gun, don't you?"

Dietrich launched another attack, even faster and more frenzied than before, because he knew that once Leeson brought a firearm into the equation everything would change. Either he would be forced to cease his attempts to kill Victor, or he might have to fight a bullet instead.

Victor backed off, keeping out of the blade's path, defending only because the fight was about to be over—however it ended—and he wanted to appear to have acted purely in self-defense. He let himself be trapped in a corner with countertops converging behind him to encourage Dietrich to lunge in—which he did—and ducked below the knife before sweeping Dietrich's load-bearing leg out from under him.

Dietrich landed on his back and immediately rolled backward over his head and onto his feet. He charged forward, rage dictating tactics, and Victor caught the attacking wrist and dropped his own blade so he could lock the arm. But Dietrich was too fast and strong to allow Victor to break it at the elbow.

They hit the floor together.

Victor went down first, Dietrich on top of him. Victor immediately wrapped his legs around Dietrich's neck, keeping hold of the knife wrist. Dietrich roared and stood, lifting Victor off the floor and slamming him back down, shoulder blades colliding with the floorboards. The breath was knocked from Victor's lungs, but he kept hold of the wrist.

Dietrich used his free hand to punch at Victor, but though they were hard blows, he couldn't get his weight behind them. Victor maintained hold of Dietrich's arm to keep the knife immobile.

Leeson had the small SIG in hand and aimed at the two men fighting on the floor. "Mr. Coughlin, take the knife out of Mr. Dietrich's hand. Mr. Dietrich, you will let him or you will get shot. Mr. Kooi, if you don't then release Mr. Dietrich, you will get shot. Does everyone understand?" He didn't wait for anyone to supply an answer. "Now, if you please, Mr. Coughlin."

Coughlin hesitantly moved closer.

Clap. Clap. Clap.

"A stirring performance," a voice said from the open exterior doorway. "But lacking a certain finesse."

Dietrich stopped punching and struggling. The aggression slipped from his face. On the floor, Victor couldn't see the speaker, but in his peripheral vision he saw Coughlin hesitate and Francesca stiffen. But Leeson smiled.

"Ah," he said. "You rejoin us at last, Mr. Hart."

· Chapter 47 ·

Victor released Dietrich's wrist and scrambled away. The fight had vanished from Dietrich. He seemed to have forgotten Victor even existed, let alone that he had been trying to kill him five seconds before. Dietrich wasn't looking at him. He was exposed. Vulnerable. But Victor didn't take the opportunity to disarm his opponent and drive the knife deep into his neck, even though he had been taught never to fail to exploit a weakness, never to give away an advantage. Such single-minded ruthlessness had seen him triumph against the odds several times, but he held himself back now. He didn't attack because there was something in the new arrival's voice that stopped him. Something intriguing.

He stood and faced the new guy, taking his gaze off Dietrich because he was no longer a threat.

A man stood outside the open kitchen door. He looked to be somewhere in his mid- to late forties. His eyes were small and deep set, pale blue bordering on gray.

His skin was weathered brown and red—naturally pale skin exposed to a lot of sun. Deep crow's-feet etched the corners of his eyes. His hair was short, a mix of blond and gray, as was the short beard that covered his cheeks and surrounded thin lips. His expression was one of contemptuous amusement.

His neck was a trunk of muscle as wide as his skull. The bones of his face were dense and prominent beneath the weathered skin. He was about Victor's height and a little broader. He looked like the few big guys Victor had known in the military: men with natural size and strength, made denser and stronger over many years of hard physical existence, not artificially gained via ritualized weightlifting that built slow-twitch muscle fiber only good at lifting and pushing and too slow and too hungry for oxygen to be of much use when life depended on it.

The man called Hart gestured to Coughlin. "Step back from the two lovers." He looked at Dietrich. "Safety that shiv."

The urgency left Coughlin's body language and he backed off. Dietrich obeyed without pause or question. He went to slip the knife back into its belt sheath.

"No," Hart said. "Give the weapon to me. You can't be trusted with it."

This time Dietrich hesitated a moment. Victor couldn't predict what he would do next, but he nodded and walked over to Hart, and gave him the knife. He was only a couple of inches shorter and probably weighed about the same, but he seemed tiny and insignificant next to Hart, because he acted as he felt.

Hart motioned and Dietrich moved aside. Hart

stepped into the kitchen and Francesca hurried over to him. She threw her arms around his neck and he effortlessly lifted her by the waist from the floor. They kissed, long and hard.

Victor watched for a moment, questions in his mind now answering themselves one by one, only to be replaced by others.

When Hart and Francesca finally stopped kissing, he lowered her down and whispered something to her. Then his gaze locked on Victor. Francesca didn't make eye contact.

"What's your name, compadre?" Hart asked Victor.

"Kooi."

"The man we've all been waiting for."

"I thought it was the other way around."

Hart ignored the comment. "Good to finally put a face to the name." He walked toward Victor. "I've heard a lot about you."

Victor said, "Funny, I've heard nothing about you."

A corner of Hart's mouth turned upward. He stopped and stared into Victor's eyes. "I see you're already integrating yourself into the team."

Victor glanced at Dietrich. "We're one big happy family."

Leeson said to Hart, "We've got a lot to discuss. Join me outside?"

"You're the boss."

They left out of the front door.

"I'm going to clean up," Dietrich said to no one in particular and headed for the interior door. As he passed Victor, he added, "One all," referencing the wound to his shoulder and the one to Victor's leg. "We'll settle the scores another time."

"You mean when your daddy isn't around?"

Dietrich's jaw muscles bunched and he knocked his uninjured shoulder with Victor as he passed.

"Never a dull moment," Coughlin said, then laughed. "I had my money on you, by the way." He exited through the front door, leaving Victor alone with Francesca.

She didn't look at Victor when she said, "I was going to—"

"It doesn't matter," Victor interrupted.

"Your leg—"

"Is fine."

He ignored her and looked through the kitchen window, to where Hart and Leeson stood talking in the driveway. Behind them stood the vehicle Hart had arrived in. Victor hadn't heard it during his fight with Dietrich because his senses had been focused on keeping him alive. Hart led Leeson to the back of the white panel van and unlocked and opened the back doors. He pointed into the interior that Victor couldn't see. Leeson smiled and patted Hart on the back.

Excellent job, Mr. Hart, Victor read on Leeson's lips. Then Leeson turned away and Victor couldn't follow the conversation. Behind Victor, Francesca cleaned up the mess caused by the fight with Dietrich.

Victor thought about the effect of Hart's arrival on the group's dynamic. Leeson was the employer, but Hart was the alpha. Dietrich and Coughlin were afraid of him for good reason. It wasn't just his physicality. He had the kind of gaze that could make anyone back down. The kind of gaze that was supremely confident because he had been born without fear, and long experience had affirmed the innate knowledge that nothing the world could offer necessitated his concern. Certainly no man. Dietrich and Coughlin had the sense to register that aura of invincibility and the experience to know it was best to concede to it.

Victor had seen that kind of gaze before. Sometimes in those who were borderline insane, or way over that line. Other times in those who had no right to it and whose faith in their own invincibility dematerialized when truly tested. Yet others, though, had every right to that confidence because they were still breathing despite a life of acute violence. Victor didn't know which applied to Hart. Until he did, Hart was a problem.

Through the window he watched Hart close the rear doors of the white panel van, slide the locking bolt across, and then fix a padlock. The van looked at least eight years old. Grime darkened the paintwork to an uneven gray. The wheels were filthy. It was the kind of van removal men used, and couriers and tradesmen of all descriptions. Dents marked the bodywork. It looked like a well-used vehicle that wasn't looked after beyond the absolute essentials. It would blend into traffic, its driver mistaken for a regular workingman, one of any number of trades that did not include professional killing.

The rear compartment might contain almost anything, but clearly it was something Leeson needed to put the job into action. And only Hart had been trustworthy or capable enough to transport it. Or whatever was in there belonged to Hart. Victor memorized the license plate to pass on to Muir. It would most likely do no good, because if Hart had been chosen for this important task he would be competent enough not to make any of the amateurish errors necessary for Muir to discover anything useful from the license alone.

Francesca had taken a seat at the table. She toyed with her coffee cup. She didn't look at Victor.

"How long have you known Hart?"

She still didn't make eye contact. "Long enough."

Victor slipped the butter knife into a pocket. It had been a poor weapon to use against Dietrich, but any weapon was better than none. The kitchen door opened and Hart walked in, ducking his head under the low frame.

"What's the job?" Victor asked Leeson once the younger man had closed the door behind him.

Leeson didn't answer. He poured himself a glass of water. Hart stood near the door, blocking the only way out, should it come to it.

"Tell me what the job is," Victor said. "Right now. Or I walk."

Leeson faced him. "I'll tell you this evening, Mr. Kooi. Now that Mr. Hart is back with us, there is no need to keep you in the dark any longer."

"Except until tonight."

"Except until then," Leeson agreed. "We shall all eat together here and after dinner is concluded I will explain the job and what your role is to be within its remit. Okay?"

Victor nodded.

Hart said to Francesca, "Time to go."

She stood and made sure to glance at Victor as she left the kitchen. This time Victor didn't look back.

"I'll see you again tonight, Dutch," Hart said, then left too.

Leeson followed and Victor watched the three through the window. The driver's door slammed behind Hart, and Victor felt the faint hit of bass wash through him. Hart drove the van with Francesca in the cab next to him. Leeson drove behind in the minivan. Victor's gaze stayed on the rear of the white panel van, and whatever valuable contents its back compartment held, until it had disappeared from view.

Victor heard Jaeger's heavy footsteps behind him. Victor faced him.

"That guy is bad news," Jaeger said.

"Tell me about it."

Jaeger stroked his stubble and said, "I'm going to kill him."

· Chapter 48 ·

Victor looked at Jaeger for a moment. He stood on the opposite side of the table. He wore the same loose khakis and T-shirt he'd worn when Victor had first met him, or identical garments. The shirt was tight around his massive shoulders, arms, and chest. His body fat percentage was almost as low as Victor's. He was hugely strong but quick and fit, and like all the men Leeson had hired, he was experienced and dangerous. Victor would happily face Dietrich armed with a knife again rather than Jaeger armed with just his bare hands. But Jaeger looked at that moment like an amateur who was in over his head in something he should have stayed well clear of. And now there was no way out.

"Why?" Victor asked.

"Isn't it obvious?"

Victor shook his head.

Jaeger didn't blink. "You've seen him, right? You've spoken to him?"

Victor nodded.

"Then you must know what I'm talking about. He's all wrong. I know you can see it too. Everything about him stinks of trouble. What's he doing here? Why did he go away and come back? Why is he all buddy-buddy with Leeson?"

"I don't know," Victor said. "You know more about him than I do. This is the first time I've talked to him."

"And what's your point? I only had to meet the guy for five seconds to know he was playing from an entirely different rule book."

Victor kept his voice even. "I don't understand what you're talking about."

"Then you're an idiot," Jaeger said, his voice edging on a growl. "I thought you were switched on. Don't tell me you're another bonehead like Dietrich and Coughlin."

"I'm switched on enough to know telling me that you're going to kill one of the team is a bad idea for all sorts of reasons. So you'd better start talking."

"That's more like it." Jaeger smiled. "That's what I was waiting for."

"I'm listening."

"How long have you been doing this kind of work?"

"Years," Victor said.

"How many jobs have you done?"

"Countless."

"How many times have you been expendable?"

"Most of them."

Jaeger nodded and rested his knuckles on the table. "So tell me, why would this job be any different?"

"You're saying Hart is the cleanup guy."

Jaeger nodded again. "Why else is he here? He looks at me like I'm nothing. I didn't have to be in the room to know he looked at you in the exact same way and I know you noticed. Coughlin pretends he doesn't see it. Dietrich gets no better, but Dietrich is a dick. He expects people to look at him like he's a piece of shit because that's how he looks at everyone else. But Hart is not wound up tight enough to snap at any point like Dietrich. Hart is like a block of ice. He knows a lot more than us. I can tell. And what he knows is the reason why we're nothing to him. Because we will be nothing. When we've done what Leeson wants doing, Hart is going to make sure there's no comeback."

"There's four of us," Victor said. "And one of him."

"Do you really think he's going to try anything when we're together? He'll get us one by one. When we're vulnerable."

"You're a lot bigger than he is."

Jaeger laughed. "Somehow I don't think he's going to try wrestling me. If you had to kill me, would you come at me head-on?"

"No."

"How would you do it?"

"I'd prefer to keep that to myself."

"If you wouldn't come at me head-on, why would Hart? He's already got it all figured out. Three seconds after I first met him, he'd worked out how he was going to kill me. Same with you."

"Why are you telling me this?"

"So you can help me kill him, of course. I'm not here

chatting for the sake of it. What do you think this is? It's recruitment time, friend."

"Why would I want to help you?"

"You want to stay alive, don't you?"

"I'm a lot harder to kill than I look."

Jaeger smirked. "Is that because you face threats like Hart all on your lonesome? Maybe, but why would you if you don't have to? And do you choose to fight on your enemy's terms? No chance. It's on your terms or not at all. You hide it well, but you're a lot smarter than you want people to see. But I see it. You're always watching. You never relax. You're always working out what your next move is going to be well before you need to make it. That's good. I like that. I know it means you're not the kind of man who blindly rolls the dice. You stack the odds in your favor first. So I know you'd rather it was two against one."

"We could just walk away. No one is here to stop us."

"No, we can't. My real name is Jaeger, just like you're really Kooi. Leeson knows who we are. He knows everything about us. We run, and Hart will hunt us down one by one. Besides," Jaeger added, "if you help me on this, then I can help you take care of Dietrich too."

"Why would I want to do that?"

Jaeger laughed. "Because you hate the prick. I don't blame you."

"I don't hate anyone."

"Then for self-preservation. Get him before he gets you. He's no Hart, but do you really want to be looking over your shoulder for him all the time when you need to be watching out for Hart?" He shook his head. "Of course you don't. And don't tell me you think that little scuffle was the end of it for you and Dietrich. That's just the beginning. He's going to come for you. Knowing Dietrich, sooner rather than later."

"How can you be so sure about that?"

"Because he told me. People have always confided in me. I look like a trustworthy guy, don't I? Plus, he wants me to help him."

"And will you?"

The wide shoulders shrugged. "That depends, doesn't it?"

"On whether I help you kill Hart?"

Jaeger rapped the knuckles of his right hand on the tabletop. "Told you I knew you were switched on."

"Why haven't you asked Dietrich to help you instead? You've only known me a day."

"Because Dietrich is a dick. I wouldn't trust him to tie his shoelaces, so I'm sure as shit not going to trust him backing me up against Hart."

"Coughlin, then?"

"Are you joking? I tell him I want Hart dead, first thing he's going to do is go straight to Hart to rat me out."

"How do you know I won't?"

"Several reasons."

"Which are?"

"You're the new guy, and after Hart, I've been here longest. Your word won't mean shit compared to mine."

"That's not enough of a reason."

"It's a secondary consideration. The reason I know you won't go to Hart is that you want Hart out of the

way, just like I do. Only you'd want Hart gone even if I
hadn't told you he was bad news."

"Why?"

"Because you want his woman."

"If you want my help so badly, you'll be happy to tell
me what you're working on in the barn."

"Oh, you'd just love to know that, wouldn't you? But
no deal. I'll show you when this is over. You wouldn't
believe me otherwise."

"How do I know this isn't a setup?"

Jaeger laughed. "What if it is? This whole job is a
setup. Haven't you worked that out yet?"

"How do you plan to do it?"

"Leeson's going to fill us in on the job tonight, right?
After dinner, he told me. We'll all be there, sitting around
this here table. What I want you to do is piss off Dietrich.
I'll leave you to decide how best to do that. Shouldn't be
hard given your relationship. Dietrich won't need much
of a push for things to get lively. Which will be the distraction I'll use to get that little pistol from Leeson and
turn it on Hart. I don't care how tough he is. He's not
tough enough to survive half a dozen bullets in the cra-
nium."

"But he tells Dietrich to stop, he'll stop."

"Dietrich's scared of Hart, sure. But he hates you and
he's dumb enough to take whatever bait you toss him. By
the time Hart tells him to back down, it will be too late.
I only need Dietrich to be Dietrich for a few seconds."

"Then what happens?"

"I'm not taking any chances with Hart. I'll unload
Leeson's pop gun into him. Then we can take care of

Dietrich together. Won't be difficult between the two of us. And Coughlin isn't anything without a gun, which he won't have. Which just leaves Leeson and Francesca. Obviously, we don't touch her. Unless you're into that kind of thing. It'd be fun. We could—"

"And Leeson?"

"Sweat the money out of him. He's got some hard currency somewhere nearby. Without Hart to protect him he'll be soaking his trousers. He'll give us anything we want to save his skin. The details of his numbered accounts. His list of clients. Whatever."

"And then?"

"Then we kill him too. Slowly. Bastard was going to have his pet clean us once we'd done his little job. I want him to know the error of his ways before he dies."

"Then?"

"We burn this place to the ground with them inside it. And we go our separate ways."

"How can I trust you?"

"How can I trust you back? I can't trust you and you can't trust me because neither of us is stupid enough to not know how this business works. But what's the point of going through all that to save our skins just to die trying to kill each other at the end of it? I want to put this shit behind me. I want to live."

"Good point."

"Told you I think of everything. So, Mr. Kooi of Holland, are you in?"

"I'm thinking about it."

"Time is of the essence here, in case you've forgotten. So you'd better stop thinking and get on with acting."

"That's the exact opposite of how I normally operate."

"Do you normally sign up for a job without knowing the target, and get put into a team you didn't know existed?"

Victor didn't answer.

"And do the people you normally work for plan for your death before you've even actually done anything to compromise them?"

"It's more common than you would think."

"If you say so. But tell me, did you get out of those holes by sitting back and letting the bastards trap you in a corner?"

Victor shook his head. "I've always found the best form of defense is to attack."

"Exactly," Jaeger breathed. "So are we going to let that bastard Leeson and his rottweiler stub us from existence the second we're no longer any use to them?"

"As you rightly said, that's not how I do business."

"So you're in?"

"I'm in."

· Chapter 49 ·

Mr. Hart. That was the blond man's name. Lucille had heard the young man in the suit call him that when he praised the blond man's good work. She was scared. More scared than she had been during the long journey in the dark. Hart had kidnapped her and Peter for the man in the suit. But why? What did he want?

"Who was that?" Peter asked. He sat next to Lucille on the mattress while the van rocked and swayed. He spoke loudly to be heard above the rumble of the engine and exhaust.

"I don't know, honey."

"I want to go back in the cab."

"Maybe later."

"I'm bored in here."

She put her arm around him and pulled him close. "Me too."

"I'm hungry."

She fumbled in the darkness until she found the bag

Hart had given her what seemed like an eternity ago. She had given up trying to keep track of the passing time. When she slept and woke, she didn't know how long she had been asleep. She felt continuously exhausted.

"Here you go," Lucille said, finding Peter's hand and placing a bar of chocolate in it.

"Ugh," he grunted. "I want some proper food."

"I'm sorry, honey. I don't have any. We'll eat some soon, I promise."

The van rocked and swayed and Lucille reminded herself to be strong for Peter's sake. He was in denial, of course. Despite his age, he must know they were in some kind of trouble, that something bad was happening, but he buried it down deep inside him and pretended it wasn't real. Lucille wished she could do the same, and maybe if she tried, she could convince herself that they were going to get out of this okay and she could find a brief moment free of terror and panic. But she needed that fear. She needed to be afraid each and every second because she had to be ready to try—to fight. For Peter.

• • •

It seemed about an hour before the van stopped again, but the engine stayed running. The padding on the walls, floor, and ceiling muffled exterior sounds, but Lucille felt as if their captor had left the vehicle for a moment and then climbed back inside. Twenty seconds later the van stopped once more and the vibrations from the engine ceased. The rear doors opened again and the man with blond hair and the wolf's eyes, the man called Hart, stood before her.

"We're here," he said.

"You're letting us go?"

"Not yet."

"But you're going to?"

He said, "Of course," but his eyes said otherwise.

She looked past him. They were outside some kind of industrial complex. She saw large buildings, crates, equipment, tanks, containers, and a forklift truck. It seemed deserted. She recognized the Italian script on a safety sign.

"We're in Italy," she said out loud.

Hart nodded.

"Why?"

"Why not?"

"Let us go. Please."

He held out his hand. "Come with me."

"I don't want to."

"Of course you don't, but you will."

His expression didn't change. He waited with his hand outstretched for her to accept. She knew she couldn't refuse him. She bit her bottom lip to stop it trembling and touched his hand with hers. He gripped it and helped her out of the van. He turned away from her to beckon Peter and she fantasized about striking the back of Hart's skull with a length of iron pipe and grabbing Peter and running. But there was no length of pipe for her to use, and if there had been, she had no strength to swing it.

Hart lifted Peter up and placed him down on the ground next to Lucille, then ruffled his hair. Peter didn't smile.

"This way," Hart said.

He gestured for her to walk to the smaller of the two buildings. The larger one was a modern factory unit, whereas the building she walked toward looked at least a century old. It had whitewashed walls and a sloping roof of red tiles. A set of arched double doors made of dark-stained wood formed the main entrance, and Lucille approached them, heart thumping, imagining what might be on the other side of them.

But Hart said, "Not through those," and led them to one end of the building. "In there."

She inhaled sharply. "No, please . . ."

"Save your tears, Lucille." Hart wiped one from her cheek and sucked it from his thumb. "You'll need each and every one for later."

· Chapter 50 ·

At a few minutes after seven p.m. Victor heard the rumble of an approaching vehicle. He finished his stretching routine and looked out the window of the upstairs hallway to see the Toyota minivan ascending the hill. It disappeared out of his line of sight as it pulled up in front of the farmhouse. The panel van and its precious cargo had been left elsewhere. The dust kicked up from the Toyota's tires drifted into nothingness.

He waited awhile to give everyone time to assemble. He wanted to be on the periphery of the gathering, close to an exit, not surrounded by killers who might turn on him at any moment.

Everyone looked at Victor as he entered the kitchen. He didn't detect any reason behind the look beyond the fact that he was the last to arrive. Hart stood at the opposite end of the room to Victor, by the exterior door, which was open to keep the air moving. He'd cleaned up since Victor had last seen him and changed his clothes, but he looked as confident and dangerous as he had that afternoon. He greeted Victor with a hint of a nod and something in the pale blue-gray eyes that Victor couldn't determine. He was still an unknown quantity, but Victor had the perfect way to test him. Dietrich was leaning with his elbows against the countertop. Victor couldn't fail to read the hatred in his gaze. Jaeger was sitting at the table, waiting to eat. Leeson was taking foil cartons from brown paper bags and placing them on the table. Coughlin nodded at Victor. He sat with his arms folded. Francesca stood to Hart's right. She looked stunning. She gave Victor a sad smile.

"Who's hungry?" Leeson said.

They ate in near silence. There were a few comments on the quality of the meal—meatballs in marinara sauce and spaghetti—but no sustained conversation. Victor wasn't sure if that was because everyone's thoughts were on what Leeson would say after dinner, or whether the atmosphere was the result of Hart's presence. He sat next to Francesca, with Leeson perpendicular to his left at the head of the table. Hart didn't seem to notice the atmosphere. He didn't look tense. He was hungry. He wolfed down the contents of the foil packet, took another from the bag, and began eating it just as fast.

Jaeger ate with his gaze locked on his food and didn't make eye contact with Victor once, which Victor took to mean he wasn't ready to make his move or had changed his mind altogether. Or perhaps there was more to his inaction. Perhaps he didn't look at Victor because he was hiding something. Perhaps he wouldn't involve himself if Victor provoked Dietrich into an altercation. Perhaps it really was a setup, after all.

This whole job is a setup.

When everyone had eaten, Leeson had Coughlin tidy up and Francesca fetch a bottle of wine from the basement.

Leeson removed a set of keys from a trouser pocket and slid them across the kitchen table. They stopped equidistant between Dietrich and Victor. "Would you be so kind as to take the Phantom from the barn?"

Dietrich reached for them.

"No," Leeson said. "I'd like Mr. Kooi to do it. If he doesn't mind."

"Sure," Victor said. He took the keys and stood.

Jaeger looked at Victor. His eyes said, *Soon.*

• • •

Last night Leeson had asked Dietrich to put the limousine away after Victor had driven it back from Rome. Now Victor was taking it out. Yesterday morning Leeson had said that Victor wasn't allowed in the barn. But now he had been given the keys to let himself inside. The padlock key was obvious on the ring and Victor used it to unlock the barn door. It shuddered and creaked as he pulled it open.

The sun was low in the sky. There was about another hour left of daylight. Inside, the barn was gloomy. Deep shadows surrounded the swath of light that fed in through the open door. It reflected off the waxed bodywork of the Rolls-Royce limousine parked inside. It had been reversed into the barn and the front grille was now less than a meter from Victor's knees.

Either side of the vehicle, the barn was full of long-handled rakes for pulling olives from the branches during harvest and nets to catch them when they fell. Stacks of brown baskets rose to the ceiling; come harvest they would be filled with fruit and packed into vans to transport to the mill. Aluminum ladders lined one wall, to be used by the farmers to reach high into the olive trees to shake out the fruit with the rakes. Rolls of nets as tall as the ladders were next. They would be spread out around several trees at a time to ensure that every olive shaken from above was collected. Dust and cobwebs nestled among the beams overhead.

Victor circled the Phantom, the rear bumper of which lay about halfway down the barn's length. The area behind was some kind of workshop. There was a sturdy workbench and metal shelving units and tools of all kinds.

Whatever Jaeger had been working on had been finished or hidden or moved elsewhere.

Victor smelled detergent. The workbench had been washed, as had the floor around it. The floor had been swept. An empty bucket and mop were nearby. The mop was damp on the back of Victor's hand.

He squatted down. The floor had been mopped as well as swept. He ran his fingers over the floor around the edges of each leg of the workbench. When he looked at his fingers he saw a gritty black substance on them that was hard and shiny. It was like the fine dust created when sawing metal, but Victor recognized it for what it was: ceramic.

From behind Victor, Hart said, "What are you looking for, compadre?"

"I'm satisfying your curiosity," Victor answered as he brushed the ceramic dust from his fingers onto his trousers. He turned to face Hart.

Hart stood on one side of the Phantom. Victor hadn't heard his approach. "Isn't that what the cat said?"

"I've got bigger claws than a cat."

Hart stepped a little closer. "I've no doubt you do." Then said, "Felix Kooi. The Dutchman," as if testing the feel of the words.

"That's me," Victor said, and immediately regretted it. Always better to stay quiet than say something that has no value. "Is there something I can help you with?"

Hart shrugged. "Yes and no."

Victor remained silent. As far as he could see, Hart was unarmed. There were wrenches and hammers and pliers all within Victor's reach. "Why don't we start with yes?"

"Sure," Hart said. "Let's start with how you can help me." He stepped closer still, until he was in front of the Phantom's rear bumper, equidistant between the brake lights, a sidestep either way from blocking Victor's route past the car and his only way out. "What should I call you?"

"Kooi. Or Felix, if you prefer."

Hart moved out of a patch of shadow and into a shaft of light cutting across the barn. His eyes shone. "I prefer Dutch."

"What do you want?"

"You make it sound so nefarious, kid. Who says I have to want anything? I simply want to get to know the new guy. Bond a little."

"I'm not here to make friends."

"I'm surprised you have any with that attitude. Me, I've got lots of friends. All over the world. It's good to be sociable. Give it a try. What's wrong with swapping a few war stories?"

"I'm not the nostalgic type."

Hart laughed. "Yeah, I can believe that about you, Dutch. Don't suppose you'll answer me if I ask about your background."

"I prefer to keep my focus on the present."

"Well, you're still alive, so I guess that's working for you. From what I'd heard, I thought you'd be older."

"I'm older than I look."

Hart stepped closer. "And there's no age in a man's eyes, and yours are as black as death. Bet you wear contacts on jobs, right?"

Victor didn't answer.

"Of course you do. I'm also thinking beard as often as not. Mix it up with the hair. All those different looks. All those different faces. Guy as private as you gets to be good at pretending to be other people because you spend every second hiding who you really are. A regular chameleon."

"What's your point?"

"Who says I have to have a point? We're just talking here."

"No, we're not."

Hart stroked the Phantom's bodywork with the fingertips of one hand. "You and Dietrich don't seem to get along too well."

"It's just playground stuff. Boys being boys."

"What about the other two: Jaeger and Coughlin? You've known them as long as you've known Dietrich, so what do you think?"

"They must be good if Leeson hired them," Victor said, thinking about Jaeger's plan to kill the team.

"Because Leeson hired you, and you're good?"

"Yes," Victor said, thinking about how Kooi had failed to kill Charters as Leeson had wanted, yet Leeson had hired him for this job regardless. Because he needed Kooi and only Kooi.

"How did you end up doing work for Leeson?"

"Long story," Victor answered.

"You'll have to tell me it sometime."

There was something in Hart's tone Victor couldn't read, so he didn't respond.

Hart walked closer. "You seem nervous."

"I don't get nervous."

"You don't trust me, do you?"

"I don't trust anyone," Victor said. "You and Leeson seem close."

"Do we? Guess that's because I was hired first, so I've known him longer than you or those other three reprobates."

"What's Francesca got to do with this?"

Hart looked at him a moment before asking, "Why am I detecting there's more to that question than just those words?"

"What is she doing here?"

"Why are you so interested?"

"She's not a professional," Victor said.

"Does she have to be?"

"She shouldn't be here."

"She's got free will, same as everyone else. And she knows where the door is."

"You shouldn't have involved her."

"Who says I did? She works for Leeson, not for me. I didn't involve her in anything. If you've got a problem with her being here, then you should take it up with her. Or him. But not me. So, are you going to tell me what all this is really about?"

Victor just looked at him.

One-half of Hart's mouth formed a smile. "She's not mine, if that's what you've been thinking."

"I imagine she'll be pleased to find out she's not your property."

"Turn of phrase."

"Sure it was."

Hart asked, "Why do I get the impression that you don't like me very much?"

Victor didn't answer. They stared at each other for a moment.

Leeson's voice broke the silence: "Have you got lost in there, Mr. Kooi?"

He appeared outside the open barn door. "For a man as keen to get to work as yourself, you seem strangely intent on delaying its initiation."

"Coming now," Victor said.

"Sorry to hold him up," Hart said. "We've been getting to know each other."

"Well, isn't that nice?" Leeson said without sincerity. He gestured to Victor. "The Phantom, if you please."

"Good talking to you, Dutch," Hart said. "Maybe we can continue this conversation another time."

Victor waited until Hart had left the barn, then climbed into the limousine.

· Chapter 51 ·

Victor drove the Rolls-Royce out of the barn, killed the engine, and climbed out. The sun was setting and a light was on in the kitchen, so Victor could see through the window to where Hart, Leeson, Dietrich, Jaeger, Coughlin, and Francesca stood. Victor couldn't see Leeson's lips, but he was gesticulating to emphasize whatever points he was making to the others, who all stood still as they listened. Those faces Victor could see were blank with concentration. Whatever Leeson was telling them was important. Victor thought more about Leeson's decision to send him out to the barn.

He approached the closed kitchen door—quieter than a relaxed man walking, but not as quiet as a man trying to be quiet. The gravel driveway betrayed him, as he knew it would, before he got close enough to hear what was being said, but as he neared and his angle to the window changed, he didn't pause to read Leeson's lips, because Hart looked his way.

Hinges quietly squealed as Victor pushed the door open. The conversation had already stopped before he stepped inside. All eyes focused his way. Eight of those eyes belonged to trained and experienced killers. Two belonged to a man armed with a gun, who employed those killers. The final two were the only pair Victor felt the need to look away from. He tossed Leeson the car keys before he could be asked for them and made his way to the sink, unconcerned about his back being to the room because there was no logical reason the crew would turn on him now when they had not done so earlier.

He helped himself to some water and as he drank it down individual conversations broke out behind him: Leeson talking to Hart and Francesca, Dietrich with Coughlin. Jaeger spoke to no one. His reflection in the window glass stared at Victor's and nodded just once.

No one saw it but Victor. He turned around and examined the room. Jaeger was on the opposite side of the room. Hart, Francesca, and Leeson formed a small triangle close to the door, to Victor's left. Dietrich and Coughlin stood near the stove, to Victor's right.

Victor circled around the table, moving past Coughlin and Dietrich. He bumped his shoulder into Dietrich's— the shoulder that he had stabbed.

Dietrich grimaced. "Watch it, prick."

"Don't tell me that little cut hurts a strong man like you?"

"Not as much as it will hurt you when I cut your tongue from your mouth."

"Gentlemen," Leeson said. "Let's not have a repeat of earlier."

"There won't be," Victor said as he continued to stare at Dietrich. "He hasn't got his knife."

Dietrich smiled but anger raged in his eyes. Victor saw Jaeger's reflection shift across the window as he neared Leeson. Hart saw Victor look.

"Back off from each other," Leeson said. "Now, if you please."

"I thought you were a real tough guy, Dietrich," Victor said. "But you're just a coward. Everyone in this room knows it. Without the knife, you're nothing."

Dietrich swung at him wildly. It was a powerful right cross that would have fractured Victor's eye socket had he not slipped the punch. Victor caught Dietrich's hand and wrist and twisted it into a lock. Dietrich responded with a left-handed uppercut to Victor's stomach, but Victor knew it was coming and turned away, making Dietrich follow him in a semicircle to avoid his arm breaking. He roared—anger rather than pain.

"That's it," Leeson said, and drew his SIG.

Jaeger went for it.

He got his hands on the weapon and wrenched it easily from Leeson's grip.

It was a small gun and Jaeger's hands were huge, and it took him a second of fumbling to get his finger into the small trigger guard. In that second Hart grabbed a mug from the table and threw it at Jaeger—a fast underarm toss aimed at the head, which wouldn't induce unconsciousness or inflict major damage but would hurt.

Jaeger flinched. He lurched backward and to his left, away from the incoming mug, which Hart had thrown at

Jaeger from his right, herding him away from Leeson and into the open space.

Hart charged.

Jaeger was huge but he was fast for his size, and he recovered quickly enough to be ready before Hart reached him. The SIG was in his hand and he brought his arm up to point at Hart. Victor saw that though it would take a few more seconds to reach its conclusion, the attempt was already over.

In the same way Jaeger was fast for his size, so was Hart. But Hart was around one hundred pounds lighter. As the gun came up, Hart went low, below the muzzle, and Jaeger couldn't react in time to stop Hart wrapping his arms around Jaeger's thighs—thighs that were too close together because Jaeger's feet were too squared.

Jaeger was huge and heavy but Hart was strong. He didn't need to lift him high off the floor for his forward momentum to tip Jaeger backward far enough for gravity to pull him crashing down to the floor.

Victor released Dietrich and Dietrich didn't attack. He, like everyone else in the room, watched Hart and Jaeger.

Jaeger was on his back and his arms had gone up over his head. He'd kept hold of the gun despite the impact, but being thrown to the floor had momentarily stunned him. Hart used that brief window to go for the gun, standing up to do so, and Jaeger rolled his head backward to keep him in view as he tried to angle the weapon.

Well played, Victor thought, because he saw what Hart had done. He didn't go for the SIG, but stamped down with his heel on Jaeger's now-exposed throat.

Then Hart stood back, because there was nothing else he needed to do.

Jaeger's whole body seemed to tense. He sat up and whipped the gun around to track Hart, but let it fall from his fingers. Because he was trying to breathe.

Panic warped Jaeger's face.

He grasped at his throat, eyes wide and staring at a point far beyond the kitchen. He opened his mouth and shoved fingers into it, but Victor knew he had no chance of getting them far enough into his throat to push open his windpipe, which had been crushed by Hart's heel. Jaeger wheezed and wretched and spluttered, his face reddening with every second that passed.

Everyone just watched.

After thirty seconds of fruitlessly trying to open up his windpipe with his fingers, Jaeger barged across the kitchen, knocking aside anyone not quick enough to get out of his path. He wrenched open a drawer, then another because he didn't find what he was looking for in the first.

Jaeger grabbed a pair of scissors, but dropped them because his heart rate was so high his fine motor skills were almost nonexistent. He fell to his knees to grab the scissors from the floor. He didn't stand again—having been without oxygen for almost a minute, he had neither the strength to stand nor the time.

He directed his gaze at the ceiling by tilting his head back and with the fingers of his left hand found the groove at the top of his rib cage, where the clavicles met and only a thin layer of skin covered the esophagus.

"Look away," Victor said to Francesca.

She didn't. At first Victor thought she was shocked and terrified and confused by his words and Jaeger's actions, but he saw that she was none of those. She watched because she was curious. She watched as Jaeger used the scissors to stab himself in the throat.

The scissors were an ordinary kitchen utensil, not a surgical scalpel, and the tip of each blade was blunted for safety. Jaeger's first stab drew blood and a breathless grunt but failed to pierce the cartilage.

Victor had no doubt Jaeger could have driven the scissors through a man's skull in other circumstances, but he was weak and dying and with such an awkward maneuver could only employ a fraction of his depleted strength. Jaeger tried again, then again, stabbing at his throat with increasingly wild and inaccurate blows as oxygen deprivation escalated. Blood soaked his hand and cascaded over his shirt. Torn skin hung in strips from his neck.

He slumped from his knees onto his left side, his face swollen and blue, eyes bulging and red. He made a slow, weak stab at his neck, then stopped.

No one spoke for a long moment. Hart picked up Leeson's gun and handed it back.

"Would it have worked?" Coughlin asked, eventually. He looked around, not certain who would know.

"Yes," Victor said. "He could have opened the scissors a little to create a breathing hole."

Hart nodded. "He never gave up. I respect that."

Francesca said, "You're an animal." It didn't sound like an insult.

Hart nodded again. "I'm human."

"He paid the price for turning on me—for turning on

us all," Leeson said. "He deserved everything that he received. He could have left here a rich man. Now he'll never leave."

"He believed you were going to betray him," Victor said. Everyone looked at him. "He believed after the job was complete you would have Hart kill him—and the rest of us—to ensure that there was no comeback."

"And how would you know what he believed?"

"Because he told me."

"Then he had an overactive imagination."

"He thought Hart would kill him," Victor said, gesturing to where Jaeger lay unmoving on the floor, scissors still clutched in hand, blood pooling on the floor around his head. "Hart killed him."

Leeson smiled a little. "Jaeger's paranoia became a self-fulfilling prophecy. I think there's a lesson in there for each and every one of us. But, fortunately, we are able to continue without him. He's already fulfilled his part."

Victor thought about Jaeger working in the barn and the ceramic dust. "You said you'd tell us about the job after dinner."

"I did. So let's go."

"Go where?"

"Outside," Leeson said. "Jaeger's corpse can stay here for now. Mr. Dietrich will drive my limousine. Everyone else in the minivan. It's time you knew what you were hired for."

· Chapter 52 ·

Coughlin drove. Leeson sat next to him. Francesca sat behind. Victor sat next to her. Hart sat on the backseat. Victor couldn't see Hart, but he knew he was watching. The reason for that, however, Victor didn't know. Maybe Hart was trying to decide if Victor really was Felix Kooi, as he claimed to be. Maybe he was wondering if Victor's provocation of Dietrich had anything to do with Jaeger's subsequent attempt to take Leeson's gun.

They drove through the winding, narrow country lanes between the endless fields of olive trees before joining the motorway north to Rome. Dietrich followed in the Phantom. The drive took fifty minutes. Leeson directed Coughlin on which turnings to take when they reached the city, navigating through the industrial neighborhoods and business developments of Rome's southern sector.

Their destination stood between a massive structure housing self-storage units and the row after row of used cars in a dealership. A high chain-link fence surrounding the compound. Steel spikes like shark's teeth protruded from a metal tube that ran along the top of the fence. Beyond the fence were two buildings. Coughlin stopped the minivan before a gate and Hart climbed out to unlock the padlock that secured it. He pushed it open and waved Coughlin through. The neighborhood was quiet. An office block stood on the opposite side of the street. There were no residential buildings nearby and little through traffic. Units were shut down for the night.

Security lights illuminated the buildings inside the fence. Both were sizable, but one dwarfed the other. The larger was a prefabricated steel structure, modern and built purely for functionality. The smaller building looked at least a hundred years older. Its walls were of rendered brick, painted white. Red tiles formed a sloping roof.

"It's owned by a consortium," Leeson explained as the team disembarked from the minivan and Hart relocked the gate. "Growers from all over the region have their harvest processed here. Some of those families have been bringing olives to this mill for two centuries; one generation after the next following in their fathers' footsteps. I think that's quite beautiful. But it's also similarly pathetic. We should strive to do better than our parents, not copy them."

"When's the harvest?" Victor asked, as though he was making conversation.

"Not for some time."

"So the mill is empty?"

Leeson nodded. "We have it all to ourselves, yes."

Victor saw that the white panel van Hart had driven

to the farmhouse was parked in the six-meter corridor of space between the two buildings. Parked in front of it, farther away from the gate, was another vehicle, almost as tall and wide as the panel van. A number of weatherproof sheets covered it, each tied down by ropes that ringed the vehicle. Victor would have recognized the dimensions even without the information supplied by Coughlin. This was the ambulance he and Dietrich had stolen, parked away from the road and hidden by sheets to ensure that it wasn't identified. It would make a good getaway vehicle, with room in the back for the entire team. Or it might be equally effective at providing a way of getting into a restricted area. He felt Hart watching him but didn't look to confirm it.

"One building for traditional production," Victor said, "and the other to utilize modern methods?"

"That's correct, Mr. Kooi," Leeson answered. "There is a feeling—or prejudice, if you will—among some that the more machinery and technology involved in the production, the lower the quality of the oil. Hence one building to pander to such elitist nonsense and one for an efficient enterprise."

He responded as if Victor was curious about olive oil production and Victor acted as if he was interested in such things and not the likely interior composition of the two buildings so he could begin strategizing for his presence in either one. Something was wrong. There was an atmosphere between Leeson, Hart, and Francesca that went beyond Jaeger's recent demise. They all knew what Victor, Dietrich, and Coughlin were going to discover and what was going to happen next. Dietrich and Coughlin were oblivious of it, but Victor saw the shift in posture and body language; Leeson's enthusiasm wasn't purely because of Victor's seeming interest in the mill's product. He was growing increasingly edgy and excited.

Victor thought back to the events of the past twenty-four hours, searching for some indication of what he was about to find. He thought back to the journey with Francesca from Gibraltar to the farmhouse, and further back to the conversation with Leeson on the phone and that first meeting in the back of the limousine.

"What are we doing here?" Coughlin whispered.

Victor didn't answer, because he didn't know. He saw cigarette stubs littering the ground near the grated drain.

"Is this where we're doing the job?"

Victor shook his head. He didn't know the mill's purpose, but he knew it wasn't the strike point. He knew enough to know that. It was obvious. It didn't need to be deduced. Coughlin should have known that too. That he didn't meant he wasn't very smart. Victor looked at him, then at Leeson, at Dietrich, then Francesca, and finally Hart. Hart had asked Victor what he thought of his teammates, including Coughlin. Victor had said Coughlin must be good if Leeson had hired him. Because you're good, Hart had said. Dietrich was good in a fight, and maybe he was good in the field too, but his attitude and mentality were just about as bad as they could be. Coughlin was stealthy but too young to have any significant experience, and he was no thinker. Victor didn't know much about Jaeger, but he'd got himself killed and death was always the ultimate separator. Kooi had been a competent killer, but he had failed to kill Charters as requested and if not for the attention drawn by the watch merchant would have been killed without incident. Kooi, Dietrich, Jaeger, and Coughlin. All average operators. All lacking. Except Hart. He had foiled Jaeger's mutiny in a matter of seconds.

It didn't make sense.

"This way," Leeson said.

He led them down the corridor of space between the two buildings, past the white panel van, and to a door that led inside the bigger and newer of the two structures. Victor noted that the fluorescent ceiling lights were already switched on, illuminating the large interior. A corrugated metal roof stood ten meters above, supported by steel girders and pillars. Gleaming modern machinery filled the majority of the floor space. Victor saw conveyor belts and centrifuges, vats and tanks, pipes and chutes, and massive presses. Everything was shut down and dormant and strangely silent. Ear defenders hung from hooks near the door for use when the mill was operational, but now the only noise was that of their footsteps on the hard flooring. The whole space was immaculate: diligently and meticulously cleaned after the last harvest had ended.

Coughlin and Dietrich shared an expression of curiosity and Victor made sure to wear a similar one. In contrast Leeson was still excited, Hart relaxed yet purposeful, and Francesca ambivalent.

A door on the far side of the mill led to corridors and to other doors that would lead in turn to testing rooms and offices, changing rooms and toilets, and other facilities. Leeson pushed open a door into some kind of meeting room, perhaps where managers and supervisors would discuss the day-to-day business of olive oil production. Whiteboards hung from the far wall. Flip charts stood before them. A wastepaper bin sat nearby. Cheap plastic chairs, which during the harvest season would no doubt be arranged in uneven rows facing one wall where someone would stand in front of the whiteboards and flip charts, were stacked against one wall to free up the room. There was another door at the far end.

"Cool," Dietrich said.

Cheap veneered tables that matched the chairs were arranged into a large square in the middle of the room. On top of the tables stood a model. It was made of white Plasti-Card, meticulously cut and glued and arranged to form a scale reproduction of a building. The model was about three feet long by two wide and two high. It had a roof, but that roof sat next to the rest of the building so its interior could be seen: individual rooms, open rectangles for doorways and stairs. The floor could be lifted out to reveal the one below it and the ones below that. The building the model represented was a grand structure, similar in dimensions to a grand country villa or hotel.

Victor had seen models like this before, if not for a very long time. He remembered memorizing layouts and angles and likely danger spots and the best points of cover and concealment. He would stand silently with men just like him as they were briefed on the coming mission.

The group spread out around the model without being told. Coughlin and Dietrich stood closest to the arrangement of tables so they could get a good look at the model, leaning over it to see inside and ducking down to peer through the windows.

Victor ignored it because the corners of the flip chart pages were curled and the covers creased, the whiteboards were smeared and marked, and the wastepaper bin was full with scrunched-up balls of paper. He moved to a position a couple of meters back from the model, at an angle where he could see without having to turn his head the door through which they had entered and the far one.

"Gentlemen," Leeson began, "this is the strike point."

· Chapter 53 ·

"**W**hat is it?" Dietrich asked.

Victor looked at Leeson as he said, "An embassy."

"He's right," Hart said.

Leeson smiled. "How very perceptive of you, Mr. Kooi. But I can't say I'm surprised at the speed of your uptake."

There was something dangerous in his voice.

"Whose embassy?" Coughlin asked.

Leeson looked to Victor. "Any astute guesses?"

Victor shook his head because he knew who it belonged to.

"It's the Russian embassy," Leeson explained.

"Where?" Dietrich asked.

"In Rome, of course."

Victor saw Hart watching for his reaction. He ensured that there was none.

"The target?" Coughlin asked.

Leeson strolled to one of the flip charts and pulled up

the cover. "This is the gentleman whose demise we're all being paid to ensure arrives before nature intends."

Four eight-by-ten photographs had been affixed to the first page of the flip chart. They all showed a man in his fifties. He looked short and overweight but otherwise likely to live naturally for a long time yet. The first photograph was head and shoulders, blown up from a wide-angled group shot. An arm belonging to someone else was draped over the target's shoulder. The target was wearing a dinner jacket and smiling, a fat cigar nestled between his teeth. The second picture showed the target in safari gear, holding a rifle and smiling next to the corpse of a lion. In the photograph the target was sitting on the terrace of a restaurant with a younger date. Like the first, the photograph had been blown up to focus on the target, and only a slice of the woman opposite him was included. The last picture showed the target's profile as he walked along a busy street among out-of-focus passersby.

"Who is he?" Victor asked.

Leeson said, "His name is Ivan Prudnikov. Mr. Prudnikov is a Russian bureaucrat and is to be a guest of the Russian ambassador, a personal friend of his, who is hosting one of his famous receptions at the embassy for all manner of industrialists, delegates, politicians, and dignitaries. They say there's enough cocaine at these parties to drop a horde of elephants."

"Why kill him inside the embassy?"

"Because that's what the client is paying for, Mr. Kooi. The specifics are of no relevance to you."

"That's where you're wrong. Every aspect of the job is of relevance."

Dietrich said, "Why don't you stop being a pussy and let the man finish?"

"Though I don't exactly approve of Mr. Dietrich's language, I agree with his sentiments. Perhaps, Mr. Kooi, you would be so good as to leave any questions you have until later?"

Victor remained silent.

"As I was saying," Leeson began. "The client wishes Mr. Prudnikov to be killed while in attendance at the upcoming reception at the Russian embassy in Rome. Here is a scale model of the embassy so you can familiarize yourselves with its layout. The flip charts contain further intel on the target and the strike point."

"Any stipulation as to the means of death?" Coughlin asked.

"I'll come to that later, but for now I'm going to leave you all for a little while so you can get better acquainted with some of the facts of the mission, instead of listening to me drone on. I'll be back before too long." He gestured to Francesca. "Come along, my dear."

He left through the second door, Francesca following.

Victor walked over to the flip charts and began examining the one Leeson had opened, to which the photographs of the target were attached. On the other pages were more photographs, extensive biographical information in the form of printed documents stuck to the flip chart pages, photocopies of Prudnikov's passport, driver's license, and birth certificate, and copies of his handwriting and fingerprints.

The embassy was the focus of the second flip chart. There were schematics and blueprints and photographs of the interior, hand-drawn diagrams and names of staff and security and descriptions of procedures and protocols. Between them the two charts contained a wealth of information that must have taken a considerable amount of time and resources to compile. It would take days to become familiar with it all, endlessly flipping back and forth between the pages of the two charts—making the bottom corners of the pages curled and soft and frayed. It must have taken a week to build the model.

Victor turned away. Coughlin was examining the other flip chart while Dietrich's interest was fixed on the model. He'd taken out the two upper floors and was peering down at the ground floor. Hart was standing on the other side of the room, leaning against the wall by the door through which they had entered, watching the other three men, but mostly Victor.

"What are your thoughts?" Hart asked.

"That you already know all about this."

"I meant about the job: the target and the strike point," Hart said.

"I know what you meant."

"Looks good," Dietrich said to Hart.

Victor raised an eyebrow. "In your expert opinion?"

Dietrich didn't respond.

No one spoke further. Victor went back to examining the background on Prudnikov and the intel on the embassy. Hart continued to watch.

• • •

Leeson returned an hour later. He looked relaxed and confident and in charge and content. Francesca wasn't with him.

"How are we getting on?"

"Fine," Dietrich said.

Coughlin said, "Not bad."

Victor remained silent. As did Hart.

"Fabulous," Leeson said. "I take it you've all had the opportunity to familiarize yourselves with the particulars of the upcoming assignment. To repeat: The objective is to kill Ivan Prudnikov while he is in attendance at a reception at the Russian embassy here in Rome. Gentlemen, I'd like to hear your initial impressions."

Victor gave Dietrich and Coughlin a chance to speak. They didn't. It was beyond their comfort zone; beyond their thinking. They followed orders. They didn't plan. This wasn't what they did.

"It can't be done," Victor said.

Leeson asked, "Why not?"

"Many reasons: Firstly, we'll be going in with no weapons because the embassy will have security with metal detectors and wands and will possibly conduct personal searches. And even if we could get weapons inside the building—which I don't believe is possible—there will be security personnel in the crowd at the party, and important foreign dignitaries will have trained aides and bodyguards. Even discounting that, we can't possibly know Prudnikov's movements during the party. Just because he's been invited to the reception doesn't mean he won't be powdering his nose with Bolivia's finest off the breasts of a hooker in the ambassador's private quarters. So that means we need two triggermen in different positions, ready to move in independently depending on where Prudnikov goes and who he goes with. But the embassy is a big building with lots of rooms and there's going to be lots of people there, so we'll need dedicated watchers not only to keep eyes on the target at all times, but also to watch embassy security and look out for unexpected problems. Which there will be, given this is to take place in an enclosed public space that's also heavily guarded. With Hart and me as the triggermen—"

"Hold it right there," Dietrich interrupted. "Who died and made you god of planning? If anyone's going to be one of the shooters, it's me."

Victor ignored him. "With Hart and me as the triggermen, and Jaeger dead, that leaves just Dietrich and Coughlin as surveillance, and they're simply not good enough."

"Fuck you," Dietrich said.

Coughlin glared.

"We need more men," Victor said. "We need at least one more inside the embassy to provide surveillance and backup. Then we need watchers outside the building to keep track of who comes and goes and to provide continuous updates to those inside. That's at least another two men. Whether it ends up loud or stays quiet, there needs to be another member of the team providing the means of extraction. And ideally another still if we want to disable the embassy's security cameras and/or delete the recordings. That's another five required, based on the current level of competence, if any of the operators actually wants to walk away without getting killed or captured."

"Don't listen to him, Mr. Leeson," Dietrich said. "We can do the job, no problem. Kooi is just scared."

"And we need more background information on the

target. We have a lot about him but nothing about his work."

Dietrich frowned. "What does it matter what the guy does for a living?"

Victor ignored him. He said to Leeson, "You said he's a Russian bureaucrat. That's a very general term. What part of the government does he work for? What does he do?"

"You make some interesting points," Leeson said to Victor. "There are some facts that you aren't yet privy to that might change your evaluation of the task at hand. Come with me, please. Everyone."

Leeson motioned for the group to follow him out of the door they had entered through an hour ago. Coughlin followed first, then Dietrich. Victor hung back to let Hart go next.

"After you, compadre," Hart said.

· Chapter 54 ·

Leeson led them back across the main floor of the mill and out of the building. He walked along the corridor of space between the two buildings, then to the older building with the whitewashed walls and red-tiled roof. Leeson pushed one of the dark-stained double doors open and ushered the team inside.

He was in an antechamber attached to the main mill area. It occupied approximately one-quarter of the building's interior and looked as though it had a range of purposes. There was a small kitchenette at one end with a wooden table and benches near it. There were hooks for outside clothing and crates of empty green glass bottles.

"Through here," Leeson said, leading the team into the mill itself.

It was a large space, if about half the size of the modern building's interior. Like the outside, the interior walls were painted white. The roof peaked above Victor's head and was supported by a framework of metal posts and struts.

There were two rows of machinery: on the left were stone grinders to pulp the olives; on the right were the presses. Three thick circular stones that had to weigh at least a couple of tons each were arranged together at an angle to a central cog that turned them to crush the olive fruit and pits into a mash. As in the modern mill, all the equipment was dormant and waiting for the next harvest. But unlike the modern mill, not all the equipment was there for the production of olive oil. There were five folding camp beds and sleeping bags, backpacks and sports bags and camp chairs and boxes of ammunition, and a wooden crate with stenciled Cyrillic script sprayed on in red paint.

There were also four men standing in and around the equipment, all facing the doorway through which Victor and the others entered.

They were a mix of ages: the youngest in his mid-twenties, two in their thirties, and the fourth in his early forties. They weren't Italians. They wore jeans, T-shirts, and sportswear. They were unshaven and unclean because the mill probably didn't have showers and they had been sleeping on camp beds and washing using only sinks and washcloths. They had the look of civilians, not military personnel, but civilians who knew how to fight and kill. As he got closer, Victor could smell the cigarette smoke on their clothes. The room didn't smell of smoke, so they didn't smoke in here. He pictured the cigarette stubs by the drain outside.

Four men in the room. Five camp beds.

It didn't look as though the four had just got up on account of Leeson, Hart, Dietrich, Coughlin, and Victor. They had already been standing. They could have sat on the chairs or on their beds, could even have been lying down, relaxed and comfortable. Instead they were on their feet when they didn't need to be. Their jaws were set and their fists clenched. Their eyes were narrow, lines between eyebrows. Nostrils flared. They were pumped up and restless. Victor had seen groups of men displaying the same signs. Their adrenaline was up and they were tense and restless because they were waiting to go into action.

"The party's tonight," Victor said, almost in disbelief.

Leeson nodded. "That's right, Mr. Kooi. The embassy reception begins in about an hour."

"That's not enough time to plan and rehearse, let alone get firsthand intelligence of the strike point. It's nowhere near enough time."

"That's where you're wrong," Leeson said. "We've been rehearsing for weeks. We've been planning for months. These gentlemen know everything there is to know about the embassy."

Victor thought about the flip chart pages, curled and frayed and softened from endless use.

"Why do you need us?" Victor asked as he began to understand.

"To kill Prudnikov, of course."

"There's no time to plan it. Even if these four have been rehearsing for the whole of the summer"—he gestured to himself, Coughlin, and Dietrich, but not Hart—"we haven't. There's not enough time to integrate us into the plan."

"You're not a part of their plan, Mr. Kooi," Leeson said. "There are two teams in this room, each with its own objective. Yours is to kill Prudnikov."

"Theirs?"

Leeson didn't answer.

"They're not following this conversation, are they?" Victor asked, but didn't wait for an answer. "Because they don't speak English. Who are they?"

"They are from Chechnya, Mr. Kooi."

"They're not professionals, are they? They're terrorists. They're going to take control of the embassy."

"Right again. You are so very perceptive, aren't you?" This time Leeson didn't wait for an answer. "I haven't hired them. They're enthusiastic amateurs who are patriots looking to strike a blow against Moscow imperialism. I can't say their cause does much to excite me, but I'm being paid very well to assist them."

"Have you heard of Operation Nimrod?"

"Of course," Leeson said.

"In 1980 six Iranians took twenty-six hostages in the Iranian embassy in London. They had a list of demands pertaining to the autonomy of the Iranian province of Khūzestān. Obviously, those demands weren't met and a hostage was killed. As a result, the British government ordered soldiers from the Twenty-second Special Air Service regiment to end the siege. They assaulted the building, killing five of the six hostage takers and capturing the remaining man in a battle that lasted seventeen minutes. All but one of the remaining hostages were rescued. The SAS didn't take as much as a scratch."

"One of the many reasons we're not in sunny London Town for this excursion."

"And what about when Chechens took control of the Dubrokva Theater in Moscow?"

"Why don't you just make your point, Mr. Kooi?"

"It won't work. These things never do. Whatever demands these Chechens make won't be realized. There'll be a siege. It will last for a few days and then the Italians will storm the building and it will be over, and anyone who goes in there will come out in a body bag."

"That's a rather pessimistic view to take."

"It's an accurate view."

Coughlin said, "If you have that team, why do you need us? Why not just have them kill Prudnikov?"

"Excellent question, Mr. Coughlin," Leeson replied. "Security at the consulate isn't likely to admit a group of Chechens while hosting an exclusive reception. It's invitation only. Fortunately, we have one courtesy of the lovely Francesca, who by legacy of her late father is invited to such gatherings."

"Who is Ivan Prudnikov?" Victor asked.

Leeson said, "He's Russian intelligence."

"FSB or SVR?"

"SVR."

"He's the head of the SVR, isn't he?" Victor asked. "You want us to kill the chairman of Russia's foreign intelligence service."

"That's correct."

"That's suicide. It would be suicide even if we had months to plan. Security at the embassy will be insane."

"We've had months to plan," Leeson said. "And we have an excellent plan thanks to Mr. Hart's tactical brilliance. Mr. Kooi, you will accompany Francesca and enter the embassy ahead of the assault team. You will go under the guise of a British businessman, George Hall, using his invitation as he is unable to attend in person thanks to Francesca's charms and an unfortunate encounter with Mr. Dietrich and Mr. Coughlin. And they say Rome is such a safe city. Once inside you are to have a good time: Mingle, drink champagne, help yourself to the caviar. Dance with Francesca. Then, at precisely nine p.m., you are to approach Mr. Prudnikov and kill him."

"That's not even a plan," Victor said, looking from Leeson to Hart and back again. "Dietrich could come up with something better than that. There's no indication in the materials as to how many bodyguards Prudnikov will have. He'll be surrounded by SVR operatives. It will be almost impossible to get close to him without alerting his security. Unless I can get to him inside a bathroom—and there's no way to guarantee that is possible at a specific time—then it will have to be done in the main reception area. There'll be chaos. Extraction will be next to impossible, and even if I do get out, then a hundred people will have seen my face. And how am I supposed to kill him? There's no way of getting a gun in there. You need to delay the job by at least six weeks to develop a new plan and new preparation."

"That's impossible, Mr. Kooi. The party is tonight."

"Then you should have hired me months ago."

"Perhaps I can offer you an incentive."

"No amount of money is going to get me to partake in something so poorly conceived."

He was arguing as himself, but nothing in Muir's intel on Kooi suggested the Dutchman was foolish enough to agree to what Leeson was suggesting. No careful and competent professional would take on such a dangerous assignment under these circumstances. For all Victor knew, the job was a bluff, yet another test set by Leeson to determine Kooi's mentality, or perhaps his trustworthiness. If Victor agreed, maybe that would be all the evidence Leeson needed to know Victor wasn't who he claimed to be.

But there was something in Leeson's expression. He wasn't staring at Victor as if to read his thoughts. He was excited. He was excited with anticipation. Not because of the job; there was something more immediate. Something that was about to happen.

Here it comes, Victor thought as he analyzed the chances of making it to the door before someone could draw a weapon and use it.

"Killing Prudnikov is going to be a lot easier than you might think," Leeson said. He gestured to Hart, who picked up a bag from the floor and began unzipping it. "All you have to do is get within twenty feet of him. You don't even need line of sight."

Hart removed something from the bag.

"Mr. Jaeger has kindly constructed a suitable weapon for us," Leeson said, and drew his SIG.

The object Hart held was constructed primarily of canvas, reinforced by leather. It had pockets and straps to keep in place the plates of explosive and the parcels of ceramic shards.

"What the hell is that?" Coughlin asked.

"It's a suicide bomber vest," Victor said.

Leeson pointed the gun at Victor. "That's right, Mr. Kooi. It's in your size too."

"Then you'd better shoot me now," Victor said. "Because I'll kill anyone who tries to put that on me."

"Oh, I don't think it will come to that."

"Then you really are insane."

"What about if I give you something precious? What if I could offer you something beyond material wealth? What if I could offer you the most valuable thing of all?"

Victor remained silent. He thought about the five camp beds and the four men in the room. He thought about the white panel van and its precious cargo. He heard the big double doors open in the antechamber. Everyone else heard too. Like him, they looked in the direction of the sound and watched the open entranceway.

The fifth Chechen appeared through it. He was a little older than the others but otherwise just like them. He wore jeans and a sports jacket and moved like a civilian, but one who had known violence and was ready to know it again. He held the grip of an AK-47 in his right hand, the barrel resting against his shoulder. With his left hand he guided two people into the room.

A woman and a child.

The child was a boy. The woman's hands were tied together with duct tape and her mouth was gagged with it.

Questions were immediately answered in Victor's

thoughts. So much he hadn't understood now made sense.

"Mr. Kooi," Leeson said with a wide smile. "What if in return I were to offer you the lives of your wife and son?"

· Chapter 55 ·

The woman looked at Victor with the same surprise he felt, but hid. She seemed about the same age as Kooi had been, but appeared older because of acute stress and tiredness. She had blond hair and pale skin. Her hair was greasy and uncombed and her clothes were creased and marked. Victor made her for a strong woman, mentally and emotionally robust, used to the knocks and setbacks of life, aware and cautious but afraid of little. She looked terrified.

The strip of duct tape over her mouth kept her lips sealed and prevented her from shouting out what her eyes were screaming:

He's not the man I married.

The duct tape that bound her wrists looked clean and shiny and had few creases. The strip across her mouth was the same, and flat, with no trace of the corners curling. So Victor knew both had been applied not long ago. The state of her clothes and hair said she had been held captive for longer, but no more than two or three days. It would show in her appearance if she had been held for more than that. Unless they had given her clothes and provided her with basic means of sanitation. But the clothes fit exactly as they were supposed to, matching and suiting her too well to have been given to her by someone who didn't care what she looked like. She had been captive for two or three days but had been bound only recently.

The boy next to the woman was about seven, but could easily have been a small eight-year-old or big for six. Victor wasn't sure. He didn't know much about children. The boy wore trainers, jeans, and a T-shirt with dinosaurs embossed on the front. The boy wasn't bound and he wasn't gagged. Like his mother's, the boy's hair was a mess and his clothes were dirty. He didn't look scared. He didn't shout out that Victor was not his father. He just stared at Victor, intent and curious.

They had been captive for two or three days, but the woman had only been recently bound. Because the circumstances of their captivity had changed. The need for security had intensified. They'd been moved from one captor to another or from one prison to another. Or both. Victor remembered Hart's arrival at the farmhouse and the white panel van with precious cargo in the back that only he had been trusted to deliver. That precious cargo being Kooi's wife and child, kidnapped two or three days ago and transported here to the olive mill, where they had been taken from the van and held somewhere else under the guard of the five Chechens, who had gagged and bound the woman. Because she had given them problems. Because she had tried to escape and they couldn't hurt her. Because if she was hurt it could change the dynamic of the threat. Kooi might be too angry to comply rather than scared.

"Is that it?" Leeson said. "You're just going to stand there? No tearful greeting? No rushing for a hug? You're a cold man, Mr. Kooi, but I didn't think you were that cold. But just as well, because I'm afraid there isn't time for an emotional reconciliation."

The woman was shaking her head and mumbling behind the tape, struggling against the fifth Chechen, who gripped her by the arm. Only Victor knew what she was trying to achieve. The boy stared at him, eyes quizzical and searching.

"Let them go," Victor said.

Leeson said, "It would hardly make much sense to go through all the considerable efforts we have made to bring them here and then to release them immediately on your request, now, would it?"

"They mean nothing to me," Victor said.

"Really?" Leeson asked. "Lucille and Peter mean nothing to you?"

Lucille. Peter.

Muir hadn't known about them. She hadn't known Kooi was married. She hadn't known he had a family. Kooi had lived alone in Amsterdam. Lucille and Peter must have lived elsewhere, outside Holland. They must have married in another country with Lucille keeping her maiden name. But it hadn't lasted; otherwise Muir would have known about it. When the separation occurred Kooi moved back to Amsterdam, the marriage not showing up on his Dutch records.

"That's right," Victor said. "They mean nothing to me."

"They mean nothing to you, yet you pay their extortionate rent and Peter's school fees using a Swiss bank account belonging to a shell corporation registered in Indonesia?"

Victor's mind worked fast. Kooi had separated from his wife and walked out on his son, but supported them financially. Yet he had no contact with them—Muir would have seen the pattern of flights or calls. Peter's T-shirt had a dinosaur design. Back in Algiers, Kooi had bought a statuette: a carved wooden reptilian man. Juvenile design. Victor had thought Kooi to have strange tastes, but he'd been wrong. Kooi had bought a present for his son.

So Kooi hadn't abandoned his family. He had stayed away from them because he operated in a dangerous world and he had been protecting them from something like this. But he'd failed.

The clicking of heels announced Francesca's arrival before she stepped into the pressing room. She wore an A-line black dress made from crushed velvet that reached her ankles. It had a slit that opened almost to her hip. Light sparkled on the jewelry adorning her ears, wrist, fingers, and neck. Her dark hair was pulled back and held up with clips. She'd never looked better.

Victor ignored her and said to Leeson, "What do you want?"

"For you to do as requested. Wear the vest. Accompany Francesca to the party. There is no metal in the vest, so you will have no trouble getting through security. Then simply plug in a mobile phone, stand within twenty feet of Mr. Prudnikov, and when the phone makes or receives a call: boom. You won't feel a thing. In return, your family will be driven back to Andorra and they can carry on with their lives."

"Let them go," Victor said again. "Let them go and I'll kill Prudnikov. I don't need the vest."

"You said it was impossible."

"I'll find a way. I can do it. Just let them go."

"I'm afraid that's no good to me. One does not assassinate the head of Russia's foreign intelligence service if one values his own life and liberty. As you said, it's suicide. I have no wish to spend the rest of my life looking over my shoulder. The only way to pull off such a job is if no one believes an assassination has taken place, which they won't if Prudnikov just happens to be one of the many unfortunate victims of a terrorist attack by Chechen nationalists. After you have blown yourself up, these five fine nationalists right here will use the ensuing chaos to storm the building. In the aftermath those that matter will believe the bombing's primary role was to give the team a means of entry. No one will ever think—nay, ever imagine—that it was an assassination. So you see, it wouldn't work to have you kill him any other way than to blow yourself up. But don't think of it as killing yourself; think of it as saving your family. After you've used the vest to kill Prudnikov, Lucille and Peter will be released without harm. Fail or deviate from the plan in even the smallest way and they will be killed. Refuse to comply and watch them die right now. But I'll do you the kindness of letting you be the one to decide in which order they take their final breath."

There was nothing to gain by revealing he wasn't

Kooi. He had met Leeson as Kooi and pretended since that moment to be Kooi. Denying it now would seem like desperation, the kind of desperate claim a man fearing for the lives of his loved ones might make. Or perhaps he would convince Leeson of the truth, but that would achieve nothing save his immediate death and the deaths of Kooi's wife and child.

"How do I know you'll let them go if I do what you ask?"

"You don't," Leeson said, as a reasonable man might, "but I have no reason to kill them unless you force my hand. I assure you I have no desire to be responsible for a child's death if it can be avoided. But if you don't believe me they are certain to die."

Victor looked at Francesca. "You're going along with this?"

Hart laughed. A deep, malevolent mirth. "*Going along with it?* Funny, kid. Using your family was her idea."

Francesca said, "I told you I didn't need your help, Felix. I don't really know why you thought I was so different from you. Maybe I used to be a good person long ago, but where does that ever get anyone?"

"You want the death of a child on your conscience?"

She shook her head. "Of course not, but if you do what they tell you to do, then I won't have one."

Victor turned to Coughlin, who said, "Don't even bother, okay? Just do your job and I'll do mine."

Dietrich laughed. "Couldn't have happened to a nicer person, Your Majesty."

Leeson held up his hands. "Enough, children. We're all professionals here, so let's all behave with some professionalism. Mr. Kooi has a simple job to do, and if you do it Lucille and Peter can go back to their lives knowing you really did love them. Peter can go back to school and play with his friends and grow up and chase girls and have a family himself one day. He'll always know what his father did for him."

Peter was still staring at Victor with the same quizzical gaze. Not frightened or overwhelmed with emotion. But curious. Then Victor understood.

The boy didn't know his father. He didn't know Kooi. He didn't tell his captors the truth because he didn't know the truth. His parents must have split long enough ago that the boy couldn't picture his father's face.

He thought Victor was his father.

Leeson squatted down on his haunches before the little boy. "They say if you come down to their level so you can look them in the eye, they'll trust you." Leeson brushed the shoulder of the kid's T-shirt. "Do you trust me, Peter?"

The boy called Peter didn't answer.

"Maybe I should start hurting him now. Would that encourage your cooperation? I wonder how loud he would scream if I cut off his thumb."

"Let them go," Victor said.

"Kill Prudnikov and they'll be released," Leeson said. "There is nothing more to discuss. All I need from you is your agreement. Otherwise by proxy you will give me your consent to have the ones you love butchered."

Victor looked around. Dietrich, Coughlin, and Hart surrounded him in a loose circle. Leeson and Francesca stood between him and Kooi's family. Five Chechens stood at the periphery of the room. He had a single advantage: they thought the woman and the boy really were his family whom he supported and protected. Leeson believed they were Victor's priority. The men in the room were positioned to stop him from trying to kill Leeson or rescue the captives. They weren't concerned about Victor escaping because they didn't consider that he would want to.

"You're probably wondering why this is happening to you," Leeson said. "Well, quite simply, Mr. Kooi, reliable suicide bombers aren't that easy to come across, and those that are reliable aren't exactly the kind of people who can get into a Russian embassy and in range of a specific target. So it had to be a professional. You weren't the only candidate, but you were so very calm when we met in Budapest, which we need you to be in that embassy, and of course you have such a lovely family to use as leverage. You need to make a decision, Mr. Kooi. Right now. You're going to die. There's nothing you can do to stop that. But you don't have time to grieve for yourself because you need to answer a question. You need to ask yourself whether you would rather die alongside your family or whether you'll die to save them."

The door was six meters away. He could cover the distance and be through it before anyone could intercept him. Leeson was pointing a gun at him, but Leeson was no marksman. Victor doubted he could hit a moving target. The mill was enclosed by the chain-link fence topped with spikes, but it was almost sunset. Shadows were deepening. The modern mill building was huge and full of machinery and blind spots—places to hide and to ambush pursuers. There would be improvised weapons. He had the valet key still. If he distracted them long enough, he could get to the limousine and charge through the gates. It wasn't a great plan. It wasn't even a half-decent one. As soon as he was out of the door, he would be improvising every step.

There was only a slim chance of a successful outcome, but a slim chance was all he needed—those inside the room had no idea what he was really capable of, and he would do anything to survive.

Victor stared into Lucille's confused, terrified eyes, and then down to Peter's. The boy didn't blink. He stared at the man he believed to be his father. The man about to run away and leave him to his death.

"I'll do it," Victor said.

· Chapter 56 ·

Leeson's expression didn't change. It didn't change because there were only two answers to the dilemma he had posed, and Kooi or Victor or any sane person would never choose immediate death for himself and his family if there was even the slightest possibility of avoiding it. Leeson ruffled Peter's hair.

"You see," he said to the boy, "your father does love you. My father loved me too. It's a good feeling, isn't it?"

Peter didn't blink. Victor found it hard to hold his gaze for any length of time.

Hart faced Victor. "This is how it's going to work, Dutch: You'll leave shortly, after you've changed into some more suitable attire. Francesca, Coughlin, and I will accompany you. The embassy is a fifteen-minute drive from here. We'll drop you and Francesca off to go to the reception. She'll be your date, but think of her as a chaperone. Me and Coughlin are going to be running the show from an apartment that overlooks the terrace where the ambassador will make a speech. That's the one time we know for certain where Prudnikov is going to be. The speech is due to take place at twenty-one hundred hours, but you'll need to be in the party an hour before that to get security used to your presence and forget about you. Turn up ten minutes before the speech and blow yourself up and too many awkward questions are going to be asked in the aftermath. Can't have that, can we? We're going to keep the comms old-school to avoid detection. Francesca will text updates to me every fifteen minutes to let us know you're behaving yourself. If anything stops her from sending a text or you're not on that balcony when you should be, then bad things are going to happen to Lucille and Peter. From the apartment we'll be able to guide you into range of Prudnikov and we'll be able to confirm the op's success after you push the button. Simple."

"You've thought of everything," Victor said.

"Do you understand, Mr. Kooi?" Leeson asked.

"Perfectly."

"What's my role?" Dietrich asked.

Leeson smiled. "Think of yourself as the motivation, Mr. Dietrich. You'll remain here with me so that you can butcher Kooi's wife and child if he does not fully comply. Is that okay with you?"

"Nothing would make me happier."

"Remember when I told you I needed Mr. Dietrich because he had no compunction, Mr. Kooi? Well, this is what I was talking about. Do you believe he will carve your brood into little chunks should I command it?"

Victor glanced at Dietrich's grinning face. "Yes."

"Tremendous," Leeson said. "Then we can dispense

with any unpleasant demonstrations to prove we mean what we say."

Dietrich looked disappointed.

"We're all set," Hart said.

"Excellent." Leeson looked at his gold watch. "I'm getting excited now."

"I need more time," Victor said.

"Why?"

"To make sure I do it right. To make sure the job is successful."

"He's stalling," Hart said.

"He can try to stall all he wants," Leeson added. "But we have a schedule to keep and if we're late for any reason his family die. You were hired in part because you are a competent professional, so if there is a problem that we have not foreseen, you will have to find a solution. It's up to you to make sure this comes off perfectly."

"It'll never work," Victor said. "You must know that."

"There's no reason for it not to. Your role is a simple one. All you have to do is approach the target and use the phone."

"The Russians won't comply with the demands. I may kill Prudnikov, but the Chechens will not succeed."

"Why don't you let me worry about that, Mr. Kooi? You worry about your family."

"But why all this for something that cannot possibly work?"

"Why should I care if this works or not? My client is paying for the death of comrade Prudnikov. Which will be achieved if you do your part and save your family. I don't care about these idiots and their ideals. Whether their objective after the fact is achieved or not is immaterial to me and inconsequential to yourself. They'll all be killed when the embassy is eventually breached, just as you said would happen. Or, who knows? Maybe it will work and they'll get what they want. Then perhaps I'll start a side business in professional terrorism. Could be the next big-growth industry. Why have fanatics blinded by cause of religion when you can have experts?" He smiled to himself. "Maybe that will be my slogan. But I suggest you concentrate on your specific role in proceedings. You can't afford to be distracted."

"There can be no greater distraction than having my family threatened with death."

Leeson smirked. "Call it incentive, then. Now let's get you dressed and ready. You'll be pleased to know I have an excellent tuxedo for you to wear. You want to look smart when you meet your maker, do you not?"

• • •

Leeson was right. The vest was Victor's size. It fit exactly as it should. That didn't surprise Victor. They knew his sizes because they had taken his clothes when he'd first arrived at the farmhouse. That had been a smart deception. It was reasonable and predictable that Leeson would be cautious and would seek to ensure that there were no weapons or recording devices on Victor's person. Victor hadn't anticipated that Leeson would want his clothes for any other reason. Jaeger had done a fine job spreading out the plastic explosives to make the vest as thin as possible and the weight distribution as even as it could be. Hook and eye straps secured it in place.

Leeson was right about the tux too. It was an expensive, high-quality outfit. The jacket and shirt were a size too big, but that was to accommodate the vest beneath. Victor dressed in the antechamber of the old mill, watched by his team.

"You plug the phone in like this," Hart said when Victor had finished dressing.

Victor nodded.

"You can't tell he's wearing it." Dietrich smirked. "You're the best-dressed suicide bomber in history."

Francesca entered the room. She carried a small serving tray on which rested a glass of water. Next to the water stood a small plastic bottle of prescription drugs. Next to the bottle sat a small white capsule.

"What's this?" Victor asked.

"It's a sedative," Hart explained. "Anxiety medication. It'll keep your heart rate low and ensure that you stay relaxed. You won't be scared. You'll be quite content, in fact. If you go into that embassy sweating and panicking, security is going to be onto you long before you get within kill range. We know you're the ice man, but this will help you keep extra cool. You'll probably feel a little dehydrated and your throat will be dry. There won't be any lasting damage. Not that that will matter, of course."

"Comforting to know."

"An added benefit is that it will make you pliable and suggestible. Which you should be glad about. If you get scared and try to back out at the last minute, you'll get your wife and child killed, and you don't want that, do you?"

"I don't need the drug."

"I'm guessing there are a lot of things about this that you don't need, but need and necessity are two different things in this case. Take the capsule."

"Do I seem like the kind of man who is going to panic?"

"No, but we've come too far to start taking risks."

"I'm not taking it. I need a clear head for this."

"You don't. Francesca will put you in position. You'll be told when you're in range. You just need to be able to push a button."

"I'm not taking it," Victor said again.

"Then Dietrich is going to get his knife wet early. What should he cut off first?"

"Just take it," Coughlin said. "For your family's sake."

Victor took the pill from the tray with the thumb and index finger of his right hand. He put it in his mouth and used the same hand to pick up the glass of water. He brought it to his lips and took a drink. He swallowed.

"That wasn't so hard, was it?" Hart asked.

Victor placed the glass back down on the tray. He cleared his throat.

"He didn't swallow it," Francesca said. "It's still in his mouth."

"He's not going to be that stupid. Are you, Kooi?"

Victor didn't answer. His lips remained closed.

Francesca was insistent. "I'm telling you it's still in there."

"Check his mouth," Leeson said.

Hart approached Victor, who backed off a step. Leeson motioned to Dietrich, who moved behind Victor.

"Hold still, compadre," Hart said.

He used one hand to grip Victor's jaw and pull open his mouth. Victor didn't resist. Hart peered inside.

"Lift your tongue up."

Victor did.

"He's clean," Hart said. "He's swallowed it."

"You heard him cough," Francesca said. "He could have brought it back up."

"There's no capsule in his mouth," Hart said.

"Make him take another one."

Hart shook his head. "One is more than enough for someone his size. He takes two and he'll barely be able to walk. He's taken it. He's not going to risk the lives of his loved ones for the sake of a little pill."

"Correct," Victor said.

"It won't take long to get into your system," Hart said. "And it won't last long either, but that doesn't make too much difference to you. Just don't drink any alcohol with it."

"Now that that's out of the way," Leeson said, "I think we're good to go."

· Chapter 57 ·

The embassy stood on Via Gaeta in central Rome, on the north side of the narrow street. It was impossible to miss with its imposing perimeter wall and fence and the flag of the Russian Federation that rippled in the breeze. The surrounding wall rose almost two meters in height and the steel fence that topped it added another three. Barbed spikes the shape of arrowheads further secured the fence, and metal sheeting ran along the rear of the posts to block the gaps between them. A pale gray paint coated the entire arrangement and provided a stark contrast both to the building guarded by the barrier and to its neighbors. Antennae and satellite dishes bristled on the roof. Lights sunk into the grounds uplit the embassy at regular intervals, creating deep shadows between the russet bricks of its facade and glowing bright off the Tuscan columns that flanked the entranceway and supported the balcony above.

Toward the east end of the building's southern facade,

the main entrance faced Via Gaeta from behind the exterior gate with a narrow stretch of grounds between the two. Vehicles had access to the compound from larger gates in the western and eastern perimeter fences. The fence to the north of the embassy was heightened by an additional three meters to secure the complex from the neighboring property. The front gate was open and manned on the outside by two Italian police officers who seemed happy enough with the unchallenging role of providing embassy security—or at least the appearance of security, because the embassy had its own Russian guards for protection. Victor knew they wouldn't be as carefree as the Italians on the pavement, who ignored him to appraise Francesca at his side.

The two officers smiled and waved them through. The grounds ran the length of the building's front, five meters wide at its greatest point, then expanded out on the western side and in the rear. Tall trees and plants dotted the perfectly maintained lawn. A terrace protruded from the west wall and overlooked the embassy garden.

A couple were in the process of being processed when he stepped inside with Francesca. Two well-dressed embassy security staff performed efficient simultaneous checks, one tracing the contours of each visitor with a metal-detecting wand while the other examined the invitations and compared the names with those on the guest list.

"Keep thinking of your family," Francesca whispered, looking at the security guards, "and don't do anything to encourage them to search you. Okay?"

Victor neglected to respond. He desired to be

searched even less than Francesca wanted him to be. Being discovered to be wearing a suicide bomber's vest beneath his tuxedo wasn't going to help him get out of this any more than it would Lucille and Peter.

"The vest won't set off the wand," Francesca whispered as they neared.

"Are you trying to convince me or yourself?"

She didn't answer because the guards had finished with the couple ahead and were turning their way. On the far side of the entrance hall, two attendants took coats from the guests and hung them on a wheeled hanger, giving them tickets in return.

The guard with the guest list said, "Good evening. May I see your invitations, please?"

"Of course," Francesca said, and opened her clutch bag to hand the man the square of card.

"Sir," the second guard said to Victor, and gestured for him to raise his arms.

Francesca was watching while the guard examined the invitation and searched for the name on the guest list. She was nervous, but she hid the fact well with a little smile that feigned amusement at the novelty of the wand. There was tension in the skin around her eyes as her gaze flicked between Victor's own for signs of rebellion and the wand that passed over, then under his arms, along his flanks, down the outsides, then the insides of his legs, and over his chest, stomach, and back. It crackled and beeped quietly as it detected the zip of his flies, his belt buckle, cuff links, phone, and watch. The ceramic ball bearings embedded in the explosives gave no reading.

Francesca couldn't stop herself sighing in relief when

the wand moved from Victor to her, but she was quick to disguise the sound with a chuckle.

"It's quite exciting," she said to the guard.

He nodded, polite and placatory.

The one with the guest list said, "Please head in that direction," and held out a hand toward a wide corridor.

"Enjoy the party," the one with the wand added.

Francesca smiled. "I've no doubt we will."

"It'll be a blast," Victor said.

She shot him a look, but controlled her expression. They walked past the two attendants waiting to collect guests' coats and then side by side through the entrance hall and into the corridor as directed. Behind them, other guests arrived and the guards repeated their checks, to the curiosity of those not used to such security and the sighs of those who were.

Francesca gestured for him to plug in the mobile phone detonator and watched as he did while shielding him from any possible onlookers. She then removed her phone from her purse to message Hart. She was careful to ensure that Victor couldn't see the screen, but from the movement of her thumbs he saw she typed out a single word. She waited for Hart's confirmation and put the phone away.

"Next code is due in twelve minutes."

Victor stopped and faced her. "It's not too late to put a stop to this."

"And why would I want to do that?"

"Because you don't want to be responsible for potentially dozens of people being killed by an explosion."

"But it's not me who will be responsible. You're the one who will kill them."

"You're making that possible."

Over her shoulder he could see guests handing coats and other belongings to the attendants. A tall man with pure white hair received a ticket for his raincoat and his wife's fur and warned the attendant that he expected both back without a single speck of dust.

Francesca huffed. "Semantics, Felix. Now stop these pathetic stalling tactics and let's get this done. Lucille and Peter need you. Let's go."

A strip of red carpet ran along the center of the corridor, appearing orange where directly under the intermittent space light fixtures in the ceiling above. Along one wall hung photographic portraits of every prime minister and president of Russia to hold office since the end of communism. Freestanding signs stood at corridor junctions to guide visitors through the building. Thick red ropes barred restricted areas and funneled tonight's guests to where the reception was taking place. Victor saw no other security personnel or overt precautionary measures—the consular section of the embassy was located in a separate building across town, so this building had no need to obstruct the wanderings of the general public. Closed-circuit cameras covered every corridor, and the footage would no doubt be monitored around the clock. Some embassies were more akin to fortresses, but Russian and Italian relations were good and Rome was far from a trouble spot, so overall security here was light. It had to be; otherwise Victor would never have gotten through the door.

"It'll be a blast," Francesca echoed with raised eyebrows when they were well out of earshot.

"Just a little gallows humor," Victor replied.

"Maybe cut the jokes, Felix."

"You're the one who gave me a sedative."

"Don't get too relaxed, and keep your focus on what you need to do to keep Lucille and Peter away from Dietrich's blade."

"That's exactly what I am focused on."

"Good."

They followed the corridor around a corner and were greeted by a smiling embassy employee who explained where they needed to go. They followed his directions, acting as though they didn't already know the way from the maps and model, walking slowly enough to take in the brass busts of famous Russians that lined the hallway and the paintings of Red Square and the Kremlin that hung above them.

Victor took a deep breath and blinked a few times.

Francesca looked at him. "Drowsy?"

"A little."

"It shouldn't get any worse."

"Good, because neither of us is going to get what we want if I pass out in the middle of the reception."

"You won't. We know what we're doing."

"I want you to remember you said that when Hart comes for you."

She smirked. "He won't."

"Are you really that sure your act has worked on him?"

"And why wouldn't it? After all, it worked on you."

Victor remained silent. They walked along another corridor past doors marked with signs as toilets for men, women, and the disabled. They reached a staircase and began ascending. Francesca's dress was long and elegant and tight and limited her movements. Victor took the side next to the banister, so that should he decide to throw her down the stairs, she would have nothing to grab on to to slow or prevent her fall. She didn't notice.

"Bet you wish you hadn't loosened the seat belt in Budapest now, don't you?"

"The thought had crossed my mind."

She chuckled. "I'm glad we can still have fun together, Felix. I never had to pretend about that."

"Then you'd better make the most of it while you still can."

"It's a pity we never had a chance to get to know each other more intimately. I think we would have been good together. I don't suppose you fancy a quick detour somewhere a little more private?"

He simply looked at her.

She laughed. "I was just joking. Well, half joking. Quick doesn't work for me."

"You're insane, Francesca."

"I prefer the term liberated."

They reached the top of the second flight of stairs together. Victor took a series of breaths and swallowed heavily. The sound of music and chatter grew louder as they made their way down a short hallway. Ahead it opened out and dozens of mingling guests were visible.

"Can you do this?" Francesca asked.

"You almost sound concerned for me."

"Don't flatter yourself. I'm concerned about the job. This is worth a lot of money to me."

He faced her. "You needn't be concerned about getting paid. Everything is going to work out exactly as Hart and Leeson have planned it."

She pursed her lips but didn't respond.

The reception was held across three rooms on the west wing of the embassy's first floor and centered in a grand music room. It was a huge, high-ceilinged space almost absent of furniture aside from a few low couches interspersed along the room's exterior in between mirrors that rose five meters in height. The ceiling was plain except for the chandelier that hung from its center. It was as wide as it was tall and dazzling to look at. The polished floor and the mirrors bounced back the chandelier's light so that no other lighting was needed. Colorful arrangements of lilies, roses, and orchids bloomed from vases that stood before the mirrors. A potted dragon tree stood in each corner, towering above the guests.

At one end of the room a string quartet performed Schubert's *Rosamunde*. They were about halfway through the first movement: *Allegro ma non troppo*. At any other time Victor would have enjoyed the quartet's seemingly effortless excellence, but he was here to blow himself up. The guests were too busy chatting to pay attention to the music. There were approximately one hundred men and women spread throughout the room, almost all dressed in black evening wear barring the occasional white dinner jacket. Serving staff made their way through the crowd carrying trays of champagne and canapés. The ambassador's aide was doing a circuit, shaking hands with important guests, making quips, and chuckling with equal measure at those of others.

There were no obvious security personnel, but before he had stepped into the room Victor's gaze was hunting them down. They were dressed like guests and blended well among them, but were notable because they never stayed in one place for long, made no attempt to engage guests in conversation, and kept their hands free of food or drink. Within a minute Victor had counted five. All men, all between thirty and forty. And good. They weren't just guards. They would be from within the Operations Department of Directorate S of the SVR. They were based at the embassy for the protection of the ambassador and his subordinates. Tonight they would be especially alert because of the presence of their organization's head. Each wore a subtle earpiece with a thin cable trailing down from his ear under the lapel of his dinner jacket. They would be armed too, with handguns at their waists, because their dinner jackets were buttoned as part of their cover, rendering an underarm holster inaccessible.

Prudnikov wasn't in the music room. Neither was the ambassador. They were probably in the ambassador's private quarters, smoking cigars and drinking cognac and telling risqué jokes to avoid the odious schmoozing required of them. When they appeared, they would no doubt be accompanied by more security.

"What are you thinking?" Francesca asked.

"That I could use a drink."

"Me too." She gestured to a waiter. "But you can only have a few sips for show. Alcohol will greatly exacerbate the effects of the drug."

"Great," Victor said. "I'm going to blow myself up and I can't even appreciate a glass of champagne first."

"You're not here to enjoy yourself."

"But you are, aren't you, Francesca? You were entertained by Jaeger dying in front of you. At the time I thought you were shocked, but I didn't know you then. Now I know better. This is one big thrill to you, isn't it?"

"So what if it is? It's not every day a girl gets to be part of something so dramatic. Every country in the world will know what happened here tonight. I'll never forget I was part of it."

"Spoken like a true psychopath."

She smiled a little. "You say it like it's a bad thing."

The waiter arrived. "Champagne, madame?"

"I should say so." She took a flute for herself.

"Sir?" the waiter said to Victor.

He nodded and took one. "Thank you." When the waiter had gone, he raised his glass and said, "So, what shall we drink to? Well, sip in my case."

She thought for a moment. "Us," she said. "Let's drink to us and the special time we've shared. It's so much more romantic to know in less than an hour's time we'll never see each other again."

She clinked his glass.

Victor said, "Is that Prudnikov?"

Francesca's head turned to follow his gaze. "Where?"

"Over by the mirror."

He pointed with his champagne flute. "That one. Near the woman in the black dress."

Francesca craned her neck. "Every woman is wearing a black dress."

"At your one o'clock. By the flowers and the woman with the big hair."

She looked for a moment and then said, "No, that's not him." She turned back to face Victor. "Too tall."

Victor took a single sip of his drink.

Francesca did the same. "I do love champagne." She took a second sip and frowned a little. "But trust Russians to go for the cheap stuff. It's probably not even real champagne but some second-rate national equivalent." She said, in a bad accent, *"Champagnovski."*

"Shampanskoye," Victor corrected.

"You're so very knowledgeable, Felix," she said, half mocking. "I bet you have lots of hidden talents I couldn't possibly imagine."

"All sorts. I can do magic tricks."

She chuckled and sipped her drink. "How charming."

"I'll show you one later if you like."

"I think I'd really rather like that, but I'm afraid it's not going to be possible." She sighed, sympathetic and almost sad. "Oh, Felix, there isn't going to be a later for you, is there?"

Chapter 58

Coughlin used the back of his hand to wipe the sweat from above his eyebrows and his top lip. His jaw ached from clenching his teeth. His nostrils flared with each heavy breath. Next to him, Hart was focused, but relaxed and calm. Coughlin didn't like him. Coughlin was scared of him. They stood near the north-facing windows of the top-floor apartment. All the furniture had been pushed away from the windows to give them the best view. The only light came from streetlamps outside, and the room was dark. Coughlin was glad of that. Hart wouldn't be able to see how much he was sweating. He might be able to smell it, however.

Hart's phone chimed. He checked the screen, then thumbed a reply before calling Leeson. "Francesca's sent the second code. Everything's on schedule." He waited a moment as Leeson said something in return, then hung up. Coughlin said, "Couldn't Kooi just force her to tell him the code?"

Hart shook his head, somewhat contemptuously. "He's at an embassy reception surrounded by security personnel. How is he going to get the opportunity to *force* her?"

"I don't know. But that's only because I'm not the one who has to blow myself up. And if I was, I'd find a way to get that code, regardless of the consequences."

"What a fine father you'll make someday. Kooi cares about his family too much to back out. But if he was as selfish as you, it would do him no good. Every fifteen minutes Francesca will send a different code that only she and I know. Don't let appearances deceive you; there's nothing Kooi could do to her in there to make her reveal the code and he won't be as stupid as you would be in his place. Which is why you're here and he's in there. Amusing, isn't it?"

"What is?"

"How by virtue of your idiocy you will not only survive while Kooi dies, but you will profit from the demise of a more intelligent man. Natural selection in reverse."

Coughlin frowned.

Through the window they could see over the crossroads to the Russian embassy. Much of the building was screened by the trees in the grounds, but from their elevation they could see above those on the south side to where the terrace stood. A couple of dozen guests were visible there, drinking and chatting. Coughlin couldn't see them all because the trees to the west of the terrace partially blocked line of sight.

"It's not a problem," Hart said, reading Coughlin's thoughts with unnerving accuracy. "The ambassador likes to make his speeches from the south side."

"How do you know that?"

Hart didn't answer.

Coughlin asked, "What if the target is watching from the northern end, where we can't see?"

"That doesn't matter."

"But if we can't see him, how do we guide Kooi into position?"

"That doesn't matter either."

Coughlin sighed. "I could do my job a lot more effectively if you didn't withhold intel."

Hart faced him. "Your job at this time is to be a second pair of eyes for me. You just have to keep watching. Nothing more. That is within your capabilities, is it not?"

"Of course."

"Then be quiet and trust and know that all factors have been considered."

"Look, I just want the job to work so I can get paid, and I'm not going to stand here in silence if there's something I think has been overlooked. If it hasn't, great, but if you won't tell me anything, how can I know that?"

"Fine." Hart stared at him. "Speak now or forever hold your peace."

"Okay," Coughlin began, happy to have got Hart to back down, albeit temporarily. "If Prudnikov watches the speech from the north side and Kooi ends up over there and out of sight, how do we know he's going to stay in kill range if we can't see and Francesca has gone?"

"The moment Kooi steps outside, he will be in range. The blast radius will kill anyone within fifteen meters, not five. He'll wipe out each and every man and woman on the terrace. We're not going to guide him into range, just like we're not going to rely on him to detonate the bomb. As soon as he joins the crowd for the ambassador's speech, I'm going to call the phone and do it for him. Kooi didn't need to know that."

Coughlin nodded, understanding the logic and feeling better about his prospects of getting paid. Then he thought of something. "But Francesca is going to be there with him. When you say you'll blow the bomb as soon as Kooi joins the crowd, you're going to wait for Francesca to go back inside out of range, right?"

Hart looked at him as if he were an idiot. "How is it going to appear if Francesca is the only survivor of the blast?"

He thought for a moment. "Suspicious."

"Correct," Hart said. He sounded vaguely insulting. "We don't want anyone asking her difficult questions, now, do we?"

Coughlin nodded his agreement, but when Hart looked away, he frowned in the dark and thought about what had happened to Jaeger.

* * *

The crowd in the music room expanded as more guests funneled through the doorway. Victor watched every new arrival. Men entered adjusting bow ties and cummerbunds. Women checked themselves in the tall mirrors. Lots of hands were shaken and air kisses dispensed. Conversations in Italian and Russian and English provided a disharmonious clatter in Victor's ears. He was fluent in all three, and snippets of small talk and serious discussion competed with each other and drowned the beautiful music of the string quartet. They had reached the last movement of *Rosamunde*, Victor's favorite, and he wanted to make the most of it before it was time to go into action. Some things couldn't be rushed.

Francesca signaled to a waiter for another flute of champagne. "I'm starting to get a taste for this," she said, sipping from her new glass. She checked her watch. It was thin and silver. "Not long now until the speech. How are you feeling?"

He didn't answer.

"You are going to go through with this, aren't you?" she whispered, quietly enough that no one nearby would hear.

"Are you concerned I won't?"

"No," she said. "I'm concerned by what Dietrich will do to your wife and child if you're too scared to go through with it."

"Do I look scared?"

"No—that's the problem. You don't look like a man who is going to blow himself up."

"That's the point of the sedative, surely."

"Even so, I didn't think it would be this effective."

"I've said already that you don't have to worry about me. I'll do what I have to do."

"If you're thinking of trying something, you must realize it won't work. I'm not going to leave your side until you're out on that terrace with Prudnikov. Then Hart and Coughlin will be watching your every move. If you try to slip away they'll know. If that bomb around your waist doesn't go off and if Prudnikov is not in the blast radius, then they're going to know about it. All it takes is one call to Leeson and Dietrich is going to start carving chunks from Lucille and Peter."

"Do you honestly think I don't know all that?"

"And," she continued as if he had said nothing, "if you leave my sight for just a second before the speech begins, then I'll be calling it in before you can be out of the building. Even if you had a helicopter waiting for you outside, you couldn't get to the mill in time."

"Again, I know. You've done a very good job of orchestrating this."

"I think you'll find we've done an exceptional job. The plan, even if I do say so myself, is perfect."

"It's interesting you say that, because in my experience no plan is perfect. Everything goes wrong as soon as the bullets start flying."

"Quite the pessimist, aren't you?" She looked at her glass. "They certainly know how to make it strong in Russia. Let's go for a little wander, shall we?" She offered him her hand. He didn't take it.

The other two rooms designated for the reception were obvious from their open doors and the guests inside. More ropes and signs made those rooms that were off-limits just as obvious. Across the hallway was a study and library. One-half of the room contained an antique bureau and swivel chair. On the wall behind the desk hung framed photographs of previous Russian ambassadors, all serious-faced men with gray hair. Floor-to-ceiling bookcases filled with Russian and Italian texts occupied the other wall. Biographies of important Russians were turned face out on eye-level shelves. Guests perused the titles.

Francesca picked a random book from a shelf. "Are you a big reader?"

"What difference does it make?"

"I'm trying to get to know you."

"What's the point?"

She shrugged. "I want to remember you accurately."

He didn't respond and she flicked through the book, frowning at pages of indecipherable Cyrillic script. "I've never seen the point in books."

"They say you get out of reading what you put in."

She nodded as if in agreement, but also absently. She struggled to slide the book back into the gap it had left.

"Let's take a look at the terrace," Victor said. "I want to see where it's going to happen."

The last room holding the reception was bathed in a soft glow from gilded brass fixtures on the walls and ceiling that colored the marble columns and arches in warm hues of yellow and pink. A conference table and chairs dominated one-half of the room. The table and chairs were neoclassical antiques, as were the rest of the room's furnishings. A fireplace stood on the wall behind the head of the table, with a neat pile of logs in the hearth, but only for appearances. The chimney would have been blocked up long ago. Above the fireplace hung a snowy cityscape by Boris Kustodiev. Victor recognized the style and signature from the many hours he'd spent in Moscow galleries, performing countersurveillance while he enjoyed the artwork. He also recognized a painting by Ivan Aivazovsky on the opposite wall, which depicted naval battleships dueling during the Battle of Navarino. Beneath it stood a Mockba grand piano, white, polished to a mirror sheen. Victor felt the urge to play.

Guests stood in small groups around the table and piano. Three sets of French doors spaced along the opposite west wall were open. Cool night air seeped in from the terrace outside, where more guests drank and laughed and where the ambassador would make his speech in less than an hour's time.

Francesca put her glass down on the conference table. The glass was about forty percent full.

"Had enough?" Victor asked, a certain tone to his voice.

"Oh, you'd like me drunk and pliable, wouldn't you?"

"You're looking a little worse for the wear."

"After one and a half glasses of fake champagne? Keep dreaming, Felix. I know my limits."

"Then why are you holding on to that chair?"

She followed his gaze and snapped her hand away from where it had been gripping the chair's back.

"Let's get you some air," Victor said.

• • •

He guided her outside onto the terrace, pausing before the closest set of French doors to let her pass through first. The terrace ran the width of the building's west wall and overlooked the embassy's small but perfectly maintained garden. Lights mounted in the ground illuminated the rows of plants and flowers. A waist-high stone wall surrounded the terrace. Guests leaned against it and rested their glasses on top. Francesca found a spot at the south wall and leaned against it herself. Victor stood in front of her.

The foliage of tall trees shielded the terrace from the

buildings across the street, but Victor looked to the southwest, to where Hart and Coughlin watched from the five-story apartment building. They had a good view of the terrace from across the four-way junction, high enough to provide line of sight over the trees to the south of the terrace, which were not as tall as those to the west. There were no lights on the terrace itself, but those from the conference room provided the space with subtle illumination. Victor's eyes followed the width of darkness that lay between the glow spilling through the French doors and that of the lights in the garden.

Francesca's phone chimed and she checked the screen. "Hart has a visual on us."

Victor nodded in Hart's direction in way of reply. Hart could see him from the apartment window. He had a good view. But not a great one, because the broad foliage of the taller trees to the west blocked line of sight from the apartment to the northwest corner of the terrace and reduced visibility to the terrace's entire northern segment. A man standing inside the area of darkness between the two light sources would be almost invisible.

All Hart had to do was dial a number and the explosives strapped to Victor's torso would obliterate him from existence. All that would be left of him would be his severed head, blown clear of his body but left intact, eyes still open.

He looked back to Francesca to avoid Hart or Coughlin noticing where he was looking and perhaps deducing what he was thinking. She had the small of her back against the wall and her elbows resting on top of it. From the apartment across the street she would look relaxed, but Hart and Coughlin couldn't see her open mouth and her eyebrows raised with the effort of keeping her eyelids from drooping.

"*Shampanskoye,*" Victor said. "It's stronger than you would think."

"I'm fine," Francesca said after swallowing a couple of times.

"Let's have a look at the gardens," he suggested, and took her hands.

He stepped away and pulled with his arms to bring her away from the wall, and walked with her across the terrace to its northern half.

"I thought we were going to look at the garden," Francesca said, voice quiet, as Victor steered her away from the wall and toward the northernmost set of French doors.

"We need to get you some water, don't you think?"

"Yes. My throat is dry." She touched her neck.

"You said it would be."

"When . . . when did I?"

Victor didn't answer. He took her hand away from her neck and led her back into the conference room. They walked by the grand piano, Francesca trailing the fingers of her free hand across its surface, taking a circuitous route across the room. He kept one arm around her waist to help her walk and gave a knowing look to a tall man with white hair who noticed Francesca's half-closed eyes and vacant expression as they neared.

She stumbled into the man's much shorter wife, much to the wife's shock, and Victor was quick to get Francesca upright on her feet again while the man helped his wife recover.

"I'm so sorry about that," Victor said to both as he stepped away from them.

He headed to the room's exit with Francesca and into the hallway beyond. The string quartet had begun playing *Rosamunde* again. Victor had expected them to play a different piece, but perhaps *Rosamunde* was the ambassador's favorite.

As they passed the music room a man said, "Is everything all right?"

He was about six feet tall, with red hair cut short enough that his scalp was visible between the strands.

"Fine," Victor replied. "She's just had a little too much."

"I have not," Francesca interjected, words slurring.

"Anything I can do to help?" the man with red hair asked.

Victor shook his head. "Thanks, but she'll be okay."

The man nodded and Victor led Francesca away, wanting to glance back over his shoulder to see if the man was watching them, but not willing to risk it because he had seen him in the music room, circling the room with his hands free and not talking to anyone.

Francesca had trouble with the stairs and Victor kept a firm hold of her to make sure they descended without a problem.

"What's going on?" she said, voice barely more than a whisper.

He led her down the corridor at the bottom of the stairs to the men's room and pushed open the door. An overweight man with a thick mustache stood at the farthest urinal. He glanced over his shoulder.

"I'm sorry," Victor said. "She's going to be sick. You don't mind, do you?"

The man didn't break stream. He cast his gaze over Francesca and responded with an approving nod. He continued to stare at her while Victor took her into one of the cubicles. He toed down the toilet seat, sat Francesca on it, and closed and locked the cubicle door behind him.

"I—"

He put a finger against her lips and she stopped talking. He waited, hearing the overweight man zip up his fly and then leave without a visit to the sinks. Victor took his finger away.

"Am I drunk?" she asked.

"In a way. But you feel okay, don't you?"

"I feel great."

He fished Francesca's phone from her purse. She watched him, but didn't speak, her head periodically nodding forward before she set it back again. He scrolled through her sent messages. She had sent two messages to the same number. The first had been after they had passed security at seven thirty-three p.m. The second had been sent twelve minutes later at seven forty-five p.m. Victor and Francesca had arrived at the embassy at seven thirty p.m. in sight of Hart and Coughlin. The first message had been sent at the earliest opportunity, as the time it took to get through the security checks couldn't be predicted. The next had been sent at a specific time. Leeson had said there would be regular updates. So there would be another at eight p.m. and another fifteen minutes later and so on. Both of the messages Francesca had sent contained just a single word, different each time.

Each was followed by a message back from Hart soon afterward: *confirm*.

The clock on the phone gave the time as seven fifty-four p.m.

He adjusted Francesca's seating position and rested her head against the wall of the cubicle. She seemed happy enough like that and wasn't likely to fall off the toilet seat.

"I'm going to leave you here now," he explained, "but I'll be back soon. Okay?"

"Why?"

"Because the less people see of you, the better."

"Why?"

"Because you can barely walk. You've had a strong dose of flunitrazepam and you've made it worse by drinking alcohol with it. You just need to stay here and wait for me."

She frowned. "But the . . . the drug was for you, not me."

"Yes, but I did a magic trick. You wanted to see one, remember?"

She nodded. The frown disappeared. She looked confused. "Yes, but . . . ?"

"And it was a good trick. You didn't see me palm the capsule instead of swallowing it and you didn't see me empty the capsule into your drink, did you?"

"No."

"So it was a good trick, wasn't it?"

She smiled. "Yes."

"Now you can do a trick of your own and stay here for a few minutes, okay?"

"Okay."

The men's room door opened and Victor put a finger on Francesca's lips. She smiled. Two minutes later they were alone again. Victor reached up, gripped the top of the cubicle wall, and pulled himself up, hooking his left leg over and then his right. It was difficult to swivel his torso around because of the vest restricting his movement, but it wasn't enough to stop him. He dropped down on the other side.

"Just wait there," he said. "I'll be back soon. Don't make a sound. Okay?"

She didn't respond. Either she had passed out or she was obeying his request, but as long as she stayed quiet he didn't care which it was. He exited the bathroom and headed down the hallway past the busts and paintings. In the entrance hall he joined a short queue of new arrivals handing over their coats. When he reached the front he handed over the ticket belonging to the tall man with white hair whose pocket he had picked while he was distracted by Francesca stumbling—tripping—into his wife.

"Tan raincoat and fur," he said to the attendant.

The young man who took his ticket nodded and left to seek out the garments from wherever it was they stored them. It wouldn't be far. There would be a utility room or closet nearby. The embassy would throw enough parties to warrant the space, and the stature of the guests would ensure the room's proximity to the entrance hall. No one liked to wait. The rich and powerful wouldn't stand for it.

He returned in less than three minutes with the white-haired man's raincoat and his wife's fur. Victor took them, thanked the attendant, and returned to the men's room. It was empty. He hung the coats over the door of the cubicle, then hoisted himself over the cubicle wall. The vest slowed him down again, but not as much as the first time now he knew what to expect. Francesca still sat exactly as he had left her.

"Are you okay?" he asked.

Her eyes stared into his but she didn't answer.

He said, "You're allowed to speak now."

She smiled. "I'm fine. I feel good. Where did you go?"

"Francesca," Victor began, squatting down so he could look into her eyes because she couldn't keep her head upright. "It's nearly eight p.m. In one minute you need to send a message to Hart. An update, right?"

"Yes."

"What word do you need to send to let Hart know everything is okay?"

Her eyes were glassy, the whites bloodshot. "It's a secret."

"I know," Victor said. "It's a code word that only you and he know, right?"

"Yes."

"Can you tell me what it is, please?"

She stared at him. "It's a secret."

"Yes, but you need to tell me so I can send it to Hart. That is what you need to do, isn't it?"

"Yes."

"And you want to do your job properly, don't you?"

"Yes."

"So what's the code I need to send to Hart to let him know everything is okay?"

"I'm okay."

"That's good, Francesca. You need to tell me the code

now. We've only got a few seconds left to send it; otherwise you'll be late."

"I don't want to be late."

"I know."

"You're handsome."

"Thank you. Can you tell me the code now, please?"

"No."

"Please, Francesca, you really need to tell me the code so I can send it to Hart. You want to tell me the code, don't you?"

The clock in the corner of the phone's screen changed to eight p.m.

"No." She shook her head and reached for the phone. "I have to send it."

"Tell me instead. I'll do it for you."

"No," she said again, and stretched her fingers toward the phone. "You're not allowed to know. I have to send it."

He let her take the phone and watched as she fumbled with it, wondering how many seconds late Hart would accept before aborting the mission. She tapped the screen with a single finger, long delays between taps.

"Done," she said, and grinned.

"Press Send."

"Oh yes." She did. "Silly me."

Victor took the phone from her and stared at the screen. She'd sent the word *apple*. There was no way to know if this was the correct code or a random word. Maybe it was the right code but sent at the wrong time.

Five seconds passed. Then ten. Fifteen. The phone vibrated.

Confirm.

· Chapter 59 ·

Victor slipped Francesca's phone into one of his pockets.

"What are these?"

"It's cold outside, so I fetched you a coat. Stand up so you can put it on."

He helped her to her feet and into the fur.

"Is it real or faux?" she asked.

Victor unlocked and opened the cubicle door and slipped on the tan raincoat. "It's whichever you'd prefer."

"Good."

He raised her left wrist and unclasped her watch. She watched him but didn't comment. He pulled back her hair and wrapped it in a bun, using the watch to keep it in place. It wouldn't hold it for long, but he didn't need it to. She reached up to undo the watch.

"You're prettier like this," he said.

She smiled. Her arms dropped back to her sides.

"We need to go," he said.

"Okay," she said.

He knew he had about nine minutes before he needed to send the next update. As long as Francesca didn't pass out, that wouldn't be a problem. She was becoming more suggestible as time passed and the drug took hold of her consciousness. He was confident that the next time he asked her for the code she would give it to him without any delays.

She seemed to be standing on her own, but he kept hold of her hand and waist as he led her out of the men's room and into the corridor beyond. A man was there, as though he were just passing, but Victor knew he'd been waiting. The man was about six feet tall with very short red hair.

"Everything all right?" the man asked for the second time, in the same tone he'd used just outside the music room.

Victor nodded at him. "Fine, but I need to get her home."

The Russian stepped closer. His expression was even and his body language relaxed, but his eyes stared at Victor. "May I see your invitations, please?"

"They were checked when we arrived."

"And I'd like to check them again," the man said.

"I really don't have time for this. I have to get her to bed."

"Of course," the man agreed. He stepped closer. "But only after I've checked your invitations."

"Fine," Victor said. He rooted in Francesca's purse for the invitation and handed it to the Russian.

He examined the invitation, then said, "What are your

names, please?" Before Victor could answer, he added, "Let the lady answer."

"She's drunk."

"I'm not drunk," Francesca said. "I'm—"

"It's okay," Victor said. "The security guard would just like to know our names. He wants you to tell him. Why don't you tell him what he needs to know?"

"I'm Francesca."

"Surname?" the Russian asked.

"Leone."

"And who is the gentleman you're with?"

Say the name on the invitation, not the name you know me by, Victor willed. *Say George Hall.*

Francesca said, "He's Felix."

The Russian stared at Victor as he asked Francesca, "Felix what?"

"Kooi."

Victor didn't blink. Neither did the Russian.

"You need to come with me now, sir," the Russian said, right hand hovering near the right hip flap of his jacket. Victor recognized the way it hung slightly farther from the man's body than the left side did.

"I had a feeling you were going to say that."

The Russian's expression didn't change. He motioned for Victor to head along the corridor. Victor did.

"Where are we going?" Francesca said.

"For a little walk. Don't worry."

"Okay."

He walked slowly, in no rush to get to wherever the man with red hair was taking them. He heard the man's footsteps following a couple of meters behind. He knew the Russian would be watching him closely. He was an employee of the SVR, responsible for embassy security. He knew what he was doing.

Behind Victor, the man whispered something. His voice was too quiet for Victor to hear, but he knew he would be making a report of the incident. Whether that was just procedure or whether it meant there would be a welcoming committee waiting wherever they were heading, he didn't know. He did know that there wasn't time for this.

• • •

The Russian with the red hair unlocked a plain door with a key card and gestured for Victor to open it and step into the room beyond. He guided Francesca in first. The room was some kind of office. It was located on the ground floor along one of the roped-off corridors past which Victor had walked with Francesca earlier. Four unremarkable office desks were spaced throughout the room. Computer terminals, phones, in-and-out trays, and other paraphernalia sat on top of each desk. Filing cabinets and shelves units lined the walls. A watercooler stood in one corner. On one wall a roster had been scrawled onto a whiteboard with dry marker pens of various colors. It looked like a place that would be busy in the daytime with phone calls and typing and discussion. Now it was empty except for Francesca, Victor, and the Russian. Victor looked at each corner of the room, where the walls met the ceiling. No cameras.

Behind Victor the door clicked shut.

He stepped back and threw a backward right elbow

toward where he knew the Russian was standing, swivel-
ing one hundred and eighty degrees with the arc of the
blow to face his target and follow the elbow with a left
hook.

Delivered one after the other in quick succession, the
blows should have been enough to knock the Russian
out, or at the very least take him to the floor, but the vest
restricted and slowed Victor's movements and his opponent was a fully trained and experienced employee of the
SVR. He saw the attack coming and slipped out of range,
the handgun at his belt already out of the quick-draw
holster and angling up when Victor completed the turn.

Victor brought his left fist down on top of the gun's
barrel, the downward force stronger than the upward
momentum of the Russian's arm, knocking the gun to
waist level, barrel pointed at the floor. He stepped inside
the Russian's reach, ripped away the thin cable that ran
down the side of the Russian's neck and connected an
earpiece to a radio transmitter and throat mike, and delivered a short head butt. It struck too high to break the
man's nose because the Russian pulled back from it, but
Victor used his enemy's resulting lack of balance to sweep
his load-bearing leg from under him while grabbing hold
of the gun and wrist.

The Russian hit the floor and the gun came out of his
hand, but before Victor could turn it around and get his
finger inside the trigger guard, the prone Russian swiveled around on his back, kicking Victor on the side of his
knee, then scissoring Victor's leg with both of his own
and heaving his foot from the floor.

Victor went down, landing on his shoulder blades and

rolling backward over his head, abandoning the gun because as he came back to his feet the Russian was upon him and he needed both hands to defend himself against the assault. Victor blocked the first punch and slipped the second, responding with one of his own. The Russian stepped inside it and grabbed the arm, turning Victor and driving him into the front of a filing cabinet. He got his elbow up in time to take the collision, denting the sheet steel front.

He kicked backward with the edge of his heel, striking the Russian on his shin, causing him to grunt and release the hold on his arm. Victor spun around, immediately punching, then countering as his attack was dodged and the Russian responded with one of his own—an elbow that Victor caught, straightening the arm into a lock. The Russian twisted out of it and stamped on Victor's foot, stepping away to create enough room for a knee that collided with Victor's stomach and would have knocked the air from his lungs had the suicide vest not cushioned the blow. There was no danger of it going off prematurely. The plastic explosives could be detonated only with an electric current supplied by the mobile phone detonator.

A shuffle backward meant the Russian's follow-up punch fell short of its intended target, Victor's nose, and a ducking sidestep caused the next attack to sail over his head, the Russian stretching off balance in an attempt to hit his mark. Victor darted under the outstretched arm to land an uppercut on his enemy's ribs and another above the liver. The Russian sagged, but didn't slow or hesitate. He slammed his elbow back and down and caught Victor on the shoulder. Then he tried another knee, but Victor wrapped an arm under the knee as it came up, grabbed his opponent's jacket, lifted him off the floor, and drove him backward until he collided with a table, then slammed him down onto it.

The monitor and keyboard were knocked away. The monitor housing cracked on the floor. The Russian crushed the plastic in-and-out beneath him. He grabbed the phone and slammed it into the side of Victor's head. Victor recoiled, bringing up a forearm to knock away the phone as the Russian threw it at him to create enough time for him to roll off the table and get back to his feet.

Victor exploited the distance between them to slip off the tan raincoat. On the other side of the table, the Russian took off his dinner jacket. Both garments dropped to the floor at the same time.

The Russian made to circle around the table, but Victor lifted his right leg and planted a front kick on the table, knocking it into his opponent. He couldn't generate enough force to cause any injury, but the blow surprised the Russian and he didn't recover fast enough to block the keyboard that Victor swept up from the tabletop and swung double-handed into his face.

The keyboard was well made, and though it cracked and warped on impact, its structure held and most of the force was transferred to the Russian. He staggered backward. Victor dropped the keyboard, charged, dipped low, and wrapped his left arm around the Russian's waist as he used his right behind the knee to lift the leg. His forward momentum tipped the Russian off balance and he hit the floor hard, the back of his head thumping against the thin carpet.

Victor went down with him, but on top. Dazed but still fighting back, the Russian didn't have the strength to stop Victor turning him over and snaking his arm underneath his jaw, the Russian's throat in the pit of Victor's elbow. He squeezed with his arm as he pushed the knuckle of his right thumb into the side of the man's neck at a downward forty-five-degree angle, his left hand closed over the right to increase the pressure. The Russian went slack in less than three seconds.

Another thirty seconds would ensure that the Russian never recovered, but Victor didn't want to kill him. He was no longer a threat, and if Victor wasn't out of the embassy by the time the man woke up, then he was never going to get away.

He found the gun on the floor near the office door and scooped it up. It was a Russian-made Yarygin MP-443 pistol. He checked the load: seventeen 9 mm rounds in the magazine. He tucked it into the front of his waistband. He didn't plan to use it, but it was of infinitely more use in his possession than left on the floor.

Francesca still stood in the same spot as he had left her. She watched him, but her eyes were focused on the middle distance. He retrieved the raincoat and put it back on. He took Francesca's hand. Her palm was cool and clammy.

"It's time to go."

"Okay."

A sound outside the door gave Victor a second's warning and he snapped up the Yarygin so that when the door opened the two SVR security guys walked straight into the line of fire. They were dressed in tuxedos like the unconscious man with red hair. Victor recognized one from the music room, but not the second. He must have been patrolling elsewhere.

"Hands above your shoulders." They did as instructed. "You on the left, kick the door closed behind you. Don't turn around." He complied. "Now, with your left hand and using just your thumb and forefinger, take the gun from your colleague's belt holster and drop it at your feet." He struggled to remove the pistol from the holster, but managed it after a few seconds. It thunked on the carpet. "Get your hand back in the air and kick the gun my way." It skidded across the floor and stopped half a meter from Victor's toes. He stepped forward and kicked it to the other side of the room. "You on the right, do exactly the same as your friend."

When the second gun had joined the first at the far end of the office, Victor approached his two captives. Stopping a meter before them, he stared hard into the eyes of the one on the right, then pistol-whipped the man on the left on the jaw while he was focused on what Victor might do to his colleague, and backhanded the gun into the temple of man to his right before he could react to the surprise attack.

They both dropped, unconscious.

He tore away their radios and crushed them beneath his heel, one after the other. Then he grabbed Francesca's hand and led her out of the door.

· Chapter 60 ·

The corridor outside the office was quiet and empty. Victor led Francesca down it and pulled aside the temporary rope barrier so they could pass into the hallway that led to the foyer. He didn't know how long he had until the three SVR guys came round, but he didn't need long to get out of the embassy. How far he would get outside before the alarm was raised was unknown. He would have a few minutes, maybe five or six. Whether that was enough time was out of his hands. He could have killed the three men to ensure a decent head start, but he didn't want to give the SVR any further incentive to come after him. And the three had only been doing their job.

He walked at a casual pace down the hallway, Francesca at his side, even though his instincts told him to run. But the precious few seconds gained by hurrying now would be lost tenfold if the alarm was raised before it needed to be. Up ahead he saw the two cloakroom attendants chatting; all the guests had arrived by now and no one was likely to leave before the speech. The two guards at the front door were similarly without anything to do, but they weren't chatting.

They were alert as they had been before. He couldn't determine whether there was an additional layer to that alertness created by the SVR guy with the red hair putting out a notification that he had a suspicious individual in custody. That notification might have gone to all security personnel, or just to the other undercover SVR operatives at the embassy. These guys were regular security guards. Competent, because they were stationed at the front door of the Russian embassy, but not trained to the same level as SVR employees and perhaps not privy to the same information.

Both guards looked Victor's way. Until the three unconscious operatives woke up, they couldn't have much to go on. Maybe they had his description or were reacting to everyone with caution and suspicion until they were given the all-clear. Alternatively, they knew nothing and were just looking at Francesca.

He walked toward them. He didn't have a lot of choice. To divert would only confirm what they already knew or create suspicion if there was none, and trying to escape from the compound another way would burn time he didn't have.

Francesca walked alongside him, holding his hand, her heels clacking on the mosaic floor. At five meters he saw that there was no tension in the guards' faces. Their eyes moved back and forth between Victor and Francesca. All one of them had to do was ask her a question and they would know she was more than just drunk. She was the kind of woman men didn't soon forget. Would they remember she had entered without the fur coat? He'd find out soon enough.

The two guards said nothing as Victor and Francesca approached and nothing as they passed between the pair and out of the embassy. Whatever information the red-haired Russian had passed on through his lapel mike had not reached these two or they believed the situation was under control elsewhere and there was no reason to stop anyone leaving.

Hart and Coughlin had line of sight from the apartment windows to the front of the embassy, but at an acute angle, and the distance was about sixty meters. If their focus was on the terrace, they might not even see Victor and Francesca leave. But he couldn't rely on that, which was why he had tied Francesca's hair back and why they both wore coats. It should be enough to fool the naked eye, though it wouldn't be enough to fool Hart and Coughlin if they turned their binoculars this way. Then the phone attached to the vest would no doubt receive a call and chunks of Victor and Francesca would be found thirty meters down the street. But there was no reason they would be watching the front entrance at this point in time. Outside the building's main entrance, the lights illuminating the front facade were bright enough to identify Victor and Francesca, but the high-perimeter fence and the trees in the grounds provided concealment from the apartment's windows. That would change once they were out on the street, but then they would be out of the glare of the uplights.

The Italian police officers outside the compound gate smiled and nodded as Victor and Francesca walked between them, exchanging amused looks with one another regarding Francesca's inebriation.

Victor turned left—east—away from where Coughlin and Hart waited in the apartment. Crossing the street first would have restricted their view, but there were no turnings off Via Gaeta on the south side of the street going east. Victor would need to lead Francesca another forty meters until they reached the end of the block and the wide boulevard beyond. Even at a difficult angle, forty meters was too long a walk and gave Coughlin and Hart too much time to identify Victor and Francesca from the rear—maybe from the shape of her legs or their respective heights. If that forty-meter walk had been the only means of escape from the street, Victor would have had her take off her shoes before stepping out onto the street, but a side street ran north alongside the embassy compound.

He led Francesca into it. It was narrow and dark. Maybe Coughlin or Hart had seen the tall, white-haired man and his wife arrive earlier. There was a good chance they hadn't arrived via the side street, but leaving a different way wasn't necessarily suspicious. There was no pavement and cars stood alongside the embassy building to Victor's left.

"Where are we going?" Francesca asked. She spoke quietly, with difficulty.

"Just to get some fresh air."

There was a set of car keys in a pocket of the tan raincoat, but they were useless to Victor. He had no way of knowing where the corresponding vehicle was parked and there was no time to search for it.

A gate wide enough for vehicles to pass through when open stood along the compound's east edge. In front of it, a well-dressed woman stood hurriedly smoking a cigarette, illuminated by lights from the embassy windows above. She wore a black gown of some flowing light material with a slit down one leg, and a shawl around her shoulders. An embassy employee, because a guest wouldn't have had access through the side gate. She glanced in the direction of Victor and Francesca, because the alley was empty and dark and no one alone in such an environment was likely to ignore someone who joined them. She kept looking for a moment, recognizing from their clothes that Victor and Francesca were guests of the reception and curious that they should be leaving so early. Not ideal—when news of what had happened to the security personnel spread, the woman would remember this—but not a disaster because by heading down this side street Victor wasn't giving away the rest of the route he intended to take.

As he walked closer he saw the problem. The woman tossed her cigarette away and turned in his direction. She was slim but toned. Her hair was tied back but when loose would be no longer than jaw length. The slit in the dress let him see her shoes: elegant but practical, with a small heel. The dim light coming through the embassy's windows disguised much of her features but caught the thin cable running down the length of her neck and disappearing under her shawl.

Her weapon had been in a purse hanging from her left

shoulder, and it was out before he could draw his own, because she'd identified him before he had her. She held it steady in a two-handed grip, aiming at his center mass.

"Put your hands against the wall."

"No."

"Do it or I'll shoot."

Victor shook his head and carried on walking toward her, leaving Francesca behind. "No, you won't. You're not in the embassy compound. You're on Italian soil now. Two meters to your right is Russia, but this ground right here is Italy. You're not part of the diplomatic staff; you're SVR. You have no diplomatic immunity. I am unarmed. You're not at risk. If you shoot me your life is over."

She stepped toward him. Her expression was aggressive. *"Hands against the wall."*

He began unbuttoning his shirt as he approached her. She was three meters away. "I'm not going to put my hands against the wall."

"I'll shoot."

"We've already established you won't." Two meters. "Besides, if you do shoot me you'll kill yourself as well." He opened up his shirt to show what lay beneath it.

He had no doubt she would know that plastic explosives would not be set off by a bullet's impact, but that didn't mean she could stop the surprise and panic she felt at seeing a suicide bomber vest so close before her.

Victor stepped forward fast while she was distracted. Using his left palm to knock the barrel of the gun to his right as his torso twisted out of the line of fire, he grabbed her wrist as he stepped left and wrenched the forearm down, making her double over, gun pointing at the ground, his one arm against her two but his weight and position defeating her off-balance strength. He used his free right hand to push up the gun barrel with the web between thumb and forefinger, stretching back her hands and weakening her grip before easily pulling the weapon away.

She realized she was disarmed an instant before the gun was in his possession and was using her left hand—the one not in his grip—to thumb her radio.

He hit her with a downward open-palmed blow to the jaw before she had a chance to speak or yell. Her head snapped back and she tipped backward and dropped. He caught her on the way down to stop her head smacking against the hard ground and eased her into a prone position. He checked her pulse to be sure he hadn't killed her with the strike, but her blood was pumping fast and hard beneath his fingertips.

"We need to hurry," Victor said to Francesca as he reached down and tugged off her stilettos, one then the other.

"Okay."

She couldn't run, but she could hustle. They hurried along the side street, past cars parked tight against the wall to the left. He took her east down the first alley he came to. He didn't know how many SVR operatives were stationed at the embassy, and how many of those were on duty tonight, but four currently down would heavily deplete the numbers available to respond when the alarm was raised, especially when the ambassador, embassy staff, guests, and the head of the SVR needed to be protected.

They wouldn't come charging out after him. They would make sure there was no threat—discreetly, to avoid ruining the ambassador's reception—and let the Rome police hunt for him. By the time the first patrol car was in the area, Victor would be long gone. The party would continue as normal and Coughlin and Hart would have no reason to suspect the truth.

Francesca vomited.

Victor didn't allow her to stop, and she retched and coughed and wiped her mouth with the back of her hand while they walked fast to the end of the alley. It opened out alongside a four-lane boulevard. He turned south, stretching his neck in an attempt to spot a taxi with its light on. Hailing a passing cab wouldn't be easy, as in Rome they mostly operated from stands or via calls, and he wasn't relying on seeing a free one and expecting it to stop for them. There were no cabs in sight and he turned west along the street that ran parallel to Via Gaeta when he was one block south of it.

He found the Toyota minivan a couple of minutes later, parked alongside the curb. An anonymous and forgettable vehicle. It was a risk coming back to it with Hart and Coughlin so close by, but he was running out of time.

He took out Francesca's phone and asked, "What's the next code?"

"Taxi."

"Is that the code or do you want to find a taxi?"

She frowned. "The code, silly."

He thumbed a message and sent it to Hart's number. Seven seconds later: *Confirm.*

He asked, "What's the next code?"

"It's too early to send it."

"I know, but if you tell me now it doesn't matter if you then forget it. Okay?"

She nodded. "Mountain."

If there was another code after that, then Victor didn't need to know it because he was due on the terrace fifteen minutes later. No further code would convince Hart that Victor was somewhere he wasn't.

He used Francesca's keys to unlock the vehicle. He took the fur coat from her and placed it in the back of the Toyota along with the tan raincoat, then helped her into the passenger seat and climbed behind the wheel.

He started the engine and headed toward the mill.

· Chapter 61 ·

Victor thumbed Muir's number into Francesca's phone and hit DIAL. She sat passed out in the passenger seat next to him. He switched the phone to speaker and continued south. It had taken about twelve minutes to reach the embassy from the mill when Coughlin drove. Victor knew he could get there in half that time, but he couldn't afford to come to the attention of the police. He couldn't do what he needed to with a patrol car chasing him through Rome's narrow streets. It was eight sixteen p.m. He had twenty-nine minutes before he was due on the balcony. If he could reach the mill in ten instead of twelve, that left him nineteen minutes before Hart knew the job was over and Dietrich was given the order to kill Lucille and Peter. Not long, but he was out of options.

Muir answered on the fifth ring. She said, "Janice Muir speaking."

"It's me. I'm in Rome. The job is a setup. Leeson has

Kooi's family captive. He's going to have them killed in less than twenty minutes."

Muir took a breath, but her voice stayed even. She had been in stressful situations before. She wasn't about to panic now. "Did you say Kooi has a family?"

"Yes. A wife and a young boy. He hid them away in Andorra in an attempt to protect them. And he did a good job too, if you didn't know they existed. Leeson built up a profile on Kooi through the contracts he had him do. A guy called Hart kidnapped them and brought them to Rome so they could be used to convince Kooi to go through with the job."

"What kind of job requires that kind of persuasion?"

"The kind you don't walk away from. I'm wearing a suicide bomber's vest with seven kilos of plastic explosives and the same weight of ceramic shards." He explained the plan to assassinate the head of the SVR inside the Russian embassy and disguise it as terrorism. "I'm out of the embassy now and on the road. I had to take out a few guards, but they'll live. Leeson and Hart are going to know that I'm gone in eighteen minutes' time. At that point, Dietrich is going to kill Lucille and Peter."

"Holy shit," Muir breathed. "You're wearing the vest right *now*?"

"Yes."

"What the hell are you thinking? Get out of it and get clear."

"I can't. Once Hart realizes I'm not at the embassy, they'll detonate it. I'm in the middle of Rome. There's civilians everywhere. Besides, I need it."

"What for?" When he didn't answer, she said, "Don't tell me you're going after Kooi's family. You don't need to. Just tell me where they're being held."

Victor thought for a moment, then said, "I can't tell you that."

"What? Why not? I don't understand."

"If I tell you, you'll pass it on to the Italians."

"You're damn right I will," Muir said. "This has gone way too far now. We're talking about a terrorist threat on Italian soil and kidnapped civilians. They need to know right this second what they're dealing with if they're going to have any chance of dealing with it."

"That's why I can't tell you. Lucille and Peter have less than half an hour left to live. That's no way near enough time for a hostage rescue team to be mobilized and a plan to be formulated. Let alone put into action. They'll be up against six heavily armed gunmen. Either the Italians rush in and get massacred or there'll be a siege. In either scenario, Lucille and Peter don't survive."

Muir didn't respond for a moment. Victor pictured her mouthing and gesturing to colleagues before she said, "Listen to me. You need to get yourself out of the line of fire. You've done your job. It's time to stand down. We need to turn this over to the Italians. You're in their country. The threat is against them. Leeson is not going to have Lucille and Peter killed once he knows this is over. They're his only leverage."

"He will. He'll remove every link between the job and him. I'm close to where they're being held. I've been inside once already. I know the layout. I know the opposition. Leeson thinks I'm still at the embassy. By the time anyone realizes I'm not, Lucille and Peter will be safe."

"That's crazy," Muir said again. "It isn't a plan and you know it isn't. Tell me where they are. The cops can be there in minutes. The mission is over, so we turn the intel over to our allies and step away. That's an order."

"I told you at the start of this that if I accepted, you're not my boss. You supply me with the information and I decide what to do with it. And in this case, you don't have any information for me."

She changed tack. "It's not your fault they're in there. They're not your responsibility."

Victor remained silent.

"They're not," Muir repeated. "It's Kooi's fault they're under threat. It's Leeson's. It's not yours."

"Had I not agreed to meet with Leeson and take this job, he would never have taken them. He had them kidnapped because I said yes. He wouldn't have needed them had I declined."

"Then it's my fault. I hired you. If I hadn't, then they would be okay. It's my fault, not yours."

"Then what are you going to do about it?"

"Tell the Italians. Let them—"

"Not good enough," Victor said. "If I don't do this, they're dead."

"That's not your fault. Listen to me. Please. Don't do this. It's suicide."

"I'll call you when it's done."

"Wait," Muir pleaded.

Victor hung up.

• • •

Lucille was scared. She could hear nothing. Noises didn't frighten her. Silence did. The world was loud and chaotic, and when humans were making no noise, trouble filled the void left behind. She sat in the corner of the underground room that was her prison. Peter slept in her lap. He was scared as she was, but he tried not to show it. He didn't want her to worry about him. She loved him so much. He was so brave.

She tried to make sense of what was happening, but nothing made any sense. This was some terrible mistake. Some bizarre misunderstanding. She was just a sous chef. Her ex-husband was a charity worker. The man they'd said was her husband was a stranger. She hadn't seen him before. Ever. There was a vague similarity between him and Felix. They had the same height and the same color hair and were of similar ages and builds, but they were also unmistakably different people. It had been years since she had seen Felix, but no one changed that much in such a relatively short period of time.

Had Felix done something in the intervening years that had warranted this situation? She couldn't believe he had. He had been a cold, emotionally stunted man who loved his family but could not treat them correctly even when he made every effort to do so. Even he had realized that in the end, but he was a decent man. He spent his life traveling the world for the good of others. How could he have done anything that would lead to the kidnapping of his family? Surely her captors would realize their mistake. Surely the man they thought was her husband would put them right.

Or was all this his fault? Was he pretending to be Felix? Had he stolen her ex-husband's identity and used it to commit crimes that had led these men to Lucille's door? That seemed more likely.

Echoing footsteps told her one of her captors was approaching. The footsteps grew louder as they descended the steps and ceased when they reached the gate. The lock squealed and the hinges creaked and a man appeared. He wasn't Hart or one of the five foreign men who had been holding her but a man she had seen only once, when she had been taken to see the man they thought was her husband. She remembered what they had called him: Dietrich.

He had a pistol tucked into the front of his trousers and carried a plate of plain boiled spaghetti in his left hand. He ate it with his fingers. He was a noisy eater.

Lucille couldn't remember the last time she had eaten a proper meal. Even though she was sure her nerves would not let her eat anything substantial, her stomach groaned at the sight and smell of the spaghetti. Peter loved spaghetti. Dietrich saw her looking at the food and seemed pleased. He stood there, staring at her.

"What do you want?" she asked when she couldn't stand the silence any longer.

He didn't stop chewing to answer. "To kill your husband. But I'm not going to get the chance."

"He's not my husband."

"Sure he isn't." He scooped up more spaghetti with his fingers, dropping and sucking it into his mouth. He checked his watch. "I hate waiting, don't you?"

"Your name's Dietrich, yes?" She didn't wait for confirmation. "You must listen to me, Dietrich. That man is not my husband. I've never seen him before in my life."

Her captor smiled a little and she saw his yellow teeth. "If you say so."

"I'm telling the truth. He's not going to kill himself for us. He doesn't even know us." She shuffled forward and whispered so Peter couldn't hear, "Then you're going to have to kill me and my son. You don't want to have to do that, do you, Dietrich?"

He smiled another yellow smile.

• • •

He stopped the car two hundred meters from the mill, next to the used car dealership, and killed the engine. The drive had taken almost eleven minutes. In eighteen minutes he was supposed to be on the terrace. He pulled off the tuxedo and threw it into the back of the minivan. He unbuttoned the shirt and dropped it into the foot well while he unfastened the vest.

Francesca came around. She groaned and stirred and raised her eyebrows and blinked and grimaced. Then she turned her head and looked at him as though she had woken up after a full night's sleep. Her eyes were still bloodshot, but she was focusing on him now and not at some point behind him as she had done. Hart had been correct when he'd said the effects wouldn't last long.

She said, "What's going on?"

Her words were quiet but clear. He didn't answer. The vest was heavy and difficult to take off in the confines of the driver's seat, but he couldn't risk doing so outside in case someone saw.

"Why aren't we at the embassy?"

He didn't answer that either. He put the shirt back on.

Francesca stared at him and the vest he no longer wore. She peered through the windshield and saw where they were. Her mouth opened to speak, but no words came out. He saw her eyes look to the passenger door a second before she went for the handle. The door didn't open. She tried a few times before reaching for the unlock button on the console.

He grabbed her arm.

"Let go of me."

He didn't. She struggled and tried to jerk her arm from his grasp. He kept hold of her while with his free hand he buttoned the shirt back up.

"Oh no, Felix. What have you done? God, what are you doing? Dietrich's going to kill them. Don't you understand? Your son is going to be killed."

"He's not my son," Victor said. "He's Kooi's son."

She stopped struggling because she heard the truth in his voice. "I don't understand. What are you talking about? Who are you?"

He didn't answer. It was eight thirty p.m., so he thumbed out the last code and sent it to Hart. He replied a few seconds later. Francesca stared, understanding.

"You're crazy. You'll never get them out of there. This can't possibly work." She shook her head, breathing heavily. "If you're not Felix Kooi, who are you?"

"That's not important, Francesca. What's important is that you tell me where in the mill Lucille and Peter are being held."

"I . . . I can't do that. Whoever you are, you must understand that. What do you think you're going to do? You can't get them out of there. Drive back to the embassy. There's still enough time. I'll tell them you panicked but you're going to go through with it. That's the only way you can save them."

"Tell me, where are they?"

"I can't."

"Then I'll have to hurt you. I have very little time left, Francesca, so I'll do whatever I need to so that you tell me what I need to know. You need to decide right now how this is going to work."

She stared across at him. She was breathing heavily. She was scared because in Budapest he'd given her a first-hand demonstration of his ability to inflict pain. But a lot had happened since then and the fear slipped away from her face. "No, you won't. You're not going to hurt me, Felix—or whatever your name is. Ever since the first time we met, you've been trying to convince me to walk away from this. Why is that?" He didn't answer. "You like me. I know you do. But it's more than that, isn't it? You care about me. You wanted to save me from this life, remember? You didn't want me to get hurt. So you're not going to hurt me now, are you?"

Victor stared straight ahead, through his reflection on the windshield glass. "Last chance, Francesca."

She smiled at him, softly, sympathetically. "You don't really believe you can get them out of there before Hart finds out you're not at the embassy. They could already be dead. But if they're not your family, why do you even care? Let me out of the car and drive away. By the time I tell Robert what's happened, you'll be long gone." She touched him on the shoulder, lightly. "Or we could go together. Just the two of us. You'd like that, wouldn't you?"

He punched her in the face.

Not hard, because he didn't want to knock her out, but hard enough to burst her bottom lip wide-open. She reeled away, blood smeared across her chin and cheek, face screwed up from the pain and shock, eyes wide with fear, the bloodshot whites showing all around the irises.

"Where are they?"

She didn't hesitate. "Beneath the older building. There's an underground mill. From Roman times. They're in there." She touched her lip and examined the blood on her fingers. "Why did you do that? You didn't need to do that, you piece of shit."

Victor pictured the terror in Lucille's eyes and the searching gaze of Peter as he stared at the man he believed was his father. Victor pictured what might happen to them because of Francesca's complicity.

He turned in his seat, reached across to where she sat, and broke her neck.

· Chapter 62 ·

Security at the used car dealership was poor. There was a nominal barrier that would stop a car being driven off the forecourt, but it took less than a second for Victor to climb over it. He carried the vest slung over one shoulder and the seventeen-shot handgun in his waistband. He kept low as he hurried between the lines of cars until he came to the chain-link fence that surrounded the mill complex. It was four meters high and topped by a tube of metal from which triangular spikes protruded in spiraling rows. An insurmountable obstacle. At least for the kind of intruders that kept olive mill owners awake at night. Whoever commissioned the fence had never imagined it would need to keep out someone like Victor. And it wasn't going to.

He waited in the dark, watching and listening until he was sure no one was nearby in the compound. The modern mill building stood three meters away on the other side of the fence, creating a near-perfect barrier to block line of sight from anyone in the old building or in the corridor of space between the two. He stepped back and threw the vest. It arced over the spikes and dropped down between the fence and the building. It made a distinctive thud and Victor drew the handgun in case some-one heard the noise and investigated. But no one did.

There were five heavily armed paramilitaries on the far side of the fence. Plus Leeson and Dietrich. Seven ene-mies. He had less than twelve minutes left before Hart realized he wasn't in the embassy.

He secured the gun in his waistband, stepped back to create enough distance, and took a running leap at the fence. He cleared a couple of meters and climbed the rest. The fence shook and rattled, but he didn't have the time to climb it quietly and it would be impossible to do so without making some noise. If no one had heard the vest land, no one would hear him climb.

When he reached as far as his fingers could grip, he walked his feet up until they were almost as high as his hands and he protruded from the fence in a right-angled U shape. He straightened his back and bent his legs in-ward until his shins were almost vertical and parallel with the fence. He then pushed his legs straight and let go with his hands so that he stood with only his feet support-ing him, jammed into the links, and only the strength of his thighs preventing him losing balance and toppling over backward.

He bent his torso forward, contorting over the spikes and reaching out downward with his hands as if going to touch his toes. He gripped the fence and felt the spikes pushing against his stomach. He locked and tensed his arms and straightened his back, lifting his legs away from the fence, then brought them up until they came in line with the rest of his torso and he was vertical and upside down. He adjusted his grip and bent his torso to one side, his legs tilting with his torso until gravity took over and swung his body the right way up. Finally, he let go with his hands, dropping the last couple of meters.

He went into a low squat to lessen the impact and turned around.

Victor hooked the vest back over his shoulder and re-adjusted the gun in his waistband so he could draw it with speed, but he couldn't risk a gunshot unless there were no other options. He had no knife or other quiet weapon. His hands would have to do the job instead.

· · ·

Coughlin waited and watched. On the terrace were close to a hundred men and women, almost indistinguishable from one another in their black evening wear. But he could see easily enough that neither Kooi nor Francesca was among them. It was eight thirty-five p.m., so there was ten minutes until they were scheduled to join the crowd outside to await the ambassador's speech. Within half an hour the bomb would explode and Prudnikov would be dead and the job completed. "You're sure I'm still getting paid even if Kooi backs out of this, right?"

"He'll comply," Hart replied. "Whether Leeson then pays you your fee is not of my concern."

"And the wife and kid will be free to go after Kooi blows himself up, yeah? Just like you and Leeson said they would."

"You mean Lucille and Peter?"

"Yeah, Lucille and Peter. The woman and the boy. Kooi's family. Who the hell else would I be talking about here?"

"Perhaps you should be more mindful of your tone when you speak to me."

"Why aren't you answering me? Kooi kills himself and buys the lives of his wife and son. That's the deal. That's what he agreed. I'm asking you now, if Kooi lives up to his end of the deal, you'll live up to yours?"

"Kooi doesn't have a choice. He'll do what we agreed."

"And will you?"

"No."

"Oh man," Coughlin breathed. "What happened to the rules of war? What happened to women and children getting a pass?"

"We're assassinating the head of the Russian foreign intelligence service. Do you believe leaving witnesses behind who can attest to that fact is a viable course of action for someone who wishes to remain breathing? Can you imagine what the SVR would do to you if they even suspected you were involved in Prudnikov's murder?"

"Yeah," Coughlin said. "I can. But that woman wouldn't say shit to nobody, not after all this. No way she would risk her son. And what about the kid? He's just a kid. Why does he have to die?"

"Why should he live? No one on this wretched planet is innocent. We all have hate in our hearts. We are all capable of barbarism if given the opportunity and means. That little boy could grow up to be worse than you or even me."

"It's still not right."

"You've left it a little late to turn to morality, don't you think?" Hart took out his phone. "Get your focus back on that terrace and tell me the second Kooi appears."

• • •

Victor kept to the shadows and hurried along the exterior of the new mill, slowing as he came to the corner. He peered around to see the Rolls-Royce and panel van parked in front of the building. The ambulance had been uncovered and moved closer to the gate. The back doors were open. Victor watched as one of the Chechens dropped out from inside the rear compartment. He wore a paramedic's uniform. He was joined by another similarly attired Chechen, carrying a big bag for medical supplies in each hand. The bags would contain weapons and other supplies for the siege. The Chechen with the bags passed one to the other man, who climbed into the ambulance with it and placed the other on the ground.

As far as they knew they would be leaving soon. They needed to be close to the embassy for when the bomb was scheduled to explode so they could be among the first responders who would be on the scene within minutes. But the ambulance was stolen and the longer it was out on the streets, the greater the chance of its being noticed and the plan's failing. Therefore they would leave at the last possible moment, which wouldn't be until after Victor was due on the terrace. They would still be within the mill complex when Hart realized Victor was no longer at the embassy. They were dangerous men with access to automatic weapons. They looked anxious but they were not alert. But all that was going to change in less than five minutes.

He waited until the second bag had been picked up and the Chechen was in the ambulance and made his way past the vehicles, keeping close to the new mill's exterior, where the shadows were darkest. When he was out of the line of sight from the back of the ambulance, he closed the distance. He waited alongside the back doors for the Chechen to appear. The man dropped down from the rear compartment a moment later.

Victor attacked him from behind, wrapping his right arm around the man's neck as he snapped his free palm over his mouth and nose to muffle the Chechen's scream and stop his breathing. He pulled him backward and down, dragging him away from the ambulance as the pressure on his neck cut off the blood supply to his brain. He thrashed and struggled, but within seconds he had gone limp. By the time Victor had dragged him between the new mill and the fence, he was dead. Not the best hiding place, but he didn't have time for anything else and no one would see the corpse unless they made a point of coming round the back of the building.

He searched the dead Chechen but found only cigarettes and a refillable brass lighter. He took the lighter and crept back around to the ambulance. Inside the back compartment he placed the suicide bomber's vest beneath the newly loaded bags. There wasn't time to hide it more thoroughly, but it should go unnoticed so long as no one searched for it. If someone did, it meant Victor had failed, and if he failed, it was because he was dead.

One of the double doors leading into the old mill was open and through the gap Victor could see the antechamber beyond. Inside it was the Chechen who had carried the bags, accompanied by another. They were packing AK-47 assault rifles into bags. Victor stayed in the shadows and moved by.

The old mill was about half as long as the new building. At the north end, Victor saw a stone staircase leading down to what had to be the underground mill Francesca had described. At the bottom of the steps was a metal gate, padlocked. Lucille and Peter were down there. No one was around. There was no one in earshot. In other circumstances he could have undone the lock in less than a minute, but he had no pick and no torsion wrench. The 9 mm bullets in the handgun would bounce off. But even if he could get them out right now, then what?

They couldn't climb the fence and he couldn't lift them over it. There wasn't enough room to get one of the vehicles up to a sufficient speed to ram the gate. Even when he had them out of the underground chamber, they would still be trapped.

There were four Chechens left, plus Leeson and Dietrich. At least two Chechens were in the old mill. It was where all five had been sleeping. It was where the supplies and equipment were kept. Victor had seen no signs that the modern mill served any other purpose except as a space in which to plan and rehearse. That time had passed. The two other Chechens were likely in there too, as were Leeson and Dietrich, but he couldn't know for sure and there was no time to check.

The big double doors were the only way into the old

mill. The windows were protected with iron bars from the days before the modern mill was built and the chain-link fence had gone up. There were seventeen bullets in his handgun. Enough to have a double tap at each enemy and still leave five in the magazine. But only if he could take them all unawares. Which was impossible. He would have to deal with the two Chechens in the antechamber first. Not a problem, but it wouldn't be silent, and then he couldn't hope to assault the main mill area without Leeson, Dietrich, and the two remaining Chechens being ready for him.

Victor backed away from the old mill, then paused and waited in the darkness between the two buildings. He saw no one. He heard no one approaching. The entrance to the modern mill hadn't been locked. Victor pushed it open and slipped inside. The lights had been left on. The machinery in the huge pressing room bounced back the light. On the smooth floor, a blurred and distorted reflection of Victor surrounded his feet. He stopped by the door and listened. He had the Russian's handgun in a two-handed grip.

He heard no one and hurried across the mill floor to the door opening onto the corridor that led to the planning room. He listened to make sure no one was immediately on the other side and slipped through, easing the door closed behind him. He heard a rustle of paper and approached the planning room. The noise grew louder. There was a snap, followed by a grunt and then a tearing sound. Victor pictured one of the Chechens on cleanup duty: gathering the flip charts and breaking the model down. He would be occupied and distracted. If he had a weapon it was almost certainly not in hand, but there was no way of knowing whether the Chechen was facing the door and would see Victor enter. Then there might not be time to get into killing range without the Chechen first employing his weapon. Victor's pistol was unsuppressed. The planning room was on the far side of the huge modern mill. There were lots of walls and machinery in between here and the pressing room of the old mill, but not enough to drown out the sound of a bullet being fired. A gunshot would be clearly identifiable to anyone in the compound and some way beyond.

Victor tucked the handgun into his waistband again, stood against the wall alongside the door next to the handle, and knocked once with his knuckles.

The snaps and tears ceased in the planning room.

There was a pause, silence. Victor remained motionless. He pictured the Chechen on the other side going through the universal pattern—surprise to confusion to curiosity to action. Footsteps.

The door opened. The Chechen remained on the other side.

Victor pivoted and punched him in the solar plexus. The Chechen doubled over, breathless. Victor grabbed him under the jaw with one hand, planted the other on the side of his skull, and wrenched.

The Chechen went straight down in the doorway.

Victor checked his pockets. As with the one outside, he found a packet of cigarettes and a lighter. He also found a Makarov pistol, a small knife, and a set of keys. There were several keys of different sizes for different kinds of locks. One was for a padlock, the one securing either the metal gate leading to where Lucille and Peter were being held or the mill's main gate. He placed the keys in the trouser pocket where he still had the Phantom's valet key and put the Makarov in the other pocket.

Inside the planning room he saw the model of the embassy, destroyed and in pieces on the floor, half of it stuffed into garbage bags as the flip charts had already been. Victor looked up to see a sprinkler in the center of the ceiling. Just as the new mill was protected externally from intruders by a perimeter fence topped with metal spikes, it was internally protected from fire by a state-of-the-art system.

Beneath the sprinkler, he made a pile of Plasti-Card fragments and strips of flip chart paper. He then took the refillable lighter from his pocket and thumbed the striker twice. A small flame rippled in the air. Slowly, he placed the lighter on its side on top of the pile. The flame continued to burn but didn't touch the paper it rested on. Without contact with a flame, paper auto-ignited when it was heated to about four hundred and fifty degrees Centigrade. The lighter was just a cheap flip top, but its butane flame burned at almost two thousand degrees Centigrade. Without knowing the exact temperature of the flame or the auto-ignition point of this particular type of paper, Victor couldn't calculate a precise time, but he estimated the paper would begin to smolder after a couple of minutes. Then it was down to the sensitivity of the carbon monoxide detector in the sprinkler system as to how long the paper would need to smoke before the sprinklers activated and the fire alarm blared. It was a modern system. He figured it would take less than thirty seconds.

He dashed back through the building, gun out and up because the fire alarm would sound in no more than three and a half minutes.

And in three minutes Hart would know Victor was no longer at the embassy.

· Chapter 63 ·

The old mill was a rectangular building, but one of its two narrow walls, the north wall, rounded into a semicircle of rendered stone. At the outward point of the semicircle, an alcove was cut into the wall and a set of narrow steps led down approximately three meters below the ground to where a door had once stood but had been replaced by a steel gate. A ventilation grille was mounted in the stone above the doorway, its rusty iron bars having survived where the door below had not. The rendering was crumbling around the opening and on the walls either side of the steps, revealing the bare bricks beneath. Victor descended along the center of the steps, as people had done over many centuries, wearing the once-square edges of the steps smooth.

It was the only entrance to the subterranean pressing room as far as he could make out. Perhaps there was another way down from somewhere inside the old mill that had been built on top of it. A chimney perhaps, or some form of antiquated dumbwaiter.

A dim orange light glowed from somewhere on the other side of the gate. Victor tried the padlock key. It worked. The gate squealed and he stepped down into the chamber. Half of the room was in deep shadow. On the other side of the opening stood a circular room, about ten meters in diameter. Alcoves and openings led off it. At the room's center, an uneven circle of stone bricks formed the wall of an olive press. A giant pressing stone lay on its side on the inside of the circular wall. No other equipment had endured. Around the wall a shallow groove had been worn into the rock floor by the endless rotations made by the mules when turning the heavy stone. The chamber had been carved out of rock and reinforced and improved with stone pillars and archways by medieval masons. On the far side, it opened out into a room that had once served as a stable for the mules that turned the pressing stone.

The ceiling was low. The air was cool and damp and smelled musty. A raised fireplace was housed on one side to keep the chamber warm during the winter months. Along one section of the wall were half a dozen square-sided holes in the floor, about half a meter wide and deep, to collect oil from individual presses. The chimney rose into the ceiling and Victor pictured it ending under the floor tiles of the mill above.

The source of the light was Kooi's son. Peter sat on the floor with his back to an uneven section of wall. In one hand he had a big flashlight that was as long as his arm. His other hand was pressed over the end of the flashlight so the bright white light shone through his palm and emerged orange.

Peter hadn't looked at him, but Victor tucked the pistol into his waistband so he didn't scare the boy any more than he presumably was already. Victor approached him.

"Where's your mother?" he whispered.

Peter didn't answer.

Victor squatted down. "Is she here?"

Again, Peter didn't answer, but a scraping noise alerted Victor to a presence in the darkness. Lucille stepped into the light, moving fast, a chunk of masonry in her hand. She swung at Victor, a wild attack fueled by terror and desperation, but her wrists were bound together and the stone was never going to reach Victor's head.

He took hold of her by the arms and removed the improvised weapon from her grip. She would have collapsed to her knees had he not held her upright.

"Who are you?" she sobbed.

"That's not important. You have to trust me."

"Where's Felix? Why do those men think you're him?"

Victor pushed the hair from her face. "There's no time to explain. You and Peter need to come with me. If you don't those men are going to kill you. Do you understand?"

She nodded and wiped the tears from her eyes.

"It's going to be okay, Lucille," Victor said. "Just do as I say and I promise I'll get you both out of this. I'm going to take out a knife, but that's just so I can cut your wrists free. Is that okay?"

Lucille nodded, and Victor took out the Chechen's knife and sawed through the tape that linked her wrists together.

"Thank you."

"Are we safe now?" Lucille said.

Victor shook his head. "Not yet."

Lucille managed to nod in response. She hugged Peter and kissed the top of his head. He didn't hug her back. He just stared at Victor.

He handed her the Makarov. "For protection."

She hesitated, then took it.

"It's ready to fire," Victor explain. "All you have to do is squeeze the trigger. Aim for the center of the torso."

She nodded.

"Bring Peter," Victor said. "I need to put you somewhere safe till this is over."

Peter resisted when she took his hand, and pulled backward when she tried to lead him away. "Come on, honey. We need to go."

He made a keening sound and pulled harder. The noise got louder.

"Shh," Lucille pleaded. "You need to keep quiet."

But Peter wasn't quiet. Victor didn't know much about children, but he knew what fear looked like. "I like your dinosaur T-shirt, Peter," he said. "I used to like dinosaurs too at your age. I still do. Which is your favorite? Mine's always been T. rex."

He didn't respond, but the noise stopped.

"Some people don't believe he hunted. They say he wasn't a fearsome beast but a scavenger," Victor continued. "I don't agree. I think he was a hunter. I think he was big and scary and chased all the other dinosaurs around. What do you think?"

Peter hesitated. He looked to his mother and then back at Victor. "That he was big and scary."

"King of the dinosaurs, right?"

Peter nodded.

"Do you think you can come with your mother and me and be very quiet?" He nodded again and Victor gestured to Lucille. "Let's go. There isn't much time."

• • •

The AK-47 was a fine weapon. Developed by Yuri Kalashnikov in 1947, it had proved itself as the rifle of the twentieth century—frequently copied and hugely popular for its low cost, ease of use, and extreme reliability in any and all conditions. Dietrich liked it because the bullets ripped huge chunks out of those unlucky enough to be hit by one. He'd used one plenty of times as a mercenary on the circuit and was a little envious that the Chechens were going to have the fun of using them tonight and not him. It was a waste. A fine weapon in the hands of an amateur who probably couldn't hit a man-sized target beyond twenty meters.

It was a waste, to which insult had been added by the fact that Dietrich didn't even have a firearm. Not that he needed one to kill Kooi's bitch wife and bastard son, but that wasn't the point. He sat in the pressing room of the old mill, throwing playing cards at a bucket, one at a time. He missed five or six for every one that went in. The boredom was killing him. Leeson was no kind of company and the Chechens were preparing to assault the embassy. At least it was almost over now. A clock that looked so old Dietrich was surprised it still worked showed the time as eight forty-five p.m. Not long until the job was over and a briefcase full of money was his.

Leeson stood, phone in hand, waiting for Hart's next update to say that Kooi was in position on the terrace, ready for Prudnikov's speech to begin.

He didn't like the bitch Lucille. She looked at him as if he were nothing, as most women did. Dietrich willed Kooi to chicken out or screw it up so he could put his knife to good use.

An alarm blared.

Dietrich sat up and turned in the direction of the noise. It was coming from the new mill. "Is that a fire alarm?"

Leeson looked at him. "Yes." He glanced at the phone and then back at Dietrich. "Go and see what's caused it."

He stood. "It can't be Kooi, can it?"

"That's what I want you to go check."

"But he's at the embassy."

Leeson tapped the screen of his phone. "Let's not hang around to find out, shall we?" He put the phone to his ear. "While I'm doing this, take two men and confirm that Kooi's family are secure. Then investigate that alarm. If it's not Kooi it still needs shutting off. Hurry."

He shouted at the Chechens in their own language and two followed Dietrich. They armed themselves in the antechamber. The third grabbed a rifle and moved to Leeson's side.

Dietrich exited the old mill, the two Chechens following him. He walked fast, the stock of the assault rifle firm against his shoulder, his eyes peering along the length of the barrel, index finger inside the trigger guard, taking no chances, ready to blow Kooi full of holes if he had returned. Dietrich hoped he had. They could finally settle their differences.

He led the two Chechens down the corridor of space between the two buildings, gaze sweeping back and forth in line with the AK's muzzle. They hurried to the north end of the old mill, where the staircase led down to the ruins of the ancient mill underground.

He saw the gate was open and dropped into a crouch, knowing now for certain that Kooi was here. He gestured for the Chechens to go down first into the darkness in case Kooi was waiting down there, ready for an ambush. Initially, the Chechens didn't understand. In return, Dietrich didn't understand what the men said to him, but he gesticulated and pointed and eventually they got the message. He followed them down, watching their flanks and rear because they were watching the front.

One used a flashlight to check the crumbling pressing room and the many chambers and alcoves leading off it. No woman. No kid. Expected, but no less bad for that.

• • •

Leeson had the third Chechen cover the entrance to the old mill's pressing room while he spoke to Hart, holding the phone in his left hand so he could keep his pistol in his right.

"He's not on the terrace," Hart said. "And I can't reach Francesca. The only explanation is Kooi's gone. The job's over."

"Detonate the bomb," Leeson said.

"There's no point, Robert. He isn't here, let alone within range of Prudnikov. We've failed. It seems you made a catastrophic error of judgment in hiring Kooi."

"Detonate the bomb," Leeson said again. "Then get back here. Right now."

"I'm afraid I'm not going to do that. The job is over, so I no longer work for you. Kooi outsmarted us all, and he's proved far more capable than we gave him credit for. So if he's already at the mill, then I would strongly recommend vacating the vicinity as quickly as possible."

"I'm ordering you to get back here," Leeson yelled down the phone.

"Good-bye, Robert," Hart said with some sympathy. "And if you do happen to get out of there, then you best find a good rock to hide beneath because if Kooi doesn't find you, I will."

The call disconnected. Leeson shook with rage and fear. He couldn't believe what was happening. He opened up his list of contacts to find the number for the mobile phone detonator.

• • •

Coughlin was sweating so badly that no amount of darkness was going to hide it. He watched and listened while Hart spoke on the phone to Leeson. He had heard Hart say the job was over and they'd failed and Kooi was gone. Shit. This was bad. All Coughlin had wanted to do was get paid, and now Kooi had destroyed any chance of that. Coughlin didn't know what to do. Taking the minivan and driving out of Rome and far away seemed like the only option. But he was owed money and he wasn't going to get far on what he had in his pockets. Plus, there was another problem: Hart.

"The job's really over?" Coughlin asked.

Hart nodded. He dropped the phone to the floor and crushed it under his heel. "No one can win them all. And neither should they."

Coughlin closed his eyes and exhaled. "I haven't been paid yet. How am I going to get my money if Kooi kills Leeson?"

"A financial contribution for your services should be the least of your worries."

"So what do we do now?"

"*We?*" Hart echoed. "There is no we. There is only you and I. And what I am doing now is ensuring that none of this debacle leads back to me."

There was something in Hart's voice Coughlin liked even less than usual. He backed away and hesitantly asked, "What should I do?"

"All you need do is not resist," Hart answered as he stepped closer. "It'll be far less painful that way."

• • •

"Back out," Dietrich ordered. He pointed when the two Chechens didn't respond. They hesitated, so he ascended ahead of them.

The ambulance exploded.

The noise was deafening. The overpressure wave destroyed the back compartment, ripping through the roof and sides as it expanded out, blowing out the back doors and tossing them away. The windows shattered. Great gouts of flame followed the wave, funneled by the two mill buildings on either side. The ground shook. Smoke billowed and mushroomed.

Dietrich dived to the ground. Heat and pressure washed over him. Debris and the ceramic shards peppered his body, but he was far enough from the blast for them to have lost their capacity to kill and injure. Oily black smoke thickened the air around him.

Behind Dietrich, the first of the two Chechens hesitantly climbed up the steps.

Gunshots made Dietrich remain prone. The first Chechen contorted and stumbled backward, collapsing down the steps, his face a bloody mess. Dietrich scrambled across the ground and followed the corpse, hearing more gunfire as he rolled into cover.

The shots had been a double tap of single shots, the distinctive noise almost a pop. Which meant Kooi was using a handgun. Close range, lacking in stopping power. No match for an assault rifle. He gestured for the other Chechen to keep clear, then crouched to keep his head lower than the ground and held up his rifle to release a burst of rounds. He wasn't trying to hit Kooi—he didn't know where he was hiding—but he wanted to grab his attention and make him get his head down.

Dietrich raised his head and shoulders from cover, sweeping the AK in a fast one-hundred-and-eighty-degree arc. Through the smoke, he spotted a figure between the two buildings dart through the doorway into the new mill. Dietrich fired another burst and the recoil lifted the muzzle up. He charged from the sunken staircase, barking orders and motioning wildly for the Chechen to flank Kooi through the other entrance at the end of the building.

The Chechen seemed to understand and hurried off to do as instructed.

Rifle aimed at the entrance to the new mill, Dietrich hurried down the corridor of space between the buildings and backed off until he was close to the open doorway to the antechamber of the old mill.

He shouted over his shoulder, "Kooi's in the other building. I've got him trapped."

Leeson appeared with his Chechen bodyguard. He held a hand up to shield his face from the heat of the burning ambulance. "What about his family?"

"I don't know. They must be in there with him." Dietrich risked taking his gaze off the door Kooi had gone through to glance back. "If I'm going in there I want more money."

"Kill them all, Mr. Dietrich," Leeson said. "And I'll triple your fee."

· Chapter 64 ·

Victor backed away from the new mill's side entrance. Fat bullet holes had been torn through it. He had the handgun up and pointed at the door, waiting for Dietrich to storm in after him. But he wasn't taking the bait. Victor backed farther away, giving Dietrich more credit, realizing he'd gone for another way in or sent one or more of the Chechens to do so instead.

He entered the corridor that led to the planning room, handgun leading. The corridor ceiling had a sprinkler every three meters and Victor rushed through a continuous shower of icy water that drenched his clothes and plastered his hair to his forehead. He hadn't seen another way in apart from the great rolling shutter doors at the front of the building, but he knew there would be another entrance in this direction, if only a fire door.

Victor hurried past the planning room and turned a corner into another bare corridor, splashing through puddles and swiping water from his face when it threat-

ened to blind him. He heard only the spray of the sprinklers and the fire alarm's shriek. He saw an exit sign
ahead, took a final right-angle corner, and saw the double
doors of a fire exit ten meters away at the end of it. They
had been forced open from the outside. The fire alarm
had drowned out the noise.

A man was kneeling down before it. The spray from
the sprinklers disguised his features, blurring the man's
face, but Victor made out easily enough the paramedic's
overalls and the weapon clutched in both hands. One of
the Chechens, armed with an AK-47 that he already had
aimed Victor's way, waited for him to appear.

Victor reacted first, diving to the side before the
Chechen could fully depress the rifle's trigger. Muzzle
flashes exploded through the rain of the sprinklers. He
heard the sonic snap of bullets flying past him before they
took chunks out of the walls and floor. The fire alarm was
temporarily muted by the roar of automatic gunfire.

He hit the floor in the adjacent corridor and scrambled to his feet, throwing his back to the wall perpendicular to the corridor where the gunman knelt, right
shoulder an inch from the corner.

The shooting stopped. Victor estimated that the
Chechen had released a third of his magazine of thirty
rounds. It had been the panicked burst of someone surprised and untrained.

He shot again, trying to anticipate Victor's reappearance. This time the burst was shorter and more controlled. Maybe three or four rounds. It was hard to be
sure. Holes blew in the partition walls, which were made
of glazed ionized aluminum covered in cheap white wall-

paper. The powerful 7.62mm rounds punched holes through them big enough for Victor to put his thumb inside. The two walls converging to form the corner behind which he hid offered no protection from the gunfire, only concealment.

The Chechen had about half a magazine of bullets left before he had to reload. Victor didn't know the exact amount, but there were three or four bursts' worth. If Victor made his move after the gunman had fired three, he might find himself facing down the corridor, trying to make a ten-meter head shot in poor visibility against an enemy with enough ammunition left to shred him. Alternatively, if he waited until after the fourth burst, that might be too long—he would be attacking against an enemy already reloaded and with thirty more rounds at his disposal.

Withdrawing wasn't an option. If Dietrich hadn't already entered the mill through the side entrance, he would have done so by the time Victor got back there. Dietrich would have heard the gunfire. He wouldn't wait any longer. While Victor was engaged against one enemy, it would be the perfect time to attack from his flank.

Another burst sent more rounds along the corridor. One round hit the corner, tearing through both aluminum walls and passing within inches of Victor's shoulder. He had no more time to wait.

He switched the gun to his left hand and, with his back still pressed against the wall, reached across his chest and past his shoulder and pointed it around the corner.

He squeezed the trigger rapidly, adjusting his aim with each shot to spread the paths of the bullets throughout the corridor.

Victor thought he heard a scream after his seventh shot. He pivoted on his right foot and swung himself around one hundred and eighty degrees out of cover and into the adjacent corridor, his left arm extending to acquire the target.

A smear of red marked one wall, already turning orange as water from the sprinklers diluted the blood and washed it down toward the floor.

The Chechen lay on his side, right hand clutching his abdomen, the other stretching for the rifle that had dropped from his grasp and slid out of reach. The right shoulder of the paramedic's overalls was frayed where another bullet had hit and splashed blood on the wall. That was why he'd dropped the gun, but the round to the stomach had dropped him. The fingers of his outstretched left hand wrapped around the stock of the AK and he dragged it closer.

Victor shot him between the eyes.

• • •

Dietrich walked down the corridor toward the sound of gunfire. It had stopped thirty seconds ago. He hoped he wasn't too late. Kooi must have guessed the plan, or more likely tried to flee like the coward he was. Dietrich kept his rifle up and ready, gaze focused along the iron sights. Where he looked, the gun pointed. He breathed slow and steady in an attempt to control his soaring heart rate. He stepped over the corpse lying in the doorway of the planning room. His feet kicked up water. The sprinklers had stopped and the alarm was silent.

He moved at a fast walk. He didn't want Kooi to get

away, but neither did he want to walk into a trap. The caution was unnecessary. Kooi wasn't inside the mill. The fire escape doors were open and before them lay the Chechen sent by Dietrich to flank Kooi. The back of the corpse's skull was missing and fragments of bone and chunks of brain were scattered across the floor behind him. All around the body, the water was stained red.

There was no evidence Kooi had been hit, but he must have fled from the fire escape. He would be rushing for the vehicles, Dietrich was sure. He turned around and headed back the way he had come. It would take less time than circling the building as his foe would be doing. With a little luck Dietrich might reach the vehicles first, or else he would catch Kooi while he tried to escape with his brood and then gun them all down in a hail of automatic fire. It would be beautiful.

He reached the main mill floor.

The lights went out.

Dietrich didn't panic. He smiled. Kooi hadn't looped around the mill to head for the vehicles. He'd looped around and come back in via the side entrance and killed the lights. He was playing dirty. Dietrich respected that, but it wasn't going to matter. Dietrich had hunted and killed in the dark before. This was nothing he couldn't handle. He stepped away from the doorway and peered into the darkness. Skylights in the roof let in a little ambient light, and metal gleamed where the light touched the great hunks of machinery: presses, conveyor belts, tubes, centrifuges. Metal shelving units protruded at ninety degrees from one wall, and upon them sat pallets of shrink-wrapped bottles, empty, ready for filling. Barrels and vats glinted. Convex mirrors were mounted on roof supports and on the ends of the shelving units to aid the driving of the forklift truck.

There were numerous places where no light reached and where the coward could hide. Dietrich knew he would be hiding. Kooi wouldn't face him head-on, like a man. Somewhere in the darkness, Dietrich's prey waited. He wanted to call out, to mock Kooi, but satisfying as such a thing would be, it would also needlessly give away his position. Kooi had killed a couple of the Chechens, but they weren't experienced operators like Dietrich. Kooi knew that, which was why he was hiding now, waiting for Dietrich to make a mistake and walk into an ambush.

He took one careful step at a time, considering likely points of attack, checking them, evaluating and eliminating, then moving on. He was patient and methodical. Despite his racing heart and aggressive temperament, in combat Dietrich found peace. He felt a calmness that he could never duplicate when he was not close to killing or being killed. He'd tried to explain it once to an army shrink, but the shrink had looked at him as if he were crazy. Dietrich knew he wasn't crazy. He was simply evolved. He moved on through the darkness, all the time narrowing down the potential locations where Kooi could be hiding, all the time getting closer to the kill.

He stayed away from the dim beams of light that filtered through the skylight—to protect his night vision, which was improving with every passing second, as well as to hinder Kooi's attempts to line up a shot.

Dietrich paused to examine his immediate surroundings. He'd searched approximately half of the main mill area. Nearby, corrugated steel drums were stacked in rows and piles that created a mini labyrinth of blind spots and areas of concealment. A good place to hide. Dietrich waited and searched with his eyes until he saw it.

The dim light coming through the skylight cast a shadow on the floor that did not belong to any man-made object. It blended into those of the drums but the dimensions were wrong. Dietrich studied the shadow and followed it back to its source—which lay behind the corner of a shelving unit stacked with bottles.

Dietrich grinned in the darkness. *You're going to have to do better than that,* he thought as he edged forward. Less than three meters to go before he was in position to strike. Just before he reached the corner, before he exposed himself to Kooi's position, Dietrich would angle the AK and spray rounds through the pallets of bottles. Maybe he would aim low and try to incapacitate Kooi with bullets in the legs. Then he could have some fun with him. Two meters to go.

Something clattered behind him and Dietrich spun around in the direction of the sound.

His gaze swept from darkness into light focused and magnified by one of the convex mirrors. He grimaced, the light stinging his eyes with their dilated pupils and ruining his night vision. Purple spots blinded him. He pivoted back around, knowing he'd been tricked.

There was an explosion of light and sound.

Dietrich didn't know he'd been hit at first, but he sucked in a breath and felt warm liquid in his throat. He squeezed the AK's trigger and nothing happened. His fingers didn't move. The spots cleared from before his eyes and he realized he was staring up at the night through the mill's skylights.

He couldn't move. He couldn't feel anything. He breathed again and liquid entered his lungs. Then Dietrich understood. He'd been shot in the neck. The bullet had ruptured his spinal cord and severed his jugular.

He lay paralyzed from the neck down and drowned in his own blood.

• • •

Leeson flinched at the sound of the single gunshot and made his move. He couldn't wait any longer. He hurried out of the old mill and ran across the open ground to where his limousine was parked, the last Chechen jogging behind him. He should have thought of it before. The moment he knew something had gone wrong, he should have got inside the Phantom. The protection it offered was immense. Even the high-powered bullet storm of an AK-47 wouldn't pierce the armored sides or windows. Leeson had insisted on that when he had the car outfitted. His enemies were well armed, so he had to be even better protected.

He unlocked the driver's door and tossed a set of keys to the Chechen, and instructed him to open the gate. Once it was open, Leeson shot him. He didn't want to have to explain to the man why he wasn't going to be striking the promised blow against the Russian imperialists he so hated.

Leeson climbed into the driver's seat and pulled the door shut. The heavy *thunk* it made sounded divine. It meant he was safe. He turned the ignition key to start the engine and noticed the valet key was missing from the ring. Someone had taken it, but it didn't matter now—Leeson was inside the vehicle. In the rearview mirror he saw Kooi exiting the new mill building. Leeson felt a surge of rage, but there was nothing he could do now to take revenge against the man who had destroyed months of careful planning. But that didn't mean it was over. Leeson knew everything there was to know about Kooi's life. He would hire people to deal with him and his family another time.

His thoughts were interrupted by a sound behind him. The partition window opened. Panic flooded through him and he twisted in his seat to see Kooi's wife. She had a gun, pointed through the little window and at his head.

"We can talk about this," Leeson said, swallowing. "I can make you a very wealthy woman."

She said, "Put your hands over your ears, Peter, and close your eyes."

· Chapter 65 ·

Two weeks later

Muir was waiting in the Piazza del Popolo before the archway of the grand sixteenth-century gate that led to the Via Flaminia. She stood sipping from a cup of coffee, dressed casually, sunglasses over her eyes. Victor had arrived early, but so had she. It was midday and the sky was blue and cloudless. The piazza was busy with Romans eating lunch and tourists taking more photographs than they could ever possibly need. They were densest around the Egyptian obelisk that stood, twenty-three meters tall, in the center of the square, but they also congregated near the ornate fountains and before the symmetrical churches of Santa Maria del Miracoli and Santa Maria in Montesanto. The number of people made it more difficult to check that she was really alone, but the crowd provided enough anonymity that he could take his time to be sure.

She didn't acknowledge his presence until he was standing right next to her. He'd allowed her to see him before then.

"I wasn't sure you'd come."

"Neither was I."

"I'm glad you did."

Victor remained silent. He kept his gaze on the crowd, searching for signs of watchers he might have missed, or who had only now arrived. It was a near-impossible task, but he did so all the same.

"How are they?"

Muir blew out some air. "They're doing okay, considering what they've both been through. There's a long way to go, I'm sure. But we have some great people. We'll take care of them, I promise. It was good thinking, dropping them off at the consulate. That's made things a lot easier."

"What do the Italians know?"

"Everything."

Victor looked at her.

"Not about you, obviously. No point trying to bluff our way out of this one when you left seven corpses at that mill."

"I'm only responsible for six of them."

Muir smiled. "Whatever. Six or seven, it hardly makes a difference. The Italians know about the embassy plot and, unofficially at least, they're pretty grateful not to have had a major terrorist attack in their capital. Perhaps not unsurprising when you think about it."

"What about the Russians?"

"Same thing. They're happier than the Italians. Putting four embassy security in the hospital is a lot more palatable than having a hundred staff and guests blown to pieces, ambassador and head of the SVR among them.

They've got you on CCTV, but they don't know who you are. They've been told that you're one of ours. A NOC. Which is pretty close to the truth, I guess. Prudnikov would like to thank you personally."

"What did you tell him?"

"That you're a very private person. He took it with a smile, and passes on his sincere appreciation."

"Noted."

Muir said, "Lucille has asked about you."

"Does she know?"

"That you killed her husband on the agency's behalf?"

"Yes."

Muir shook her head. "She doesn't even know he's dead at this point. They didn't have any contact. Kooi paid her money, regular as clockwork, but she hadn't seen him in forever. And I'm not sure what good it would do for her to know who Kooi really was. Better for Lucille to believe this was all some big misunderstanding and that Kooi was the victim of a mugger and not killed because he was a piece-of-shit contract killer." She paused. "No offense."

"None taken."

"Listen," Muir said. "I want to say I'm sorry."

"I already said I didn't take offense."

"Not that. I'm sorry I put you through all this. I never would have sent you after Leeson had I any idea what you were going to walk into."

"Yes, you would."

"Okay," Muir conceded. "But I wouldn't do it again."

"I know."

"I'm glad you came out of it in one piece."

"So am I." He started walking out of habit. He didn't like to stand in one place for long. Muir walked alongside him. "Any progress on the client?"

"There is no client. At least, the broker and client are not different people. Robert Leeson, otherwise known as Ruslan Lisitsyn. He was SVR, privileged background, educated in the U.K. and the U.S., and was hotly tipped to make director someday. He fell off the grid a couple of years ago after a botched assignment in Odessa where he was running an operation that tried and failed to kill the head of the Georgian mob. They've been after him ever since according to the guy you left in that trunk. He also claims Leeson's own people set him up." She paused for a moment. "I have a theory: Let's say Lisitsyn made himself an enemy of Prudnikov, perhaps he found out something he shouldn't, but whatever, our boy Lisitsyn was too slick for the setup. He goes underground, only traveling by boat or car to keep hidden from his hunters in the Georgian mob and SVR. He uses his private wealth and contacts in the intelligence world to reinvent himself as a broker, but all the while working on a plan to erase the threat posed by Prudnikov without the blame turning his way. He bides his time, and to make his plan into a reality he assembles a team of killers from those he's been hiring out to other people.

"Rome police found the body of a Clarence James Coughlin in an apartment overlooking the Russian embassy. He killed himself. Slit his own wrists. No sign that anyone else was in there with him and no trace of anyone going by the name Hart matching your description."

Victor nodded. "Coughlin didn't kill himself."

"I believe you. Hart's still out there, but he must be long gone by now."

He reached into his inside jacket pocket and withdrew an object wrapped in acid-free tissue paper. He handed it to Muir, who unwrapped it.

"Would you give it to Peter for me?" Victor asked. "It's important."

"Sure," Muir said as she turned the carved wooden figurine over in her hands. "But it looks like it'd give the kid nightmares."

"It won't. Trust me. He'll like it."

"Okay. Should I tell him it's from you?"

Victor shook his head. "Just say it's a present."

Muir nodded and rewrapped the figurine. "You ever thought about coming to work for us full-time?"

He raised an eyebrow. "Take care of yourself, Miss Muir."

She offered her hand and he shook it.

· Chapter 66 ·

Iceland

Victor's cabin had been built in the late nineteenth century as the summer house of a wealthy trawlerman on land that Norwegians had once settled, and a millennium ago Vikings had wintered here before undergoing the final stretch of the long voyage home across the Atlantic from adventures in faraway Vinland. The strategic benefits of the cabin's remoteness had been the primary reason for its purchase for use as a safe house, but the history of this particular swath of land had been the deciding factor between this particular cabin and others like it. Victor felt a kinship with the warriors who had come before him, though he wondered if he would have stood in the shield wall and survived that hellish test of prowess, where cunning and guile came second to strength and ferocity.

He estimated there was another week's work to do on the cabin to finish the security renovations, and then he would be concentrating on the aesthetic qualities of his building. It was a safe house, not a home, but it didn't seem right to secure it and not restore it to the best possible standard. He'd never liked leaving a job half-finished. He would be making several long-distance trips in the Land Cruiser to pick up furniture, and would have made progress on that front had he not been bringing in boxes full of secondhand books with each supply run. The spare bedroom was nearly full of them. He had novels and nonfiction in a variety of languages, and not all in languages he could read. He selected a novel at random and took it to his kitchen, where he placed it on the table along with his pistol while he worked on the boiler.

Victor had reached the end of the first chapter when he looked up to see Hart standing on the far side of the kitchen, next to the doorway that led farther into the cabin. He held a gun in his right hand. The muzzle began a straight line that ended at a point between Victor's eyes.

"I knew you'd come," Victor said.

"Then you really shouldn't have let me get the drop on you so easily."

"How did you find me?"

Hart said, "Does it matter?"

"How did you get past the alarms?"

"Does it matter?" Hart said again.

Victor shook his head.

Hart stepped forward. "You know how this works, don't you? Leeson hired me to ensure that there was no comeback, and now he's dead but you're still alive and well. Who sent you after Leeson? Americans? Brits? Russians?" When Victor didn't answer, Hart said, "It doesn't really matter. But what matters is there are no loose ends leading back to me."

Victor nodded. "So what are you waiting for?"

Hart shrugged. "I thought we could talk a little first."

"About what?"

"About you, for a start. I know you're not Kooi. I know this place was bought under a bogus identity. I know you travel under several different passports. But what I don't know is who you really are. What is your name, kid?"

"People keep asking me that."

"So, tell me. In a couple of minutes it's not going to make the slightest bit of difference."

Victor's lips remained closed.

"Suit yourself. I thought maybe we could end things on a cordial note. You know that this is nothing personal. I like you. You remind me of myself, but I don't think even I could have pulled off what you did. You fooled us all so easily, didn't you?"

"Nothing about it was easy."

"Take the compliment. It won't hurt you." Hart exhaled. "I like this place you've got here, compadre. It's secluded. Self-sufficient. Maybe I'll keep it."

"You can have it, but I don't really have the time to talk."

"Sure you do, kid. You've got as much time as I'm willing to give you."

"That's not what I meant." He looked to his left. "We'll pass out soon."

Hart looked too, just a glance so he didn't take his eyes off Victor for longer than a split second. But he had to glance again, then again, until he understood what he was looking at.

On the wall was a standard gas-powered boiler. Pipes ran down from beneath it and disappeared behind the kitchen counter, leading to the two-hundred-and-fifty-pound gas canister outside the house. The pipes were copper and segmented, those segments secured together with bolts. Two bolts sat on the kitchen counter. As did one small length of pipe. On the adjacent windowsill was a basil plant. Its leaves rippled from a localized wind.

"Natural gas," Victor explained. "Straight from the earth. It fills a canister, which in turn feeds the boiler and the generator. It's one of the reasons I got this place. Secluded. Like you said, self-sufficient."

"I don't smell anything."

"That's the thing about natural gas. It has no smell. Gas smells because they scent it, so you know if you've got a leak. So you don't blow yourself up lighting the stove." Victor stared at Hart. "Or when you fire a gun."

"You're bluffing."

"If you don't believe me, then just wait a few minutes until you start feeling woozy. I already feel a little light-headed. You do too, don't you?"

"You're bluffing," Hart said again. "You'd die too."

Victor cocked his head to one side. "I knew if you tracked down Kooi's family, you'd find me too. I knew you wouldn't leave such a loose end. So if I'm going to die anyway, I may as well take you with me."

Hart said nothing.

"So squeeze the trigger and send us both to hell."

Hart said nothing.

"Else keep waiting until there's more gas in the air than oxygen. You're closer to the pipe, in case you hadn't noticed. Perhaps you'll drop first and I crawl away." Victor smiled.

Hart smiled too. "I don't think I'd like that very much." He stopped smiling. "But you're not thinking two moves ahead." He stepped forward and placed the pistol down on a countertop. "I don't need a gun to kill you, whoever you are."

He took out a folding knife and extended the blade. It was only a couple of inches long, but it would be enough. He stepped around the table until only two meters separated them. Victor didn't move.

But he did pick up the FN Five-seveN handgun from the table.

Hart froze. Two meters away. Out of range for a knife attack. But point-blank range for a bullet. He glanced at the boiler, at the removed segment of pipe, at the basil plant with its leaves rippling in odorless natural gas ready to explode when ignited by a firing gun.

"You'll kill us both," Hart said.

Victor shook his head. "Not unless the bullet does a U-turn after it exits you."

Hart started to say, "The gas . . ." but stopped himself.

"Won't explode," Victor explained. "Carbon monoxide isn't flammable. But it would eventually have killed us both if you'd waited long enough. I wasn't lying about *that* part."

Victor squeezed the trigger and a hole exploded through Hart's chest.

He stumbled a step through the mist of blood and fell facedown on the slate tiles. He didn't move. Victor held his breath for the minute it took him to reaffix the removed section of copper pipe and left the kitchen door open while he went outside to fire up the incinerator.

ACKNOWLEDGMENTS

A big thank-you to the brilliant and talented people at Little, Brown, for doing all the essential behind-the-scenes magic on this book, and I do mean magic. They are: Nick Castle, Jade Chandler, Thalia Proctor, Hollie Smyth, Tom Webster, Jo Wickham, Emma Williams, and Ed Wood. Also, thank you to Danielle Perez and all those who've done such a great job at Signet.

Thanks to my agent, Philip Patterson, for years of support, guidance, and friendship, and to Isabella Floris and Luke Speed at Marjacq for all their hard work. Thanks also to Scott Miller for his efforts across the pond.

Thank you to Mike Farmer, whose expert advice on hand-to-hand combat ensured that Victor triumphed over his foes and lived to fight another day. Thanks also to Hank Smith for his skills in causing pain and the exceptional proofreading of John Kriegel.

Finally, thank you to my brother Michael for heaps of advice and encouragement at every stage of this process.

Don't miss Tom Wood's

The Enemy

Available now from Signet

Bucharest, Romania

It was a good morning to kill. Impenetrable gray clouds obscured the sun and the city beneath was dark and quiet. Cold. Just how he liked it. He walked at a relaxed pace, in no hurry, knowing he was making perfect time. A fine rain began to fall. Yes, a particularly good morning to kill.

Ahead of him a refuse truck made its slow way along the road, hazard light flashing orange, windshield wipers swinging back and forth to flick away the drizzle. Refuse collectors followed the vehicle, hands buried under armpits while they waited to reach the next pile of trash bags on the sidewalk. They chatted and joked among themselves.

He interrupted the group's banter as he passed through the spiraling cloud of exhaust fumes condensing in the spring air. He felt their gaze upon him, taking in his appearance for the few short seconds before he'd gone.

There was little for them to note. He was smartly

dressed—a long woolen coat over the top of a dark gray suit, black leather gloves, thick-soled Oxford shoes. In his left hand he carried a metal briefcase. His dark hair was short, his beard neatly trimmed. Despite the cold, only the bottom two of his four overcoat buttons had been fastened. Just a businessman on his way to the office, they would assume. He was a businessman of sorts, but he doubted they would guess the nature of his uncommon profession.

Behind him, a trash can clattered into the road and he looked briefly over his shoulder to see black bags split open and refuse spilling across the asphalt. The garbage-men groaned and rushed to gather up the trash before the wind could spread it too far.

After a short walk, the businessman arrived at a large apartment complex. It stood several stories taller than the surrounding buildings. Balconies and satellite dishes jutted out from the dull brown walls. He made sure not to appear rushed as he took the half-dozen steps up to the front door. He unlocked it with his day-old key and stepped inside.

There were two elevators, but he opted for the stairs, climbing twenty-two flights to the top floor. He reached his destination with little trace of fatigue.

The corridor beyond the stairwell door was long and featureless. Spaced at regular intervals were numbered, spyholed doors. Dirty linoleum lined the floor. The paint on the walls was faded and chipped. The cool air smelled of strong detergent. Somewhere a baby cried softly.

At the end of the corridor, where it intersected with another, was a door marked *maintenance*. He put his briefcase down, and from a pocket removed a small packet of butter taken from a nearby diner. He unfolded the wrapper and carefully smeared the butter onto the hinges of the door. He placed the empty wrapper back into the same pocket.

From inside his coat, he removed two small metal tools: a tension wrench and a slim, curved pick. The lock was significantly better than most, but the businessman unlocked it in less than sixty seconds.

A door opened behind him.

He slipped the lock picks back into the pocket. Someone said something in gruff-sounding Romanian. The man with the briefcase spoke several languages, but not this one. He stayed facing the door for a moment in case the speaker was talking to someone inside the apartment. A slim chance, but one he had to play nevertheless.

The voice called again. The same guttural words, but louder. Impatient. His back still to the speaker, the businessman reached inside his coat. He withdrew his right hand and kept it out of sight by his hip. He turned side-on, to the left, to look at the resident, keeping his head tilted forward, eyes in the shadow of his brow.

A heavyset man with several days' worth of stubble was leaning out of his front door, fat fingers white on the frame. A cigarette hung from thick lips. He looked over the man with the briefcase and removed the cigarette from his mouth with a shaking hand. Ash fell from the end and on to the marked linoleum.

He swayed as he spoke again, words slow and slurred. A drunk, then. No threat.

The businessman ignored him, picked up his briefcase

and moved down the adjoining corridor, walking away from the drunk before he made any more noise. When a door clicked shut behind him, he stopped and silently retraced his steps, peered around the corner, saw no one and placed the 9 mm Beretta 92F handgun back inside his overcoat. He reset the safety with his thumb.

Total darkness enshrouded the room on the other side of the maintenance door. Water dripped somewhere unseen. The businessman flicked on a slim flashlight. The narrow beam illuminated the room—bare brick walls, pipework, boxes, a metal staircase along one side. He negotiated his way across the space and ascended the stairs. His shoes were quiet on the metal steps. At the top, a padlock secured the rust-streaked roof access door. The lock was marginally harder to pick than the previous one.

Eleven stories up, the icy wind stung his face and every inch of exposed flesh. It subsided within a few seconds as the pressure equalized between the stairwell and roof. He crouched to reduce his profile against the sky and moved across the roof to the west edge. The wind was pushing the clouds northward, letting the glow of the rising sun spread across the city. Bucharest extended out in front of him, slowly awakening. Present location aside, a particularly beautiful city. This was his first visit, and he hoped his work would bring him back before too long.

He turned his attention to his briefcase, unlocked it and opened it flat. Inside, a sheet of thick foam rubber surrounded the disassembled Heckler & Koch MSG-9. He removed the barrel first and attached it to the body of the rifle. Next, he fixed the Hensoldt scope in place, followed by the stock and finally the twenty-round box magazine. He folded down the bipod and rested the weapon on the roof's low parapet.

Through the scope he saw a 10x magnification of the city—buildings, cars, people. For fun, he positioned the crosshairs over a young woman's head and, anticipating her movements to keep her reticule in place, tracked her as she sipped her morning coffee. She passed beneath the branches of a tree and he lost her. Lucky girl, he thought with a rare smile. He took his eye from the sight, repositioned the rifle and looked through the scope once more.

This time he saw the entrance to the Grand Plaza Hotel on Dorobantilor Avenue. The eighteen-story building had a modern façade, all glass and stainless steel, appearing both strong and sleek at the same time. The businessman had stayed in several hotels of the Howard Johnson chain while plying his trade around the globe, but not this particular one. If the Grand Plaza met the reasonable-to-high standards of the rest of the franchise, he imagined the target would have enjoyed a pleasant stay. He thought it only fitting that the condemned man should get a good night's sleep before his morning execution.

The man with the rifle took a laser rangefinder from his briefcase and aimed the beam at the hotel entrance, finding it exactly six hundred and four yards away in central Bucharest. Well within acceptable range, and only six yards under his estimate. He rotated the elevation wheel to correct for the distance and elevation.

Outside the hotel entrance, a craggy-faced doorman revealed his bad teeth by yawning. Close to him, tied to a nearby streetlight, a purple ribbon fluttered in the breeze. The man with the rifle watched it for a moment, calculating the wind speed. Five, maybe five-and-a-quarter miles per hour. He adjusted the Hensoldt's windage wheel, wondering how long it would be before someone realized the significance of the seemingly innocuous ribbon. Maybe no one ever would.

He adjusted the scope's power ring, decreasing the magnification to see a wider view of the hotel. There were few other people nearby. Some pedestrians, the occasional guest, but no mass of people. This was good. His marksmanship was excellent, but with just seconds to make the kill, he required a clear line of sight. He had no compunction about shooting whoever was unfortunate enough to stand between the bullet and its true mark, but such killings tended to give targets advance warning of their own impending demise, and as long as the target wasn't mentally deficient, they moved.

The man with the rifle checked his watch. Today's unfortunate subject was due to appear shortly, if the itinerary included with the dossier was accurate. The businessman had no reason to doubt his client-supplied information.

Another adjustment of the scope and he saw the entire width of the hotel's front side and two-thirds of the way up its single tower. Light from the rising sun reflected off the windows of the top three floors within the scope's view.

The rain had ceased by the time a limousine pulled onto the hotel's drive from the adjoining road and stopped outside the main entrance. A large white guy dressed in a beige overcoat and dark jeans climbed out and ascended the steps with the brisk efficiency of a bodyguard. His head swept back and forth, fast but efficient, gaze registering every nearby person, assessing for threats and finding none.

The man with the rifle felt his heart rate begin to speed up as the time grew rapidly closer. He breathed deeply to stop it climbing too high and negatively affecting his aim. He waited.

After a minute, the bodyguard reappeared and took up position midway down the steps. He looked around before gesturing back up at the entrance. In a few seconds the target would come into view. According to the dossier, the target—a Ukrainian—typically traveled with several bodyguards who would naturally have stayed at the same hotel. The bodyguards were all ex-military or ex-intelligence, who would no doubt surround the Ukrainian and make an otherwise completely clear shot difficult.

The man with the rifle had selected the MSG-9 because it was semi-automatic and would allow him to fire several times inside of just a few seconds. The 7.62×51 mm full-metal-jacketed rounds carried enough power to pass through a human body and still kill someone standing behind, and these particular bullets incorporated a tungsten penetrator to account for the body armor the target and his guards would likely wear. A wall of flesh two-armored-men thick could shield the Ukrainian and he would still die.

Before the businessman could zoom in closer to prepare for the shot, a tiny flicker of light from a window of the hotel's thirteenth floor caught his attention. He quickly raised the barrel of the MSG-9, angling up the scope to check out the light source. He feared a guest was better enjoying the view of the city through a telescope or pair of binoculars. From an elevated position they might inadvertently spot him, and if so, he would have to forget about the contract and make a quick escape. No point completing the kill if the police apprehended him afterward.

Once the reticule centered over the window he increased the magnification of the scope, and saw the source of the flicker was not the reflection of sunlight on the lenses of binoculars or a telescope but a rifle scope like his own.

A suppressed muzzle flash transformed the businessman's surprise to alarm for the two-thirds of a second it took for the bullet to reach his head.

Pink mist swirled in the air.

From *New York Times* bestselling author

STUART WOODS

The Stone Barrington Novels

**Available wherever books are sold or at
penguin.com**